Praise fo

#1 *Saturday Times* Bestseller

"*Awakened* is a taughtly written, brilliantly unexpected thriller from authorial duo James S. Murray and Darren Wearmouth . . . *Awakened* hits the high notes of Douglas Preston and Lincoln Child's *Relic* and Scott Snyder's *The Wake* . . . but its scope actually extends much further."　—*Kirkus Reviews*

"Murray and coauthor Wearmouth . . . sculpt a briskly moving narrative that includes a plethora of short-burst action sequences and pacing fit for a Brad Meltzer novel. Along the way, they plant the seeds for sequels and craft a tight, pulse-pounding story that practically cries out for a film adaptation."
—Booklist

"*Aliens* meets *The Taking of Pelham 123* in this fast-moving science fiction thriller."
—Publishers Weekly

"*Awakened* is a thrilling read."
—New York Journal of Books

"A great book with both science fiction and horror elements, along with some mystery. I highly recommend this."　—SciFiMoviePage

"Short, tightly plotted and as grounded in reality as monster stories can be, it's a cinematic read."
—Serendipitous Reads

"It took James S. Murray many years to get his debut thriller *Awakened* finally published . . . It was well worth the wait. The thriller is a page-turning great debut."
—Red Carpet Crash

"*Awakened* is an action-packed, fast-paced and exciting read, one to switch your brain off and just enjoy for what it is, a fun-filled creature-fest."
—The Tattooed Book Geek

"If you're looking for a good scare delivered in a fast-paced, blockbuster-style novel with thrilling action and horror, this novel should do the trick. Overall, I thought it was a fun and thrilling read."
—BiblioSanctum

AWAKENED

A NOVEL

JAMES S. MURRAY WITH DARREN WEARMOUTH

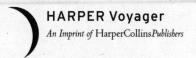

HARPER Voyager
An Imprint of HarperCollinsPublishers

AWAKENED. Copyright © 2018 by James S. Murray. All rights reserved. Printed in the United Kingdom. No part of this book may be used or reproduced in any manner whatsoever without written permission except in the case of brief quotations embodied in critical articles and reviews. For information, address HarperCollins Publishers, 1 London Bridge Street, London, United Kingdom SE1 9GF.

First Harper Voyager international printing: February 2019
First Harper Voyager hardcover printing: June 2018

Print Edition ISBN: 978-0-06-289503-5
Digital Edition ISBN: 978-0-06-268790-6

Cover design by Richard L. Aquan
Cover photograph © Shu Ba/Shutterstock
Map by James Sinclair

Harper Voyager and the Harper Voyager logo are trademarks of HarperCollins Publishers in the United States of America and other countries.

HarperCollins is a registered trademark of HarperCollins Publishers in the United States of America and other countries.

Printed and bound by CPI Group (UK) Ltd, Croydon, CR0 4YY

10 9 8 7 6 5 4 3 2 1

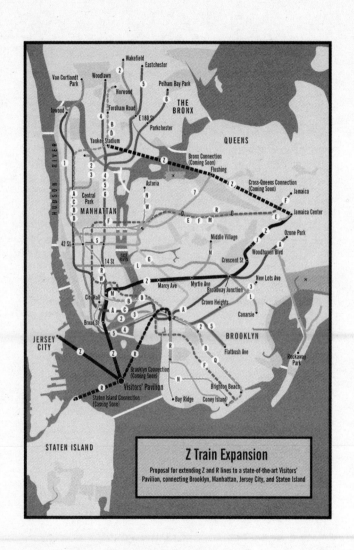

Wakefield
Eastchester
Van Cortlandt Park
Woodlawn
Norwood
Pelham Bay Park
Fordham Road
THE BRONX
Inwood
E 180 St
Parkchester
Yankee Stadium
QUEENS
HUDSON RIVER
Central Park
Bronx Connection
(Coming Soon)
Flushing
Astoria
Cross-Queens Connection
(Coming Soon)
Jamaica
MANHATTAN
Jamaica Center
Ozone Park
42 St
Middle Village
Woodhaven Blvd
14 St
Crescent St
Marcy Ave
Myrtle Ave
New Lots Ave
Broadway Junction
City Hall
Crown Heights
Broad St
Canarsie
BROOKLYN
JERSEY CITY
Rockaway Park
Brooklyn Connection
(Coming Soon)
Flatbush Ave
Visitors' Pavilion
Staten Island Connection
(Coming Soon)
Brighton Beach
Bay Ridge
Coney Island
STATEN ISLAND

Z Train Expansion

Proposal for extending Z and R lines to a state-of-the-art Visitors'
Pavilion, connecting Brooklyn, Manhattan, Jersey City, and Staten Island

AWAKENED

CHAPTER ONE

Grady McGowan hunched behind the controls of the tunnel-boring machine and wiped sweat from his brow. A giant cutter wheel slowly rotated in front of his cabin's shatterproof window. Twin conveyor belts rumbled beneath it, transporting the excavated bedrock back to the waiting supply trains.

The cabin's digital temperature reading flicked to ninety degrees, eight times higher than the brutal winter aboveground. His T-shirt clung to his body, and he banged his fist against the faulty vents for the hundredth time.

Eleven hours of gouging a path below the Hudson River had mentally and physically drained him, and he still had one to go, but double shifts went a long way toward paying for college tuition. He glanced at the photo on the console, showing his wife and daughter at the top of the Empire State Building. Caitlin was so small in that picture, but Daddy's girl was growing every single day.

Grady straightened in his seat and focused. Drilling was about timing: knowing when to push forward, when to pull back, when to readjust. He increased the cutter wheel's revolution speed and pressure, powering the machine as hard as possible without compromising its integrity or direction of travel.

Construction of the Z Train subway line extension had progressed around the clock for two years. Grady loved the overtime, but cash wasn't his only driving force. One day in the future, he imagined sitting around a crackling campfire with his grandkids, telling them how Grandpa helped build the most advanced subway system in the world.

This boldly conceived expansion, capable of handling eight subway trains at speeds of over seventy miles per hour, would connect four of New York City's boroughs with New Jersey in a matter of minutes, with express stops in the city going as far as Jamaica Center and the Bronx and expanding the actual subway service into places like Jersey City and Hoboken (thus sucking more and more of New Jersey into the "official" metroplex). It was the most ambitious infrastructure project since the time of Robert Moses . . . and probably just as controversial. The cost alone was a staggering number. But to hear the politicians speak of it, the benefits would outweigh the expenditure in a matter of months. Especially with the pièce de résistance: the state-of-the-art underwater Visitors' Pavilion, the crown jewel of the Z Train—and the place Grady and his team were close to reaching. He was a small component of the overall plan, but knowing the importance of this current push, he couldn't help but feel he was playing a vital role in a project that could completely change the city.

It was a good feeling.

A screen on his console displayed the progress of the other four drilling teams, each closing in on the same location. The onboard GPS calculated his arrival in fifty-five minutes at the current speed of thirty feet an hour. It left just enough time to get home and see the Giants fail to make the playoffs. Some called his football predictions cynical; he called them inevitable.

Grady nudged the power lever, upping it to the maximum safe level.

The axle's grind increased in pitch.

Smaller rocks bounced on the conveyor belts. Shards of granite spat in every direction and battered his window. Everything held steady, though, and the machine churned him inches closer to the taste of buffalo wings and an ice-cold Coors Light.

Suddenly, the cabin jolted.

A warning alarm buzzed on the console and the controls shuddered in his hands. The cutter wheel's normally steady rotation increased to a blinding whir.

"What the f—"

The machine lurched downward before he could finish his thought.

Grady slammed forward, the harness that the union insisted he wear knocking the wind out of him. He gasped, reached out his left hand, and, going by feel more than anything, yanked the emergency brake.

Nothing happened.

The geology had been surveyed precisely, and he had expected a wall of dense bedrock for the remainder of this stretch. Whatever was happening, though, meant the survey was very, very wrong.

He grabbed the gear lever, downshifted, and slammed the machine into reverse—but its momentum continued without slowing.

Grady tried the brake and gears again, forcing the levers backward and forward, attempting to gain any kind of traction, any kind of *control*. The left side of the machine jolted against jagged rock formations, throwing him sideways, and his shoulder smashed against the locked door, hard enough for him to know there was going to be a nasty bruise tomorrow. He hung there, leaning against the door, tensing for the inevitable crash.

Rocks pounded the glass, leaving white shatter marks.

Thank God for protective glass . . .

And then a length of rigid steel flipped from the cutter wheel, speared through the cabin's window like it was paper, and impaled itself into the part of his seat where his shoulder would have been if the machine hadn't been tilted.

The machine continued to plummet on its side, letting out a deafening metallic screech. Grady swallowed hard and closed his eyes. Images of his family raced through his mind:

Standing by a hospital bed as a proud father . . .

Snapping out a picnic blanket in Prospect Park for his two favorite girls . . .

The heart-bursting joy of hearing his daughter's first words . . .

The cabin bucked hard. His handheld radio hit the ceiling and shattered into pieces. A booming crunch came from the axle area, and—finally—the machine juddered to a halt.

Shouts echoed in the distance.

Grady grasped the still swinging emergency cord and ripped it down. An air horn blasted, alerting workers of a tunnel collapse.

His next priority was to get the hell out of wherever he had crashed. He swept the photo off the console, slipped it into his jeans pocket, and unlocked the door, which was now pretty much his roof. The machine had come to rest at a forty-five-degree angle in thick mud. Its body and working parts resembled scrapyard junk. A hundred feet above, thin light streamed into the darkness, marking the beginning of his violent descent.

The machine vibrated and he sensed downward momentum again. Looking over the edge, he saw that mud was consuming the cutter wheel at a startling pace, and the cabin was slowly sinking toward the same fate.

Grady heaved the door open, maneuvered around the steel jutting out from the back of his seat, and leaped out, his boots squelching against the ground. His ribs and shoulder hurt, but that didn't stop him from running as hard as he could for solid rock, racing to get clear of the twisted wreckage before a part snagged his clothes and dragged him into the same filthy grave.

Workers in hard hats appeared at the top of the collapse. Their four flashlight beams crisscrossed through the dusty darkness.

"Down here," Grady shouted, throwing up his arms.

The beams focused on him, and he found solid ground.

Adrenaline fueled him as he clambered up a steep rocky incline, ignoring the nicks on his arms and legs from the sharp outcrops. As he made his ascent, someone threw down a length of cable, and it slithered to within thirty feet. He found his next foothold and thrust upward . . . but the ground gave way, snapping like a shell, and the loose gravel swallowed his calf.

Grady's heart thumped against his chest and beads of sweat rolled down his face. He hauled himself free and climbed to a small plateau. Cries of encouragement echoed down as the workers waved him forward. The end of the cable neared, and he rushed the final few steps toward it.

A deep rumble reverberated inside the collapse. The ground shook and cracks forked across it.

He peered over his shoulder for one last look at the machine, but all that was left was a deep void. Shuddering, he looked back up only to see fist-sized rocks dropping from the ceiling. He ducked his head and tried to press flat against the wall, but one battered his thigh, causing Grady to cry out in pain.

The workers shouted and pointed, but the noise

of splitting granite drowned out their words. The ground beneath Grady's feet disintegrated. He lunged for the cable, clutched it in a white-knuckled grip, and dangled over the newly formed black abyss.

A moment of silence followed.

"Pull me up," he yelled.

The workers' lights disappeared from the ledge, now an overhang with only darkness beneath, and he was close to all-out panic, thinking they had abandoned him. Despair washed over him, knowing he didn't have the strength to climb up by himself, but then the cable rose a foot at a time as they heaved.

Grady hung twenty feet from a future with his family.

After five shuddering breaths he reached within ten feet.

He couldn't face the idea of a cop knocking on his front door and delivering the news of his death to his wife. Or not living to see his daughter grow up.

Eight more pulls brought him within an arm's length. He stretched out his right hand and grabbed the ledge. A heartbeat later, he viewed the smooth, dimly lit tunnel. Four workers crouched forty feet away, by the side of a supply train, tug-of-warring the cable in single file.

Grady scrambled onto solid ground. Cuts peppered his body, his palms stung, and his head throbbed. He was certain he had at least one cracked rib, and his shoulder and thigh were a mixture of burning and numb. As he lay on firm footing for a second, he was pretty sure he'd never felt better in his whole life.

Grady pushed himself up, only to pause once more. He rested his hands on his knees and exhaled, puffing his cheeks at the enormity of what he had just experienced and had barely escaped from.

The man at the front of the cable dropped it and removed his hard hat. "You're one lucky son of a bitch."

"Tell me about it," Grady said, and they both forced a smile.

An earsplitting crack quickly wiped away those expressions.

A black fracture line tore between him and the workers, and his side of the ground dropped a few inches. He thrust forward, realizing the overhang had snapped, and he had only seconds, if that, to reach a secure part of the tunnel.

Grady went to plant his boot and make his final lunge for safety, but the rock disappeared below him.

His boot hit stale air, and he plunged into the abyss.

CHAPTER TWO

Pride swelled inside Mayor Tom Cafferty as he gazed at the vast steel-and-glass vaulted ceiling of the underground Visitors' Pavilion. Today was a landmark day. Today was the moment his legacy finally came to fruition, three hundred feet below the Hudson River. Even President Reynolds' party crashing could do nothing to take away from his moment of triumph. He watched as the president, wearing his trademark gray suit, climbed the steps of the temporary stage and joined him behind the microphones.

His smile never wavered.

A large assembly of people had been shuttled through the brand-new subway tunnel to witness the opening ceremony and inaugural run of the re-christened Z Train. The press' TV cameras rolled and their rapid-fire flashes flickered. Beyond them, several of the sixty handpicked guests, made up of

New York's elite and the Z Train's MTA team, extended their phones in the air to capture the moment. Cafferty shook President Reynolds' hand and held the pose for the array of lenses.

Reynolds leaned close, away from his mic, and increased the power of his grip. "I was amazed you invited me, Tom."

That almost made Cafferty frown, but he kept it together. "I didn't. You invited yourself, Mr. President."

The splendor of the Pavilion outshone the presence of Reynolds. On the far side, past the central platform that separated the east and west lines, twenty glass-fronted stores lined the wall, including the likes of Cartier, Gucci, Louis Vuitton, and Prada. A food court that opened up to their left was for shoppers with any money left over to enjoy the array of international flavors on offer. To the right of the stage, an IMAX screen displayed the silver-and-blue MTA logo, and the semicircular walled command center, designed to withstand a nuclear blast, radiated an aura of quiet authority.

Everything sparkled. Everything was perfect. It was hard to believe all this was built underneath the intersection of the Hudson and East Rivers.

A cool breeze blew through the crowd, courtesy of the two hundred ventilator fans refreshing the air every few minutes. Cafferty tugged his hand free from Reynolds' grip and nodded toward the *New York Times* reporter.

"Mr. Mayor," she said, "how do you feel now that the big day has arrived?"

"Like I've been working on this all my life."

Some laughed, though he meant every word. A protracted eight-year fight had been the prologue to this day. Partisan political disputes, territorial pissing contests, construction problems, and slipping timelines had all dogged the project through its various stages. Yet Cafferty and his team had fought hard to overcome every obstacle and hit their deadlines—miraculously for government work, some of the talking heads opined. He had defied the critics who had claimed it would take over two decades, and now he had the proof of his promise kept.

How many politicians can claim that?

"Are you pleased with how the Pavilion came out?" a reporter asked.

"More than pleased. I'm elated."

"Lucien Flament from *Le Figaro*," another reporter said in a thick French accent. "Mr. President, ten years ago you fought funding for the Z Train. Have you changed your mind?"

Reynolds cleared his throat. "I helped pass one of the largest transportation bills in the last fifty years, granting more money to this and many other mass-transit projects. Personally, I consider the Z Train one of my administration's greatest achievements."

These bullshit words raised Cafferty's pulse a couple of notches, but he maintained his grin as the president continued to reel off his other nationwide successes. A decade earlier, both attended a Senate committee meeting about the costs and benefits of the Z Train. The then senator from Virginia was as stubborn as a mule. He called it a vanity project and wanted federal appropriations spent on highway construction and improvements . . . in Virginia, of course. Thankfully, his motion was struck down. Everyone else saw the logic of extending the subway to New Jersey, finally bringing a single, integrated interstate network to one of the busiest cities in the world.

"I've known the mayor for ten years," Reynolds said in closing. "He's always been courteous and the epitome of professionalism. Isn't that right, Tom?"

Some of the press gave the president a quizzical look after his final comment, likely remembering the two as old sparring partners. Tom knew Reynolds' real motivation, for he had retained the same grudge for years: Cafferty, a city planner at the time of the Senate meeting, had left a voice mail for Reynolds a few months later. *I just received word that Congress approved a full funding grant agreement for the Z Train. So on behalf of all New Yorkers: go to hell.* His message felt petty the next day, and he momentarily considered sending an apology. This morning, though, he smiled at the thought of his brash thirty-six-year-old self still rattling Reynolds after all these years. But that was just icing on the cake, and he wasn't going to let *anything* steal his thunder today. "Thank you for those kind words, Mr. President. Now, let's get this show on the road."

On the giant screen, a digital timer flashed through a luminous ten-second countdown. Stirring music pumped through speakers at either side of the stage, composed by one of Broadway's pre-eminent talents, Lin-Manuel Miranda. No expense had been spared.

The timer reached zero. An animation played showing the construction phase of the numerous tunnels throughout Manhattan, Brooklyn, Queens, New Jersey, the Bronx—even the start of the next phase from Staten Island. Machines ground through the rock and met at the Pavilion, and the image transformed into a three-dimensional diagram of the newly created extension. It spun five times before melting into the brushed-metal MTA logo.

The introduction ended and the screen switched to a live video feed of the Jersey City station. A train, silver in color, with a sleek bullet nose and red trim around the doors and windows, sat on the track by the spacious platform (also brand-new and state of the art, though not quite as grandiose as the Pavilion). A marching band played the same song at the far end. Sixty-five specially selected travelers, including Cafferty's wife, Ellen, waited to board.

The three sets of doors on the front car smoothly parted. All passengers embarked for an event Cafferty knew would go down in the city's history.

The digital board in the Pavilion displayed an arrival time of 12:05.

"Mr. Mayor, Christopher Fields from WNBC—"

"I know who you are," Cafferty said. "Have you come to spread some of your special joy?"

Ignoring the comment, Fields said, "Sir, today's

the first time in nearly three months we've seen you and your wife together. Is it fair to say the project has impacted your personal life?"

"No," Cafferty snapped, though Fields, a renowned thorn in the side of city hall, had called it right—except that the rocky period was closer to three *years*. "Ellen and I lead busy lives. Let me know the next time you'd like a photo—we should have a chance in less than five minutes!"

The crowd let out a murmur of laughter.

On the overhead screen, the train glided from the platform. Plumes of confetti exploded from the sides of the track. The cars sped through the glittering cloud and disappeared inside the tunnel. Within minutes, the sound of its smooth, humming engine would carry into the Pavilion.

"Speaking of my wife," Cafferty said, "why don't we see how everyone's doing on board. Ellen, can you hear us?"

The left speaker crackled. "Greetings from the best subway train in the world."

"Hi, honey. How's the ride?"

"Smooth sailing. I'm here with sixty-four passengers including the mayor of Jersey City and our two governors in the first car. The champagne is sweet; I'll give you a taste in two minutes."

Claps rippled through the speaker.

"Don't drink too much," Reynolds said.

Ellen laughed. "We'll save you a glass, Mr. President."

"Thanks for the live update," Cafferty said, and faced the cameras. "My fellow New Yorkers, our neighbors in New Jersey, President Reynolds, distinguished guests, it's my pleasure to christen New York's newest technological innovation. This achievement pushes us ahead of any other city in the world. Ladies and gentlemen, in less than ninety seconds, I give you the Z Train!"

The crowd burst into applause and a few members of the MTA team whistled. Cafferty took a deep breath. His decade-long dream was about to be realized, and with the project complete, his vow to rebuild his marriage could finally be attempted.

A time of 12:04 displayed on the platform's clock.

"Ellen, can you see the Pavilion yet?" Cafferty asked.

Nobody replied.

"Ellen?"

A short shriek erupted through the speaker, followed by a static hiss.

The time changed to 12:05.

The camera crews swung to face the tunnel. Quiet chatter filled the air, punctuated by several more static hisses. Cafferty checked his watch to make sure the platform's clock wasn't faulty. It displayed a time of 12:06, and he watched the second hand carry out a complete revolution.

Reynolds stepped across to him. "Two minutes late, Tom."

"Patience." Cafferty inclined toward the mic. "Ladies and gentlemen, because of an earlier incident, the Z Train is running three minutes behind schedule."

A few of the guests laughed at his mocking of

the typical intercom announcement by a subway conductor. However, the apprehensive faces of the MTA team matched Cafferty's internal emotion. He couldn't detect even the faintest noise of the train approaching.

The platform clock flicked to 12:08.

Three faint bangs rumbled from somewhere deep in the tunnel, and nervous mutters rippled through the crowd. At the same time, five of Reynolds' Secret Service detail, stalking near the entrance to the semicircular walled command center, moved closer to the stage.

But all eyes were focused on the tunnel, and another sixty seconds passed. Four minutes late confirmed something serious had gone wrong, and without any information forthcoming, Cafferty decided to find out for himself.

Reynolds, now flanked by two human tanks in typical dark suits and dark glasses, blocked his path. "What's the problem?"

"Wait here. I'll be a moment."

Cafferty calmly descended the stage, headed around the back of it, and entered the sturdy command center. Internally, his mind raced through the possible aftermath of a failed first run. He imagined front-page pictures of the train being towed into the Jersey City station, along with mocking headlines.

He could feel things falling apart, just as they had with Ellen . . .

He shook those thoughts from his head and

headed toward Diego Munoz. As the Z Train's head of operations, Diego sat inside the command center with his eight-person team. Each peered at the measurements and reports displayed on the monitors that filled the walls of the basketball-court-sized room. He twisted in his chair to face Cafferty and mirrored his look of concern.

"What's up?" Cafferty asked.

"We don't know. The train just vanished from the tracking display."

"What does that mean?"

Munoz shrugged. "Tom, it vanished. Like it lost all power in an instant, without warning."

Cafferty rubbed his eyes with his index finger and thumb. He was seething but knew that exploding with rage wouldn't help anyone. The team members here had been selected from the MTA's star employees, and if they didn't know the problem, nobody did. Raised voices outside broke him out of his thoughts and he returned to the main area of the Pavilion.

David North, his reliable head of security, joined Cafferty as he made for the side of the track. "Everything okay?" he asked.

"Looks like a power outage. What have I missed?"

"Listen."

Metallic squeaks echoed in the distance. Cafferty quickened his stride and joined the crowd on the platform, peering into the pitch-black tunnel.

The silhouette of the train appeared out of the darkness, rolling down the shallow incline toward the platform. Its silver nose emerged out of the tunnel, and its powerless body drifted to a standstill in front of the assembled crowd.

The Pavilion echoed with sharp intakes of breath and the shuffling of shoes as people toward the front staggered back. Only a few small shards of glass remained around the edges of the front car's twenty windows.

Cafferty's heart raced as he pushed his way forward.

Blood smothered the interior. The walls. The ceiling. The seats. The floor. Everywhere. A crimson handprint on the opposite side of the car extended into four finger lines and stopped at a set of doors. The blood overwhelmed the train with both its dense color and coppery smell.

But it was empty of passengers.

CHAPTER THREE

Diego Munoz had grabbed a tool kit and left the command center shortly after Cafferty. Without any obvious clues in the reported data, he wanted to inspect the track before the maintenance team arrived. The sight of the train rolling to a halt fifty yards in front of him stopped him midstride.

The black plastic case dropped from his hand.

No one heard it fall, though, as shouts and screams swept through the Pavilion.

People on the platform burst away from the train, stumbling backward in shock. Cameras flashed in front of the damaged car, brightening its bodywork and grisly interior. Cafferty and North stood frozen by a set of its mangled doors. Several cops drew their guns and aimed at the tunnel. Others barked orders, attempting to control the chaos.

Nobody listened.

Hundreds of footsteps pounded against the polished stone floor.

A man lost his balance and crashed to the ground.

A wave of guests and MTA workers trampled over him as they headed for the shopping concourse.

TV cameras near the stage continued to roll, capturing the mayhem.

"Diego," a woman's voice called.

Munoz spun to face the command center.

Anna Petrov, his second-in-command, wearing a dark blue jacket and with her brown hair pulled back in a tight ponytail, waved him forward.

As he made his way back, two Secret Service agents grabbed President Reynolds and dragged him from the stage. Five more agents flanked them, sweeping their guns in all directions as they headed for the command center.

Realizing what was about to happen, Munoz sprinted for the doorway and reached it first. Inside, shouts filled the air. His team had left their work-stations and clustered around the console, peering at a video feed of the Pavilion. Structural alarms, critical warnings, and network failure alerts from the Jersey City tunnel flowed across the overhead monitors.

"Back to your damned positions," Munoz shouted. "The president's coming."

One of the agents hurtled inside with Reynolds under his arm, twisted to face the Pavilion, and shouted, "Guard the door from the outside!"

The Secret Service detail fanned out into an arc and raised their guns.

The agent with Reynolds, shaven-headed and built like a heavyweight boxer, scanned the command center. He drew his fist level with a waist-high button protected by safety glass.

"Stop!" Munoz shouted. "Don't touch that—"

The agent punched through the glass and depressed the button.

Dazzling red ceiling lights and a piercing siren engulfed the room. The floor-to-ceiling circular blast door began whining across the entrance, designed to protect the command center from fire, a nuclear blast, or ten thousand pounds of water pressure per square inch if the tunnel ever imploded. It was a marvel of engineering . . . and nothing could stop the lockdown once it was initiated.

"Who's in charge?" Reynolds asked.

"Diego Munoz, Z Train operation manager, Mr. President."

"This is Agent Samuels, head of my Secret Service team. He's here to protect us, so do as he says."

"We didn't need to activate lockdown," Munoz said. "Not unless—"

"It's not your call," Samuels said, and turned to Reynolds. "Stand back. Now."

The siren had attracted the attention of at least forty guests and the press. They switched their direction of flight toward the command center.

The president's detail shouted warnings. Two of them extended their palms, gesturing the mini-stampede to halt. Munoz waved the people away, fearing for their lives if they attempted to surge past the six leveled guns, but he doubted they even saw him.

Samuels tilted his head and raised his hand to his earpiece. "Negative. Stay outside. I'll handle it in here."

Munoz glanced at Reynolds, who stared open-mouthed at a video feed covering the area between the platform and the command center. The siren's wail had triggered an extra layer of panic. Some people raced for the restrooms, others tried maintenance doors. Cops tried to ease the throng as at least a dozen tried to seek shelter in a Starbucks. Two figures, holding each other in a mutual headlock, crashed through the already splintered window.

"Follow protocol," Samuels transmitted again. "Any of them might be a threat. Hold the line. No one enters this command center. No one . . . That's an order."

The blast door moved to within two feet of closing.

The baying crowd screamed at the agents to let them inside, assuming—perhaps correctly—that the command center was the only safe place to be.

Munoz took a step back and avoided eye contact with the people beyond the weapons. He hated himself for doing it, but he couldn't help but acknowledge that Samuels' judgment of isolating President Reynolds in a safe environment was a sound one.

A red-haired Secret Service agent glanced over his shoulder and must have come to the same realization, because in seconds he broke from the defensive line and dove for the command center entrance, seizing a last opportunity before the blast door sealed entirely. His head and chest made it inside before the door's steel edge forced itself against his stomach. He planted his hands on the wall and attempted to squirm his way through, flipping like a salmon but managing to move only a few inches. The increasing pressure suspended him three feet above the ground.

A gunshot rang out in the Pavilion, close enough for Munoz to guess a civilian had tried to take advantage of the agent wedged in the tightening gap and rushed to gain access to the command center, only to suffer the consequences.

The blast door's pistons increased in pitch.

The redheaded agent, suspended in midair, stared at Munoz with fear in his eyes. "Help me . . ."

"Save him!" Reynolds yelled.

"We can't reverse the lockdown procedure," Munoz said, helpless. "It's impossible."

The agent clenched his teeth and reached out a hand. He tried to speak but his breath rasped in his throat, as the door crushed the life out of him, inch by inch.

"Look away, Mr. President," Samuels said. He stood over his stricken colleague, drew his gun, and placed the muzzle against the top of his head. "I'm sorry."

A gunshot split the air.

The pistol kicked up. Blood spattered Samuels' face and created an outline of his body on the command center's wall. The agent's head sagged, his arms flopped to his sides, and his gun clattered onto the tiled floor.

Munoz's team had frozen, staring with horror etched across their faces, and flinched at the sounds of snapping bones as the door traveled its final few inches.

No MTA training had prepared Munoz for this experience. Neither had anything in his thirty-five years on the planet.

The blast door's ten steel bolts slammed into their locking positions.

The agent's upper body hit the floor like a bag of wet cement.

Munoz recoiled and shuddered.

Samuels shouldered past him. He ripped a fireproof blanket from the wall, unfolded it, and draped it over his dead colleague.

For a moment there was seemingly no sound. Finally, though, the president said, "We need a phone and an update. Right now."

"Use my office," Munoz said. "I'll tell you what we know, but it's not a lot, Mr. President."

Glancing at the blanket-covered body, Munoz couldn't help but wonder what kind of situation they were in. The sight of the train had shaken him to his very core, never mind the brutal efficiency with which Samuels euthanized his dying colleague.

Munoz led Samuels and Reynolds through the command center. He increased his pace as he neared his poky office, slipped through the door, and swiped his *Star Trek* action figures into his desk drawer before they entered. As much as he loved science fiction (he even worked as an audio engineer in his spare time for a conspiracy podcast), having Captain Picard, Lieutenant Worf, and a tribble standing between him and the president didn't seem like a good idea.

Reynolds circled the desk and sat in the chair. Samuels twisted the door's lock and lowered the blinds.

Munoz lifted the cordless handset from its base station. "Dial nine for an outside line."

"Not yet." Reynolds shifted his focus to Samuels. "Who gave the order to drag me in here?"

"I did, sir," Samuels replied. "It's the safest place right now. You saw the chaos outside."

"At six o'clock tonight, one hundred million Americans are going to see the president of the United States protecting his own ass, leaving dozens of people outside. Not to mention my Secret Service detail gunning down civilians."

"And they'll know that our actions were necessary and justified, Mr. President. The Secret Service can't concern itself with optics—the only thing that matters is that *you're* safe. We don't know what we're facing, and until we do, you need to trust my lead, sir."

Reynolds slammed his fist on the desk. "Damn you, Samuels. I didn't spend a career in the Marines for you to make me look like a coward and kill civilians at my expense."

"And with all due respect, sir, it's not up to you. The state of the train suggests a terrorist attack. There's a chance somebody outside is part of the same sleeper cell."

"With slightly less respect, if you're wrong, you just cost me the reelection."

Samuels didn't respond, and Munoz wasn't sure he even registered the president's words. They resonated with him, though. He remembered Reynolds sweeping through the primaries with his decorated war hero background and "man of the people" rhetoric, and he won the bitterly fought election using the same message. Things hadn't gone well for him in the subsequent three years, mainly due to his alienating his own party, rising unemployment, and his blunt international diplomacy. It was easy to see his side, considering his usual tough talk, though Munoz doubted anyone would view his protection as *cowardly*.

"What do you think?" Reynolds asked Munoz. "Are we under attack?"

"It's impossible to say. My team is sifting through the available data as I speak. Sir, if you only want secure communications leaving the Pavilion, I suggest we cut the relays, Wi-Fi access, and cellular boosters."

"Do it. We don't need a bomb being triggered by a cell phone. Let's control the flow of information until we know what's happening. Anything else?"

"Gimme two seconds."

Munoz crouched beside the desk and twisted a monitor toward himself. Nothing stood out on the network management system. Or, more accurately, everything did. He supposed whoever had carried out the attack had also damaged the tunnel's electrical cabling. The position where the train had vanished from the tracking display, in between the Jersey City station and the underwater Pavilion, and its powerless state as it freewheeled into the Pavilion remained his only solid clues.

"Visually, we know the grid's down. I've got maintenance teams waiting at the Jersey City station and Broad Street station in Manhattan if needed."

"The grid?"

"The electrical grid. There's no power in the third rail. Whatever happened, it looks like it took down the whole system."

Reynolds gave an appreciative nod. "Stand down your maintenance teams for the moment. We need to rule out terrorism first. If this is an attack, we have to secure the Pavilion and get these people to safety before they strike again."

"What makes you think it's terrorism?"

"How else do you explain all the blood?" Reynolds asked dismissively.

Somebody outside the room knocked three times. Samuels unlocked the door and pulled it ajar.

Anna's face appeared in the gap. "There's something you need to see."

"Can it wait?" Reynolds asked. "I'm about to call the secretaries of defense and homeland security."

"Mr. President, this cannot wait."

The group followed Anna into the main body of the command center and surrounded her chair. Munoz knew she rarely acted on impulse and nobody knew the integrated systems better. The ventilation management system measurements above her workstation confirmed his fear.

"What are we looking at?" Reynolds asked.

Anna pointed to a screen with eight fluctuating bars: seven green at a similar height, one twice the size and red. "Sir, this system monitors the ventilation in the subway tunnels and alerts us in the event of a biological or chemical attack. Methane levels are at three percent in the Jersey City tunnel and rising. We don't know the source or cause, but at this rate, it'll reach the LEL in a matter of minutes."

Reynolds frowned. "LEL?"

"The lower explosive limit, sir. Methane explodes when it reaches five to fifteen percent of air density. Once we reach the LEL, any kind of spark could make the Jersey City tunnel blow."

"Including the Visitors' Pavilion?"

"Not the Pavilion," Munoz said. "Not yet, anyway."

"But we're reading smaller leaks in the Manhattan and Brooklyn tunnels," Anna said. "At its current rise, those tunnels could reach the LEL in roughly fifty minutes."

"Sir," Munoz added, "the Manhattan tunnel is the closest exit from the Pavilion. I suggest we evacuate everyone along that route."

Reynolds walked over to the blast door, gazed at the fire blanket, and shook his head. After a moment of silence, he spun to face Anna. "Negative. I'm not risking another life today by sending people into the muzzles of terrorists. They could be waiting for us to try to evacuate. You say we've got time to send our counterassault teams through the Manhattan tunnel?"

Anna nodded. "If they're quick. There's no telling if the methane leak will continue at this pace."

"Sir," Samuels said, "you need to execute the order for our special forces to come from Manhattan and call the DSRV."

"DSRV?" Reynolds asked.

"A deep submergence rescue vehicle," Munoz explained. "Basically, a submarine that connects to a docking station under the Hudson. An emergency tunnel leads from this command center to the docking station. Sir, the DSRV can be here within the hour."

"The DSRV is the best way to get you to safety, Mr. President," Samuels added.

"Call it, but I'm only boarding as a last resort." Reynolds studied the fluctuating bars monitoring the methane levels. "What happens if the cavalry doesn't arrive in time?"

"They need to arrive in time, Mr. President," Munoz replied. "Because in less than an hour, everyone in the Pavilion dies of asphyxiation."

"If the terrorists don't get us," Samuels said.

"Or if the tunnel doesn't explode first," Anna muttered.

CHAPTER FOUR

afferty stood staring at the train, frozen. Fear, anger, guilt, and desperation warred within him and rooted him to the spot. He had persuaded Ellen to join the inaugural run, telling her the project's end signaled a significant change in their lives, but obviously he had not meant it like this. Instead of greeting his wife for a mutual renewal of their relationship, he faced an empty car, potentially stained with her blood.

David North snapped him out of his trancelike state by grabbing his shoulders and twisting him away. Cafferty blinked and surveyed the Pavilion.

Three deathly still bodies lay in front of the Secret Service agents, who roared warnings to anyone moving within close proximity. Behind them, two legs protruded from the blast door.

Four cops wrestled with a woman and man outside the Starbucks; a jet of orange pepper spray splashed over the store's shattered window. Inside, three bloodied figures sat slumped against the counter. Others peered over tables.

Several casualties lay between the platform and the command center, likely the victims of the surge after the train arrived; none was receiving treatment.

People crouched by the side of the stage, behind trash cans, or hugged the walls. Others fumbled with their phones. Cafferty could barely hear himself think above the confused mix of shouts. He forced Ellen and the passengers from the front of his mind.

First, a semblance of order needed restoring.

Cafferty hustled to the stage and climbed the steps, ignoring a camera crew who tracked his moves as he made his way back to the mic.

"Everyone calm down," he bellowed. *"Right now!"*

Voices shouted back at him in rapid succession.

"Are we in danger?"

"Is this a terrorist attack?"

"How come the president is in there and we're out here?" a man yelled from the side of an empty newsstand.

"Because he's the goddamn president of the United States," Cafferty shouted. "Now start acting like New Yorkers and pull yourselves together. First, I want everyone to calmly head to the food court. In the meantime, I'll coordinate with emergency personnel and the command center. Once I get the all clear, we'll evacuate. But we need to work together right now."

"What if they come here next? What if they at-tack again?" a woman asked, her voice riddled with panic.

A serious-faced, white-shirted police lieutenant with a bushy mustache approached the stage. "I've sent twenty of my squad to cover the tunnels. Who-ever attacked that train isn't getting in here without a fight."

"You're damn right about that," Cafferty said. He pulled the lieutenant aside. "What's your name, officer?"

"Lieutenant Arnolds, sir."

"Good work with deploying your men. We need a plan for the casualties and injured."

"I'll set up a triage area in one of the stores."

Cafferty peered at the growing number of faces gathering to his front. Raising his voice to the group, he said, "There's a lot of hurt people here. Anyone with medical experience, speak with Lieu-tenant Arnolds. The rest of you, let's get moving."

The majority headed to the food court while shooting nervous glances toward the train. Cops, now free from the burden of chaos, helped the in-jured to their feet and escorted them to triage. The five dead—one from the stampede, another shred-ded by the café window, and three at the hands of the Secret Service—were placed in a line and had jackets draped over their faces.

Cafferty descended the steps, where he was met by North, and they made their way to the sealed command center. All five of Reynolds' Secret Ser-vice team eyed him as he neared. None saw the anger flaring inside him at the thought of people getting shot for trying to save their own lives.

One of the agents advanced and met them before they reached the blast door. "The president's secure, sir."

"Why did your team shoot these three civilians?" Cafferty asked.

"We followed a direct order to secure the door."

"That doesn't answer my question."

"As harsh as it looks, if one of those people wore a suicide vest . . ."

"But they didn't."

"If they did? We didn't have time to chance that. In this moment, everyone is a threat to the president until they're not." His tone was no-nonsense, almost patronizing.

The thing was the agent had a point, and one Cafferty mentally conceded. The action still seemed disproportionate, like using a sledgehammer to crack a walnut, considering the vetted guests and MTA workers in attendance. But he'd have to worry about that later.

"Everyone in this Pavilion needs to be searched," the agent said. "Immediately."

North nodded. "I'll see to it."

"If you want to make yourselves useful," Cafferty said to the Secret Service, "shut off those goddamn TV cameras and help us guard the entrances to the Pavilion."

"Sir, we're not moving from this blast door."

"Superman couldn't smash through that," Cafferty said. The stone-faced agents didn't respond or move an inch. "Please. I'm asking you for help protecting these people."

"Sorry, sir. As long as the president is behind this door, we're not moving."

Cafferty knew he couldn't win this argument. In his mind's eye, the safer option was more guns guarding the tunnels in case of a second attack, but he understood the Secret Service's primary duty. The logic of it didn't make him any happier, though.

With the Pavilion secured and organized as best as possible under the current circumstances, Cafferty headed into the men's bathroom and locked the door. He tore his tie loose, turned on the faucet, and splashed cold water on his face.

The blood-soaked subway car appeared fresh in his mind. Nausea swelled inside him and his hands trembled. He rushed into a stall, hunched over, and dry heaved.

Ellen had been on the train at his request.

A couple of corners had been cut during the construction to meet deadlines, but they wouldn't have led to this. Slashing costs on materials and quietly settling an industrial accident out of the public's eye had no tangible link to the appearance of the train when it rolled into the Pavilion.

The blood surely meant terrorism.

All that blood . . .

This wasn't his fault. He had no control over the action of terrorists.

His eyes teared up and he heaved again. A string of saliva dangled from his bottom lip. He knew he had to get a grip for the sake of everyone in the Pavilion and the passengers—if any of the latter remained alive, of course.

No. They have to be alive. Ellen *has to be alive.*

Cafferty rose from the bathroom floor, straightened his suit, and glared into the mirror. His salt-and-pepper hair had sagged over his forehead from his side part. The blaze from the overhead lights accentuated his wrinkled forehead and crow's-feet, making it appear as if he had aged ten years in the last ten minutes.

Nothing like the fresh-faced man who had somehow gotten Ellen's number all those years ago. She was the love of his life for the best part of fifteen years. He remembered locking eyes with her for the first time and her radiant smile from across a packed Williamsburg bar. A driven, independent woman, and a good listener when he regularly came home late and blew off steam. She had put up with his Z Train obsession while he neglected her . . . or as much as a person could stand being neglected.

He had been working so hard for so long that he couldn't remember when he stopped seeing his wife. He just realized it one day. He hadn't been intimate with her in almost a year.

And then, just pure stupidity. Looking back, he couldn't believe he even did it. One stupid mistake. He had won an award from . . . he didn't even remember anymore. Ellen couldn't make the ceremony. He was drinking, she was young. Ellen was a shrewd enough businesswoman to keep his indiscretion private for now, but it was just another nail in the coffin of their marriage. That was nearly six months ago.

Now she was gone before he could make amends.

Get a grip, he told himself again.

For all Cafferty knew, dazed passengers might be staggering out of the Jersey City tunnel right now as his mind raced with speculation and dread. He slipped his phone out of his jacket and hit the redial button. "Ellen Cell" flashed on the screen. The call began connecting . . .

. . . and then the signal bars vanished and the call cut.

The public Wi-Fi also dropped out.

Unless the terrorists had damaged the communication systems, somebody in the command center had disabled the network boosters and routers. It made sense—cell phones were an easy remote trigger for bombs. Not only that, but it's always a good idea to control the story, and with a few dozen civilian "reporters" to go along with the actual reporters, cutting off the cellular signal wasn't a bad idea. But it meant *he* was also cut off. He racked his brain for a second, pushing past the frustration, and finally remembered there was an internal landline in the AV room.

He shoved open the swing door and reentered the main area of the Pavilion.

North acknowledged him with a nod. "Are you okay, Mr. Mayor?"

"Relatively speaking, yes."

"I hear you," North murmured.

"What's going on?"

"I've sent our team to recheck civilians for suicide vests or weapons of any kind."

"Let's hope they don't find any. Give me a minute—I'm calling the command center to get us an update."

A faint buzz of chatter came from inside the food court. The NYPD had dragged tables and chairs into the central eating area and attended to the injured. A few cops stood by the train, while ten each lined up in front of the Jersey City and Manhattan tunnel entrances.

Cafferty walked to the left of the command center, down a short corridor, and entered the AV room. Pinhead lights illuminated a bank of computers, which controlled the advertising displays and the projection on the Pavilion's wall. He picked up a telephone with an alphanumeric keypad and small video screen, entered his PIN, and raised the handset.

The phone rang four times.

The image of Diego Munoz's face appeared and he offered a thin smile. "Mr. Mayor, I thought you'd call."

"Is everyone all right in there?"

President Reynolds nudged Munoz out of the way. "We're fine, Tom. I see you're controlling things outside. Great work."

"What happened to the networks? We've got no cell service, no internet, no broadcast signal."

"Emergency services only. We don't need false information getting out and panic spreading in the city. And if this attack isn't over yet . . ."

Cafferty nodded in agreement. "What about the response?"

"We're working on it," Reynolds replied. "Rescue teams are coming your way through the Manhattan tunnel."

"Why not the Jersey City tunnel? The missing passengers are in there."

Munoz leaned back into shot. "We're monitoring—"

"The decision rests in capable hands," Reynolds said. "Keep everyone calm and inform them help is on the way."

"I'll do my best," Cafferty said, still puzzled as to why teams weren't descending from both directions. "Any info on the passengers?"

"Like I said, Tom, we're working on it. Hang tight and we'll let you know as soon as we have any further information."

Munoz looked like he was about to say something else, but Reynolds rested a hand on his shoulder and squeezed.

Cafferty shook his head. "The attack happened in the Jersey tunnel. Surely canceling the threat first makes the most sense?"

"For the third time, we're on it, Tom," Reynolds said. "Have your team inspect the train for any clues and we'll keep you updated. Sound like a plan?"

"All right. And what's your plan, Mr. President?"

"We called the DSRV, but I'm only boarding as

a last resort. We'll see this through together. Good luck, Tom."

"Likewise." Cafferty hung up the phone. "Not that you'll need it behind twenty inches of steel."

It all seemed reasonable, yet something didn't add up. Reynolds, as a fellow politician, should have known he couldn't bullshit a bullshitter. Cafferty drummed his fingers against the desk and scanned the AV room. A closed laptop sat on a bench to his left. He reached across and flipped open the lid, and the operating system blinked on. Commercial communications were down, but he guessed the MTA's private network remained active.

The laptop searched for available wireless networks. A wave of relief washed over him when "MTA-P" appeared in the box and automatically connected. He launched the browser and input his government username and password.

Cafferty navigated to the contacts list and only the command center staff appeared online. He selected the private message envelope next to Munoz's name. With no cameras or president to kowtow to, he dropped the niceties.

TC: Diego, what the fuck is going on?

CHAPTER FIVE

A message notification beeped from Munoz's workstation. He wheeled his chair from the telephone to his laptop, and as he had hoped, the on-screen speech bubble contained Cafferty's name. In his peripheral vision, the hulking frame of Samuels moved toward him.

Munoz quickly tabbed his display to a spreadsheet.

"What're you doing?" Samuels asked.

"Nothin'."

"You look guilty of something."

"I am: not telling Mayor Cafferty about the methane leaks."

Samuels glared down at him with a laser-like intensity. "Every move made in this command center is subject to my or the president's approval. I don't like loose cannons rolling around my deck. Don't even consider a unilateral course of action. Do we understand each other?"

"As clean as a whistle."

"It's clear as a whistle."

Munoz shrugged but held eye contact. "Let's just do our respective jobs. But let's also be clear: you don't need to treat us like children."

"Act how you like when I'm not here protecting the president. For now, you follow my instructions. Period."

Munoz shrugged once more. Nothing much intimidated him, not after growing up in Brownsville. He had been sucked into a street gang as an impressionable teenager. It hadn't lasted long—he soon realized that kind of existence ruined the lives of those around him, not to mention the agonizing toll it took on their families. The drugs. The guns. The senseless territorial disputes. But it had been long enough, and he spent years constantly looking over his shoulder and wondering if he would live to see another sunrise.

Munoz had faced down threats from people with far worse intentions than *this* guy. So to have someone try to stare him down when they all had a job to do? It wasn't going to happen. Munoz didn't go straight and claw his way to genuine respectability for people like Samuels to kick sand in his face. Not today.

Not *any* day in the future.

Everyone in the command center wanted the same thing but had different roles to play. His team still hadn't gone through all data relating to the attack, and anything they found could prove vital in the current shit-storm. So for now he'd focus on that, but he would find a way to get in touch with the mayor.

You can count on that, Samuels.

Another critical alarm pinged through the wall-mounted speakers, breaking the silence. Munoz rose to his feet, skirted around the agent, and joined Anna at the console. On the overhead screen, a bar representing the methane level in the central section of the Jersey tunnel had reached the 5 percent lower explosive limit. The Manhattan tunnel fluctuated at a steady 2.5 percent. That was worrying, but more alarming was the fact that the methane in the Pavilion had risen to a similar level.

Munoz spun to face Reynolds. "Mr. President, I don't get why you're not telling Mayor Cafferty about the gas leak."

"My job requires tough decisions. I know you're all under tremendous pressure, and I'm grateful for your help in this crisis. Have faith in what we're doing. Our special forces are coming and I truly believe it's wisest if we keep the danger under wraps. The moment we think informing the mayor will save more lives, I'll speak with him personally."

"How is not telling him saving more lives?" Anna asked.

"You saw what happened earlier. If we spread more panic, it might send innocent lives straight into the hands of terrorists. We don't want to create a nightmare scenario of people fleeing when our teams are trying to identify the enemy. I'll tell the mayor once we know there's not another attack imminent. You have my word."

The response made partial sense, but it still lacked an internal logic the more Munoz thought about it. It just didn't make sense to not let *Cafferty* know the potential danger his group faced. If worst came to worst, and everyone outside the command center had to attempt their own escape, at least it gave the mayor time to devise a strategy. Still, he bit his lip rather than continuing to question the president. The man had made a decision, and knowing what he did—or thought he did—about the president, Munoz knew there was no changing his mind.

So Reynolds was a nonstarter. But it didn't mean Cafferty had to be kept in the dark. In fact, having worked with the mayor on a few projects, Munoz knew he wasn't the type of man to create hysteria; his actions in the Pavilion showed that. The moment Samuels stopped being Munoz's unwanted shadow when he neared his laptop was the moment he intended to reply to the mayor's private message.

The desk phone rang.

Anna hit the loudspeaker button. "Command center."

"Hello. Mr. President, it's Mansfield again."

"How are things proceeding?" Reynolds asked the secretary of defense, Blake Mansfield.

"Extraction teams are minutes away from the Broad Street station in Manhattan and we're working alongside Homeland Security. We're clearing the Jersey City station and setting up a perimeter. We can't risk some dumb hero cop or fireman triggering an explo—"

Reynolds ripped up the handset. "Great work, Blake. I'll let you know if the situation changes in the Pavilion." He paused, listening and murmuring in agreement, and looked directly at Munoz. "Don't worry, nobody is straying into the tunnels. Send my best to our brave men and women. Thanks for the update and keep me posted."

Anna tugged on Munoz's arm and gestured her head toward the ventilation management system measurements. The methane level in the Pavilion had crawled up to 3.25 percent in the time taken for the brief call.

"Mr. President," Anna said, "how long until the teams arrive?"

"Agent Samuels?" the president replied.

"Realistically," Samuels said, "special forces will take twenty minutes to coordinate a response and another twenty minutes to clear the tunnel of any hostiles. My best guess is forty in all."

"We don't have forty minutes," Anna said. "We have to reverse the ventilation fans. Like now."

"But it's risky," Munoz added.

"Explain," Samuels said.

Munoz brought up an electronic map of the Z Train systems on the console's central display. Tiny blue arrows rushed along the Jersey tunnel toward the Pavilion. "What you're seeing is the ventilation flow, drawing fresh air from the Jersey City entrance and pumping it through the system.

As it is right now, methane is being blown directly our way."

"And reversing the fans solves our problem?" Reynolds asked.

Anna said, "But it probably makes most of the Jersey tunnel highly explosive, and it increases the likelihood of suffocation for any passenger that might still be in there. On the flip side, it buys time for the people in the Pavilion to escape through the Manhattan tunnel."

"With the Manhattan level rising," Munoz said, "we're fighting a losing battle, but it's our only option of improving the situation. All tunnels are reporting leaks, but we'll at least be blowing one a little clearer."

"Let's get it done," Reynolds said. "This might sound harsh, but our priority is saving those who we know are alive. And judging by the state of the train, most, if not all, of the passengers are already dead."

Munoz hated to admit it, but he agreed with the president.

CHAPTER SIX

irst came a pounding headache, the same kind as waking in the morning after too many gin and tonics, but without the parched throat and a comforter stretched over her entire body. The cold rocky ground sent a chill through her torn trouser suit, and she had lost a sandal. She gulped and forced her eyelids open.

Total blackness cocooned her. She patted the loose stones to her sides while attempting to focus on anything that might give a clue to her location and fate.

A crackle echoed in the distance, like the static sound an old vinyl makes before spinning to the first track.

A metallic stench filled the air.

Her ribs ached from where somebody had grabbed her.

Memories crystalized in her mind.

It had all happened so fast. Boarding the train to the strains of classical music, champagne corks popping in the car, and the high spirits of the passengers on the inaugural run. Then the savage halt, throwing everyone out of their seats. The power cut. Total darkness. Glass shattering. So many screams. So much . . .

Strong hands had ripped her into the dark tunnel and carried her at speed. She thrashed her body, attempting to break free from the powerful grip, until the final memory of turning her head as the tunnel wall raced toward her face.

The vivid recollections sent a chill down her spine. Whoever attacked the train had used overwhelming speed and force. She had no idea how long she had been unconscious or if help was coming. Survival for her and the ten-week-old fetus in her womb was the only immediate goal.

Footsteps crunched over the stones toward her.

She bolted up stiffly and her heart rate spiked.

"Stay away from me," she shouted into the darkness. "What the hell do you want?"

Nobody replied.

She shuffled away on her backside, but a muscly arm rushed out of the gloom and pinned her shins against the ground. She kicked out. Her remaining wedge-heeled sandal connected with something solid and unmoving. The arm slid up her legs and applied excruciating downward force on her thighs.

An acrid breeze invaded her nostrils.

"Get the fuck off me!" she screamed as she leaned up and swung a fist at her attacker. It was like punching solid rock, and clearly it didn't faze this person in the slightest. She struggled harder, but hands grabbed her shoulders and forced them against the stones.

A hulking figure towered over her in the darkness.

Hot saliva dripped onto her neck.

She had to think of something. Anything to get away. Anything at all . . .

She had nothing.

A single finger, with a long dirty nail, prodded against her shirt.

The pressure increased against her shoulders and thighs, driving her against the hard ground. She didn't have the strength to match this power.

Tears streamed down the sides of her face and her chest heaved.

The dirty fingernail sliced off her shirt buttons one by one and parted the material.

She gasped, reached back, and grabbed a thick pair of forearms. No amount of trying moved them an inch.

"Wh-what do you want from me?"

The fingernail jabbed into her stomach and spiraled around her belly button like a corkscrew, scraping off a layer of skin. The pain was so sharp, so intense, she was shocked to the point of muteness. But while her voice wouldn't work, her body still responded, and she struggled again to free herself, twisting sideways enough that her cell phone dug into her hip.

The fingernail tapped her stomach three times and circled again, peeling away another layer of flesh, as if it were strip-mining into her body.

As if it were digging right for her unborn child . . .

She reached into her pants pocket, fished out her phone, and hit the unlock button.

A faint glow brightened the immediate space and the massive figure rushed away.

"What the hell do you want?" she cried, as a trickle of blood dripped down her belly. She got no answer.

Closing up her shirt as much as she could, she pressed the material against her wound, hoping to stanch the bleeding. Not wanting to turn the light away from the tunnel, lest her attacker come back, she nevertheless risked flipping her phone over only to see "No Service." She quickly angled its face upward with her trembling hand, casting light outward once more, this time at the ceiling of a cave.

To her right, the shadow of a figure moved beyond a dark circular entrance.

A smaller hole to her left had enough space for her to squeeze through, though not enough for her much larger captor to give chase. She didn't hesitate and rolled onto her front and started crawling on her hands and knees. Using every ounce of strength—and ignoring the phantom sensation of those strong hands grabbing her calves and dragging her back—she made it inside the cave.

Her moment of safety was quickly destroyed when footsteps crunched toward her again and stopped at the mouth of the hole. She struggled to move deeper, the pain in her stomach amplified by it being scraped across the ground, when something razor sharp reached in and sliced through her sandal's heel. With a shriek she wriggled her foot free and pushed deeper inside, grabbing the outcrops and hauling herself forward.

The walls widened into a tunnel and the crackling grew louder. She rose to a crouch, extended her arm, and angled the phone to illuminate her path.

Debris littered the ground: A clay pipe. Musket balls. A crumpled stovepipe hat. Shards of pottery. Rust-speckled tin toys. A faded family photograph. It was like a museum had exploded down here, and her brain whirled, trying to figure out what was going on. The only things that made sense were her inner dread, the gruesome cut on her belly, and the burning desire to escape from wherever her attacker had taken her.

The space opened out into another cave, and she edged back, not wanting to enter an area where she could be grabbed for another round of torture. She strained to hear anything above the crackle, and while she waited, the events finally sunk in. No signs of any other passengers. The probable mayhem in the city and the Pavilion when it dawned that they were under attack. The reactions of her family and friends.

Total chaos.

A scraping sound came from behind, growing louder by the second.

Somebody small enough had followed her inside the tunnel, which is when it dawned on her.

Nowhere was safe.

She scrambled to her feet and advanced deeper into the cave. She was running blindly now, the faint light on her phone enough to see just barely ahead of her, but she had no choice. Ahead of her was darkness, but behind her was a nightmare. She just had to keep moving for—

A heavy weight battered her right shoulder, and she dropped to her knees. Her phone cartwheeled across the ground and landed facedown, plunging her back into total darkness.

Hot breath brushed her ear.

Arms clamped around her chest and flipped her over forcefully, and the dirty fingernail corkscrewed into her flesh once again.

She knew nobody would hear her scream.

But she screamed anyway, until her lungs emptied, until her throat was raw.

She screamed, and screamed, and screamed.

CHAPTER SEVEN

The smooth, collective hum of the Pavilion's ventilation fans wound to a halt. Seconds later, they whirred back to life. Cafferty stared at the wall-mounted grilles and wondered why somebody had restarted the system. Munoz knew the answer, of course, but he hadn't replied to the message yet.

"What do you reckon?" North asked.

"I'm not sure. Reynolds wants us to inspect the train, though, so let's worry about that. We'll check on the injured along the way."

"Sounds like a plan."

Cafferty tucked the laptop under his arm and they headed past the stage toward triage.

"You don't have to do it," North said.

"Do what?"

"Check the cars for evidence. I'll handle it. You—"

"What? David, just say it."

"Well, aren't you going out of your mind right now?"

"We all knew passengers aboard that train, David. All we can do is gather any useful information and pray the rescue teams find them."

But even to his friend, he gave a politician's answer. The truth was Cafferty couldn't stop thinking about Ellen. Many in the Pavilion were in the same position, having a missing relative or friend, and likely shared his sense of helplessness. There was nothing to be done for it, though, and for the moment at least, he had to focus on things within his control. *Not* doing something would truly drive him crazy.

A dozen people lay on blankets and couch pillows inside the café. He approached the closest: a stocky bearded man wearing a bloodstained white T-shirt and holding a towel packed with ice over his left shoulder.

"You look like you've seen better days," Cafferty said.

"What's up, Mr. Mayor? Have we caught the terrorists yet?"

"They won't be leaving the tunnels alive. But that's not something you need to worry about—between the NYPD and whatever the president can call in, we've got it covered. What happened to you?"

"I was caught in a crush at the Starbucks door and forced against the broken window. Any word on when we're getting out of here?"

"Soon. Try to relax."

The man winced a smile. "Easier said than done."

Cafferty moved among the injured and NYPD,

repeating the assurances from President Reynolds. He also instructed Lieutenant Arnolds to pass on the message to those in the food court and to tell his squad at the mouth of the Manhattan tunnel that help was coming from that direction.

And while all this was just Cafferty being a good politician—and a generally good person—he had also used these interactions to help mentally prepare himself for facing the macabre scene of the subway car. Finally feeling he was as ready as he would ever be, he tapped North on the shoulder and motioned his head toward the platform. They left the store and made their way to the track, where a makeshift barrier had been set up around the train. He gave two cops an authoritative nod and ducked under the tape.

North wrenched open a set of doors on the front car and slithered through the gap.

If one person in the Pavilion could figure this out fast, Cafferty knew it was his trusted head of security, David North. In law enforcement circles, they had nicknamed him "X-Ray Man" because of his uncanny ability to spot critical forensic evidence whole teams of detectives had missed. Quite simply, he could imagine the execution of a crime, just like the criminal had done, while efficiently going about his work without any fanfare.

Cafferty followed him inside the car with a sense of optimism that they'd get to the bottom of it in short order . . . and froze.

Everywhere spelled violence. Seats ripped from the walls. A gray slip-on shoe lying on its side.

A deep scratch across the ceiling. A tablet with a smashed screen. Torn commemorative flyers on the floor. A Gucci purse by his feet with a snapped strap.

All caked in blood.

"There's no glass," North said.

Cafferty glanced up sharply at North's tone. The normally staid man's voice was just a touch strained, clearly affected by the brutality of the crime scene. *If* he's *nervous, what the hell should* I *be?* But he had chosen to check out the train, and he wasn't about to back down now.

"Meaning what?" he asked, forcing the words out.

"The windows were shattered *outward.*"

"You think the terrorists set off an explosion inside the car?"

"I'd say yes, but that's the weird thing—I don't see signs of any shrapnel damage. Or burn marks. The blood spatter isn't typical of a blast zone, either. It's random."

The flash from a camera popped on the platform.

Lucien Flament, the French reporter, lowered his camera. He looked every inch the Continental European, with a pink sweater tied around his shoulders, circular framed glasses, and a large leather satchel that hung by his side.

"Get back to the food court," Cafferty snapped at him.

"I witnessed the immediate aftermath of the Paris Métro attack. Do you want me to check for similarities?"

"I want you to do as you're told."

"Mr. Mayor, I'm here to help. And it looks like you need it."

"You came over to take photos. This is the wrong time to test my patience, Mr. Flament."

The two cops guarding the line stepped in front of Flament. He shifted to the left and raised his camera.

"Escort this pain in the ass back to the food court," Cafferty said. "And stop anyone else from leaving."

One of the cops grabbed Flament's elbow and led him away. The Frenchman shrugged free of the grip, glared at the cop like he'd just found him on the bottom of his loafer, and headed across the Pavilion.

With the minor irritant dealt with, Cafferty returned his focus back inside.

North had crouched at the far end in the conductor's compartment. "They came in here," he said. "And through another hole at the opposite end of the car."

"They?"

"It had to be a large group."

"Why?"

"This isn't the work of a lone wolf or a small cell. Whoever tore out two sections of the floor used special tools and needed enough power and speed to deal with sixty-five passengers."

Cafferty moved to North's side, past the empty radio docking stations, and peered at a gaping hole in the floor, big enough to fit at least three people through at once. Congealed blood stained its jagged edges and a shred of clothing dangled toward the track. "How did it go down?" he asked.

"I'm still working on it, but I'll admit I'm not really sure what happened. For instance, why they came in this way makes the least sense. It's convoluted. I mean, if it were me, I'd just force open the doors and order everyone off at gunpoint."

"Found any bullet holes?"

"Not yet. But I don't think guns were involved— the blood spatters are consistent with lacerations. From what I've seen so far, the evidence suggests the terrorists entered, destroyed the controls and lights, and sliced the passengers with sharp knives or machetes."

"Jesus . . ." The word hung in the air for a minute as both men pictured the chaos a group of men armed with machetes could do in a crowded subway car. Finally, softly, Cafferty asked, "David, can you tell if anyone survived?"

"I'd guess quite a few bled out before being removed." North stood, walked along the aisle, and paused in front of a window. "Damn . . ."

"What?"

"It's . . . You're not going to like this next part."

"I don't like any part, but go on."

"There's a piece of skin on this window's remaining shard," he said, pointing at a dangling piece of gore Cafferty had been trying to ignore. "Forget about explosives blowing out the windows. It looks like the passengers were thrown *through* them."

"What the *hell*?"

North grimly nodded.

The nausea returned, along with a vision of brawny men, decked from head to toe in black clothing, grabbing Ellen by her arms and legs and hurling her headfirst through the glass. Cafferty's left knee buckled and he thrust his hand against the wall to support himself, only to pull his hand away when he felt something sticky.

I'm in a goddamn slaughterhouse . . .

"Mr. Mayor, you don't need to see—"

"Continue," Cafferty said.

North hesitated but, after a firm nod from the mayor, went on. "It happened fast. To pull this off, you'd need a well-trained and well-financed team with night vision, advanced access to the tunnels, and several plants in the car when it left Jersey City."

"I personally checked the passenger list. It's hard to believe terrorists infiltrated the group. No, that scenario makes no sense—I don't buy it at all."

"I'm having a hard time with it, too. But an attack this complex requires extensive planning and coordination on multiple levels and a degree of sophistication unheard of in typical terrorist strikes. Don't be fooled by the barbaric nature of the attack. This took planning."

"What are you saying?"

"I'm saying, Tom, that I've never seen anything like this before."

Perhaps more than anything, that chilled Cafferty's blood. If North was *admitting* he was spooked, things must be even worse than he thought. Trying to salvage some logic out of this horror, he said,

"They must want hostages, right? Otherwise why not just blow up the train?"

"It's possible they knew the media were here and the car arriving in this state would incite the maximum panic. That said, I still don't get their method of boarding the train, or why they individually shattered the ceiling lights instead of just flipping the switch in the conductor's compartment."

"None of this adds up."

"I know. Tom, I . . ." North trailed off, and it was clear enough to Cafferty that it wasn't because he was hiding something.

It was because there were no words at this moment.

"What the hell should I tell the president?"

"I don't know. But wait till I've checked the outside of the train before saying anything, okay?"

Cafferty followed North back to the platform. They walked the length of the train. Scratches and dents peppered the front car, along with a few deep gouges the same as the ones in the ceiling.

"Why beat the crap out of the bodywork?" Cafferty asked.

"Maybe for effect," North said, although there was doubt in his voice. "There's something else bugging me, though. For all the strategizing and execution this took, the terrorists can't have thought too hard about an extraction plan."

"Why do you say that?"

North focused on the Jersey tunnel. "If they did take any hostages, it's almost certainly to use them as human shields or bargaining chips to gain freedom. But it's naive if that's their intention. It won't work."

"Why?"

"Every exit is covered. There's no way out. Unless there's something I'm missing, these terrorists don't plan to escape."

Cafferty suffered a second unwanted vision of a terrorist with an arm around Ellen's neck and a muzzle jammed against her temple, wearing a suicide vest, heading through the deserted Jersey City station under the watchful eye of snipers.

"I'm not sure we've found anything of immediate use," North said, distracting Cafferty from the image in his mind. "The only thing that's clear is that we're facing an armed and capable enemy who's . . ." North paused and looked intently at the mayor. "Who's still inside the subway system."

"Thanks, David. I'll let the president know."

This attack was clearly not over, that much was obvious from his security chief's words. And it frightened him, but that wasn't his only problem . . .

A light headache that had developed during the inspection was now growing into a stabbing throb. Cafferty put it down to the stress. He had a recent history of migraines, usually when confronted with a list of potential delays to the Z Train's inaugural run, and those times had put him only mildly out of his comfort zone. While this might seem like the worst thing he'd ever faced, it wasn't even close to the migraines he got asking the state legislature in Albany for more funds. He could handle this headache.

He crossed the Pavilion and headed for the AV room. Inside the food court, though, a sight brought him up short: a few guests and MTA workers were rubbing their temples and resting their heads in their hands, displaying the physical signs of suffering the same ailment. Having seen New York through a number of tough moments (a brutal superstorm that leveled the southern end of Staten Island; a lone wolf car crash during the New York City Marathon), he was well aware of what shock and PTSD looked like . . . and this wasn't it.

Something definitely wasn't right.

Cafferty glanced up at one of the security cameras and thought about the ventilation system restart again. Munoz had given him a guided tour a couple of weeks back and explained various measurements. He instantly regretted tuning out the technical details and letting his mind wander to issues he considered more important. But he was pretty sure those fans had something to do with what was going on. He reached the AV room, picked up the handset, and dialed the command center.

Reynolds' face appeared on the video screen. "That was fast work, Tom."

"Is there something you're not telling me, Mr. President?"

"About what?"

"I've got a killer headache and it looks like others do, too. What's going on?"

"There are no current dangers in the Pavilion. Did you find anything on the train?"

The use of *current* set off all sorts of red flags

in Cafferty's head, and he ignored the question. "I heard the ventilation system restart. Why?"

"The situation is being handled," Reynolds replied, maintaining a neutral expression. "Help is coming. Now, tell me about the train—"

Cafferty shook his head. "What situation?"

"You're in no immediate danger, Tom. Stay safe."

"But—"

The call cut and the image of Reynolds shrunk to a dot.

Cafferty growled with frustration. That Reynolds was lying to him was no surprise—the man was a snake, and he wouldn't trust him to keep a cactus alive for a week, let alone the lives of all these people down here. But that he was lying *now* of all times—it was too much. He flipped open the laptop, connected to the secure network, and selected Munoz's private message contact once more.

> TC: Diego, I want some straight answers.
> TC: NOW.

CHAPTER EIGHT

Another notification pinged from Munoz's laptop. He remained facing away from his workstation to avoid Samuels storming over and questioning him again. The big agent took micromanagement to an aggressive new level, and he outwardly trusted nobody. He stalked among all nine MTA employees with purpose, treating every move as a potential risk to the president's safety.

Reynolds rested his hands on his hips and watched a muted news channel on an overhead screen. Shaky images of the initial panic played, and headlines scrolled beneath about a terrorist attack and the president confirmed as safe.

"The rise of the methane levels are slowing," Anna said. "Look."

Everyone turned toward her position. The Pavilion's methane measurement bars had crept up only a tenth of a percent since reversing the fans. The Manhattan tunnel's fluctuated at the same height. And as predicted, two-thirds of the Jersey City tunnel now reported above the lower explosive limit at 6 percent.

"That bought us some time," Munoz said. "But not much."

"It's now down to our rescue teams," Reynolds said. "That's thanks to the crucial work of this command center."

"Mr. President, while we're waiting, I'd like your permission to check the audio files from the train," Munoz said. Truthfully, he didn't need permission, but thought it better to ask given Agent Samuels' persistent icy glare. "We might be able to piece together more of what happened."

"Audio files?" Reynolds asked.

"Subway trains communicate with each other and dispatch through radios," Munoz said. "We record those, including the feeds from the Z Train cars, and archive them here. It might lead to nothing, but it could give us a clue."

"You'll do this?"

"He's Mr. Audio," Anna said. "Diego runs this podcast—"

Munoz flashed her his shut-up glare. Once they were safely out of the Pavilion, the last thing he wanted was the Secret Service checking out his guest appearance on a podcast he helped produce. During the one-hour show, he speculated about Area 51 and the likelihood of alien races living on distant exoplanets. Those opinions often attracted attention, and a little further digging would likely reveal his gang links. He didn't want anyone knowing his past outside his old neighborhood, especially people in official circles.

"It'll only take a few minutes, Mr. President," Munoz said.

"Do it."

Munoz sat in the corner cubicle and put on his Sennheiser HD 800 S headphones. He navigated through the system to today's date, selected the train's last downloaded audio file, and imported it into a bootleg copy of Pro Tools that he used to edit his podcasts. He hit play.

"Greetings from the best subway train in the world."

"Hi, honey. How's the ride?"

"Smooth sailing. I'm here with sixty-four passengers including the mayor of Jersey City and our two governors in the first car. The champagne is sweet; I'll give you a taste in two minutes."

He skipped the file forward.

"Ellen, can you see the Pavilion yet?"

[Static.]

"Ellen?"

[A piercing collective shriek.]

Munoz looped the audio back and listened to the shriek again and again. He slowed the speed during the fifth pass. A distinct mix of desperate voices came through his headphones. With the audio slowed down, the shriek had separated to component parts. A woman's cry. Shattering. Scraping sounds. A child's scream. A name being called out. Several names. Munoz sampled the rhythmic sound of the train rolling on the track and applied a phase cancellation filter to the clip, knocking out any background noise. Then he applied a hiss removal filter and a high-pass filter, removing the static of the transmission and the popping sounds. He focused on the male voices, dropping the levels on the equalizer and bringing up the lower frequencies one by one.

A chill ran down his spine.

Screams. Dozens of them.

"Fuck."

"Help."

What sounded like *"Get the fuck—"*

"Holy shit."

"Jennifer."

". . . everywhere."

Munoz focused on that stream and isolated "everywhere." He pushed the headphones closer to his ears.

". . . are everywhere."

He slowed it again.

"They're everywhere."

But who the hell are "they"?

Not finding an answer there, he raised the frequencies on the EQ to isolate the female voices.

"Mommy."

"Jesus."

"What the hell . . ."

Just as abruptly as they invaded his headphones, the screams turned to silence. Munoz sighed as his shred of optimism faded along with the voices. He reached for his headphones.

"Tom, h . . ."

Munoz bolted in his chair. He isolated the clip and played it again.

"*Tom, help . . .*"

He ran it again to make sure.

"*Tom, help me . . .*"

There was no mistaking the voice of Ellen Cafferty, crying out a second after the main body of sound had ended, as if she were still alive after the attack had ended.

Munoz ripped off his headphones and spun to face Reynolds. "I've found something."

"Something?"

"A single voice shortly after the main attack. It's Ellen Cafferty, Mr. President."

"What do you mean *main attack*?"

Munoz passed him the headphones and replayed the full slowed recording.

The president's eyes widened and he waved Samuels over. "What do you make of this?"

Samuels planted a single headphone to his ear, listened, and shook his head. "I agree with Munoz's assessment, but there's nothing we can do. We don't know if she's still alive and we can't risk our teams. Consider the terrorists might want us to go in that tunnel so they can blow it up with a spark. They're filling the tunnel with methane for some reason, and that's the most logical purpose if they want to create maximum damage."

"Agreed," Reynolds said. "But it gives us a glimmer of hope."

"Can I offer a suggestion, Mr. President?" Munoz said. "We have MTA police officers stationed at the tunnel entrance in Jersey City. Let's send in two of our men on foot and try to locate any survivors or find the methane leak. No engagements. No sparks. They leave at the first sign of trouble or when our teams enter the system. We'll stay in radio contact."

Samuels shook his head once more. "That's not happening."

"Why not? Mr. President, my team knows the tunnel infrastructure through and through. If any of those passengers are alive in the Jersey tunnel, this might be their only chance."

Reynolds broke away and looked along the overhead screens showing the methane levels, the guests and MTA workers in the food court, and the damaged train sitting next to the platform.

"I strongly advise you against agreeing to this plan," Samuels said. "One wrong move and that tunnel could ignite."

Reynolds listened again to the cries from Ellen Cafferty playing on loop and glanced once more at the video monitors.

"Let's go for it," he said. "Diego, make the call. But only two officers, and tell them not to blow us all to kingdom come."

OFFICERS JIM DONALDSON AND CARL BRADSHAW CREPT SIlently down the Jersey City tunnel wearing gas masks. The dim orange glow of the emergency lighting illuminated their path, and they rounded a shallow bend that led toward the Pavilion. They could barely see three feet in front of them in the darkened tunnel, but they didn't dare use the powerful flashlights on their belts. If there were terrorists still here, the cops didn't want to alert them to their presence.

Donaldson was in front, avoiding the subway tracks in case power returned and they transformed into a death trap. Munoz had given him clear instructions not to use their weapons or engage the terrorists, just to search for survivors and the source of the leak. It made him feel like bait, especially as they were descending into a choking atmosphere, but he understood the importance of the task. By now, the whole world knew about the attack on the Z Train and lives were at stake.

They pushed deeper, closing on the halfway point.

Donaldson stopped midstride. "What the hell?"

A few feet to his front, rubble surrounded a gaping hole in the middle of the track that dropped into an unknown darkness.

"No idea what caused this," Bradshaw said. "But it doesn't look good."

"No shit."

Bradshaw pressed his back against the tunnel wall and edged to the side of the hole. He flicked on his flashlight and aimed the beam downward; it speared into the dark, dusty air. Donaldson grabbed a rock from the pile of rubble and tossed it down.

No sounds returned.

"I'm no geologist," Donaldson said, "but that ain't right, is it?"

"It's safe to say we've discovered our breach."

"Call it in."

Bradshaw unclipped the walkie-talkie from his belt, depressed the transmit button, and pulled away the lower end of his mask. "Diego, we've found part of the problem."

The speaker let out a static squelch. *"Go ahead, Carl."*

"We're by marker 119. It looks like the railroad ties buckled under the track. There's a pretty deep hole. We don't know how far down it goes."

Nobody replied.

"Did you get that?" Bradshaw asked.

"Roger. Is the track still intact?"

"It's bent upward on both sides of the hole, but the track hasn't ripped off the ties entirely."

"Is there any way you can block or fill in the hole?"

"Not unless you send down a backhoe and a shit ton of dirt."

"Any signs of life?"

"None."

"In that case, you and Jim pull back and return to the station. Don't forget to keep your weapons holstered and stay alert."

"Understood."

The men turned to retreat, and Bradshaw's shoe made a squishing sound. He looked down to examine the ground and gasped.

"We're standing in a goddamn pool of blood." He nearly gagged. "And what are those clumps on the floor? Is that . . . ?"

Bradshaw leaned down to get a closer look.

A liver. What looked like a giant hock of flesh. Severed digits.

Bradshaw stumbled back in shock, nearly tripping over his own feet. The walkie-talkie slipped from his hand and plunged into the abyss.

"Fuck!" Bradshaw yelled futilely.

"That's the least of our concerns," Donaldson snapped. "Let's get outta here."

The officers retreated up the tunnel. At the next marker, the walkie-talkie on Donaldson's belt crackled. He ignored it and continued until it chirped twice, as if somebody on the same channel had double-tapped a transmit button.

"Come on," Bradshaw said. "Keep up."

Donaldson unclipped his walkie-talkie. "Wait. You hear that?"

"No?"

"It sounded like . . . I'm not sure. Something." He hit transmit. "Diego, did you just pick anything up?"

"Nothing. What are you hearing?"

"Give us a minute."

Donaldson slowly walked back in the direction of the hole. The crackling cleared, and in the faintest regions of audible discernment, he thought he heard a faint voice calling out. He drew closer.

The speaker hissed, followed by a whisper. A child's whisper.

"It sounds like a kid," Bradshaw said.

Both men froze, silently waiting for another transmission.

"*Help me*," a little girl said more clearly through the speaker.

Donaldson pried away his gas mask and raised his walkie-talkie. "What's your name?"

"*Help me*," she repeated.

"You're not hearing this, Diego?" Donaldson asked.

"*Just hearing you. What's going on?*"

Donaldson didn't answer as he took in the situation. He knew he wasn't imagining things, because Carl definitely heard the girl, too. Which meant that Munoz was probably out of her range. And since her voice became clearer when he neared the damaged part of the tunnel . . .

He was pretty sure a passenger who had fallen into the hole had Bradshaw's radio.

Donaldson sprinted for the hole and lifted his walkie-talkie. "We have a passenger alive. A little girl. May need medical assistance. We're going back, over."

"*Negative*," Munoz replied through the speaker. "*Return to perimeter. Immediately.*"

"To hell with that. There's a kid down there." Donaldson skidded to a halt by the marker post and flipped open one of the MTA emergency boxes lining the tunnel. He grabbed a basic medical pack and unhooked a coil of orange rope and an LED lantern.

Bradshaw knelt by the hole and raised his mask again. "Sweetheart, can you hear me?"

"*Help me*," came through the walkie-talkie.

"We're coming," Donaldson yelled. "Carl, tie this end to the track."

"Are you nuts? You can't go down there. Hell, you don't even know how far down it goes!"

"Are you prepared to leave that kid to die?" Donaldson tore off his jacket and slipped on a pair of gloves. "We have to at least try, don't we? Tie the goddamn rope, Carl."

Bradshaw hesitated for a moment before he secured an end to the track.

Donaldson cast the other end into the abyss. He wrapped the rope around his gloved hand, latched the lantern on to his belt, and passed Bradshaw his walkie-talkie. "Keep Munoz in the loop. And be careful with it this time."

"You got it."

Donaldson planted his feet, leaned back, and lowered himself into the pitch-black shaft. The dim orange light from his swinging lantern bounced off the walls. He descended slowly, careful to avoid brushing against the jagged edges of the rock.

"You see anything, Jim?" Bradshaw called.

"Not yet."

The shaft narrowed toward an opening and he had twenty feet to go.

"Sweetheart," Donaldson said. "I'm almost there. Can you hear me?"

"Help me," echoed from below. "Help me."

Hearing the little girl's voice directly for the first time struck him as odd. It sounded the same every time, like a talking doll. He paused to catch his breath and listened more intently.

The rock snapped below his boots and gave way. He plummeted a dozen feet, crashing against the sides of the shaft, and sharp outcrops tore into his left side. He clamped his hands around the rope to stop his slide.

Dirt and rock rained on him, showering into his eyes and battering the top of his head and shoulders. The light from the lantern cut. Donaldson winced as strength drained from his body.

The rope slipped from between his fingers.

He plunged toward the opening and braced himself for the moment of impact. His boots crashed against solid ground sooner than he expected and pain seared in his left ankle, and he collapsed in a heap over a pile of rubble.

Bradshaw yelled something.

Donaldson coughed. He shook the lantern and tapped its side. It flickered back on and he held it in the dusty air, illuminating the walls and ceiling of a small cavern. The points of sharp stalactites hung down, making it impossible to stand if he wanted to search the place, but he had enough room to crawl.

"Jim," Bradshaw's voice echoed from above. "Can you hear me?"

"I'll live but I think I broke my ankle."

"Do you see the girl?"

Something rustled in the darkness.

"Sweetie, is that you?" Donaldson asked. "Are you hurt?"

"Help me."

"Darling, head toward the light. I'm here to help you."

Nobody replied.

"Don't be scared. I'm a police officer."

Donaldson crawled through the cavern and entered a tighter space where the stalactites scraped his back. His lungs burned and his ankle throbbed, but his determination to save the girl drove him on.

His hand hit something soft, and he lifted a child's tattered and bloodstained white dress. "Sweetie, my God, I'm coming. There's no need to be afraid."

A figure darted across his front. He extended his lantern, inched closer to a dark corner and toward the sound of the girl's coarse breaths.

"Reach for my hand, honey."

Donaldson's shirt snagged on a stalactite. He lowered the lantern and reached back to free his shirt.

In his peripheral vision, the figure lunged at him. With no room to maneuver, there was nothing he could do as hands grabbed his shoulders, nails pierced his flesh, and his body lifted in one sudden movement.

The glistening ends of two stalactites exploded through the center of his chest and stomach and held him in the air. Blood spurted from his mouth and his vision blurred.

"Jim," Bradshaw screamed in the distance. "Jim, are you there?"

Through the darkness, a snarling face appeared below Donaldson's torn-open torso. A scaly hand lifted Bradshaw's walkie-talkie, and a dirty fingernail hit the transmit button.

"Help me."

Not . . . terrorists . . . was the last thing that went through Donaldson's mind before the scaly hand choked the little life he had left out of his throat.

*   *   *

REYNOLDS AND SAMUELS STOOD ON EITHER SIDE OF MUNOZ AS he listened to Bradshaw's increasingly frantic and incoherent transmissions about losing contact with his partner. Guilt burned inside Munoz at the mission's apparent failure, but he needed confirmation before carrying out a full internal self-flagellation.

Munoz leaned toward the mic. "Calm down. What's happening? Over."

Static.

Sweat beaded on his forehead.

He squeezed the mic harder. "Officer, what's—"

"*It's a trap!*" Bradshaw screamed over the walkie-talkie. "*Goddamn it, someone help us!*"

"Calm down and tell us what's happening."

"*There was a girl's voice. Jim climbed into the hole to rescue her and . . . My God, I think he might be dead. Now she's trying to lure me down.*"

"He's losing it," Samuels whispered to the president.

"Get the hell out of there and return to the station now," Reynolds said.

"*I can't just leave him. What if—*"

"Follow the president's order," Munoz said. "You've located the breach and the enemy. We'll let the rescue teams know about Jim Donaldson."

"*I can't just—*"

A hiss came through the speaker, followed by silence.

"Bradshaw?" Munoz said.

Static.

"Bradshaw!"

Nothing.

Munoz rested his head in his hands.

"It's time to focus on that sub, Mr. President," Samuels said.

"What's the ETA?"

Samuels and Reynolds headed for the monitor displaying the sub's GPS coordinates superimposed on a map of the Hudson.

Even as the grief and guilt coursed through him, with Samuels' shadow gone, Munoz seized the opportunity at hand. He flipped open his laptop, read Cafferty's messages, and composed a quick reply.

> DM: Tom, some kind of breach in the Jersey City tunnel. Methane leak at dangerous levels. Extreme explosive hazard. Terrorist attacks still possible. DO NOT enter Jersey City tracks. Rescue team on its way thru the Manhattan tunnel. Pavilion not at explosive level yet, seek shelter fast. Half hour tops. Protect against possible suffoca

Munoz hit enter and quickly folded his laptop lid down right before Samuels turned his attention back his way.

He prayed Cafferty got the message in time.

CHAPTER NINE

Protect against possible suffoca

Cafferty read it over and over. His blood pressure soared at the idea of Reynolds purposefully holding back this information. Playing politics was one thing; treating him like an untrustworthy fool was another story.

He typed an immediate reply.

TC: When are the rescue teams arriving?

No response from Munoz.

TC: Diego, are you still there?

Nothing.

Cafferty guessed Munoz was back under the control of Reynolds and his Secret Service detail. He slowly spun in the AV room chair while digesting the rest of the message. It seemed inconceivable that terrorists had mined a route under the Hudson to attack the train. Unexpected methane pockets were found during the construction process, but all were filled, and a ground-penetrating radar survey confirmed the absence of any potential breaches. To dig a tunnel of that magnitude underneath their whole operation—it just wasn't possible. And yet . . . clearly it was. Something was missed, and it was costing people their lives.

Is this because I rushed the project through? The tunnel collapse that had claimed the life of that construction worker—*what was his name, McGoins? McGowan?*—had been a true accident, but Cafferty couldn't help but wonder if his obsession had led to more than just his marriage's struggles. He had pushed, and pushed hard, but . . .

No. Maybe we missed something, but it wasn't for lack of looking. This was especially true after the collapse—safety had been the top priority moving forward, and thorough inspections of all the tunnels and their routes had been instituted, even though it could have meant serious delays. Terrorists caused this mess. They were to blame.

Still, the Z Train extension was his project—his *baby*—and even the most observant parent was to be blamed if the child got hurt, regardless of if the fault lay elsewhere.

Blame would have to wait, though. Right now, a more pressing fact remained: he had to come up with a contingency plan if help didn't arrive in time.

North leaned his head around the door. "All civilians searched, Tom. We found nothing."

Cafferty stayed glued to the screen.

"What's up?" North asked.

"Our dear president hasn't been forthcoming with certain details," Cafferty said, twisting the laptop to face him.

North inclined toward the screen and read the message. "Jesus Christ. Do we know when the teams are coming?"

"I asked Diego the same thing. But we don't have time to wait. Grab one of the senior MTA workers and bring them here fast. We need a backup strategy."

North hustled out of the room, leaving Cafferty alone with his thoughts. Precious time had been wasted by the president not looping him in to the situation. If they got out of this alive, regardless of Reynolds' position, a score required settling. A *new* score. That was for later, though. The question right now was how they were going to get out of this, and he pondered his options.

Footsteps rushed back up the short corridor.

North reentered with a vaguely familiar-looking man wearing an MTA polo shirt. "This is Paul De-Luca, one of the project's technical managers. He knows this place like you know baseball."

Cafferty rose and shook his hand. "Thanks for coming, Paul. We need your help, and we need it fast."

"Whatever you say, Mr. Mayor."

"I'll get straight to the point: you've probably got a headache, like me, and it's because of a methane leak in the Jersey tunnel. If rescue teams don't arrive in half an hour, we're . . . well, we're dead."

DeLuca's face sunk. "What?"

"I know it's a lot to take in on top of what we're already facing, but we have to come up with a solution. Forget the command center. We need to create a sealed environment out here where we're shielded from an explosion *and* won't choke to death before rescue teams arrive."

"I don't . . ." DeLuca said. "I mean, I'm not . . ."

Cafferty rested his hand on his shoulder. "Take your time, buddy. Not thirty minutes, obviously, but digest it. Keep your cool and think."

DeLuca slipped his hand inside his satchel, retrieved a tablet, and scrolled through technical drawings. Cafferty paced the room, thinking about the consequences of the leak for Ellen and the passengers. He came to the stomach-churning conclusion that if any had survived the attack, the methane drastically cut their chances of leaving the subway system alive.

"What about the train?" North asked, interrupting his thoughts.

"What about it?" Cafferty said.

"The rear car is intact and untouched. Only the first car where the passengers were was attacked. Can we use it?"

They both looked to DeLuca.

"I guess it's possible. But we'd need to create an airtight seal in the car." DeLuca pulled up a list of materials stored in the Pavilion. "Okay, let's see . . .

We've got oxygen tanks, spare wall panels, and should have four blowtorches in the maintenance room. If we block the vents, seal the doors and windows, it might work. The thing is . . ."

"What?" North asked.

"I just don't know if we'll have time."

"Mr. DeLuca, you've got time," Cafferty said. "You've got twenty minutes. Get it done. Our lives depend on it."

DeLuca swallowed, then nodded.

"Good—let's go."

Cafferty left the AV room and jogged over to the food court, but slowed his stride before anyone could see him rushing anywhere. The appearance of him, North, and DeLuca drew curious looks from the seventy or so guests, MTA workers, and cops who sat around the tables, and he knew he needed to appear calm if they were going to get through this. The fact that most had the pallor of corpses, courtesy of the leak Reynolds had forgotten to mention, was not helping him keep his emotions in check.

But you don't become mayor of New York by losing your shit in public.

He climbed on top of the nearest empty table. "Ladies and gentlemen—"

"What's going on?" someone shouted.

Cafferty held up his hands. "I know you have questions, but right now, we don't have time. The reason for your headache is the level of methane in the air. Help is on the way, but we need to take a precautionary measure and seek shelter now before the methane level rises further."

The crowd murmured, and some looked toward the train.

"We'll see this through," Cafferty said. "But I need your help. I need a dozen people to help Mr. DeLuca with gathering materials from the maintenance room. Anyone with welding experience, report to David North."

"What's happening?" a woman he recognized from city hall asked.

"We're sealing the second car of the train and taking refuge inside."

"Are you mad?" the *Washington Post* journalist called out. "There's not a chance in hell I'm going near that subway train."

"Suit yourself," Cafferty said, half expecting this response. "The second car is completely intact. The methane level is okay at this moment, but it won't be soon. So until the rescue team arrives, it's your choice—seal up that train and stay safe, or stay out here and take your chances, buddy."

The man shifted uneasily in his seat.

"This isn't a debate, folks," Cafferty said with a sharp clap. "Speed is of the essence. Let's go."

Twelve people approached DeLuca and he led them out of the food court. Five approached North—which was more than the available blowtorches, but it wouldn't hurt to have as many on hand as possible—and his group crossed the Pavilion toward the train.

Cafferty assumed that by now President Reynolds

had likely seen the plan falling into action, though it didn't matter. He was safely behind a wall of steel with a submarine on the way. Perhaps more important, Cafferty didn't care: these people were sick and in danger, and if the president was just going to sit by and do nothing, it was up to *someone* to act.

A sea of nervous faces remained in the food court. They had every right to feel this way, though Cafferty had no other option but to move fast and keep the information brief. At least he had given it to them straight, unlike a certain person in the command center.

He could only hope that actually mattered.

CHAPTER TEN

Sal Kirsch surveyed the scene outside the MTA maintenance shed through the cab window of a diesel locomotive, used for hauling subway trains. Bright early-afternoon sunshine reflected off the Z Train Exhibition Center's glass pyramid. Beyond it, police and firefighters packed a line surrounding the three-story Jersey City station, blocking the press, who had steadily gathered on Marin Boulevard.

"Over there," Sal said to Mike Esposito, his fellow operator, who sat next to him paying more attention to his ham sandwich. "Two Blackhawks and an Apache over the Hudson. Shit's escalating real fast."

Four army trucks roared down the boulevard, crashed over the speed bumps leading to the newly christened Krumgold Avenue, and screeched to a halt outside the station. Soldiers armed with M4 carbines jumped out of the back and spread themselves inside the line.

"Mike, you listening to me? People are dead and you're stuffing your face. What gives?"

"You heard the boss. We go as soon as we get the all clear from the command center." He sounded almost bored.

"I don't get it. How are you not the least bit interested?"

"I'm interested enough, but what are we supposed to do?"

And that summed up exactly what was bothering Sal. He shook his head. "Sixty-five people up and vanish, some reported dead in the Pavilion, and God knows how many injured, and we're sitting here jerking off."

"In case you haven't noticed, you're a train driver, not Jason Bourne."

Sal grunted. "Betcha it was really an accident. The mayor is down there shitting his pants, trying to figure out how to break it to the press without losing face."

"You know what?" Mike popped the remnants of his sandwich into his mouth. "You're a real dick, Sal."

"Why, 'cause I tell it like it is and don't talk with my mouth full? You got a better explanation?"

"Yeah. Terrorism, you dumbass. The news says it's an attack. You think the army shows up for train accidents? Check out the pictures on your cell phone."

Sal sighed and slipped his phone out of his pocket. Mike had never taken a chance in his life. The two men had grown up in Bay Ridge together, both going to Fort Hamilton High School and, later, taking five different MTA exams, and they now operated one of the seventy-two service diesel engines in the subway system. Through all the thirty years of knowing him, he had always played it safe. Mr. I'm Not Risking My Butt for Anyone or Anything. Steady Eddie. Usually it was a good trait. Made Mike someone Sal could rely on.

Sometimes—like today—it drove him fucking nuts.

Four sturdy SWAT vans arrived outside. Police, dressed in green with black body armor, disembarked and pushed the press back toward the staff parking lot. In the sky, the three helicopters banked over the shimmering towers that lined the Jersey City waterfront and thumped back over the station.

Sal selected the CNN news app.

The headlines confirmed Mike's words. He scrolled to "Photos of the Attack" and swept through the images. Mayor Cafferty giving a speech. A confused-looking crowd. The bloodstained front car. Diego Munoz, an old drinking buddy, with his mouth hanging open and a tool kit by his feet. A member of the Secret Service dragging President Reynolds by his lapel. The command center blast door closing with a line of agents, guns raised at a crowd of desperate faces, standing outside them.

A chill ran down his spine.

"See what I mean?" Mike asked.

"It's insane. I've got three pals down there. You?"

"Same. Jess wanted a selfie with the president."

"She likes Reynolds?"

"Nah, she does duck-face photos with anyone famous."

Sal shook his head, swept back to the shot of the train, and scrutinized the image. "Mike, take a look. The train isn't derailed. It's still mobile."

"Yeah, but the power's out. The train's dark."

"So what? We barrel in there with the diesel engine, we could hitch that train up and drag everyone out, including the president."

"Including the president? We're not Train Force One, buddy. Those are terrorists down there."

"That's my point. Our friends are trapped in that Pavilion. I'm not leaving them to get picked off by those assholes."

"Look at all those soldiers and cops. Nobody is leaving anyone. Not to mention that no one is going to let us go."

"Who said anything about 'let' us?"

"You're an idiot, Sal," Mike said, opening a bag of chips.

And you're a pussy, Mike. Sal opened a video embedded in the news article.

The footage showed the powerless train gliding into the Pavilion. A moment later, the crowd on the platform charged in all directions, shouting and screaming. A couple of people fell and disappeared under the hail of shoes. The recording ended, frozen on the face of a panic-stricken woman who had darted in front of the camera.

His hand tightened around the phone. The mayhem reminded him of 9/11, when he hid behind an ambulance on Fulton Street as clouds of debris and smoke belched between the buildings toward him.

"We're going in," Sal said. "Right now."

"Yeah right."

"I'm serious. We have to do something!"

"Calm down. Besides, don't you think teams are already on their way?"

"Have you seen anyone entering?"

"This isn't the only entrance, Einstein."

"Don't patronize me, Mike."

"Did you stop and think *why* no one is going in? Something's not right here."

"Exactly!"

"No—I mean something more than even the news is telling us, idiot."

He hated to admit it, but Mike had a point. He hated to admit it so much that he decided to ignore it and focus on what was important: the diesel engine they were sitting in was only a railroad switch away from being able to charge into the sunshine and through the tunnel. The line of tape outside stretched across the tracks, and two cops chatted with a soldier in front of the shed, but they were no match for more than two hundred tons of accelerating steel . . .

As if reading his thoughts, Mike said, "We're not doing it, Sal."

"I'm not waiting until it's too late."

"You'll get us both fired."

"I can live with that. Could you sleep at night knowing we had the chance to save lives and just sat here and did nothing?"

"Can you live with getting us killed? There are terrorists down there. Can you sleep at night knowing you're fucking dead?"

Sal groaned—not just at the faulty logic but at what it implied. "If it's terrorists—and I still say it's a big *if*—fuck 'em. Let's see how they deal with American steel riding down their throats. We have a chance to save these people."

"Give it some time, Sal. Let the cops do their job."

Sal battered his fist against the dashboard. That was the problem—the cops *weren't* doing their job from what he could see, not unless their job was to stand around and do dick all. And having grown up with some guys who became cops, that might actually be the case . . .

Give it some time. He asked himself if those trapped people had any time left. With the clock ticking and the means to aid in the rescue at his disposal, Sal made himself a promise. If nothing happened in the next forty-five minutes, this diesel engine was heading for the Pavilion to rescue his friends, whether Mike liked it or not.

As Mike crunched away on some chips, Sal quietly set an alarm on his watch.

CHAPTER ELEVEN

All eyes in the command center were fixed on the live news broadcast. Special forces teams, wearing black helmets, gas masks, and tactical clothing, pounded along the deserted road and streamed down the steps of the Broad Street station. The image switched to a stern-faced reporter outside Federal Hall, who glared into the camera and announced the operation to free the people in the subway system was under way.

If the terrorists were stupid enough to be in the Manhattan tunnel, they were about to meet America's most elite and deadly fighting team.

Reynolds sat with a handset planted against his ear, his face rigid with concentration while he received live updates from the secretaries of defense and homeland security.

Samuels focused on the monitor displaying the DSRV's GPS coordinates as it powered to a depth of two hundred feet, heading directly for the docking station.

Munoz kept half an eye on the slowly rising methane levels and figured they had roughly twenty-five minutes until the Pavilion reached the LEL.

Anna leaned across to him. "Not long now."

"I'm sure we'll be all right. It's the passengers I'm worried about. And Jim and Carl."

"You did what you thought was best. And those two might be okay."

"Don't kid yourself. They aren't and it's my fault."

"You don't know that."

"It was a bad call. I fucked up and now two officers may be dead."

Every few minutes since his failed idea, Munoz had glanced across to Samuels. The big agent remained focused on the screens, frowning at the flurry of activity around the train, and he regularly checked his watch. A petty man would have stomped over to Munoz's chair and said "I told you so" with a shit-eating grin plastered across his face. But not Samuels. He remained a cold and hard hallmark of professionalism.

For some reason that bothered Munoz more.

On the Pavilion video feed, a line of people carried metal panels and oxygen tanks toward the train. North organized them at the rear car. Cafferty stood behind somebody holding a blowtorch toward an internal vent, and sparks fizzed against a window.

Munoz winced. "I need to keep Mayor Cafferty updated with the methane levels. They've got minutes until those torches ignite the whole place."

"Mr. President," Samuels said, shooting a nasty

look at Munoz, "it appears we've discovered the source of our internal leak."

"Not right now," Reynolds said. "Special forces are a quarter of a mile through the Manhattan tunnel with no problems encountered."

Silence filled the air, broken only by a regular electronic pulse from the ventilation management system, reporting the Jersey City tunnel's critical methane level. The sound, coupled with the array of controls in the command center, made the place feel like a huge submarine. And just like in a submarine, they were trapped inside . . . and in incredibly dangerous waters.

Munoz reached for the console's keyboard to mute the alarm—and two electronic pulses reported in quick succession. Glancing over to the monitor, he saw that the methane level in the midsection of the Manhattan tunnel had jumped to 4 percent, meaning another larger breach must have opened up suddenly, right where the special forces were.

Distant gunfire crackled through a speaker in the command center, and Munoz's eyes flew to a video monitor. More beeps drew his attention back to the methane monitor: the measurement bars surged upward to 6 percent and transformed from green to red, marking most of the Manhattan tunnel as highly explosive.

"Oh shit," Anna said.

Munoz twisted in his chair. "Mr. President, tell the rescue teams to stop firing! There must be another breach."

"What?" Reynolds lowered the handset. "Are you serious?"

"Dead serious! The leak. It's rocketed—"

A distant thunderous explosion boomed. The ground shook. A thin layer of dust dropped from the ceiling.

Munoz tensed, hoping the lower methane levels toward the Pavilion meant it wouldn't ignite and the blast wave would be snuffed out before incinerating everyone outside the command center. He rated the chances at fifty-fifty, though that was pure guesswork at this point. Some of the team members bolted from their seats, as if they'd be able to see something from this closed-off bunker. Others instinctively ducked. Still others were frozen in place.

Alarms blared through the console and the control panel lit up like a Christmas tree.

On the overhead video feed, Cafferty and his group dove inside the train. Cops rushed away from the mouth of the Manhattan tunnel. Seconds later, flames briefly licked out before dense smoke billowed into the Pavilion, shrouding it from view and almost certainly doing nothing for the air quality outside.

"What was that, Blake?" Reynolds shouted at the phone to the secretary of defense. He listened to a quiet, tinny voice reply and color drained from his face. "It did *what*?"

The news channel cut out to solid blue.

The DSRV tracking monitor cut out.

A link to the AV room cut out.

The ventilation management system reported fan failure in every tunnel . . . then cut out.

"Blake?" Reynolds said. "Blake, can you hear me?"

The ceiling lights flickered in the command center before returning to their consistent glare. Munoz knew that meant the backup generators had kicked in, which further meant external power was lost. Judging by the sound of the president, communication with the outside world was lost as well.

Only the view of the Pavilion remained live. The IMAX projector's blue beams stabbed through the gray haze, highlighting figures moving around the train. Munoz switched the console screen to a system-wide view, and every external source reported as disconnected.

"Blake!"

"It's no use, Mr. President," Munoz said. "The explosion destroyed our physical connectivity. We're on our own, running on localized backup power."

Reynolds slowly replaced the handset.

"Mr. President," Samuels said, "it's time to head for the sub while we still have some form of power. If that goes, we won't be able to get through the emergency passage doors."

Nobody said a word and all eyed the president. Reynolds leaned back in his chair, closed his eyes, and rubbed his temples.

"We need to move," Samuels said. "They might come here next."

"Let me think, goddammit," Reynolds barked.

Samuels backed away and turned toward Munoz. "What did I tell you about not taking unilateral action?"

"Back off me," Munoz countered aggressively. "With the fans now out, every tunnel and the Pavilion might be at an explosive limit in minutes. At least they have a better fighting chance."

"Listen very carefully." Samuels stepped closer. "When the president gives a goddamned order, you follow that goddamned order."

Willfully keeping people in the dark put their very existence at risk, especially with the welding work continuing outside. More than that, Samuels' attitude was so callously . . . *inhuman* that something snapped inside Munoz. He sprung from his chair, wrestled off his jacket, and pushed up the sleeves of his blue shirt.

"You wouldn't last five seconds," Samuels said, holding the ground between Munoz and the president. "Be a professional and get back to your position."

"Diego," Anna said, grabbing his arm, "this is not the fight to have right now."

"Stop!" Reynolds yelled at the same time. "We're not fighting in here. I need information. Now."

Munoz took a few deep breaths to calm himself while scanning his team's anxious faces. The more time he spent locked inside the command center, the more he felt selfish and frustrated about not keeping Cafferty fully in the loop. He mentally kicked himself for not staying strong and letting the pressure of the situation get to him. Samuels had done nothing wrong; they simply had competing priorities.

"The methane in the Manhattan tunnel sharply spiked moments before we felt that explosion," Munoz said in a calmer voice.

"The special forces team must have come under attack," Reynolds commented. "What's the status of the Manhattan tunnel?"

"The status? Sir, it's gone. It's all gone," Munoz replied.

Silence overtook the command center as the gravity of the situation sunk in.

"We need another plan," Reynolds said.

"Mr. President," Samuels interjected, "your plan is simple. The sub was twenty-two minutes away last time I checked. We need to leave."

Reynolds swallowed hard. "I meant for the others. Cafferty needs all available information before I step foot out on that sub. Deactivate lockdown and we'll bring everyone inside in case the terrorists come here next."

"Mr. President, we're under attack. We can't rule out anyone being a terrorist. Don't think because they haven't yet shown themselves that there isn't one still in the Pavilion, waiting for an opportunity like this. That blast door needs to stay closed. Once we've left on the sub, they can deactivate lockdown, but only then."

"Can we get Cafferty on the phone then?" Reynolds asked.

"The internal phone in the AV room," Anna said. "But he won't hear it from the train."

"How have you been in contact with him?" Samuels asked Munoz.

Munoz moved to his workstation and flipped open his laptop. Thankfully, the connection to Cafferty remained live on the local area network, and a new message popped up.

> TC: Diego, what the fuck?

"Mr. President," Munoz said, "you can message Mayor Cafferty here."

Reynolds moved to his side, hunched down, and squinted at the screen. "How much does he know?"

"I told him about the methane, sir. That's why they're securing the train. It'll save their lives if the fans don't restart. The mayor's online."

Munoz slid the laptop across to Reynolds.

> DM: Reynolds here. Are you okay?
> TC: What happened?
> DM: A second attack. Manhattan tunnel is compromised. Methane rising fast, fans down.
> TC: Open the blast doors. Let us in.
> DM: Once I'm in the DSRV, MTA will let you in.
> TC: That'll be too late.
> DM: I cannot open the door.
> TC: Open the fucking door.
> DM: I'm sorry, Tom.
> TC: We're sealing ourselves into this train.

Ask for SWAT Team 415. We need a clear exit.
Give me your word.

   DM: I will. Good luck, Tom. My thoughts and
prayers are with everyone.

On the overhead video feed, Cafferty folded his
laptop under his arm, stepped off the train, and
went about organizing his group around the subway car.

Reynolds shoved the laptop across to Munoz.
"You can manage the situation once we head for
the sub."

"You need me for the docking procedure."

"We're going on our own," Samuels said. "I know
the door codes."

"It's not just the door codes. The sub cannot
dock without someone on the inside to operate the
air lock. And the emergency tunnel needs to be secured after you leave."

Samuels nodded in acceptance without any argument.

"Before we leave," Reynolds said, "I need you to
call the SWAT team that Cafferty asked for."

"Phones are completely down," Munoz reminded
him.

"How about reaching out the same way we just
messaged Cafferty?"

"That's through the local server here. We're cut
off."

"Is there no way to get a message out?" Reynolds
said.

"I can try the radio, but I suspect everyone's out of range."

Still, Munoz shifted over to the comms panel, more in hope than expectation. He depressed the transmit button and leaned over the mic. "Any station, any station, this is the command center. Please respond, over."

The speaker hissed and let out a static squelch.

"Any station, this is the command center. Please respond, over."

A distorted voice crackled a reply.

"Please repeat that last. This is Diego Munoz. Who's there?"

"It's Officer Carl Bradshaw, over."

Munoz sighed with relief. "Great to hear your voice, buddy. Where are you?"

"Heading out of the tunnel. I'll be topside in a few minutes."

"We need you to relay a message, Carl. Ask for SWAT Team 415 to head for the Pavilion. It's a direct order from Mayor Cafferty. He wants them to lead everyone out. Tell them the whole place is explosive, so no weapons fire."

"Was that what the bang was?"

"No time to explain. Tell SWAT that we've lost power. The president is safe, and he's leaving shortly through the DSRV."

"Roger, over."

"As fast as you can."

Bradshaw attempted a reply but his voice broke up.

"Carl?"

The speaker hissed.

Munoz guessed that without relay assistance, he had caught Bradshaw in the nick of time before he went out of range. It gave him consolation that on top of delivering Cafferty's message and updating the outside world on the state of affairs, at least one of the MTA cops lived.

"It's time to go," Samuels ordered.

"We stay here until the sub arrives," Reynolds said.

"Mr. Pres—"

"We stay."

arah Bowcut knelt by the side of her SWAT team's van, aiming her M4 Commando at the empty Jersey City station. They had been swapping intelligence with the local New Jersey police teams when the call came in, and this was the nearest entrance to the Pavilion. Messages through her tactical headset confirmed operations command in Manhattan had lost contact with the special forces team that had entered the Broad Street station and a mound of rubble now blocked the route.

"They can't keep us here twiddling our thumbs," Captain Larry Dumont said. "What next?"

"If they want to secure the Pavilion first, I'm guessing we'll go in from here next, regardless of the gas leak."

"What's the wait? It might get worse and we've got missing passengers down there," he said, jabbing his muzzle toward the tunnel entrance. "Homeland Security is keeping us in the dark about something."

"I'm sure they'll tell us when the time's right," Chris-

tiansen, another team member, responded over the radio.

I'm not so sure, Bowcut thought. She peered across the river to Manhattan's skyline, sparkling in the bright sunshine. Her family had a deep history of law enforcement spanning a century in New York City, and the view served as a constant reminder that her brother and father had raced to the scene after the planes struck the World Trade Center. Both perished when the South Tower collapsed. She had vowed to honor them by carrying out her duties with equal bravery in the face of depravity and knew that next unwanted day had arrived after the Z Train footage hit the airwaves.

Not only that, David North was in the Pavilion. Some said opposites attract, but he proved equally as useless with women as she was with men during their first four dates. They bonded by theorizing about unsolved cases and through a mutual love of pastrami sandwiches at Katz's Deli. A clumsy kiss on the cheek had ended each meeting, along with stuttered promises to do the same again the following week. Somewhere along the way, they fell in love, and those awkward kisses had turned into something that took her breath away.

She didn't want to lose that feeling today.

"Captain Dumont, Officer Carl Bradshaw just re-emerged from the tunnel," Dalton said through Bowcut's earpiece.

"Let's go," Dumont said. He sprinted from the SWAT van, Bowcut following suit. They ran to the entrance of the Jersey City tunnel.

Bradshaw staggered forward, clearly traumatized. He clutched a gas mask in his left hand, and his face had the complexion of a wax figure.

Dumont ran up to the officer and grabbed him by the shoulders. "Are you all right? Carl, what happened?"

"I . . . we came across a breach in the tunnel, at marker 119," Bradshaw replied. "A massive deep hole. There was blood . . . there was . . ."

"Easy. Tell us slowly. Where's your partner?"

"He . . . we heard a voice so he climbed down into the breach, and . . ."

"And what?"

"It was a trap. He's gone."

Bowcut stared intently at the police officer and knew instinctively he was telling the horrible truth. "Carl, did you make it to the Pavilion?" she asked.

"No, but I got a message from the command center on the walkie. The mayor gave a direct order for your team to head to the Pavilion and lead them out."

"What else?" Dumont asked.

"The tunnel's filling with methane. It's highly explosive. You cannot fire weapons of any kind. The people are holed up in the Pavilion without any power and the president's heading to the DSRV."

"Thank God," Bowcut said. "Carl, we need you to tell us everything you know about the terrorists. How many are they? What kinds of weapons did they have? What did you see?"

"Nothing," Bradshaw replied. "I saw nothing."

"What do you mean?"

"They were ghosts, invisible. I saw nothing but carnage."

Bowcut's skin crawled at Bradshaw's words. It wasn't so much what he was saying, which really didn't make a lot of sense to her, but the *way* he was saying it. There were so many unanswered questions in the officer's story, but she knew he was telling them everything he knew . . . and what he knew was scaring the crap out of her.

"All right, Carl, head to the DHS coordinator for a full debrief," Dumont said.

"Yes, sir."

Bradshaw let out a deep breath and headed between them. A group of cops escorted him from the line to the back of a tactical response truck.

Dumont turned to Bowcut, concerned. "Sounds like we don't have much time," he said. "What do you think?"

"If a hundred of us go down and somebody fires a shot, we all die." Bowcut scanned the weapons bristling behind the line and the hundreds of cops staring in her direction. "I think we follow the mayor's order and move in with a small team. We load up with batons, knives, and whatever else we can find, and we move fast."

"Agreed. I'll brief the coordinator and deal with Bradshaw; you ready the guys."

They returned to the SWAT team van and Bowcut conveyed the captain's order. "All right, guys, we're a go. Let's gear up and move out."

Dumont headed for the driver's door of their van to call the details in to HQ.

Bowcut looked over weaponry with the stocky Christiansen and another SWAT team member, the tall Dalton. They grabbed their gas masks and borrowed some personal fighting knives from soldiers to go along with their nightsticks.

Dumont headed over to the DHS coordinator after confirming his plans with the boss. They grilled Bradshaw for a few minutes before he returned to the van.

"Homeland Security agreed to let us go in to establish their location, but we only have a small window," Captain Dumont explained. "Operations command is preparing more teams, so let's get down there fast and get them the information they need."

"Do we engage?" Bowcut asked.

"Only if necessary, and if we reach the Pavilion, we're bringing everyone straight out. It's going to be dark so use your rifles' hybrid sights, but whatever you do, don't fire a shot. We still haven't established if the first escape teams triggered an explosion in the Manhattan tunnel by opening fire. Any questions?" Nobody replied. "Okay, Bowcut, you take point. Let's do this quickly."

Bowcut led the team to the station. Some of the cops on the line stared at her impressive rifle. They didn't even know the team was piloting a new sight with night vision and thermal imagining that fit comfortably on the eyepiece, meaning they didn't need to bring goggles. The rifle could also double as a club and had a powerful beam of light mounted on top.

A weapon even when it wasn't exactly the weapon it was supposed to be.

Adrenaline coursed through her body as she neared the glass entrance to the Jersey City subway station. Her team had served together for the last four years, arresting or killing some of the smartest and stupidest criminals in New York. They worked like a well-oiled machine. Most encounters ended peacefully, probably because the sight of laser-guided submachine guns pointed at a criminal's chest tended to quell even the most violent assholes. Today, though, they didn't have that option.

We're still the best, Bowcut thought, *and we're going to get this done.*

They entered the station, moving past the snipers on the mezzanine level and the soldiers tucked inside store entrances with their weapons pointing toward the track. A banner stretched over the stores, announcing the inaugural Z Train run. Shafts of sunlight shone through the vaulted glass ceiling, creating a checkered pattern on the ground. A paper cup lay on its side, next to a pool of black coffee.

Bowcut headed toward a signpost for the Z Train, descended a set of marble steps, and reached the confetti-covered platform. She jumped onto the track and faced the mouth of the tunnel.

Dalton crept to her left, Dumont and Christiansen behind in their typical overwatch formation, and the team pushed into the darkness.

"Gas masks now," Bowcut instructed the rest of the team. She slid hers over her face. "No flashlights to give our position away. And remember what the captain said, only use your sights for identifying targets. Keep your weapons locked. Nobody pulls their trigger or we'll all be kissing our asses good-bye."

A quick series of nods confirmed they heard, and she moved forward, knowing they followed tightly behind. The emergency lighting in the subway had failed and the tunnel changed to pitch black the farther in they went. Bowcut switched her scope to night vision. She proceeded past the markers at a quick pace, closing on 119 faster than she was comfortable with, but the clock was ticking for the survivors in the Pavilion.

"Keep it tight," Dumont said through her headset. "We're close."

"Scan the tracks," she replied. "Look out for anything suspicious."

"Roger," Dalton said.

Bowcut searched for wires crossing their path, stray packages—basically anything that appeared out of place. Anyone who had infiltrated the subway system, taken out an entire train, *and* eliminated a special forces team was smart enough to booby-trap the tunnel.

Marker 118. They were close now.

Around a shallow bend, close to the breach, a whole section of the tunnel glowed bright green. Bowcut dropped to one knee and the team took up defensive positions.

"What the hell are we looking at?" Christiansen asked.

She had no idea. "Wait here," she said.

Bowcut edged toward the 119 marker. On the left wall, an MTA safety box door hung open.

Her boot squashed against something. She cupped her hand over the front of her weapon-mounted light system, switched it on, and thin rays burst between her fingers.

Red spatter stained the wall. On either side of the track, maroon lumps of unrecognizable body parts lay in shallow pools of blood. A sense of gratuitous violence hung in the air.

Her heart hammered against her chest. She aimed the beam down and her boot rested on top of what looked like a length of intestine.

Bowcut staggered back.

"What have you got?" Dumont asked.

"We found where they attacked the train, Captain. It's . . . it's bad."

The rest of the team crept forward. She focused her streams of light on the pools of blood.

Dumont gasped. "My God . . ."

Christiansen silently shook his head.

Dalton ripped up his gas mask and heaved.

A few feet ahead, a rope ran from the track and disappeared inside the hole. An NYPD vest lay next to it on a pile of rubble.

"This must be the breach Bradshaw mentioned," Captain Dumont said.

"Something's not right," Christiansen said. "We need backup."

"We don't," Bowcut replied. "If the terrorists want to live, they can't fire, either."

"Or they do and kill us in a suicide attack," Christiansen retorted. "Who takes a knife to an explosive gunfight?"

"Listen up," Dumont said. "Whoever did this might reach the Pavilion at any minute. We're those people's only defense, so stay sharp. Nobody else is getting butchered today. Christiansen, you and Dalton take point."

Dalton cleared his throat, spat on the ground, and replaced his gas mask.

Bowcut stayed in her crouching position, waiting for her team to ready themselves and continue with their mission.

Nobody else is getting butchered today.

Sarah Bowcut prayed he was right, especially in David North's case.

CHAPTER THIRTEEN

Sweat poured down Cafferty's face as he inspected the train's retrofits. Since the explosion and the fan failure, the temperature and humidity had climbed, and his soaked shirt clung to his back. To say things had taken a turn for the worse was putting it mildly.

A thin cloud of smoke still partially cloaked the area. Cafferty thanked God the explosion snuffed itself out when it hit the Pavilion's higher oxygen density, but he knew they wouldn't get lucky a second time with the methane levels slowly rising. His pounding headache had returned with a vengeance, and he paused to catch his breath.

Thankfully, the welding of a steel plate onto the final vent of the train was almost complete when he'd received the messages from Reynolds. One of his team stood on a seat and went about finishing the job with some high-strength adhesive. Others attached plates over the windows using heavy-duty bolts and screws.

"If what he says is true," North said, "I hope the tunnel collapsed on the terrorists' heads."

"It's the ones in the Jersey tunnel I'm worried about. I'll feel safer once Reynolds splits and we're in the command center."

"Agreed. It's down to us to hold out."

"And that's exactly what we'll do."

Several police officers wheeled four more industrial tanks of compressed oxygen from the maintenance room to the train, giving them a total of ten on board. Paul DeLuca and his crew carried over MTA lanterns, flashlights, tools, and steel poles from the stage. Shooting wasn't an option, but if the terrorists attacked again, Cafferty had no intention of surrendering without a medieval-style fight to the death.

"My head's killing me," North said. "You look like crap, too."

"Thanks," Cafferty said wryly. "Listen, we better load up the train. Let's wrangle everyone on board. The explosion might not have kicked off another wave of panic, but if people start losing consciousness . . ."

David North nodded and headed straight to work.

Cafferty knew his rock-solid head of security was good—he never doubted that—but he never understood how great until today. Having North by his side gave him the strength to focus on their immediate situation, instead of becoming consumed by the thought of Ellen's fate.

Although, of course, now that he was thinking about her . . .

No. Focus!

Cafferty crossed the Pavilion and entered the food court. The people inside had retreated from the entrance and clustered around tables in the far corner.

"Mr. Mayor," a man asked weakly, "is help still coming?"

"What was that explosion?" another voice said.

"Are we still under attack?"

The questions came fast and furious, and Cafferty sensed the panic.

"I don't know," he said firmly, and something about his tone silenced the questions. "The truth is I just don't know. We've lost communications with the outside world. The tunnels are full of methane and the fans are no longer working. The explosion could've been anything. An accident. A spark. A single gunshot. I won't lie to you—it could be another attack. So here's what we do. We stick to the plan. I need you all to calmly proceed to the train's rear car before we can't breathe anymore out here. Once we're sealed inside, we'll figure out what's next."

"What if the terrorists attack here?"

"Then we fight back." He smiled grimly. "You all know that New Yorkers don't lie down to let someone stomp on our faces. Now, let's get to the train."

Cafferty returned to the train, followed by a procession of roughly fifty people. He had lost count of the exact numbers in the Pavilion but figured they needed to squeeze around one hundred souls inside the car, like sardines in a tin.

Like the 6 Train during rush hour, he thought. *I have to work on that next . . .*

He almost burst out laughing. Here he was, facing a catastrophe, and he was already thinking about what his next project should be.

This methane must really be getting to me.

He looked around. Guests, MTA workers, the press, and police filed into the train. The ones by the doors and newly armored windows grabbed hammers, wrenches, pipes—anything that could be used as a weapon.

Cafferty waved over the five Secret Service agents in front of the blast door, but they maintained their positions guarding the command center. He didn't expect them to leave their post anyway, but they were no less susceptible to the methane than anyone else, so he figured he'd ask. He scanned the Pavilion for any strays before calling in the cops from the tunnel entrances. It would leave them exposed, but if those officers passed out from the methane, it wouldn't matter if they were still guarding the tunnels—the attackers could just step over them.

God, this plan has *to work.*

Having rescue teams arrive to a train full of corpses didn't bear thinking about. The sight of the blood-spattered front car was bad enough.

"Do you know of anyone missing?" North shouted from the far end of the train.

Nobody responded.

Three gunshots split the air, coming from the

Jersey tunnel, and Cafferty's heart leaped into his throat as he braced for the inevitable.

By the grace of God, the methane didn't ignite.

But it meant someone was out there and willing to risk shooting. And that there was something worth shooting *at*. All of which meant they didn't care if the methane exploded. Cafferty wondered if that was because they *wanted* it to ignite or because they thought whatever they were shooting at was a bigger risk than a tunnel full of explosive gas . . .

People pressed toward the door to look toward the Jersey tunnel, while others pushed to get deeper into the car. The last thing they needed was a stampede on a crowded subway car.

Mustering all his strength, Cafferty shouted, "Everyone stay on the train!"

The cops worked to keep people inside, urging them with a professionalism that gave Cafferty a sense of pride. *The best damn police force in the world*, he thought.

That is, until a police officer sprinted out of the mouth of the tunnel, barreling through his line of colleagues, screaming, pistol drawn, face bloodied and full of pure terror. He scrambled onto the platform and aimed back toward the tunnel entrance.

"Hold your fire!" Cafferty bellowed. "You'll kill us all!" Even as he said it, though, he could see the officer's finger edging toward the trigger. And while the previous shots hadn't set off an explosion, the risk was too great . . .

But Cafferty was also too far away to stop him.

*   *   *

LUCKILY NORTH WAS AT THE OTHER END OF THE CAR, AND THE big man sprung from the train and dove on top of the officer like a linebacker, ripping the gun from his hand before it discharged. Other officers rushed to help.

"Get the fuck off me," the cop said, struggling to break free of North's grip. "We've gotta get outta here. They're in the tunnel and heading our way!"

"Who is?" North asked.

"There's hundreds of them." He coughed. Blood spouted out of his mouth and speckled his face. "We're dead. We're all dead."

North let go of him and raised his bloodstained hands in front of his face. He leaned back down and ripped open the cop's shirt.

Three diagonal gashes had torn open his chest and stomach, and every heartbeat sent more and more blood pumping from his torso.

"Who did this?" North asked. "What are they armed with?"

The cop's eyes closed and his head flopped to the side.

"What happened?" North asked desperately. He shook the cop's shoulders. "Tell me!"

"They followed me back," he whispered. His limbs went limp and his body relaxed in death.

CAFFERTY PUT HIS FINGER AND THUMB IN HIS MOUTH AND whistled. The cops at the mouth of the Jersey tunnel glanced over their shoulders. "Fall back, now! Into the car."

That was all the impetus they needed. They started making their way back as quickly as possible when one officer was seemingly sucked into the darkness at lightning speed.

His cry rang through the tunnel.

In the blink of an eye, another cop disappeared, yanked into the pitch black by an unknown force.

Cafferty's eyes widened. "What the fuck?"

The remaining seven cops didn't even look back—they sprinted for the train. One stumbled and fell flat on her face. Before she had a chance to drag herself back up, a long black arm reached out of the tunnel and clasped her ankle.

She grabbed a rail tie, looked toward the train, and screamed.

The arm must have been incredibly strong, and in a second it had ripped her free. She clawed at the ground but couldn't stop being dragged away.

Cafferty stood frozen, watching as three cops vanished in a heartbeat. *What the hell is going on?*

What the hell was that . . . thing?

As he tried to parse everything, he didn't even notice his head of security charging toward him.

North wrapped his arms around Cafferty and strong-armed him inside the car. But Tom had to see, so he shook free enough to lean out the open door, praying the rest of the cops made it to the train where everyone could make their final stand.

One boarded.

Then another.

Three. Four. Five.

A single cop remained outside, overweight, and he puffed his cheeks as he bounded along the track.

"Come on, man—run!"

The officer tried. But it didn't matter, because a jet-black creature burst out of the tunnel with lightning speed, and it was clear the man had no chance.

Yet as horrible as that was, all Cafferty could think was: *A creature.*

He took a sharp intake of breath.

The creature raced forward on two muscly legs and its shriek echoed around the Pavilion.

A mix of shouts and screams filled the car.

"What the hell's that?"

"God!"

"It can't be . . ."

"Jesus Christ . . ."

"Run," Cafferty shouted to the cop. "Fucking run!"

"Please run," he whispered to himself.

The creature hunched down, leaped forward, and pounced on the cop within five yards of the train doors. The cop collapsed to the ground. The creature's claws shredded his trousers and gouged his calves as it seemingly climbed up the officer's body.

Flesh and fabric tore off the cop's torso.

Lucien Flament, the French journalist, shoved past Cafferty and thrust between the open doors with a claw hammer raised over his head. He aimed a kick at the creature's gut, knocking it back.

The cop scrambled on all fours inside the train

and collapsed on his back, wincing and taking rapid shallow breaths. A few passengers moved to help with his wounds.

The creature's movement had slowed, and it rose on its legs to a height of seven feet, shrieking once more. It was a chilling sound, and its open mouth revealed three rows of razor-sharp teeth, a horrific sight. It had sleek scaly black skin, a bulbous head, a thin tail with jagged spikes running along it, and four muscly arms, each with three talon-like fingers.

Flament swung the sharp end of the hammer down and smashed it into the creature's skull. Dark brown blood dripped from the two steel prongs.

The creature lurched to the side and let out a piercing howl.

Cafferty staggered back and hit the throng of people inside the car. "Get back!"

He turned around again to see the Frenchman swing the hammer downward once more, going in for the kill. A split second before it reached its target, though, the creature leaped back into the darkness of the subway tunnel, leaving a trail of blood in its wake.

The train fell silent.

So did the Pavilion, apart from the footsteps of police officers racing from the other entrances and boarding the car. Everyone focused on the pitch-black tunnel, waiting for another living nightmare to appear.

Cafferty balled his trembling hands into fists, utterly staggered at what he had just witnessed.

Flament simply pushed his glasses up his nose, straightened his sweater, and stepped back inside the car.

A cacophony of high-pitched shrieks emanated from the darkness of the tunnel.

Everyone tensed.

Cafferty recalled the dying man's words. *There's hundreds of them.* He had never subscribed to conspiracy theories or the far-fetched stories about monsters, but he couldn't deny what he just saw. It hardly seemed believable. They were under attack from a new kind of evil, unknown to the world. Until today.

This wasn't terrorism. It was pure terror.

CHAPTER FOURTEEN

Munoz froze in horror as he watched the command center's live video feed of the Pavilion. Three police officers were dragged into the darkness, and a black creature surged out of the tunnel and attacked another cop. He broke out of his state and shouted, "We're under attack!"

"What?" Reynolds sprung from his chair, followed by Samuels, and they rushed to Munoz's side. "Show me."

On the video feed, nothing moved in the Pavilion. Cafferty and his group had packed themselves inside the rear car and were in the process of blocking the final set of doors with steel plates. Blood soaked the tracks behind the train.

"What am I looking at?" Reynolds asked.

"There was . . . this thing . . . it just attacked the police, dragged them back into the tunnel. It happened so fast."

"Roll back the tape," Reynolds commanded.

The rest of Munoz's team crowded his chair. He

gripped a small joystick on the console with his trembling hand and twisted it to the left, reversing the feed.

Frame 01:32:07:10. North wrestling with a cop.

He nudged it forward.

Frame 01:32:07:20. A cop's legs disappearing into the tunnel.

He tapped the joystick again.

Frame 01:32:07:32. The creature in midair, arms outstretched, lunging toward a cop on the platform.

It all happened lightning fast.

Somebody behind Munoz screamed. Others muttered in disbelief.

"My God," Reynolds said. "Go back to live."

Munoz fast-forwarded back to real time.

Cafferty's team had covered the final set of train doors, and the rear train looked like a custom-built silver torpedo. Something, or some *things*, moved at the mouth of the tunnel. It was impossible to see with any clarity because of the resolution and the smoky atmosphere. Arms reaching out of the darkness and retreating. Not just two.

Hundreds of arms.

Reynolds moved closer to the screen and scrutinized the image. "I thought it wasn't true . . . This can't be . . ."

"It can't be what, Mr. President?" Anna asked in a shaky voice.

"Enough," Samuels said. "It's no longer safe for you here, sir. We're heading for the sub, right now."

"Mr. President," Munoz said, "do you know something?"

Reynolds' eyes darted between the team and the video feed.

"Mr. President," Anna said with increasing fury.

A row of the Pavilion's overhead lights next to the tunnel exploded.

All eyes went back to the screen.

The next row shattered.

And the next.

The grid of lights cut out in sequence, sending a dark staccato wave rolling across the Pavilion and plunging it into blackness. Only the deep blue beams of the IMAX projector and the timestamp remained visible on the screen.

"Mr. President," Samuels said, "we need to leave. *Now.*"

A thunderous crash shook the walls of the command center. The screams of the Secret Service members guarding the outside of the blast door echoed through the speakers.

"What the hell is that?" one of the command center operators asked.

Another crash hit the blast door.

The MTA team recoiled toward the back office.

Samuels grabbed Reynolds' arm and dragged him in the same direction.

Munoz crouched behind his chair. It didn't take a genius to work out that the creatures were attacking the door with weapons . . . or mind-blowing strength. He feared for the people barricaded in the train, though held out no hope for the Secret Service guys and could only pray their deaths were quick.

"What the hell?" one of his team members shouted.

A moment of silence followed the rhetorical question.

Then another shuddering crash rocked the command center.

The hinges on the blast door—built to withstand just about all known conventional strikes—groaned.

A calendar dropped off the wall, pens rolled off workstations and bounced on the tiled floor, and a chair toppled over.

"Holy shit," Anna said. "What are these things, Mr. President?"

Another wince-inducing crash buckled the door, but it held.

"How long until the sub arrives?" Reynolds asked, his voice trembling.

"Fourteen minutes," Samuels said.

"How many passengers can it hold?" Anna asked.

"A maximum of twelve," Munoz replied.

"We'll all go."

Samuels drew his pistol. "Mr. President, it's you, me, and the one closing the hatch behind us. Nobody else. The door will hold. We cannot risk your life any further."

"Are you insane?" Anna said. "You can't leave us here."

"Nobody is coming with us," Samuels snapped. "The safety of the president of the United States is at stake and we follow clear protocols. I'll do this as fast as I can and send the sub straight back."

"Are you fucking mad?" Anna replied. "Mr. President, you can't leave us here."

Another crash rattled the walls and something inside the blast door cracked, but again it held. Samuels stood unflinching, uncompromising. Munoz knew nothing was getting past him or changing his mind.

"*Mr. President!*" Anna repeated.

"Mr. Munoz," Reynolds said, trying to compose himself, "you'll come with us, seal the door once I'm safely on the sub, and head back for your colleagues. I don't like this as much as you, but if we act fast, we'll all get out of here. Now, grab the gun from under the fire blanket. We don't know if those things have infiltrated the emergency passage."

"I don't want him armed," Samuels said. "He's a former gang member, sir."

Munoz stood glued to the spot, stunned at the revelation. All eyes focused on him and he couldn't find any words to counter or explain the truth. "How did . . . ?" he said.

"Secret Service plans for every eventuality and carried out a deep-dive background check on everyone in the command center," Samuels replied coldly. "You cannot hide your past, Mr. Munoz."

Munoz shot daggers at the Secret Service agent. He hated being judged for mistakes he'd spent his life making amends for. And seeing as they were all in shit, now seemed like an irrelevant time to rake up his past.

"We need to move," Samuels said. "I don't want him armed."

"Gather around," Munoz said to his team. "Quickly." Once they were all close, he whispered, "This'll only take a few minutes. Once the president is safe and I'm back, we'll all head for the docking station. Use my laptop to get in touch with Cafferty. My password's HanS0l0. Capital *S* and *H*, zeroes for the *o*'s."

"Let's go!" Samuels said.

"Mr. Munoz," Reynolds said, "I know you probably don't trust me, but I'm putting my trust in you." The president walked over to the dead agent, crouched next to the fire blanket, lifted it, and visibly shuddered at the sight of the agent's pale skin and lifeless eyes. He reached a hand underneath and patted around, grimacing, and eventually located the blood-soaked weapon. Reynolds returned with the gun and approached Munoz.

"Mr. President, I strongly disagree with—" Samuels said.

"Enough," the president said.

Reynolds handed the gun to Munoz. For the first time in years, Munoz wrapped his fingers around a pistol grip, something he had promised himself he wouldn't do again. It felt familiar, though, like riding a bike, and he stared at the weapon, wondering if he still had the same cojones after all this time.

Guess I'll find out.

Munoz led Reynolds and Samuels down a short corridor to the circular electromagnetic hatch. He keyed in the code on the digital pad and the steel locking bolts snapped open.

"Be careful where you point that," Samuels said,

peering down at Munoz's gun. "Only fire on my command."

"You don't need to worry about me."

"Actually, that's exactly what I need to be. And to be very clear, if you point the gun anywhere near the president or me, you're a dead man."

The hatch opened with a mechanical grind, revealing a brightly lit concrete corridor that climbed out of view.

Samuels ducked through and extended his gun forward.

Reynolds followed.

Munoz glanced back at his team, gave a reassuring nod, and stepped inside the emergency passage. He keyed in the code on the opposite side.

The hatch slammed shut. They were on their own.

CAFFERTY HELD A STEEL POLE ACROSS HIS CHEST AND STOOD next to North in front of a set of the train's blocked doors. The overhead lights shattering and the ear-splitting booms coming from the direction of the command center had spread panic through the tightly packed car, but the mayor, the cops, and the MTA employees worked quickly to calm everyone down.

"Listen up," Cafferty bellowed. "I don't know what the fuck those things are, but we're all in the same boat—"

"We're on a train," a young voice piped up.

Nervous laughter rippled through the car.

"Same *train*," Cafferty said with a tight grin. "We have to fight them together. If we do—and if we don't panic—we *are* going to get out of this alive. And if you don't trust me, trust in New York's finest."

He didn't think that would really sell it to the frightened passengers, but he did see the cops on the train stand up a little straighter. They were scared, too, but if they could show the mettle he'd seen from the NYPD time and time again, Cafferty felt they at least had a fighting chance.

He just wasn't sure what they were fighting *against*.

Well, I'm sure we'll find out soon.

Cell phone lights and MTA lanterns illuminated the interior of the car, casting thin light on the sweaty but now determined faces of others who stood by the windows and doors with their improvised weapons raised.

The injured cop lay in the aisle, groaning as two fellow police officers applied pressure to the gashes in his legs.

Nobody said a word as they waited for the creatures to attack.

CHAPTER FIFTEEN

The SWAT team had halted barely a stone's throw from the breach after faint sounds of panic rumbled up the Jersey tunnel. Dalton and Christiansen knelt to Bowcut's front on either side of the track. Dumont crouched to her left. She drew her knife and peered through her sights, searching for any signs of movement.

"See anything?" Dumont asked.

"Negative," Dalton said.

"Nothing here," Christiansen said.

Bowcut shuffled across to Dumont. "If that's coming from the Pavilion, we need to move faster."

Dumont rose to his feet and indicated the team forward. Christiansen quickened his pace and took point, leading thirty yards ahead.

They advanced away from the grisly scene, and Bowcut hoped she'd never have to witness anything like that again. Yet it had also increased her already steely determination to make whoever had attacked those innocent people pay for their actions. If justice was to be served by her cold steel blade, so be it. Right now, she *really* felt like getting her hands dirty.

"Hey," Christiansen said. "Flip on your night vision."

Bowcut had previously switched for a clearer view of the tunnel, and she was certain the rest of the team had done so as well.

"Flip on your night vision," Christiansen said again.

"We have," Dumont replied. "You don't need to tell us twice."

"Tell you what?"

"To change the setting on our sights."

The team moved forward. Erratic booms continued to echo up the tunnel, increasing in volume as they closed in on the Pavilion. Bowcut knew it wouldn't be long before they faced the enemy, catching them like bilge rats before they escaped.

"Flip on your night vision," Christiansen said.

"I did," Dalton said. "What the hell's your problem?"

"What are you talking about?"

"That was the third time you told me."

"I told you once."

Christiansen turned and headed back. "I haven't said anything three times."

Bowcut stared at the man, baffled. It was clearly Christiansen who had spoken.

"Flip on your night vision."

Christiansen stood in front of her. Mouth closed. The group dropped to an all-round defensive formation, kneeling with their backs to one another, knives extended.

"Switch to thermal," Bowcut said. She changed her setting and searched for any heat signatures.

Nothing beyond specks of blood on the wall that had sprayed this far.

A breeze whipped through the tunnel, coming from the direction of the Pavilion.

"What the hell was that?" Dalton asked.

"Someone's fucking with us," Dumont said. "Stand by."

They silently held their positions, twenty feet apart.

Bowcut scanned every part of the tunnel again. Nothing.

"Someone's fucking with us."

"That wasn't me," Dumont said.

Something thudded against the ground behind Bowcut. She glanced over her shoulder.

Christiansen's head lay by his side. Blood squirted out of his neck. The knife dropped from his hand and his lifeless body collapsed to the track.

Bowcut scrambled to her feet. "Fall back—now!"

The remaining three sprinted up the tunnel. She had no idea how their attackers had not shown on the thermal image, but she'd worry about that later. Right now, the team needed to regroup and come up with another plan.

Right now, we need to fucking survive.

Someone let out a gurgled scream.

Bowcut stopped just short of the hole, spun back to face the lower side of the tunnel, and looked through her sights. She drew in deep breaths, the gas mask sucking around the edges of her face and sweat pooling below her chin.

Dumont skidded to a halt next to her and raised his Commando.

Dalton staggered forward thirty yards from her position, missing his right arm. She urged him to close the gap, but something sharp and glistening thrust out of his stomach and lifted him off the ground like a paperweight.

Bowcut unslung her rifle and rose to attack.

Dark blood oozed from Dalton's mouth. His left hand dropped by his side, unclipped his holster, and drew his Glock.

"No!" Dumont screamed. "Dalton, don't fire that weapon."

But if Dalton heard the captain, he clearly was beyond caring. He aimed over his shoulder and pulled the trigger . . .

. . . and a methane-fueled ball of fire flashed around him.

The blast shattered the railroad ties, and wooden splinters battered Bowcut's body armor and helmet. "The hole!" she yelled.

A wave of fire raced over their heads as more methane ignited.

Dumont's foot slipped in a pool of blood and he crashed to the ground. He scrambled to his knees and looked down with an openmouthed expression at a large splinter that had become embedded in his thigh.

Bowcut grabbed his chest rig with both hands,

dove for the hole, and used her falling body weight to drag him inside.

They plummeted at breakneck speed, battering against rocks, straight downward into the abyss. Bowcut reached out to try to grab anything to slow her fall, but Dumont's body kept crashing against her, tearing her grip. A blanket of flames rushed overhead, and a deafening boom roared through the tunnel.

The hole narrowed.

Bowcut thrust out her arms and legs, planting them against walls, and slowed her descent, gritting her teeth at the sharp jolt to her joints. Dumont did the same, but he was unable to keep his pain in, roaring in agony as blood dripped from his thigh into his boot.

"I can't hold it any longer," he said. "My thigh . . ."

He dropped, knocking Bowcut back into a free fall.

Her back hit the ground hard, and her helmet slammed against rock. Staggered for a moment, she lay motionless, staring straight up at the gas burning through the shaft. It was mesmerizing, and for a moment its eerie beauty made her forget what had happened to Dalton and Christiansen.

But then she remembered, her training kicked in, and Bowcut mustered her remaining strength to roll on her side. She activated the mounted light on her Commando and swept the beam on her immediate surroundings. Dumont's unconscious body sat slumped against a boulder in the small cavern. Farther inside, where the ceiling lowered, the body

of a police officer hung in the dusty air with two stalactites protruding through his stomach and chest.

She crawled over to Dumont and shook his boot.

He didn't move an inch.

I'm fucked.

CHAPTER SIXTEEN

Something thudded on the roof of the train. Cafferty and the rest of the group looked up and listened as slow footsteps pounded the metal, traveling the length of the car. For a few seconds there was silence, and then the creature dropped in front of the barricaded doors. North forced his shoulder against the recently secured steel plate, gripping a screwdriver in his right hand.

Silence returned once more. Then small sounds. Nothing like the previous explosion they had heard coming from deep inside the Jersey tunnel.

A cop coughed into his palm.

Near the center of the car, a woman whispered the Hail Mary.

Cafferty's held breath released with what sounded like an explosion in his ears. It woke him from whatever fear had frozen him in place, as if hearing his own breath was a reminder that he was still alive and wanted to make sure he kept on living. He wasn't prepared to accept that his day of reckoning had arrived. Not yet. Not without battling until he drew in that *final* breath. Maybe he wasn't a former marine like President Reynolds, but he knew about battling in a political arena and wasn't going to back down from a physical fight.

And he was ready.

A shrill screech moved along the train's outer body like fingernails down a chalkboard, sending a shiver down his spine. He imagined a claw shaving off a sliver of metal. Considering the damage to the front car, he realized it was only a matter of time before the creatures forced their way inside.

Tap, tap, tap came from a blocked window.

More taps on the roof, windows, and doors.

Hundreds of them built into a metallic clatter, as if a hailstorm of ball bearings pelted the train, and the noise increased the pain of Cafferty's splitting headache.

"What the hell are they doing?" a woman cried.

"Testing us," Cafferty said.

"No," North said. "They're *teasing* us."

The taps slowly died down.

Nobody said a word for the next few minutes as they waited for the monstrosities outside to make their next move. The regularity of coughing inside the car increased.

"All right," North said. "Let's make it more breathable in here. Open a tank of oxygen at both ends and one in the middle."

DeLuca crouched, heaved a tank to a standing position, and twisted the valve. Potentially lifesaving oxygen hissed out.

It took less than a minute to experience a tangible difference. The excruciating throb in Cafferty's head reduced to a dull ache and his nausea eased. The plan working gave him little satisfaction, though, given the danger lurking right outside the train. They had to find an effective way of combating the creatures, and fast.

"David, now that we can think a little clearer," he said, "got any other ideas about how to beat these fuckers?"

"Our best idea is to stay here. Do you fancy heading outside?"

"No, and I guess they could be in any tunnel."

"How the hell did they even get inside the subway system?"

"From below?" DeLuca said. "Otherwise we'd know about them. Think about it—we've had a rise in methane and we know pockets exist underneath this new subway system."

"Do we?" North glanced over his shoulder at Cafferty. "Do you?"

Cafferty's mind turned to the industrial accident three years ago, when a tunnel-boring machine crashed into a prehistoric, methane-filled cavern. They filled the hole, he swept the accident under the rug to avoid a lengthy investigation, and the site of the Pavilion moved three-quarters of a mile west, under his strict orders.

And now the stars were aligning for him in a chilling way.

Because the Pavilion's original location was roughly halfway up the Jersey tunnel—probably right near marker 119. When the search party had failed to find Grady McGowan's body in a timely fashion, it was called off. And the methane was considered an unfortunate anomaly and quickly forgotten.

But if he had gone by the book and been more thorough, it might not have come to this. Investigation teams would have explored the cavern, found the dead body, and, by doing that, discovered the creatures.

A trainload of people would be alive. *This* trainload of people wouldn't be in danger.

Ellen wouldn't be lost . . .

Regardless of what was outside the train, he had to shoulder the responsibility for today's events. Not for the existence of the creatures, obviously, but the timing of their discovery and the consequences.

"Is there something you're not telling me?" North asked.

"I . . . I don't know." Cafferty swallowed hard.

"Tom, if you know something, now's the time to come clean for all of our sakes."

"What's it matter now?"

"Because we all might die because of you!"

The words rocked him, especially coming from North. But he couldn't deny the inherent truth in the accusation. Cafferty played the events through his mind again and came to the same gut-wrenching conclusion:

He had blood on his hands.

"Tom," North said more forcefully, "what do you know about those creatures?"

"Nothing. Absolutely nothing."

"And the gas leaks?"

Cafferty avoided eye contact, overcome by his own guilt. Everyone in the car stared in his direction, and he had no easy way to explain the sequence of events.

"Tom," North pressed. "The leaks."

"Three years ago, a construction worker died when he accidentally drilled into a cavern full of methane, close to where we originally planned on building the Pavilion."

"Grady McGowan, right?"

Cafferty nodded.

"Christ, Tom, remember the state of McGowan's wife and kid standing next to his empty casket? You said it was an accident."

"It was an accident! There was no way to know it would happen."

"But this, right now—it's not an accident, is it?"

"We were so close. So . . . we cut corners." Cafferty met North's glare. "*I* cut corners to keep the project on track. You have to understand, it would've cost us millions and wasted precious time."

"How about *lives* wasted, you son of a bitch?"

"I didn't know it'd lead to this. How could I? I swear to you, I know nothing about these creatures. I'll take full responsibility for everything else— and that's bad enough—but you have to believe me. We've known each other a long time, David. I might have cut some corners, sure, but to think I'd willfully throw people to these . . . *things*? I'd never."

But even those words weren't exactly true. Because Cafferty knew his ego and pride had ruled his decisions, and monsters or no, this project was his entire life. He had fought long and hard to make the Z Train happen, made so many enemies, sacrificed so much, and it had all blinded him from doing the right thing. He never wanted to admit defeat and face the jeers from people like Reynolds. This tunnel was meant to be his legacy, his footnote in the city's rich history, and now it had materialized with unimaginable repercussions.

Maybe I'm just as bad a monster as those creatures out there.

Christopher Fields, the WNBC reporter, barged between two MTA employees and confronted Cafferty. "I heard every word. You're finished, Mr. Mayor."

"We're all finished if help doesn't arrive or until we figure out a way of getting past the creatures. After that, I'll take whatever's heading my way."

"Unbelievable. Un-fucking-believable." Fields spun to face the packed car. "In case you haven't heard, the mayor invited us down here for the opening of Jurassic Park. Those things out there are from caverns he knew about and covered up."

"That's not what he said, and you know it," North said, stepping toward the reporter. "Keep your cool, Fields. Now isn't the time for this."

"I'd say now is the perfect time. Hands up if you think we should throw the mayor off the train."

The crowd murmured, but nobody raised a hand.

"I told you I'll answer for my actions," Cafferty said, "and I promise I'll do just that."

"Your promises aren't worth shit, Cafferty."

"Then listen to *my* promise," North said. "I promise you that whatever you're trying to accomplish means nothing at this moment. Let's focus on keeping everyone alive, rather than starting an unnecessary panic."

"Unnecessary? How about the fact that we're trapped down here surrounded by things that want to tear us apart? I figure if we're all going to die, we might as well have the satisfaction of seeing that lying motherfucker die first!"

"You really want to throw him to the wolves," North said, incredulous.

"I don't want to die!"

The reporter practically sobbed the last words, and it hit Tom in the gut. As much as he detested the man, Fields was right—he had brought them all down here to get killed. He wanted to say something to make things okay, but there were no words. It *wasn't* okay.

Fields must have seen his reaction, because he jabbed the stubby antenna of a handheld radio toward Cafferty's face. "Don't try to wiggle out of this, asshole! You're going down for this, you piece of—"

North grabbed Fields' wrist and twisted it, revealing the radio's screen. It displayed a grainy image of the injured cop with the creature partially out of the shot and a green check mark with "sent" in the bottom right corner.

"What the hell?" Cafferty stepped closer, resisting a strong urge to punch the reporter in the face. "You've got *comms*?"

"The world deserves to know about you."

North ripped the radio free. He slammed his hand in Fields' chest, holding him at bay, and studied the device. "It's a short-range UHF communicator."

"Can we use it?" Cafferty asked.

"The battery's at two percent. Maybe for a single transmission."

"To who?"

"To whoever he sent this image."

"Who's on the other end of the communicator?" Cafferty asked Fields.

"Go to hell."

"You idiot—this message could save everyone," North said. "Who's on the other end?"

Fields paled as the realization dawned on him. "My—my assistant. She's outside the Jersey City station."

"I should strangle you for sending that picture," Cafferty growled. "All hell will be breaking loose in the city, thanks to you."

"Screw your self-righteous indignation. All hell's already broken loose here, thanks to *you*."

Two thunderous booms from the direction of the command center stopped Cafferty from doing what he had daydreamed about in several press conferences.

"We're not finished yet—" Fields shouted.

He never got to finish that sentence. A serrated jet-black tail punctured the roof. It thrust diagonally down with blinding speed and punched through Fields' left shoulder, and its glistening end stabbed out of the right side of his shirt.

Screams filled the car.

The tail whipped back through the reporter's body, lashed the ceiling—creating a crimson dent— and slithered out of the train.

Everyone ducked, watching the ceiling expectantly.

Everyone except Fields.

His shoulders wavered, his eyes glazed, and his arms hung loosely by his sides. A patch of blood rapidly expanded on the side of his chest, and drops pattered the floor around his suede boots. The man looked about to speak, but Cafferty, figuring the yelling had drawn the creature's attack, placed his trembling hand over Fields' mouth, whispering urgently into the man's ear while his other hand tried to put pressure on the wound.

The car fell silent while blood seeped between Cafferty's fingers.

Fields let out a short, bubbling breath, his eyes rolled upward, and he collapsed with a twist on top of Lucien Flament. The French journalist eased his lifeless body to the floor, checked his wrist for a pulse, and shook his head. *"Il est mort."*

"We need to get this message out," North whispered to Cafferty. "Rescue teams need to know what we're facing."

North keyed in the message and went to thumb send.

The communicator's screen died.

"For God's sake!" North said.

Another shuddering boom came from the direction of the command center.

Lucien Flament shuffled over to Cafferty. "May I offer you a piece of advice?"

Cafferty stared at the French reporter, still numb after witnessing the ease of Fields' death and unable to process anything beyond their immediate survival.

"We should think about this logically," Flament said. "Why they didn't attack the Pavilion sooner or enter the train, for example."

"You've seen the state of the front car. Getting in isn't a problem."

"But they *didn't* come in. What's changed?"

Cafferty glanced down at the hissing tank. "A drop in methane?"

"You took the words out of my mouth, Mr. Mayor. Perhaps they can't survive in our natural environment."

"I buy that," North said. "Which is why they attacked the train right next to the breach and appeared here when the fans died and gas spread into the Pavilion. If they've been sealed in caverns for God knows how many years breathing methane, it makes sense."

"That implies a rather high level of sophistication," Cafferty mused, "to know the gas would spread."

"I'd say they're *extremely* sophisticated," Lucien said.

"Who exactly *are* you, Mr. Flament?" Cafferty asked. "You don't strike me as a pen pusher."

"I don't really care how I 'strike' you, Mr. Mayor. But you're right—I wasn't always a reporter. I served in the Thirteenth Parachute Dragoon Regiment for ten years before pursuing a career in journalism. *Le stylo est plus puissant que l'épée*, Cafferty. 'The pen is mightier than the sword.'"

"Not today it isn't."

Flament shrugged. "It is when there aren't any swords lying around."

North snorted.

Cafferty ignored that, failing to find anything remotely amusing in their current plight. "So you were talking about their intelligence?"

"Yes. It's clear the creatures have some form of cognitive function well beyond a normal animal. They probed our car, perhaps testing our strength. Maybe they'll turn their focus on us after they've finished with the blast door."

"Why do you think that?" North asked.

"Because they haven't torn the roof off yet. I suspect the oxygen tanks are helping us in more ways than we think."

"You're a useful guy to have around, Mr. Flament," Cafferty said.

"I told you I could be of help. You had cops drag me away, if I recall."

"I made a mistake."

"A few, apparently. But if you can admit them, then there may be some hope for us. Call me Lucien."

"Okay, Lucien. As long as we're clear: the only thing I care about is getting these people out safely."

"That's good, because my only interest is in staying alive."

This time it was Cafferty who snorted, shaking his head. But since those two goals weren't mutually exclusive, he would take any help he could get, and right now that meant they had to grasp the small advantage Flament's reasoning had uncovered. Cafferty started wondering how he could use oxygen beyond lowering the methane levels in the car, forcing the creatures back until help arrived.

"What are you thinking?" North asked.

"Can you mount a welding torch on to an oxygen tank?"

North hunched over and inspected the valve. "Yeah, no problem."

"Good. Set up four of them as fast as you can. If any of those things tries to get in here, we'll suffocate the bastards."

CHAPTER SEVENTEEN

gent Samuels moved up the emergency passage's steady incline to the DSRV docking station, followed by President Reynolds and Diego Munoz. Unfastened wires and exposed pipe hung from the ceiling. Boxes of light fittings and other cosmetic fixtures lined the wall. Munoz wasn't concerned—this was how it had looked this morning. To the public eye, before the attack, everything looked shipshape in the Pavilion. Behind the scenes, though, the construction teams had been scrambling to meet the deadline. This tunnel was a low priority, publicly at least, and the crews had been led out before the guests arrived.

"How much farther?" Reynolds asked.

"Not long. The passage extends half a mile from the Pavilion. We're rising above the bedrock and silt."

A crash echoed in the distance.

Munoz picked up his pace and sucked in deep breaths. He had walked this route close to a hundred times, and each previous trip was never as tiring as today. It led to the ominous conclusion that methane had bled into the passage. He was by no means in the greatest shape, but he shouldn't be winded from just this slight incline.

But that wasn't what had him truly frightened. The footage of the creature remained strong in his mind. Its rapid and slick movements. Charging forward on its muscly legs. The precision leap. If Officer Donaldson had come across one of those things inside the breach, the chances were high he was most certainly dead.

"Diego," Reynolds said, "tell me about your gang."

"Those days are long gone, Mr. President. I was young and stupid."

"And I'm old and stupid," he said, and for the first time since all this happened, Munoz saw a bit of the charm that had won Reynolds the presidency in the first place. "I'm genuinely curious. You should be proud of transforming yourself."

"Maybe, but I'm not proud of being an impressionable idiot. I've worked for the MTA for the best part of a decade. That's my real story, like the other guys in my team. I was a prick, realized it before it was too late, and did what I needed to improve my life."

"Well, you succeeded."

A thin smile spread across Munoz's face.

The docking station's polished steel door came into view two hundred yards ahead. A green light flashed on the entry pad. Munoz glanced up and thanked God. Sending the president on his way meant he could quickly head back before the blast door caved.

"Mr. President," Munoz said, "may I ask you a question?"

"All right."

"Please don't take this the wrong way, but your reaction to the video of the creature suggested you at least had an inkling about its existence."

"Is that a question or a statement?"

"Both, I suppose."

The president stared at Munoz without answering. Another crash echoed through the tunnel. "We'd better get moving. After you."

Munoz headed up the final stretch of the passage, dissatisfied with the president's nonanswer, and he reached the docking station just as Samuels punched in the access code. Bolts thudded out of their locking position and the door groaned open.

They walked into the pristine cylindrical white room. At the far end, a circular hatch with a dark central window led to the air lock, and humming computers sat beneath a long desk. Flat-screen monitors lined the walls, reporting all docking station systems in working order and the methane level at 4 percent. Samuels inputted the code on the internal entry pad and the door closed and locked.

Munoz lifted a headset from the desk, placed it on, and activated the sub's communications link. "Rescue One, are you there, over?"

The overhead speaker crackled.

"*Rescue One here*," a man said in a gruff New York accent. "*How you doing, Diego?*"

"I'm fine, Steve."

"Is the president safe?"

"He's here with a Secret Service agent. You're on loudspeaker."

"Mr. President, this is Captain Steve Hillard. We're gonna getcha out of there real soon. The DSRV will dock in five minutes. Once you're on board, we'll ascend straight to the surface. You're in safe hands, sir."

Reynolds put on the other headset. "Captain Hillard, thanks for the update. Are rescue teams heading for the Pavilion?"

"I don't know, sir. I'll find out and get back to you."

"Tell them they need to act ASAP. The Pavilion's under attack."

"I'll get on it right away, sir."

"Hey, Steve," Munoz said. "Let's make this one clean."

"Roger that. Out."

The speaker crackled off.

Samuels frowned. "'Clean'?"

"We've only done this in simulation. The live tests were slated to begin next week. I can assure you Captain Hillard is excellent—"

"Is *anything* finished around here?"

"Other than a few peripherals, we're all good."

"Really?" Samuels nudged a ventilation grate with his shoe. "Where's this from? I don't remember seeing it during my sweeps."

Munoz peered at the top left corner of the ceiling. A warm breeze blew through a dark square shaft and warmed his face. He tensed and stumbled back. The ventilation system connected to every part of the new subway extension, meaning a creature could reach here by breaking through a grate in the tunnels.

Samuels, seeing Diego's reaction, drew a sleek black pistol from inside his jacket, dropped to one knee, and aimed at the shaft. The weapon hummed as if it were warming up. The pistol had a transparent handle that glowed pink around Samuels' fingers and a smooth black body with no visible markings. It appeared a million miles away from the cheap junk guns Munoz and his gang had sought out to protect their turf—hell, from the gun in his hand now.

"What in God's name is that, Agent Samuels?" Reynolds asked, clearly as bewildered as Munoz was.

"It's newly issued," Samuels said, maintaining his focus on the ceiling. "I'm protecting the only entry point, sir. Munoz, start your docking procedure."

Reynolds eyed the Secret Service member suspiciously, but he returned to the desk and replaced the headset.

Munoz tucked his gun away and perched in front of the computer, ran a successful structural integrity check. Once he was satisfied everything was in order, he activated the pressurization process.

On the other side of the hatch, vacuums opened and sucked out any water. Air blasted through nozzles, and light powered on, brightening the chamber.

A tone pinged, confirming a successful operation.

"We're ready to open our side," Munoz said. "Once the sub gets here, it'll open the outer hatch."

"Once you open it, we're good, right? No more further steps?" Samuels asked.

"Uh-huh."

Munoz moved over to the wall-mounted electronic keypad next to the hatch. He pressed 2-1-0-8-9—each digit letting out an electronic beep—and he raised his finger to input the final number.

Something made him pause, though. Something in the agent's tone when he asked if that was all that was needed. Looking in the reflection on the hatch's window, Munoz saw Samuels reach his left hand inside his jacket, draw his conventional pistol, and silently point it at the back of the president's head.

Munoz froze for half a second . . .

Without giving it another thought, he dropped to a crouch, whipped out his gun, aimed at Samuels, and pulled the trigger.

The blast reverberated inside the docking station.

Samuels sank to one knee, clutching his thigh and wincing, but he still swung both guns toward the air lock.

Munoz shouted to the president, "Get down!"

Reynolds was already moving, though, and Munoz saw him dive to the ground. At the same time, Munoz fired again, hitting the big agent in the left shoulder. Samuels toppled back, his shoulders slamming onto the ground, and one of his guns skidded under the desk. Reynolds leaped on top of the agent, and they fought for Samuels' remaining weapon.

A shot split the air.

Sparks fizzed from the air lock's electronic keypad, inches from Munoz's head.

Reynolds ripped the gun free from Agent Samuels and threw it clear, and it clattered across the floor. Even without guns—and even shot twice—Samuels wasn't out of the fight and connected with a bone-crunching right hook to the president's jaw, sending him crashing into the desk. He started to scramble toward the gun under the desk.

"Move another inch and I'll blow your brains out," Munoz said as he quickly closed in and fixed Samuels' face in his sights. "It seems I'm not the only one with an *interesting* background."

"You haven't got the balls," Samuels said defiantly.

"I've got two, which is the same amount of times I've shot you, asshole."

Reynolds reached under the desk and retrieved the gun, his face twisted into a grimace. "You fucking traitor. How much is Van Ness paying you?"

Van Ness? Who the hell is he talking about?

Samuels laughed, clutching his bleeding shoulder. "Mr. President, one way or another, you're not leaving this subway tunnel alive."

Reynolds spat blood at him. "Fuck you."

"I think I'm missing something here," Munoz said, stunned at what had just unfolded. "Who the hell is Van Ness?"

CHAPTER EIGHTEEN

Sarah Bowcut knelt next to Dumont's unconscious body and shone her flashlight through the cavern. Pain throbbed in her right shoulder and hip, but the injuries were the least of her worries.

The brutality of the previous attacks had stiffened her resolve to hit the enemy hard, but their speed and power sent a chill down her spine. *Nothing* was that fast. And yet her dead team members were proof of just how wrong she was. That scared the crap out of her, because how the hell do you fight something that Bradshaw had accurately described as a ghost.

By not giving up, Sarah.

With that thought, she gripped a knife in her right hand, ready to slash or stab anyone who showed their face.

Whoever killed Christiansen and Dalton had no time to follow them into the breach, meaning they were caught in the explosion that ripped through the tunnel. It gave the murders a minuscule silver lining, but that was about as good as it got. All the other evidence told her they were dealing with something well beyond her experience.

Hell—beyond anyone's *experience.*

She looked around, trying to get a better sense of her surroundings. This place was obviously the entry point for the attackers into the subway system, and the other end of the cavern had to lead to the outside world. Anything else didn't stack up. Thousands of pick marks scarred the walls, bolstering her theory of a large-scale operation involving a wide array of skills, though by who or what, she had no idea. How it went undetected . . . she had no clue.

Dumont moaned and his head rolled to the side. "Water," he whispered.

Bowcut grabbed the bottle from her pouch, lifted Dumont's gas mask, and trickled liquid into his mouth.

He coughed. "The others?"

"Both dead."

Dumont winced and reached for the wooden shard protruding from his thigh. "Where are we?"

"Dalton discharged his weapon, igniting the methane. The tunnel transformed into a fireball. You were hit by shrapnel from the first blast. I dragged you into the hole. But don't worry, the ground broke our fall."

He smiled, still grimacing in pain. "Thanks for saving my life."

"Don't mention it. We're lucky the gas didn't ignite down here."

"Any idea why?"

"I'm guessing it hit a pocket of low methane density and burned itself out. But I could also be talking out of my ass. The main thing is we're alive."

Dumont said nothing, echoing her own thoughts for her glass-half-full statement. He activated his weapon-mounted light.

The beam sliced through the dark, dusty air toward the breach. The rope Officer Bradshaw and his colleague had previously secured still dangled into the cavern, though it hardly inspired confidence. Bowcut suspected the fireball had scorched the rope to a crisp where it knotted around the track, and a gentle tug would bring it down.

It didn't matter—she had no plans on going back up the way she came down. This cavern led somewhere, and she was going to find out where.

Dumont had other thoughts. "We need reinforcements," he said. "We'll head back up the tunnel and establish radio contact with the topside teams."

"You're not going anywhere till I've treated that leg. Find something to bite on. This is gonna hurt." Bowcut slipped two field dressings from her rig, tore them open, and unraveled the bandages. "Ready?"

Dumont clenched his teeth and lowered his mask.

First, she used one bandage to tourniquet his leg. Then she wrapped her glove around the splinter and yanked it out of his thigh.

He bolted stiff and let out a muffled gasp.

Bowcut placed the dressing's pad over his blood-soaked cargo pants, applied pressure to stem any bleeding, and wrapped the bandage tight.

Dumont's wheezing gradually steadied. He heaved himself to a sitting position and slumped against a pile of rubble.

"Wait here," she said, and rose to her feet. "I'll be back soon."

"Get back to the station as fast as you can."

"I'm not going that way." Bowcut aimed her light to where the stalactites dipped toward the ground and the cop's dead body hung. "I'm going this way."

"Jesus Christ. Who's that?"

"It looks like Bradshaw's partner, Officer Donaldson."

"Head up the tunnel. We need more boots on the ground."

"Think about it, Captain: teams are coming into the subway system regardless of what we do. This cavern leads to somewhere else aboveground."

"How do you know?"

"How else did terrorists get to the Z Train? Look at the pick marks around you. They hacked their way here. What better way to bring weapons right to the heart of the city without being traced?"

Dumont focused his light on the wall. "I guess they could've widened the cavern below the stalactites . . ."

"Got a better explanation?"

He shook his head. "Digging out this cavern must've took years. I don't know. The scale of it all . . ."

"The plans have been public for a decade. If this is the way they attacked the train, then we need to see where these tunnels go. I refuse to let whoever killed all those passengers and half of our team escape."

"Okay, but listen. You come across these assholes, I don't want you picking a fight alone. We go with my plan and find help. Understood?"

"You got it."

Distant thumps resonated through the cavern.

She placed her hand over her light.

The noise grew louder and sounded more like footsteps. Someone in a hurry, heading in their direction.

Bowcut crouched behind an outcrop and raised her knife.

The footsteps slowed and stopped, she guessed around one hundred yards away, but the echo made it impossible to estimate. Whoever it was, an opportunity had presented itself.

"We'll ambush them here," Dumont said quietly.

"I'm tired of waiting. It's time we fought back."

"We're better off—"

But Bowcut was already moving off in a crouched run, ducking below the stalactites, and dropping to her elbows and knees. She crawled over the rocky surface, ignoring Dumont's whispered calls, and edged around a purple pool beneath the dead cop.

The quicker she informed Homeland Security about the entry and exit points, the faster they could shut down the route and begin their hunt for those responsible. But any attacker still lurking underground was hers. The memory of her dad, her brother, Christiansen, and Dalton would drive her blade. And the thought of David North, and those in the Pavilion, suffering a similar fate urged her forward.

Not that it was easy going. The ceiling rose into another pitch-black cave. She twisted her light's head, reducing its output to a minimum, and a weak beam brightened her surroundings. A radio and a tattered dress lay on the ground in front of three dark passages.

Bowcut crept to the middle one, paused by its mouth, and listened for any suspicious sounds.

Water dripped into a distant pool. Nothing else.

She peered back toward the breach.

Dumont's light cast a glow on the low-hanging stalactites.

Bowcut extended her knife and headed down the passage, softly placing her boots between the rocks and straining to catch any signs of movement. As the route twisted and turned and headed downward, though, she saw nothing.

The darkness was cloying, even with the little bit of light. She'd been in the city during a few blackouts, and that had been intense, but there was always *something* creating light, even during the darkest night. This was a solid black, though, pressing down around her, reminding her not just that she was alone, and not just that above her were tons of rock and millions of gallons of water, but all around could be the people trying to kill her.

She turned her light up just a bit.

A breeze yawned through the tunnel, carrying a faint crackle.

After several strides, smaller passages led off

to the left and right, but she kept her direction of travel simple. Still, all the side tunnels were starting to concern her—it was starting to feel less like the work of a focused group mining toward the Jersey tunnel and more like an underground maze.

The crackling grew louder.

She continued to advance, ready for anyone who lay in wait. A part of her hoped she had the chance to get some revenge. A part of her hoped she didn't meet anyone.

The ground and walls disappeared to her front.

Bowcut's light speared into the blackness beyond, illuminating the ceiling of a cathedral-like cavern. She crawled to the edge and swept her aim across the far wall, highlighting hundreds of other dark holes. Both ends curved around, making it look like a giant underground arena, but it didn't have a natural appearance. It felt like an underground Grand Canyon but bigger. A landlocked Mariana Trench.

A vast black abyss straight to hell.

Across the canyon, something moved on a distant ledge. She tracked back to it and squinted her eyes, shining her light toward the ledge.

What the hell?

Six women knelt in a circle facing one another, trapped inside some kind of thick transparent shell.

Passengers? Are they alive?

A mix of determination and excitement rose inside her. People *had* survived the train wreck. But if they were here, imprisoned, it meant her prey lurked somewhere in the darkness . . .

Bowcut had to find a way through the maze of

passages to the ledge and needed to move fast in case the enemy had already spotted her. She aimed the beam down to gain a quick appreciation of the cavern before turning the brightness down.

Her jaw dropped as she stared in disbelief.

Two hundred feet below, a mass of figures circled a man lying flat on his back. A greasy, translucent coating covered his naked corpse. Jeans, a T-shirt, and a hard hat lay by his side. It was a gruesome, jarring sight—one that she couldn't quite make sense of.

What made even less sense were the figures close to him. They were near human in size but were definitely *not* human. Each had an extra set of arms, scaly skin, sharp claws, and thrashing tails. As she moved her focus to the outer circle, past twisted pieces of wreckage, their shapes gradually grew larger to nearly double the size of your average man.

She was so transfixed by the monstrous display that she didn't notice until it was too late that a single huge creature, perching on a rusty cutter wheel at the end of the cavern, had rotated its bulbous head in Bowcut's direction and locked its beady eyes on her.

The creature roared, revealing three rows of pointed teeth.

Hundreds of heads turned upward.

For a moment everyone and everything was still. And then creatures in the outer circle burst toward the passages. Others scaled the wall directly beneath her, grabbing rocks and dragging themselves up at breakneck speed.

"Oh *fuck!*"

Bowcut jumped to her feet and sprinted back in the direction of Captain Dumont. Her boots hammered against the rock. Her light flashed around the walls. This living nightmare was way beyond anything Bradshaw had tried to convey. The appearance of such creatures was enough to destroy a person's mind. But the pure malevolence that seemed to emanate from them—it was way beyond words.

Heavy footsteps crashed behind her, closing in by the second. She retraced her previous path, straining every sinew to move as fast as possible, but the tight quarters and low ceiling made this much more difficult. Finally, though, she reached one of the caves and looked around at each of the branches.

Shrieks rang through all four passages.

They were coming at her from all directions.

I'm trapped.

That almost locked her in place, but you didn't get to where she was in the NYPD SWAT without experiencing some of the shittiest situations imaginable. For once she thanked some of those scumbag drug dealers and the firefights they put her through, because that kept her moving. Bowcut continued forward and rushed into the next cave. Dumont's light still brightened the far end of the stalactites.

"Captain!" she yelled. "Check the rope!"

She dove to the ground and scrambled on her hands and knees, passing underneath the dead cop, who still dangled from the stalactites. As she

crawled, her tac harness got stuck, and she frantically worked to free it, all the while listening to the
snarls and shrieks blasting from the tunnel behind
her. They were closing fast.

*Not dying on my stomach below the stinking Hudson
River.*

Not.

Going.

To.

Die.

With the last thought, she unsnagged herself and
bolted forward, making it to the breach.

Dumont sat against the rock. Mask raised. Head
slumped on his shoulder. Eyes closed. In no state to
escape or defend their position.

"Captain!"

His eyes flickered open for a moment.

She considered firing, taking everyone and everything down in a ball of scorching flames. It beat
being torn to pieces before the creatures moved on
to their next victim. She knew that would always be
an option, but for now, she wasn't ready to give up
just yet.

That was until dark, snarling figures emerged
from the passages, at least twenty that she could
see: a gleaming black mass hunched below the stalactites.

Too many. My God, how are there so many?

Bowcut twisted her weapon-mounted light to the
maximum output, shouldered her rifle, and aimed
at the nearest creature. For some reason, it was
incredibly important she see at least one of these

monsters get fragged before being consumed by the inferno.

Okay, motherfuckers—let's see how you like a bullet to the head before you get fried to a crisp.

She curled her finger around the trigger, knowing what had to be done . . .

But the creature screamed and retreated before she fired a single shot. Bowcut aimed at the next, focusing her powerful shaft of light on its chest . . .

It shot back into the passage.

She swept her rifle from side to side, covering the area underneath the stalactites. Every creature backed into the darkness. None reemerged.

Bowcut maintained her aim while catching her breath. Bright light from her rifle bathed the area around her and Dumont.

The discovery of the creatures astounded her, though not as much as pushing herself to within a second of detonating the methane, killing everyone in the close vicinity of her muzzle flash. She moved across to Dumont while keeping her light blazing toward the passages and dragged his gas mask over his face.

They were safe for the moment. More important, six women remained in the huge cavern. Going back meant facing near impossible odds, but she refused to leave the hostages behind, especially now that she had found a way of driving the creatures back. And it was about her survival, too . . .

But a single light wouldn't do it. Not against the mass of creatures she saw in the cavern.

Bowcut needed a plan to fight something she knew barely anything about. Something the world knew nothing about.

But that was about to change.

ELLEN CAFFERTY KNELT ON THE LEDGE IN A CIRCLE OF SIX women. She drew in a shuddering breath, still finding it hard to believe she was still alive. But for how much longer?

The beam of light that had focused on the transparent outer shell surrounding them—roughly a dome shape that looked like a thick layer of blistered skin—had given her hope, as well as her first view of her fellow hostages and the massive cavern, before the inky blackness returned.

The creatures hadn't taken her far after grabbing her from the smaller cave, and she expected Tom to spearhead a team for an immediate rescue. Nobody would leave them down here.

Unless, that is, whoever—or, as she started thinking more and more, *whatever*—had launched a wider-ranging attack.

Two creatures hunched by her side, prodding, snarling, and flexing their claws in front of her face, blasting it with their acrid breath. The same noises came from the direction of the other women.

The thing she found odd after her brief glimpse around at the other hostages was she didn't recognize any of them from the train. That wasn't completely impossible—it was an exciting, busy event, and she hadn't had time to meet everyone—but none of them wore the formal clothing of the other passengers.

That mystery would have to wait, though. First thing she needed to figure out was where the hell she was. Ellen thought back to her capture in the smaller cavern, searching for any clues to her location. A creature had carried her through twisting and turning passages into this huge underground space. Then a giant creature, who, unlike the rest, had glowing red eyes, had leaped down from the top of it and had scraped her in the same way as before, twisting a claw into her belly. After the literally gut-wrenching inspection, the place fell silent and she was dragged toward the ledge.

She shuddered at the memory.

But it gnawed at her, the strange, painful prodding. It clearly meant something to these creatures, and she couldn't help but think they had a purpose—a *goal*. They were more than simple killing machines.

Otherwise we'd be dead already.

So one more piece of the puzzle that didn't fit. And she was no closer to knowing where she was. The only thing she knew for certain was they had taken her deeper underground. She had no idea what was planned for them, but if someone didn't arrive soon, she expected they would find out.

If she couldn't find a way to escape.

Or kill herself . . .

CHAPTER NINETEEN

Nothing had attacked the train since Christopher Fields' death. The creatures sounded like they were focusing their efforts on the command center's blast door, and the constant shockwaves rocked the train's body. Cafferty expected them to shift their focus to the easier target soon, but he was happy for the reprieve—as long as they weren't coming after the train, the chances of a rescue team arriving to save them increased.

North wheeled one of the modified oxygen tanks to Cafferty's end of the car. He propped it in the aisle and squeezed the blowtorch trigger, and a concentrated stream of air hissed out of the stainless steel flame guard.

"Great job, David," Cafferty said, hoping the oxygen was as lethal to the creatures as methane was to humans.

"Let's pray it's enough."

"It has to be enough. It's the only defense we've got."

"*Ce n'est pas vrai*, Mr. Mayor," Flament said from behind. "This is not true. We've got these lanterns."

Cafferty gave the Frenchman a quizzical look.

"When the light shone on it, the creature's movement slowed and the scream sounded like it was in pain. This gave me the courage. In France, we say *il faut le voir pour—*"

"I don't mean to be rude, but please, cut to the chase."

"Seeing is believing, Mr. Mayor. Oxygen *and* light are our friends."

Cafferty examined the reporter more closely again. "You're very observant, Mr. Flament."

"I've made a career out of observing things. In the army, it was an enemy at close range. I'd record their actions, look for potential weaknesses, process the information, and report to my superior. In my journalistic career, it is much the same. In all cases, accuracy is everything. Every detail can make a difference. 'No stone unturned,' as you say in English. The best path to success is knowing—"

"Again, Mr. Flament—"

"Call me Lucien."

"Lucien, the short version is fine."

Flament did a typical Gallic shrug, lifting his shoulders, opening his palms, and raising his eyebrows. "What can I say? I'm methodical. We leverage any observations that might be productive."

"I mean you quickly put two and two—"

Heavy thuds shook the car's roof at both ends.

"Well, we need to find something productive *fast*," North said. "It sounds like they've stopped attacking the command center."

"Raise the lanterns and anything else that lights up," Cafferty shouted along the car. "Let's blind these sons of bitches."

Cops' flashlights flicked on, smartphone flashes activated, and the orange glow of ten MTA LED lanterns were lifted high among an assortment of raised weapons, brightening the brilliant white interior.

A set of shiny black claws punched through the ceiling above North. They rapidly gouged out jagged lines in a rough square shape, similar in size to the holes in the front car's floor. History was repeating itself.

Why change tactics? Cafferty thought. *It clearly worked well the first time. Of course, last time the others weren't ready to fight back. I just hope this Frenchman is as observant as he likes to believe he is.*

Otherwise we're screwed.

One of the MTA workers, holding his iPhone like a mini-shield, stood on his tiptoes and battered a wrench against the claws. The claws curled inward and pried off a section of the ceiling above Cafferty, opening the car like a pull-tab can of soda.

North aimed his blowtorch at the dark gap and blasted it with oxygen. The creature shrieked away from the roof.

At the far end, another section of the ceiling tore away. A creature's tail whipped inside and thrashed backward and forward, carving three people to pieces in seconds. Blood spattered over the walls and the conductor's cabin door, and screams erupted throughout the train as the crowd surged toward the middle of the car.

"Blast it with oxygen," Cafferty shouted. "If we lose one side, we lose the whole fucking train!"

It was easier said than done, though. Still, he was proud when a cop crawled underneath the swinging tail. He reached the tank, raised the blowtorch, and pulled the trigger. At the same time, a woman spun and raised the flash on her phone upward. Others quickly joined them, swooping below the tail and reinforcing the defenses.

The tail rocketed out.

The relief was momentary, and soon shrieks in the Pavilion drowned out the screams in the car.

"Good job," Cafferty yelled. "Just a little while longer, and help is coming."

I hope.

Claws raked the outer body, creating deafening metallic screeches.

A man in a suit flew back from a window. His back skidded against the aisle and a steel panel that had been secured on the inside of the car thudded against the ground. Tails immediately lashed both sides of the car, and the whole thing rocked side to side.

"The holes will increase the methane," North said through gritted teeth as he tried to keep his balance. "We can't sit around while they turn this place into a cheese grater."

"You're right." Cafferty grabbed a cop's flashlight and moved to the broken window, where a resolute-faced woman fired blasts of oxygen into the darkness. He cast his beam across the platform.

Several creatures scampered from the glare.

Looking across the Pavilion, Cafferty saw that the command center's blast door had been battered inward by the creatures. The bright light from inside the command center spilled out into the Pavilion, keeping the creatures at bay, but illuminating the body parts and torn clothing of the Secret Service agents in its path. The IMAX projector's deep blue beams highlighted a throng of creatures, stalking at either side of the light, hovering in the darkness just along the edges of the shadows.

"Oh my God!" a woman cried. "Someone help him!"

Cafferty stopped and turned.

Two scaly arms had reached through the gap at the far end of the car, grabbing the cop who had been wielding one of the air tanks and lifting him by his head. His body swung as he threw uppercuts, but if he was doing any damage, it wasn't apparent to Cafferty. Mostly all he could see was the blood trickling down from where the claws dug into his cheeks and temples.

"Grab his legs," somebody yelled.

Two women and a man latched on and tried to drag him down.

Thick veins throbbed on the creature's arms. This one seemed more determined than the others, and its claws sunk deeper into the cop's face.

The cop screamed. His legs kicked. Blood streamed down his neck.

Flament shoved his way through the people, extended his SLR camera toward the gap, and repeatedly activated the flash so that burst after burst of brilliant light hit the creature like the bullets from a semiautomatic gun.

The creature roared and twisted the cop's head sideways.

The crowd gasped at the sound of a dull crack.

Still Flament moved closer, within reach of the creature and the cop's twitching body, and his camera continued to strobe.

With a snarl, the creature's arms vanished in the blink of an eye, and the cop landed in a crumpled heap.

"Listen up," Cafferty shouted. "Any of the press with cameras, get those flashes working on the gaps!"

Women and men retrieved cameras from cases. They moved to the two holes in the ceiling and the broken window, and the car lit up, looking like a warped version of an early-nineties rave party. One of the guests wrestled off his jacket and laid it over the dead cop before taking over the officer's duty, blasting oxygen through the blowtorch flame guard.

"It's working," someone shouted. "They're backing off."

With the respite, another cop dragged his dead colleague into the conductor's compartment, out of the sight of the few children on board, while two others dragged the three lacerated corpses through. Cafferty knew there was no hiding the sight outside, but he was glad the death didn't seem as close. He rushed back to his end of the car, ducking between people and weapons.

"How's it looking outside?" North asked.

"Like shit, David. We're on a knife edge," Cafferty said. "Those camera batteries won't last forever. Neither will the oxygen. But . . ."

"What?"

"I think there might be another way."

"How?"

"We get someone in the command center to configure the IMAX to blast the screen with a pure white image."

North nodded. "Flood the Pavilion with light. It's a good idea . . . if anyone's still alive in there."

"That's going to be the theme of the day, isn't it?" he said. "But the creatures are crowding the entrance, which means they haven't gotten in yet. So we might be in luck."

"God knows we need it."

God? A devout Catholic, Cafferty couldn't help but wonder where the hell God had been.

How many Hail Marys is that *going to cost me?*

Shaking his head, Cafferty flipped open his laptop and breathed a sigh of relief as the internal LAN registered full bars. He maximized the private messenger app.

TC: Diego, are you there?

He peered across the nervous faces in the car while waiting for a reply. At the far end, Flament stood between two members of the press, camera raised toward the gap. The Frenchman had already saved a lot of lives with his quick thinking and deserved a medal if they got out alive.

Someone else would have to pin it on him, though. Cafferty knew if he survived, his reward would be a cramped cell, an orange coverall, and a plastic tray of food. He deserved it.

The laptop chirped.

"We're in business," he said.

> DM: Anna here. U OK?
>
> TC: For the minute. What happened at your end?
>
> DM: Those things smashed in the door. We hid in the back but they wouldn't come too far into the light of the command center.
>
> TC: Switch on the IMAX.
>
> DM: We have no remote connection anymore. Can only be controlled directly from the AV room.
>
> TC: Do you have anything else?
>
> DM: Wait—we've got spotlights in the supply room. 2 secs.

Cafferty leaned down and peeked through a gouge in the side of the train. A minute later, three thick shafts of light blasted out of the command center and carved across the platform, sending scores of creatures scattering. The shafts focused on the length of the car, bathing it in brilliant white light.

"Thank God," someone in the car said. A few others echoed the sentiment.

Thank Anna, Cafferty thought.

> DM: How's that for you?
> TC: You're a champion.
> DM: Glad to be of service.

North ducked next to Cafferty and scanned outside. "Nice. What about the IMAX, though?"

"They can't control it from the command center anymore."

"Of course not—our luck wouldn't be that good," North said.

But then he nodded, looking around. Cafferty could see his mind working, and with a final nod, he knew David had an idea. "What are you thinking?"

"Couldn't they shine out another spotlight, this time creating a path from there to the AV room? We can run toward the door through this beam and then down the other beam to turn on the IMAX. That thing will light up the *entire* Pavilion like a Christmas tree."

Cafferty smiled for the first time in a couple of hours. He felt like leaning forward and kissing the top of North's head.

> TC: Got a spare spotlight to focus on the AV room? We need a route from here to switch on the IMAX.

> DM: Great idea. I knew there was a reason
> I voted for you. We'll do it now.

Less than a minute later, two more shafts of light stabbed out of the command center and focused on the short corridor leading to the AV room, creating an L-shaped path from the car.

> DM: Want one of us to do it?
> TC: It's my responsibility. I'll come see you after we're done.
> DM: No sweat. You've given us hope.

He wasn't so sure about that, but it was clear from the reactions in the car that the light had brought palpable relief to the people stuck inside. If he could pull off this one last job, he might actually be able to truly force the creatures back from striking distance.

This will be my penance . . . and maybe all of our salvation.

First, though, he had a final question for Anna.

> TC: Did Diego leave with the president?
> DM: Yeah, and his creepy agent. He's coming back after they leave on the sub.
> TC: When's that?
> DM: Should be any minute now.

Cafferty snapped the laptop shut and stared at the lines of light crisscrossing the Pavilion. Pulling himself out of his reverie, he scanned the car for anything that would aid his mission. He wasn't really a betting man, but he rated his chances at fifty-fifty.

If I don't go, though, then I'd put our chances at zero. Cafferty had to take the risk.

CHAPTER TWENTY

The DSRV powered into video range, and its feed appeared on one of the docking station's screens, displaying the murky depths of the Hudson. Algae-covered objects sat among the riverbed's gently swaying vegetation. Munoz ignored it for the moment. He stood behind Samuels while President Reynolds covered him with a gun.

Munoz looped a cable tie over Samuels' wrists and pulled it tight, then added another three for good measure, securing him to the chair. The two gunshots to his thigh and shoulder had incapacitated the big agent, but Munoz wasn't going to make the mistake of underestimating a highly trained individual.

Especially a treacherous one.

"You're signing your own death warrants," Samuels said. "I'm your only realistic way out of here."

Reynolds scowled. "You just said my only way out of here was in a body bag. So why don't you shut the hell up and save it for the court-martial."

"Look at the screen," Munoz said, shoving him in the back. "The sub's arriving and you're heading for a lethal injection."

"You're both fools," Samuels replied. "You've no idea what you're facing."

Munoz let out a deep groan. They had already witnessed the creatures, and Reynolds appeared to have some prior knowledge of their existence, so he just chalked up such nonsense as a last-ditch attempt by the agent to confuse them. With the sub right there, he was going to keep his mouth shut and get the job done. He'd grown up in a neighborhood where chumps tried to talk their way out of things, and even though Samuels had shown himself resourceful, he was tied up, neutralizing the threat.

As much as Munoz wanted to see how many times he could punch the man in the face, he simply focused on the hatch's keypad.

Samuels' earlier gunshot had pierced the edge of the air lock's pad, though a green light still glowed around the digits, hopefully meaning it wasn't broken. They had the lung-busting option of a manual crank, but that took up precious time. He depressed the number 2 . . .

And a satisfying *beep!* echoed in the small room. He let out a breath he didn't realize he was holding.

The speaker above the desk crackled. *"This is Rescue One, are you there, over?"*

Munoz moved back to the desk and put on a headset. "Diego here. We're receiving your live transmission. Steve, we're bringing up a prisoner who requires medical treatment."

"*A terrorist?*"

"Might as well be." Munoz eyed Samuels. "And a piece of shit."

"*Huh?*"

"It's the head of President Reynolds' Secret Service detail. He just tried to assassinate him."

"*Jesus, Diego, are you serious?*"

"One hundred percent. Make sure you let everyone know it's Agent Samuels."

"*Jesus . . . okay. What kind of injuries?*"

"Gunshot wounds to the shoulder and thigh. Unfortunately, he'll live."

"*Roger. Out.*"

Samuels glared at him. "Did that make you feel special?"

"Why would it? I just wanted them to be aware of what they'd be dealing with—a dangerous, traitorous cocksucker. But let me be clear: I don't give a shit about you. My main concern is getting the president to safety and then doing the same for my team."

"Wow, a noble gang member."

Munoz strode over to Samuels and casually nudged the agent's wounded thigh with his shoe. It was petty, but seeing the man wince was worth it. He spun back to face the screen.

The docking station appeared through the gloomy water: a solid steel square rising out of the silt. The sub adjusted its course toward the external hatch, slowed its speed, and drifted the final few feet.

A metallic clank boomed from the other side of the air lock, followed by a mechanical whir.

"Successfully locked on," Steve said through the speaker. *"Securing the seal. This'll only take a moment."*

"Roger that."

"Seal secured. I'm opening the first hatch and equalizing the pressure. Stand by for my order to open the second hatch."

Munoz moved back to the window.

The external hatch fanned open, revealing the brightly lit interior of the DSRV. Steve Hillard climbed from behind the controls, wearing his dark green coveralls, and gave his trademark warm smile. He stepped through into the air lock chamber, pistol in hand, and focused on the control room window.

Munoz gave him a mock salute through the glass. Only one hatch separated the president and the traitor from a safe evacuation . . . and making it out of this living nightmare in one piece.

He started to press in the code: 2-1-0-8-9—

The chamber's overhead light flickered off.

"No . . ." Munoz said. "It can't be . . ."

"What?" Reynolds asked.

The light from inside the DSRV cast a weak glow onto Hillard's confused face.

"Get back in the sub!" Munoz shouted.

Hillard frowned and pointed to his ear. He couldn't hear the warning.

Munoz banged his fist on the protective glass.

It didn't matter.

Two creatures sprung from the darkness and rammed Hillard, crushing him into the chamber wall and forcing him to the ground. One locked its teeth around his neck and forced its claws into his eyes. Blood flowed down his temples and squirted from underneath his jaw.

Hillard's mouth opened and he let out a silent scream, and the fact that Munoz could hear nothing made the scene somehow even more chilling.

It wasn't over, though. The second creature tore at Hillard's coveralls, slicing it to ribbons and gouging deep purple lines in the captain's stomach. A claret streak splashed the window, obscuring the view, but not enough to keep Munoz from seeing the creatures quickly transforming Steve's body into a shredded mess before they dragged him out of view.

Reynolds darted to Munoz's side and peered through the glass with a look of horror.

Only a dark trail of blood remained.

"H-h-h-ow did they get into that air lock?" Reynolds asked.

Munoz staggered back a couple of paces and peered at the ceiling. "They've been in here. The grille. The creatures could be anywhere in the ventilation system."

"Which is why I covered the vent," Samuels said. "And when they're done in that submarine taking out the rest of the crew, I promise you they're coming back in here to tear us apart limb from limb. Mr. President, it's time we make a deal. First, cut me loose."

"You're getting no deal." Reynolds aimed up at the dark square in the ceiling. "We'll go back to the command center and wait for the rescue teams."

"Already dead," Samuels said.

Anger consumed Munoz as he stood over the big agent. "You claimed the blast door would hold."

"I lied. This wouldn't have happened if the president had paid his bills. Ask him."

"So it's all about money." Reynolds shook his head. "Van Ness unleashed this on America—on me—because I won't be blackmailed?"

"Money, respect, common sense, national security, take your pick. The world is a less dangerous place with you out of the White House."

"You really are a piece of work. I don't know why I couldn't see it."

"Because you're usually too busy with your head between your secretary's legs."

As incredible as this exchange was, Munoz's immediate interests lay elsewhere. He rushed back to the computer and switched to the structural view. All tunnels glowed red and reported breaches and high methane levels, as expected. He zoomed in on the command center, flagging multiple failures, and he maximized the crucial one:

The blast door reported as open and nonfunctioning.

The creatures had broken through.

Having just watched Hillard's uncompromising and savage death, his imagination exploded with the thought of what had happened to his team. Their last thoughts were probably that of pure terror . . .

and disgust at him for having abandoned them. First Donaldson and now his team. Munoz bowed his head, rage coursing through his veins. He hated himself for leaving them, but he knew he had little choice. He could only hope they had found peace quickly.

And with those somber thoughts, he knew there was only one thing left to do: he had to save Reynolds.

"Mr. President," Munoz said, "the command center isn't an option. I believe it's been compromised by the creatures."

"Contact them to make sure."

"Negative. The explosion took down our internal comm link."

"Don't we have another sub?"

"It can't dock with another one already locked in position."

"What about securing the vent and staying here?"

Samuels let out a single sharp laugh. "If they can bash through a blast door, a few screws won't be a problem. That hatch won't hold and the vents have been compromised. There's only one way out—with my help."

"Forget it," Reynolds said. "We've already got your weapons."

"Good for you. Problem is *you* can't operate them. Nobody can except me. Take a closer look at the grip of my gun. Tell me what you see."

Munoz grabbed the futuristic-looking weapon from the desk. It weighed at least five times more than an average pistol. He checked it from a side view, in case Samuels had a sly way of remotely firing.

"It's a fingerprint-activated laser," Samuels said. "And it's the only defense we've got against these creatures. Bullets are useless unless you get a lucky shot, and that's without the methane problem. This, however"—he nodded at the gun—"will slice them up into pieces. *If* you've got my fingerprint, that is."

"Who the hell are you?" Munoz asked incredulously. "And what the hell are these creatures?"

Samuels ignored the questions.

"This gun doesn't ignite the methane?" Reynolds asked.

"It was designed with that in mind—it can fire at higher methane levels. I guarantee it's enough to use in the tunnels, but only with me using it."

"How can a gun know that?" Munoz said.

"It's got an internal air sampler. Green light, the methane level is low enough to fire. Red light, the laser locks. Otherwise, you'll blow yourself up. Remember, our weapons are specifically designed for dealing with these scenarios. But you didn't think these scenarios actually existed, did you, Mr. President? So, about that deal . . ."

"I want answers first," Reynolds snapped. "Why did you sell your country out for money?"

Samuels let out a dismissive grunt, but sure enough, he started talking. "Money? Yes, a lot of money. But that's not why I'm here. I'm here because I was ordered to be here. It's my mission. It's my firm belief in the project. Don't think for a second I did this just for money. None of us do this for a financial reward. Our cause is greater than national governments."

"You purposely ordered the rest of the Secret Service to stay outside the command center," Reynolds said. "So the plan was to isolate me, kill me here, and hijack the sub?"

"Now you're figuring things out. And I came within a Brownsville pimp of pulling it off."

Munoz ignored the barb. Hell, where he grew up, being a pimp was considered a compliment. No matter what, though, he wasn't going to let Samuels' weak attempts at mind games bait him into doing something rash. *The a-hole might underestimate me, but that's his problem.*

"Who does he work for?" Munoz asked. "And what the hell do creatures have to do with money?"

Samuels smiled coyly. "The president can tell you all about the Foundation for Human Advancement and our global fight against the creatures on his own time. Let the adults speak for a moment."

Munoz resisted a strong urge to punch the big agent in his smarmy face. As much as he wanted to know more about the conspiracy, survival remained at the top of his agenda. Samuels being part of an escape plan wasn't an option, regardless of what the president wanted, though he suspected Reynolds also had no intention of striking a deal. They didn't need Samuels weighing them down.

"How did you know about the attack?" Reynolds asked.

"I guess you *don't* actually get it. Know about the attack? I *started* the attack, asshole."

"You piece of shit—"

"Spare me, Reynolds." Samuels grimaced and repositioned himself in the chair. "I saw the signs of an imminent breach during my security sweeps. A small piece of carefully placed C-4, timed to go off at twelve-oh-three, ensured a path for the creatures."

"You *wanted* the creatures to attack," President Reynolds muttered to himself, as if trying to convince himself of the madness of that. He glared at Samuels, eyes narrowed and jaw clenched. "The mayor didn't invite me to this event—*Van Ness* did."

"You'd be amazed how easy it was to forge your invitation. Van Ness knows all about your ego. Like he said, you couldn't resist a chance to upstage Cafferty."

Van Ness? Munoz thought once again. *Who gives a shit about Van Ness, whoever he is. We need to get out of here. And if it means chopping off his finger to use the laser . . .*

"No—it couldn't be that simple, though," Reynolds replied. "Van Ness needed help. Who else in my administration is involved?"

"Now, Mr. President, you know the Foundation has many friends. Why, you wouldn't have won the election without the Foundation's help."

The president ignored that. "I want names. Who in the administration?"

"No," Samuels said firmly. "This is where the

talking stops. Creatures might be in here at any moment. If you want to know about the others and more about Van Ness' plans, I help us escape and walk out of here a free man. I believe the Constitution is pretty clear about your power to pardon me."

"You expect to be *pardoned*?"

"I expect this to never even come to public light . . . except when you pin a medal on me for bravery."

"You've lost your mind," Reynolds said.

"We leave with my help or we all die. It's that simple. The sooner you realize that, the sooner I'll get us out of here. Ever heard of the Australian prime minister Harold Holt?"

"No."

"He talked like you. In 1967, twenty-two months into his leadership, he went for a swim off Cheviot Beach and never returned. Play the game or suffer the same fate."

Reynolds scoffed. "Bullshit."

"Do you seriously believe it's all over if you make it out of here alive? Once you've been greenlit by Van Ness, it's game over. Let me provide a little more localized clarity. No president has defied him or his father since 1963. You don't need to be Columbo to figure that one out."

"I don't believe you."

"If I were in your shoes, I'd start drinking the Kool-Aid."

"We'll get everything out of you. I'm sure you already realize that—"

"Mr. President, I ran a black site and know every trick we've got. I cannot be broken. And wherever you take me, you'll put everyone's lives in danger. Nobody's beyond the Foundation's grasp. They'll come for me. They'll come for you. They'll even snuff out poor little Diego here. Whoever stands in their way dies."

"We'll see about that."

"When will it sink into your thick skull? What do you think happened to Michael Rockefeller? His family resumed their payments after Otto Van Ness sanctioned his murder. It was that or be picked off one by one."

"That's a lie. You'll be telling me they whacked Jimmy Hoffa next."

"No, but Van Ness thought about it."

A decade ago, Munoz had been mildly obsessed with Rockefeller's disappearance and had visited the Peabody Museum to flick through pictures of his New Guinea expedition before the young man mysteriously vanished. Still, with their planned escape in ruins and creatures in the ventilation system, the overall conspiracy was the least of his worries. The talking had to stop, and fast.

"Believe what you want, Mr. President," Samuels said. "You're a dead man walking. Like it or not, I'm the only person who can stop your wife weeping over your casket."

Munoz grabbed the futuristic-looking pistol from Reynolds and inspected it again. He found an almost imperceptible small switch at the top of the trigger guard and flicked it. The weapon hummed to life, the grip glowed around his fingers, and the smug expression disappeared from Samuels' face.

"It seems you've lost your only bargaining chip," Reynolds said. "Thanks for the information, but we don't need an injured traitor slowing us down."

"The laser alone isn't enough," Samuels interjected, looking desperate for the first time. "I can guarantee you safe passage!"

Reynolds motioned his head toward the injured agent. "Frisk him. Let's see what else he's hiding."

Munoz patted down Samuels' trousers, retrieved an oval-shaped black device, and pocketed it.

"Nice to see you've finally shown your true colors, *homey*," Samuels said sarcastically. "How many of those have you stolen in the subway?"

"Shut the fuck up." Munoz unbuttoned the big agent's jacket, revealing two bandoliers strapped around his chest holding lines of golf ball–sized silver orbs. "What the hell are these?"

"We get out using these and my laser. I'll show you how to operate everything, giving us our only guaranteed shot at freedom. Deal?"

"That depends on how much you tell me," Reynolds said. "Keep talking, or I swear I'll leave you here to die."

Munoz plucked one free of the bandolier. Just like the laser, it weighed more than he expected and tiny black holes covered its surface at uniform intervals.

"The Foundation calls them strobe grenades," Samuels said, "or strobes for short. The creatures hate flashing light. Between these and the laser, we'll still probably die if you keep me tied up. Cut me loose and I'll take everything down."

"Am I missing something here?" Munoz said. "Again, what's the deal with the creatures? What are they capable of and what do they want?"

"They exist worldwide and are your immediate problem. A big problem that'll tear you to pieces. Like I said, though, Reynolds can explain once we get out of here. I won't waste my breath."

Reynolds didn't respond. Instead, he grabbed several silver spheres from the big agent's bandolier and pocketed them.

Munoz twisted a strobe in front of his eyes, not quite believing he held a specially designed weapon created by a clandestine organization. His podcast guys would think this kind of information was a dream, but they weren't living through the actual nightmare.

"How does it work?" Reynolds asked.

"Squeeze the sides and throw it. If you're epileptic, close your eyes."

Munoz gently crushed it with his finger and thumb. The strobe clicked, let out a high-pitched whistle, and vibrated.

"It's armed. As soon as you release the pressure of your grip it activates."

"Hold on a second," Reynolds said. "What if this blows up in Diego's face? What if it blows all of us up?"

Samuels smirked.

Munoz took a step back and threw the strobe between Samuels' legs. If it were a bomb, at least it'd take the big agent's balls off first.

Blinding flashes engulfed the docking station, like they were stuck inside a giant camera bulb.

"Shut the damned thing off," Reynolds shouted.

Munoz grabbed the strobe grenade and squeezed again, and it deactivated. "How long do they last?" he asked.

"Long enough," Samuels said. "But I wouldn't hang around much after two minutes."

Munoz grabbed six of the strobe grenades from the bandolier and stuffed them into his pockets.

An electronic beep echoed in the air lock.

Then another.

The digits 2 and 1, instantly recognizable to Munoz's audiophile nature. He spun to face the hatch and froze. A creature's snarling black face peered at him through the window. Water had flooded into the chamber, and the level rose around the creature's body, meaning they had damaged the DSRV's seal. It bellowed, baring its bloodstained teeth, and smashed its claws against the glass, leaving tiny white shatter marks.

The creature's claw tapped against the keypad and input a 0, 8, and 9. The code to open the door— except for the last digit. Munoz had never pressed the final digit after seeing Samuels raise his gun in the reflection.

"It knows the code," Munoz said. "Let's get the hell outta here."

"Are you serious?" Reynolds said.

"It listened to you typing earlier," Samuels said.

"They're more intelligent than you think. They aren't dumb animals and won't stop once they have you in their sights. I know how they think. You need that knowledge to stay alive."

The creature input a 1.

A negative tone replied.

It started again with a 2, 1, 0, 8, 9, and a 2.

A negative tone again. Only eight more possibilities and the hatch would fly open, unless the failsafe locked the pad after ten incorrect attempts.

Munoz's heart raced as he practically dove for the keypad by the internal entrance. He input the code to get back into the emergency passage. It seemed like an eternity, but finally the locking bolts thudded out and the door whined open.

The creature repeated the sequence of numbers.

"Untie me, now!" Samuels shouted, for the first time with a sound and look that matched the desperation of their situation, which wasn't good.

"You're staying right in here," Reynolds said to Samuels, and shoved him and the rolling chair he was tied to back toward the air lock. "I'd like to wish you luck when the air lock opens, but . . ."

"Wait!" Samuels shouted at the president. "You'll never make it out of this tunnel without me!"

"We'll take our chances, asshole."

Even as the president was moving toward the door, keeping his aim on Samuels, Munoz had started to key in the digits to close the docking station. But his hand quivered so hard that he hit the wrong number. He tried again, pressing slower, trying not to make the same mistake.

In the chamber, the creature input the numbers again . . .

The air lock hatch fanned open.

Keeping calm, Munoz hit the last digit. As the inner door started to close, water gushed into the room from the outer hatch and spilled down the passage.

The creature shrieked, raised its claws over the screaming figure of Samuels, and jumped up and smashed the overhead lighting, leaving only the lights from the screens casting a thin glow across the cylindrical room.

Samuels fell on his side and wriggled toward the door, pleading for his life.

"Reynolds!!!" Samuels shouted futilely, as the door slammed shut and the steel bolts thudded into place, leaving him behind to face the devil.

Reynolds let out a deep breath and sunk to a crouch. "Thank God . . ."

"I think it's safe to say that's the last we'll be seeing of him."

"Excuse me if I don't shed a tear."

"You won't see any on my face."

A shuddering boom rocked the docking station door. It held firm but was quickly struck with another blow. This time, leaks sprang from around the edges. Munoz staggered back a few steps and turned to face the descending passage.

"What now?" Reynolds asked.

Munoz weighed their options. He couldn't take them back to the command center if creatures had smashed the blast door. But they also couldn't stay here, or they risked being torn to shreds or drowned by millions of gallons of the filthy Hudson.

That left only one option.

A door forty yards down the passage led to the docking station's engineering bay. From there, they could descend the subway system levels to the Jersey City maintenance tunnel. He had little doubt they'd face more creatures down there, but it was the only way to avoid certain death.

"We fucking run." Munoz checked his newly acquired laser again and nodded at the president. "Follow me."

CHAPTER TWENTY-ONE

Sarah Bowcut shifted her beam of light between the passage entrances as she attempted to process the recent events. A vague recollection about a tunnel-boring accident explained the corpse and the mangled wreckage at the foot of the vast cavern. She had no frame of reference for the rest of the scene.

Door-smashing drug raids were one thing, but creatures . . . and scores of them living right below New York City. The attacks and the perfect mimicking of Christiansen's and Dumont's voices showed this species had intelligence and cunning, and they treated humanity as their enemy.

As *prey*.

In her mind's eye, she pictured herself on the cavern ledge with the other six women, unarmed and surrounded by a terrifying force. It chilled her to the core. She had to dismiss her fears, like her father and brother had done during the last major attack on New York City, and rescue the hostages.

Dumont groaned and strained to a sitting position. "I feel like shit," he said. "How long was I out?"

"Not long. You must have taken off your mask and passed out. Don't do it again."

"I guess I owe you twice. Did you find what you were looking for?"

"Not exactly. Brace yourself."

"For what?"

"For something I can't explain."

Bowcut cupped her hand over her lens, transforming the cavern into blackness.

A second later, growling figures thrust out of the passages and hurtled directly for them. Their feet crashed over rocks and their tails whipped through the air.

Dumont lurched back and drew his knife.

She swung up her Commando, washing five creatures' scaly bodies with a ray of bright light. They halted in their tracks, contorting and thrashing as she rapidly switched her focus between each one.

Shrieks filled the cavern.

A tail lashed the stalactites, slicing three clean off.

Dumont raised his rifle, twisted his light to full strength, and assisted her in forcing the creatures back inside the passages.

Bowcut remained silent, allowing him time to comprehend what he had seen while they maintained their aim on the dark entrances.

"What the fuck?" he eventually said.

"Exactly. What. The. Holy. Fuck."

"What the hell was that?"

"Creatures. Insects. I don't know. These are what attacked the Z Train, what attacked us in the tunnel."

"Seriously? Tell me I'm having a nightmare."

"I wish I could. See the claws?"

"Of course I saw the goddamn claws! How many of these things are we talking?"

"Hundreds, maybe thousands." Bowcut focused her light on the middle passage. "Down that way is a huge cavern, bigger than anything I've ever seen, and it's full of them. Captain, I think we've stumbled on their nest."

Dumont stared at her, dumbstruck.

"There's something else," she continued. "There are six hostages alive down there. Six women, kneeling in a circle, side by side in a cocoon of some kind. I can't explain it, but they're alive."

"This is crazy. We need backup, now."

"You saw those creatures. If we fall back, those women are as good as dead. We need to act as fast as we can."

"What I saw means we can't fight hundreds of those things. We can't even fire our weapons or we're toast."

"Who says we fight? What's inside those MTA safety boxes?"

"Safety boxes?"

Bowcut looked toward the breach where the train tracks were. "The ones attached to the tunnel wall every hundred yards."

"First aid kits, rope, flashlights . . ."

"Exactly. Here's what we do. I'll climb up, snag the lanterns, and secure a new line of rope. Then we'll use the light to keep those creatures at bay while we free the women and get the hell out of here."

Earsplitting shrieks blasted out of the passages.

"Are you out of your mind?" Dumont asked.

"We know they hate light, right? Would you think twice if your sister was trapped inside the cavern?"

"That's different."

"It isn't. Those hostages have brothers and sisters."

"I can't allow a suicide mission."

"It's only suicide if you want to die. I'm not planning on dying. I'll head back up and check the next box. You make sure nothing comes within striking distance. It'll take a few minutes."

"I swear you'll be the death of me."

"Hopefully not."

He gritted his teeth. "Get going."

Bowcut slung her rifle, headed over to the burned rope and gave it a firm tug. It predictably snapped free, dropping through the shaft and bunching on the ground by her boots. She coiled it around her shoulder, intending to attach the undamaged end to the tracks if nothing else was available.

A mound of rubble led up to the left edge of the breach. She wasted no time in scrambling up, grabbing the lowest outcrop of jagged rock, and heaving herself upward into the shaft.

Rookie climbers always made the mistake of thinking it was all about arms. Engaging her full upper body made it easier to hoist herself, and she powered upward. Sweat trickled down her face, and her thighs and shoulders burned, but she trusted in her technique.

After energy-sapping minutes, Bowcut reached the top. She raised her head into the now silent subway tunnel and rotated her light 360 degrees, checking for any signs of movement.

Dalton's corpse lay sprawled in the distance, charred to a crisp, unrecognizable from the man who had entered the tunnel. His dreams of early retirement had ended in a brutal fashion. A creature nearly twice his size smoldered by his side, its claws still sunken inside his body.

Deeper into the tunnel, several more dismembered creatures were spread around the track, all previously undetectable with thermal imagining. It confirmed her suspicion that the explosion triggered by Dalton had inadvertently saved her and Dumont's lives.

Bowcut climbed out and sprinted toward the Jersey subway station, turning every few seconds to ensure nothing had followed. She passed marker 117, reached the next safety box, and unlatched the door.

It contained a length of rope, two bright LED lanterns, and a first aid kit.

She threw the rope over her shoulder. Both lanterns worked, bathing her immediate surroundings in an orange glow. They radiated nowhere near the power or range of her rifle light, but they provided her with two extra sources for the high-risk rescue attempt.

Being back in the tunnel left her feeling exposed in the wide space. The explosion had killed creatures close to the breach, but there was no telling how many might be left and if they were heading in her direction.

Bowcut accepted Dumont's concerns about the danger, and the gruesome evidence backed up his point. He had a deep sense of duty and always put his team's welfare high on the agenda. However, she could not accept leaving the hostages at the creatures' mercy. They were the only two people currently capable of acting, and this sense of duty overrode her fear.

A breeze wafted through the tunnel.

The same thing had happened before Christiansen's death.

Bowcut dropped to one knee.

She swept her light's beam across the walls and punched it directly over the track. A creature hunched and glared at her through its beady eyes. Strings of saliva dangled from its teeth.

It screamed and leaped out of the glare of the light.

The strength of her resolve forced away any lingering trepidation. She advanced, following the creature's movements. It sprung to different sides of the track and retreated out of sight.

Bowcut rounded the shallow bend at pace, making sure it had no respite from her light, and forced it away from the breach. The creature's steps thudded into the distance as it swerved from side to side, and it disappeared into the darkness. She waited for a minute, expecting it to return the moment she trained her light away from its direction of travel.

No creatures returned.

She tied off one of the ropes around some pipes and ran it under the track into the breach. She attached the lanterns to her chest rig and scanned the area for a final time.

Faint shrieks rang out from the direction of the Pavilion.

Hundreds of them.

A rumble echoed up the tunnel, quickly building into a thunderous clatter.

She guessed the creatures had dropped their stealth techniques and were storming toward her position for a collective assault.

I can keep one at bay, maybe a group in tight tunnels, but hundreds in an open space?

Thinking fast, she tied one of the lanterns to a railroad tie at the entrance to the breach. If those creatures were coming for her from the Pavilion, this would slow them down.

Bowcut wrapped the rope between her legs and over her shoulder in the Dülfersitz position, for rappelling without mechanical tools, and lowered herself. She controlled her speed by letting the rope slide through her break hand and moved fast before the creatures arrived and severed her descent.

Her boots hit solid ground.

She shone her light toward the top of the breach, hoping to deter any creature from jumping straight down and slicing her or Dumont with a swing of the tail.

Dumont glanced over his shoulder. "That was quick."

"Not as quick as the creatures heading our way."

"What?"

"We need to move. Now. Some are heading up the tunnel."

"Jesus Christ. We don't know if this'll even work."

"We don't have a choice. I'll lead, you cover our back." Bowcut passed him a lantern. "There's another at the top. It might hold them for a while."

She headed across the cavern, ducked below the stalactites, and crawled underneath the suspended cop's body. Dumont limped after her, wincing with every step. He dropped to a reverse crawl and focused his beam on the breach while shuffling to her side.

From here, the objective was clear. In and out of the huge cavern as fast as possible and returning to the subway station with six freed hostages.

No more waiting.

No more debating.

No more losing.

Hundreds of creatures lay in wait. Hundreds more were heading in their direction. It was do or die time.

Bowcut took a deep breath and prepared to advance.

As she took her first steps forward, the shattered remains of the lantern she had placed at the breach dropped into the cavern.

CHAPTER TWENTY-TWO

A thin trail of smoke had risen above Manhattan after the first underground explosion. Every time Sal gazed across the river, his desire to take his diesel engine into the subway system increased. A flurry of activity on the police line had followed the second boom from inside the Jersey tunnel, but so far, nobody had followed the small SWAT team toward the Pavilion.

The alarm on his watch chirped, signaling his personal cutoff point.

He went over in his head what they knew, and it wasn't much. They still had no word on the safety of the passengers, the mayor, the president, and, most important, his friends. An hour had passed since Mike and he were ordered to board their diesel engine, ready to move at a moment's notice. But since then, they'd heard nothing. Either the police and MTA had done a great job at keeping silent, or they were as equally in the dark.

Sal cut his alarm and reached for the cabin's door.

"I told you," Mike said. "Don't even think about it."

"The shit's hitting the fan. Big time. The only person who's come out is a sickly looking cop. Enough is enough, Mike."

"You think you're tougher than that SWAT team?"

"Our engine is. We could barrel in, grab everyone, and be out before those terrorist assholes knew what hit 'em. This morning, two guys from Bay Ridge; this afternoon, national heroes. Right?"

"Or this afternoon, two dead idiots from Bay Ridge. Don't be a douche. We've no idea if the explosions wrecked the track."

"There's only one way to find out."

"Yes—wait for the cops to tell us."

Asshole. Mike still wasn't on board. And while Sal could probably go in by himself, it was definitely better to have his partner along for the ride. He shook his head and glanced around, hoping for more ammunition to persuade Mike. His eyes landed on a bunch of reporters in the parking lot gathered around a woman at the back of a blue-and-white WNBC van. Some recoiled from the open doors. Others stood staring with openmouthed expressions. Cell phone cameras flashed and raised voices drifted across to the maintenance shed.

"Betcha it's an update," Sal said. "I'm taking a look."

"Stay here, buddy—we could get the call at any moment."

"Oh, now you're ready to go? We haven't gotten the call yet, so might as well see what's going on."

Sal opened the cabin door, climbed down the short steel ladder, and headed along the platform. He couldn't stop thinking about the footage from inside the Pavilion and the photo of Munoz's shocked face. Those were his people down there. If the activity in the parking lot revolved around their fates, he had to find out.

More press flocked around the van, pushing forward to gain a better view of whatever had attracted the sudden interest. Sal reached the back of the throng and rose on his tiptoes, but he couldn't see past the sea of heads. He squeezed his way past four people.

"What gives?" he asked a man in a suit.

"It's a new photo from the Pavilion."

"What the hell?" a woman said near the front.

Sal wrestled his way forward, squeezing his wide frame through the crowd. Inside the van, a female reporter sat next to a screen displaying a low-quality image from inside the Pavilion.

A cop lay flat on his back. Blood pooled underneath his shredded legs. A distorted black figure stood halfway out of the shot. A huge figure. Sal squinted, trying to figure out what he was looking at. It looked barely human, but that didn't make any sense. Still, he couldn't quite tell.

"What the hell is that?" he asked the reporter, pointing at the figure.

"I'm not sure. It's the last image our reporter Christopher Fields sent. I've asked him four times, but he isn't replying."

"Is there any way to clear up the photo?"

"Don't you think we've tried?" she asked, exasperated. "Who are you?"

"Someone who gives a shit. Did Fields say anything else?"

"There's a gas leak or something. I don't know where or how bad."

"That's it?"

She gave him a blank stare.

With no other information forthcoming, Sal forced his way clear of the crowd. The reactions on the faces around him matched his confusion. One thing was clear, though: that was a *cop* and he was being torn apart. By what, Sal couldn't tell, but he knew that the photo had finally snapped his wafer-thin patience. Waiting and hoping were no longer on his agenda if the attack was still ongoing with the added threat of a gas leak. He had no way of knowing the true danger, but he had to act.

With or without Mike.

Sal walked calmly past a bunch of cops and headed back to the maintenance shed, resisting the temptation to break into a sprint and give away his intentions. He reached the push-button railroad switch halfway along the platform, glanced in either direction, and depressed it. His engine's track silently aligned with the tunnel. A few cops and soldiers on the police line peered toward the shed, but nobody said anything to him.

Mike glared through the cab's window suspiciously.

Sal picked up his pace, knowing his last action had already been flagged in the MTA operations command center. Any unscheduled changes guaranteed an immediate call from his boss. Usually, anyway. Today he was hoping all the chaos had that crew off their game. Still, he didn't want to tempt fate, so he quickly climbed the cabin's short ladder, entered, and sat behind the controls.

"Are you nuts?" Mike demanded. "They won't let us through."

"They can't stop this train. The rescue failed and there's a gas leak. It's down to us now."

"A gas leak? This is a goddamn *diesel* engine."

"I'll take it slow once we're inside the tunnel. Those two explosions will've burned off the gas, giving us a window to get in and out."

"You can't know that."

"Look, I'm not staying here any longer. If we do nothing, those people die no matter what. At least we're giving our friends a fighting chance."

"Or we're bringing the match that lights the whole thing to kingdom come! We're not going."

"We *are* going."

Mike shook his head. "You are one stubborn son of a bitch. There's no way I'm going down there."

"Then get off my train and suit yourself."

Sal gunned the throttle and the engine roared. He reached forward to release the brakes and sent them on their way.

"Sal, for once in your life don't be an asshole."

He had no response to that, so he let his train do the talking. The engine's sound had attracted more glances from the police on the line, but it didn't seem they had quite caught on yet. He gazed directly beyond them at the dark tunnel. This was his time to make a difference and nothing was going to stop him.

"Oh, fuck me," Mike said. "We're really doing this?"

"You got a few seconds to jump."

"You asshole. I'm not letting you go in on your own."

Sal smiled at his best friend. They always came to the same conclusion by using different logic. He always looked at the positives and jumped in head-first. Mike complained his way to always doing the right thing.

The engine picked up speed and barreled out of the shed in the direction of the subway tunnel entrance. Sal gave an extended blast of the horn. Most of the cops and soldiers turned to face the shed.

They clanked past the Exhibition Center's sparkling glass pyramid and closed to within seconds of breaking through the police line. He stooped behind the controls in case any cop got an itchy trigger finger at the sight of a slowly accelerating diesel engine.

Don't shoot. Don't shoot.

He shouldn't have worried—uniformed men and women scattered away from the track, way too concerned about being run down by the rogue train. Someone among their ranks *did* have the presence of mind to at least shout through a bullhorn, instructing them to stop.

Sal slid the cabin's window shut instead.

He was past listening, past the point where he

considered anything other than storming to the Pavilion. If these guys weren't prepared to help those trapped inside the subway system, that was their problem.

I'm coming, fellas!

Mike ducked down, covering his head with his arms.

The engine snapped the line of tape, rushed past the confetti-covered platform, and dipped inside the dark tunnel. Sal flicked on the headlights, blasting out two powerful beams. He eased their speed to avoid creating sparks. "What did I tell you?" he said. "Nobody fired a shot."

Mike rose and let out a deep sigh.

They slowly clanked deeper into the tunnel. Sal focused on the route ahead, searching for any signs of the enemy. The image he just saw in the van defied logic. It defied the laws of nature. But no living thing could defy the brute force of a diesel engine.

CHAPTER TWENTY-THREE

The command center's spotlights continued to bathe the train compartment and form a clear path to the AV room. Hundreds of creatures swarmed in the darker parts of the Pavilion, their shadows occasionally flickering on the walls. Every few moments, a stocky arm or leg would test the edges of the glare before the creature would screech and retreat into the safety of the dark.

So far, so good, Cafferty thought.

During this lull in the action, he had ordered Paul DeLuca and his team to repair the damage to the train as best they could. They busily went about stretching lengths of duct tape over the gouges and tears in the car's body, attempting to keep the atmosphere inside relatively breathable.

In the meantime, Cafferty had spent the last few minutes preparing for his mission. He and North had borrowed body armor and flashlights from members of the NYPD and attached makeshift handles on two of the smaller steel plates. He knew the rudimentary shields provided little protection, considering the state of the distant blast door. But if they stuck to the middle of the spotlight shafts, he figured they were just out of the creatures' range.

A young cop with a bloodstained face approached. "Mr. Mayor, I think you could use an extra pair of hands."

"Stay and protect the people," Cafferty replied, scanning the sea of nervous faces in the car. "We don't need to give the creatures a bigger target."

"But there's only two of—"

"The good citizens of New York and New Jersey, officer. Those are your priority."

Lieutenant Arnolds muscled through the crowd. "We can spare Officer Spear. Take him along, Mr. Mayor. You need the help, and he's one of my best."

"Okay, but no more."

North removed the final plate from the car's set of doors, revealing its battered outer side and fragments of shattered glass on the platform. Officer Spear held a steel pipe over his shoulder like a baseball bat. Cafferty drew in a deep breath, ready to make his move, until someone tapped his shoulder.

"I'm coming with you, too," Lucien Flament said.

"This isn't your fight. Help the police protect the car."

"It's everyone's fight. Is anyone else here ex–special forces?"

"Probably not. Still—"

"Mr. Mayor, don't be stupid. You've seen I can handle myself, and we clearly work well as a team.

God forbid something happens to those spotlights, I'll cover you with my camera's flash."

It was hard to deny the Frenchman's points. Flament's reasoning had definitely aided in their survival, and the injured cop lying in the aisle owed him his life. He was also highly trained and had proven how fast he could think on his feet. Something about him irked Cafferty, though, and it wasn't just the fact that his initial two-person team had doubled in the space of a minute.

"Let him come," North said. "He's the type of guy I want by my side."

"You've changed your tune," Cafferty said.

"The game changed after the creatures appeared. If it boosts our chances of success, I'm all in."

"Honestly," Flament said, "I don't really care what you think—I'm coming. I must insist."

"You must *what*?" Cafferty said.

Flament stepped closer. "If my old colleagues find out I stayed on the train and did nothing, I'll be shamed throughout the French special forces community."

"That's not the real reason, is it?"

"It's a part of the real reason. The other parts are mine to know. I told you, though, I aim to live, and right now, your plan is crucial to making sure that happens. So the most important thing we do is making sure *you* succeed. I'm your best chance at that."

"You're pretty sure of yourself."

Flament shrugged. "What can I say? I'm pretty extraordinary."

Cafferty actually laughed at that. Or maybe it was just his nervousness. "All right, Lucien. Get yourself ready and stay by my side. Spear, cover us."

Flament talked to Officer Spear, who directed him to another cop, and after a brief exchange, the Frenchman was stripping down to a fitted undershirt and pulling on black body armor. Once he'd donned the vest, he slung his leather satchel over his shoulder and removed his glasses. It wasn't quite a Clark Kent transformation, but for the first time, Cafferty noticed a steely determination in the man's eyes. His previously baggy shirt had also hidden a muscular body. He was starting to warm to the idea of Lucien joining them.

Cafferty stood on one of the seats and waved his hand to draw the passengers' attention. The car fell silent, leaving the hissing oxygen tanks and snarls and grunts outside as the only sounds.

"Attention, everyone," he said. "We're heading to the AV room and configuring the IMAX. In a couple of minutes, we'll have this whole place lit up like Times Square, driving those creatures out of the Pavilion for good. Do what you have to do to stay safe in here."

"Won't the creatures smash the IMAX when you light it up?" DeLuca asked.

"It projects from over the command center. They'd have to cross a large, well-lit space to reach it. This could be the chance we need to survive."

"I agree," Flament added. "The creatures seem to be getting better at avoiding the light. The first one we saw raced directly into it before backing away. But then they wised up and smashed the near-est set of the Pavilion's overhead lights from the confines of the tunnel. The ones attacking our car only dipped in and out briefly so as to avoid direct contact with the light. They are getting smarter, and quickly. Bathing the area in light is a better bet than the concentrated beams we have right now."

Cafferty glanced down at the verbose Frenchman. Flament's logic felt too precise, too surgical to come up with based on the few interactions they'd had with the creatures. His suspicions about the reporter resurfaced, but those questions could wait. Right now, he was certain he needed the man, no matter what he was hiding.

This isn't over, though. Not by a longshot.

"Let's move out," North said. He forced open the doors and slipped between the gap, raising his makeshift shield and sweeping his flashlight around the Pavilion.

Cafferty jumped down from the seat and followed. His shoes crunched on the fragments of glass spread across the polished stone floor. Flament quickly moved to his side, aiming his camera around but saving the battery on his flash for the time being. The young Officer Spear came out last, twisting from side to side, searching for signs of movement.

They headed toward the command center's powerful glare to complete the first leg of their journey. Cafferty's heart pounded against his chest, and he tensed, expecting a tail to lash down at any moment. He told himself to stay cool—easier said than done—but somehow he was able to keep moving forward, his confidence growing with each step down the middle of the twenty-foot-wide shaft of light.

The light blinded his peripheral vision, but he could still hear the creatures surrounding him, taking guttural breaths, matching his stride as he reached within fifty feet of the command center. Once again, his fear crashed against him, knowing how close the nightmares were from tearing the life from him, North, Spear, and Flament. It was a claustrophobic feeling, the weight of all those bodies pressing in from the sides, and for the first time since he'd come down here, he was aware of how trapped they really were. Their breathing, their occasional shrieks, screamed, *We're going to slice you open and pull your organs through the holes . . .*

But none attacked.

The plan was working.

The plan is *working. We can do this. Just stay in the path of the light. Stay in the light . . .*

The creatures' footsteps grew more frantic when he reached within twenty-five feet of the command center, hammering through the darkness at an incredible speed, as if they were throwing a temper tantrum at being outsmarted, as if they understood Tom's plan.

They're learning, Flament had said.

That might have been the scariest thought of all.

And then the Pavilion fell completely silent.

Cafferty had no idea what game the creatures were playing, but for some reason, their feet no longer thudded alongside the group. Their acrid stench and their faint wheezes betrayed their continued presence in the blackness, though.

Something's wrong . . .

North reached the command center and turned into the next shaft of light, leading toward the AV room's short corridor. He paused and looked back toward the battered entrance. "Is everyone all right in there?"

"We're okay," Anna shouted.

At least they had survived, and Cafferty raised his arm to wave. His body veered to the left, as if somebody had shoved him, and he broke into a stagger toward the edge of the light. He skidded to a stop and quickly stepped back, wondering if a nervous twitch had propelled him toward certain death.

"Be careful, Mr. Mayor," Flament said.

"No shit. It won't happen again."

He wasn't exactly sure why it had happened in the first place. Shaking his head, Cafferty reached the second spotlight's path and followed North toward the AV room, quickening his stride . . .

. . . and his body veered to the left toward the darkness again. He planted his feet firmly against the ground and glanced around.

What the hell?

Twice in under a minute he had come within a foot of the creatures' tearing him to shreds. He told himself to focus. It had to be the methane. Nothing else had ever affected his body in this way. Cafferty cautiously took another few steps and, again, veered to the left. He threw himself to the ground to stop his momentum and clutched the floor.

Flament crawled to his side, taking slow, deliberate movements, as if at the bottom of a swimming pool. The Frenchman's usually blank expression had transformed into a wide-eyed look of terror.

"It's not just me?" Cafferty asked.

"I don't understand. It's like we're puppets on strings."

North dropped to his hands and knees and looked over his shoulder. "Keep moving. Whatever this is, it's getting stronger."

Cafferty stifled a cough and rubbed his eyes. Coming back into the methane-filled Pavilion this time felt twice as hard physically. His joints ached and his pounding headache had returned in spades. Even in his prone position, the unseen force pulled at his entire body, as if the creatures had attached invisible ropes around him and were hauling him toward their claws. Spear had also dropped to the ground and leopard-crawled forward, grimacing with each shuffle.

"We need to move swiftly," Flament said anxiously. "The creatures' power has increased. This is something I haven't seen before."

"You haven't *seen* before?"

"We need to move now while we still have our strength," Flament replied, ignoring the mayor's question.

North reached to within ten yards of the corridor. He veered hard to the right, straining to counter the force. Flament copied his technique and advanced. Cafferty also followed suit, moving closely by the Frenchman's side. It was easier said than done: the muscles in his arms and legs burned as he fought the increasingly strong pull. *Fight it, fight it*, he said to himself, forcing himself forward. It felt like he was on the edge of a cliff with a howling gale blasting his side. He couldn't think of anything that could have this effect on him, and that was as frightening as the image of what would happen if he succumbed.

A metallic rattle broke the silence. Spear's pipe clattered past Cafferty and raced out of the light.

"Dammit!" Spear yelled.

"Forget it," Cafferty said. "Just keep moving."

Flament collapsed again and his leg flipped into the darkness. He quickly spun on his back, raised his camera, and let out a series of blinding flashes.

Three creatures, all squatting in the shadows, had been reaching for his ankle. They shrieked and lurched away, scurrying back to the rest of the group, which had collected in a tight circular formation in the center of the Pavilion.

"They're doing this," Cafferty said. "There's no other explanation."

"You're right," Flament said. "But never this strong."

"How, though? And how do *you* know so much about it?"

Before Flament could respond, North scrambled to his feet, sprinted down the corridor—looking all the while like he was running along a banked track, doing everything in his power to not fall over—and flung open the AV room door. He backed inside and waved in encouragement toward Cafferty, Flament, and Spear, shouting, "Get your asses moving!"

Cafferty steeled himself and then pushed on toward the beckoning door. He strained every sinew as the pressure against his body increased. His knees slipped sideways every time they hit ground. He felt sure any more force would send him skidding out into the shiny black mass of creatures.

Strangely, it was at that moment that images of Ellen flashed through his mind:

Excitedly discussing the inaugural run with her last night after agreeing to their new pact . . .

Sharing a glass of wine to toast it . . .

Waving her blouse in front of him this morning for an opinion while he sat up in bed and ate eggs, home fries, and bacon . . .

Kissing her good-bye outside the subway station . . .

It gave Cafferty the strength to lunge forward and stretch out his arm . . .

. . . only for North to grab it and drag him into the AV room.

The pressure instantly left his body and he crawled toward the servers, feeling a mixture of relief that he had made it and shock at the sinister power deployed by the creatures to stop them.

Flament closed in. Sweat soaked his hair and trickled down his face, and he reached out a hand. North clasped it and yanked him inside.

Officer Spear muscled his way forward . . . only

to stop within eight feet. The young man thrust out a quivering arm, only to roar in agony as his body flipped over at an unnatural speed.

"On your front!" North shouted. "Keep moving."

Cafferty edged to North's side. "Spear! Don't stop! That's an order!"

The force took hold of the mayor's body again, threatening to drag him outside, and he, Flament, and North lurched back into the room.

Spear's arms and legs stretched out to his sides, and his star-shaped body lifted a few inches off the ground. He roared once more, struggling to combat the overwhelming force.

Cafferty frantically scanned the desk and opened a cupboard for a rope, a pole—anything to help. North's mutual expression said it all, though: if they headed out attempting to save the cop, they'd end up with the same fate, caught in the collective power of the creatures. "Hurry—configure the IMAX," Cafferty said. "That's the only thing that'll save him."

North rushed to the workstation and hit the keyboard. The monitor burst to life.

Spear's roar transformed into a gruesome scream. His arms cracked out of their sockets and hung loosely by his sides. His legs followed, as if he'd been stretched to the breaking point on a medieval rack, and he let out a howl more bloodcurdling than any creature.

"*Mon Dieu,*" Flament said, and bowed his head.

Cafferty grabbed a small metal case from the desk and hurled it into the darkness. It did nothing, because there was nothing he could do except watch while hoping the tapping of keys behind him brought about a quick result.

"Not long," North shouted. "Hold on, Spear."

Spear's arms tore free of his body, thumped against the ground, and slid out of the light, leaving two glistening trails of blood.

"Jesus Christ," Cafferty gasped.

The cop's head flopped back as he lost consciousness. His legs ripped free and veered into the darkness, leaving his dripping torso still suspended off the ground.

"For fuck's sake," North said. "It's rebooting."

A moment later, Officer Spear's body hit the ground like a sack of potatoes, and the imposing silhouettes of creatures moved to the edge of the light.

Cafferty whipped his head away, unable to look at the horrifying sight of the young officer torn to pieces by forces he didn't understand.

Lord help us . . .

The Pavilion grew quiet again, as if the creatures were satisfied for the moment with their collective carnage.

Flament, Cafferty, and North sat on the ground, their backs against the cabinets, and took a few moments to catch their breath as the computer restarted.

Cafferty had never expected a straightforward mission, but he shuddered at the thought of the creatures' frightening new complexion, and its result. Their physical superiority was obvious, but this latest power was beyond anyone's understanding.

Or perhaps not everyone's.

"Why are you staring at me like that?" Flament asked.

Cafferty narrowed his eyes. "I think you know something about this."

"What do you mean?"

"Don't be coy, Lucien. I can accept you *maybe* figuring out the light and oxygen as their weaknesses—that made a certain sense. I might even believe that you are ex–French military. You're certainly trained. But out there, you said you've never seen *this* before, and you were scared as hell. I think you're lying to me about what you actually know."

Flament gave his Gallic shrug—a gesture that was starting to infuriate Cafferty. "You're overreacting, Mr. Mayor. I meant no one has ever seen anything like this before. Maybe it's my English, something lost in translation or misinterpreted."

"I don't believe you. There's a cop lying dead outside. Start talking."

"Think this through, Mr. Mayor. If I knew anything about those creatures, why the hell would I be down here? Why would I let anyone else be here? Why would I join you on this mission?"

Cafferty eyeballed him for a moment, searching for the hint of a lie. He had learned to spot the signs in politicians: looking to the right, pursed lips, rapid blinking, eyes darting back and forth—all classic symptoms of spewing bullshit.

But Flament's face had returned to his neutral

expression. "I've helped you, and you accuse me of lying?" he asked. "That is not how you thank someone, Mr. Mayor."

Cafferty didn't like the man's tone, but he also couldn't deny Flament's reasoning. And besides, the reporter had indeed helped him and saved lives. He couldn't shake that he was missing something crucial about Flament, but finding out his real motivation and background would have to wait. Right now their priority was clearing the creatures back into the tunnels and taking back the Pavilion before anyone else died.

An MTA logo screensaver bounced around the IMAX projector's control screen, showing the deep blue that projected onto the wall. North hit the return key, brought up the configuration screen, and switched it to test mode. He selected the background color as white, changed the range to cover the whole Pavilion, and accepted the changes.

An hourglass spun on the screen, and for a moment Tom was afraid it wasn't going to reboot, scuppering his plan. But then the MTA logo disappeared and the screen flicked to white.

Piercing shrieks rang out.

Cafferty inched toward the door.

The projector pumped out fifteen thousand watts of brilliant light, spearing it to all areas, illuminating the train, the platform, the command center, and the shattered front of the Starbucks. What mattered most, though, was that it also illuminated the creatures as they escaped from the fierce glare, siphoning into the tunnels at breakneck speed.

All of them.

"We've done it," Cafferty said. "We've damn well done it."

North breathed a deep sigh of relief and slumped into a chair. "But it hasn't gotten rid of the methane."

That—plus losing a good man—knocked the shine off their success, but it had improved their chances of survival. Cafferty now had a personal decision to make—one he'd put off long enough. But with everything in the Pavilion back to relative safety, he allowed himself to focus on Ellen. He still didn't know if she or any other passengers had survived the attack, but he wasn't going to sit around wondering.

He had to find his wife and the other passengers, dead or alive.

CHAPTER TWENTY-FOUR

Seawater sprayed from the seams of the docking station door and had formed into a steady stream in the escape passage. The two black monstrosities continued to batter themselves against the opposite side, trapped inside the flooding room with Samuels, who was now likely a floating corpse. The solid bolts held, giving Munoz small consolation, but they'd been able to breach the control center's blast door, so unless they died in the water, it was only a matter of time before they came crashing through. On top of all that, the new rescue plan had already run into a problem in the first few seconds: the steel locking wheel that opened the route to the engineering bay wouldn't budge.

Munoz gripped the top and bottom, clenched his teeth, and heaved. Even if they got through this one—and he certainly had his doubts now—he expected the creatures to swiftly follow, always keeping them just a single hatch from survival in a deadly game of cat and mouse.

"Are you sure this is our only way out?" Reynolds asked, keeping both of their guns aimed at the docking station. "If what Samuels said about the laser is true . . ."

"I'll test it when we get through," Munoz grunted, attempting to twist the wheel again. "Knowing Samuels, when I pull the trigger, a little flag will unfurl from the barrel with 'bang' printed on it."

Munoz stopped talking after that and focused his energy on the wheel. The creatures pounded the docking station door again, and increasingly powerful jets of water hissed through the cracks. It wasn't just the threat of them coming through, obviously—it was also the millions of gallons from the Hudson that would blast inside the passage and quickly end things.

Which might be the cleanest death we get, Munoz thought.

Munoz twisted the wheel using every ounce of strength in his body.

It didn't move an inch.

He unbuttoned his shirt and stripped it off, revealing his BRING BACK *FIREFLY* T-shirt. To hell with what the president thought of him; he was beyond caring about that, let alone the comeback of *Serenity*'s renegade crew. At this moment, he only cared about them both seeing sunlight again.

"You'll get there, Diego," Reynolds said.

"I fucking hope so. For both of our sakes."

"Keep trying."

Muffled electronic beeps came from the docking station. Munoz froze and listened: 3-4-5-6-7 . . .

"Don't tell me they know that code, too?" Reynolds shouted.

"Not this time. They're simply hitting the buttons in sequence."

Not that he wasn't worried. The volume of freezing water entering the passage and flowing around his shins was rising by the second.

Munoz wrapped his MTA shirt around one of the locking wheel's chunky spindles, leaned back, and used the new leverage to pull on the wheel even harder.

Again, nothing happened . . . until the wheel's central barrel let out a metallic squeak.

He yanked it again.

The wheel rotated an inch.

Thank God—

A deafening boom rattled the docking station door, shaking all thankful thoughts out of his mind.

The bolts groaned.

The tunnel shook.

The creatures would break through at any second.

A torrent of foaming water raced past Munoz's knees and sloshed down the passage. He guessed they had a minute, if that, for either of the deadly options to come true: torn apart by monsters, crushed by a wall of river water, or both.

Reynolds shot him a nervous glance. For the first time, the president genuinely looked like he had shit his pants. Munoz didn't blame him.

The water level continued to rise past their thighs. Munoz grunted, ripping his soaked shirt downward, and the wheel finally gave, rotating with a fast spin.

His triumph was mitigated by a massive boom as the docking station door rocked again. A foot-wide gap now appeared at the bottom, increasing the flow. A dangerous tail thrust out of it and thrashed from side to side, causing the president to back away, almost knocking into Munoz.

"Jesus!"

Munoz agreed but didn't respond as the mini-bolt finally clanked. He dragged open the engineering bay's door just wide enough for them to fit through—which was rather difficult, considering the water pressure trying to slam the door back shut. "You first, Mr. President," he said. "And make it fast."

Reynolds didn't even hesitate as he handed off the laser and rushed through the gap.

Munoz followed, slipping inside the brightly lit bay, and turned to seal the entrance just as the docking station burst open. A wall of water thundered toward him with a creature at its center, a diabolical body surfer aimed straight at him. Adrenaline coursed through his body as he heaved the door shut, spun the internal locking wheel, and breathed a massive sigh of relief.

A tremendous roar came from the other side of the door as water rocketed past. Munoz imagined his MTA shirt floating in the swamped emergency passage along with Samuels' body parts . . . and a creature tearing everything to ribbons. He rested his head in his hands, coming down from the flood of hormones and chemicals his body had dumped into his bloodstream, aghast at the nonstop stream of shit hitting the fan. Today had pushed him so far beyond anything he had experienced. Hell, beyond what he could have imagined. The creatures made the Brownsville Bloods gang look like pussycats.

"Great job, Diego," Reynolds said. "Where from here?"

"Down a few levels to the Jersey maintenance tunnel. It's our fastest way out."

"Good." Diego could feel the president hovering nearby, and he finally looked up. With a mix of gentleness and resolve, Reynolds said, "We need to keep moving. Lead the way."

Munoz nodded, took a shuddering breath, and stood up. Taking another deep breath, he moved past Reynolds and splashed by the docking station's generators. As he moved, he continuously swept the area, aiming the laser at the dark spaces between the machinery—spaces that could easily fit more of the creatures. The bright fluorescent lights provided some comfort, but not much. If anything, the shadows they created were as bad as the light they provided was good.

And, of course, there was always what they already knew was behind them. As if on cue, something pounded on the emergency passage door.

Both stopped and spun to face it.

A jet of water sprayed into the engineering bay.

"Oh, for fuck's sake," Munoz cursed.

"They're not going to stop, are they?"

"I'm guessing we've created a desperate situation

for them. They want their prey, and we're drowning them. And this door is a piece of cake compared to the one they just busted through. We have to move." And with that, Munoz rushed for the far end of the bay where it narrowed into a curving passage.

"Where exactly does this lead?" Reynolds asked, following close behind.

"It corkscrews down to the Jersey tunnels."

"Wait—that means we're going farther down," Reynolds said, as the truth of what they were about to do finally dawned on him. "The water . . ."

"Yeah. But it's the only way to get back up from here. Marines know how to swim, right, Mr. President?"

"Oo-rah."

"Then let's go."

Their footsteps slapped against the concrete as they descended, echoing through the passage, and they passed entrances to supply rooms containing nothing of immediate use. While he had made the swimming comment to get the president focused on moving, the fact was that Munoz knew if the creatures battered a path after them, it was only a matter of time before the Hudson flooded the *whole* subway line.

There was no swimming out of that.

A massive implosion was almost inevitable at this point, and Diego knew it. As if to remind him, a thin sheet of water overtook them, darkening the ground.

"Shit," Reynolds said.

"Just keep moving. They're not in yet or we'd be soaked. Not far now."

A locked hatch appeared around the next bend and they sprinted toward it.

"Another one?" Reynolds rested his hands on his knees and gulped in air. "You're kidding me."

"Ever seen *Titanic*?"

"Who hasn't?"

"Each level is sealed into sections, separated by a hatch that creates a watertight seal," Munoz said while punching in the code. "It's designed to contain small disasters."

"The *Titanic* sunk."

Munoz had no response for that. He'd been thinking the same thing.

The hatch opened with a mechanical grind. Reynolds climbed through the circular gap, finally into a dry environment. Munoz followed, locking it from the other side.

They repeated the process several times, descending the levels and putting distance between them and the creatures (and water), until they eventually reached the safety of the entrance to the Jersey maintenance tunnel.

Safety being an incredibly relative term.

"I need a minute," Reynolds said. "This old body isn't what it was."

"Take two." Munoz needed a rest himself. But while his body recovered, his mind continued to run wild, and he said, "While we're waiting, though, I think I deserve to know more about Van Ness."

"Let me catch my breath—"

"Mr. President, with all due respect, fuck that. We're in deep shit and you know something about why. I've got a goddamned laser in one hand and the brightest set of silver balls I've ever seen in my pockets. If we're gonna die down here together, I deserve to know what's going on."

"People always say that. They always say they *deserve* to know what's going on. I never quite got that sentiment, never quite got why anyone would be swayed by such loose logic."

Munoz looked at Reynolds skeptically, and the president studied him right back. Eventually, though, he shrugged.

"Sorry. You're not wrong about wanting to know. Maybe wrong about why I should actually tell you, but fuck it—you want to know about Albert Van Ness?"

"Anything that might help us get out of here, but yeah, that's a good start."

"All right," Reynolds replied. "Of course, you're not going to believe this. I mean, I didn't. Until today."

"I think I've got a healthy suspension of disbelief at this point, Mr. President."

"Touché." Reynolds took a deep breath at the same time Munoz held his in anticipation. "I took a meeting in the Oval Office right after I was inaugurated. Literally my first week. It was with a guy named Edwards. Not quite sure if that was his first name or last. Just 'Edwards.' I was told I needed to hear him out. Again, not really sure why, but people

I trusted were very insistent. So I sat there while he gave me a presentation about this organization called the Foundation for Human Advancement. Said every former president had been briefed on the Foundation since World War II. Now, this was probably my fiftieth meeting that day, and at first I thought this Foundation was just some think tank looking for government money or influence."

"But it wasn't, was it? What did he show you?"

"I remember it distinctly, as it sounded so ridiculous at first. The story went like this. Apparently, the Foundation was created right after World War II by a Nazi architect named Otto Van Ness. During the final days of the war, Otto was the project manager on the deep expansion of the Führerbunker in 1944. The war was going poorly, and the Nazis wanted to ensure their survival should the Allies reach the capital. Hitler's bunker in Berlin was already a marvel of engineering, the deepest mankind had ever dug into the earth in modern times. And Van Ness' mission was to make it even bigger—even *deeper*. The Nazis stumbled on a nest while digging, and Otto was the only man to make it out of the Führerbunker alive."

"Okay," Munoz said slowly.

"A few years after the war, Otto Van Ness created the Foundation for Human Advancement."

"This sounds like a myth," Munoz said, dumbfounded. "It's *always* the damned Nazis."

"That's what I thought, too. Edwards claimed Otto Van Ness hunted creatures across the planet to learn about their weaknesses. He developed his

arsenal after each encounter, in Europe, the Ameri-
cas, Asia, and Africa, slowly proving himself to
national governments with local witnesses and displays of his weaponry. Everyone was sworn to secrecy. Word of mouth spread and the Foundation
secured long-term funding contracts."

"You mean Van Ness learned to extort the governments of the world for protection money. So
why didn't you take him seriously?"

"I thought that was all he was doing—extorting
money from us. Because while Edwards presented
a fun little story, I was presented with no actual
proof. Nothing. Just a demand for an insane amount
of money to continue protecting the United States
from these nests—which he wouldn't disclose the
locations of, by the way. You have to understand, I
thought this guy was fucking insane. I didn't sign
the contract, so to speak. This Edwards fella just
shook his head and advanced to the next slide. All it
said was that as humans dug deeper and deeper into
the earth over the past century, these breaches have
become more and more common. When I asked
how come there had been no incidents with these
creatures reported, he said, 'Because of the Foundation.' That was the last straw. In my first week, I had
been getting intelligence reports from all over the
world, stuff that would scare the shit out of you—if
these creatures haven't already done that," he said
with a rueful grin.

Munoz didn't respond, and Reynolds sighed before continuing.

"The last thing he said before I had him escorted

out of the Oval Office was 'The Foundation is literally saving the world every day.'

"I laughed at him . . ."

Munoz wasn't sure whether to be pissed at this crazy-ass story or infuriated at the president's lack of foresight. Ultimately, he shook his head. "Anything else?"

"For a while, there was only silence on this front. Those trusted advisers were quietly moved out of my initial sphere, and I heard nothing else. Then, one day, my private cell rings. A phone only my *wife* knows about. On the other end, a man with a German accent tells me he's allowing me one more opportunity to reconsider my decision and I should thank him for *allowing* me to win the presidency."

"Let me guess: Van Ness?"

"Yes, but not Otto. It was Albert, his son. And now the price for his protection was *double*. Again, all I could do was laugh. This guy was a thug. No different than the Mafia. If there's one thing I can't stand, it's a bully, especially one with nothing to back up their bravado—or so I thought. At the time, though, the only thing I heard was the money, and the yearly sum he demanded from us was insane. So I refused to be part of it. I remember thinking at the time, *If he believes he can extort the United States government, he's made a big mistake.*"

"So . . . ?"

"So I told him to fuck off and that I was launching an investigation into the Foundation immediately."

"And did you?" Munoz asked.

"I ordered the CIA to look into Van Ness and my secretary of defense to dig up any records relating to his foundation."

"And they found nothing."

"Nothing. It's like he's a ghost. There was no record of my cell phone even receiving a call. NSA couldn't find anything. Defense Department, nothing. Homeland Security, nothing. But my secretary of defense told me maybe I should take the threat seriously, in case the story was true . . ."

The president paused, lost in thought. Munoz was going to ask another question, but then Reynolds let out a quiet "Son of a bitch," as if something had just dawned on him. He pulled a smartphone out of his pocket and scrolled through his messages. "That scheming bastard."

"Who?" Munoz asked.

"Blake Mansfield. The goddamn secretary of defense. The man who's supposed to be coordinating our rescue with Homeland Security and has been doing a shitty job of it the whole time. That motherfucker *has* to be working for Van Ness. Remember what Samuels said? They knew there was a nest down here and wanted revenge. And if they can't get to me, why wouldn't they have a contingency plan in my cabinet? I'm such a fool."

Reynolds slammed the heel of his hand against the wall.

Munoz couldn't believe how the conversation had progressed. It all seemed far-fetched, but it fit perfectly with what he had already witnessed. The creatures. The specialized weapons. The traitor.

Traitors. Anger rose inside of him at the thought of his team dying in a dangerous game they knew nothing about, over what appeared to be a high-end shakedown.

And Samuels had the balls to call me *a gangster.*
Assholes!

None of this mattered, though, if they didn't make it out alive.

A bloodcurdling screech rang out from the other side of the door.

The president bolted stiff. Munoz was pretty sure his face matched Reynolds' look of dread. All thoughts of what led them to be here vanished as the engineer focused on what faced them now. He guessed creatures were waiting in the tunnel, and they were also still following from the emergency passage. They were freakishly fast and strong, and the methane made most weapons obsolete—not to mention it was making breathing increasingly problematic. Luckily Munoz and Reynolds had Samuels' laser and strobe grenades, but they'd yet to put them into action.

They'd find out soon enough if the Foundation's weapons worked at all.

CHAPTER TWENTY-FIVE

Ellen Cafferty knelt on the ledge's cool stone, suspended over a mass of snarling creatures somewhere in the dark depths below. A thick, sticky mucus covered her body, holding her firmly in place, and she guessed it was the same for the other women. She felt like a fly in a spider's web. And the more she struggled, twisting and turning, the tighter the web clung to her. When it seemed as if she or another woman had moved a little bit, the creatures were vigilant in nudging her back into the exact same spot. A faint, eerie glow illuminated the darkness just barely enough for her to make out her surroundings. She guessed it was her cell phone nearby in power save mode.

If there was a positive, it *was* easier to breathe in the pitch-black cocoon, as if the creatures were supplying the women with just enough oxygen to survive. That didn't amount to much if it only meant sustaining their lives until they became victims like the rest of the passengers on the train. It also was barely worth it at all, as the mucus-like substance they were covered in was revolting, both in texture and in how the creatures delivered it. And every time Ellen tried to move, the creatures showered her with more viscous liquid from membranes hanging above. For some reason, the fact that they collected and stored the mucus made it even more alien.

She shuddered, and that little movement was enough for a creature to force her back into position and explode another sac. The substance dripped down her face like maple syrup and tightened around her body, welding her firmly in place once more.

The creatures had to be doing this to them for a reason. Nothing else made sense considering the brutal efficiency they had used to tear apart the rest of the passengers. She wondered if they planned on using the hostages as their next meal, and the mucus was the seasoning. But even that made her pause. Because why *her*?

And why these other five women?

And why were they arranged in a circle facing one another, as if in some ceremonial sacrifice?

She had decided to attend the event only yesterday, after Tom made a commitment to reinvigorate their marriage. They had barely spoken a word during the past six months apart from late-night, liquor-induced arguments. The Z Train project had consumed him, relegating everything else in his life to irrelevance. And his one-night indiscretion . . . He'd spent the past few months torturing himself for his mistake, trying to do what he could to rectify things—even confessing almost as soon as it happened—but the damage was done. He had hurt her badly by his inattention and hurt her even worse when he had found time for passion with another woman, when he claimed to have no time for her. With all that, he had pushed her into doing something she deeply regretted to this day, which in turn had made her feel guilty enough to agree to coming today.

And all of that meant absolutely nothing, because the hurt and sorrow of a failing marriage felt so distant compared to the horror and pain she was living now.

A broken marriage was better than this. Anything was . . .

The creatures stalked outside the cocoon, moving around the ledge with heavy footsteps, tails swishing and teeth chattering. It was unnerving, because there was something in their gaze when they came within inches of her face, appearing out of the blackness—something beyond just an animalistic hunger. An intelligence and deliberateness that chilled her blood. Combined with their vast numbers and brute strength, it was becoming harder and harder to believe there was a world in which a rescue was coming or an escape was possible.

Ellen thought back to her brief glimpse of the women when salvation seemed possible. The semiconscious lady on the opposite side of the circle had a bulging belly.

Did the one to her left also have a bump? She couldn't recall, but if she did . . .

The lady to her right in a summer dress looked to be with child.

The connection crystalized in Ellen's mind, and she shuddered again.

All these women, like her, were pregnant.

She reasoned that was why they had been spared. Nothing else explained their survival. And that couldn't be a coincidence.

If she wasn't so afraid she'd choke on it, she thought she might throw up, knowing that a single, terrible mistake two months ago had temporarily saved her life. He had caught her at her weakest moment and lavished her with compliments and vintage bottles of Bordeaux. His accent was charming, and he was handsome and, truth be told, a great lover. They spent the night together at that countryside hotel. At the time, it had felt amazing. It had felt right, a release from her frustration and anger at Tom. The next morning that release had transformed into the shackles lies so often become, and she instantly regretted it. And, of course, the man had disappeared.

Now those screams of passion that echoed in her head were turning into screams of horror. She thought to escape again, but the gruesome mucus held her in place. She grimaced and attempted to struggle free once more, only to stop when she realized the crackling had ceased and the cavern had fallen deathly silent.

Ellen held her breath, motionless, afraid to make a sound.

A faint scratching sound rose from below, like something was being dragged up the jagged rocks. The scratching drew closer.

Without warning, the mucous membrane she was trapped in popped. Creatures dragged the thick layer of skin off the women and flung it to the side.

A woman in the circle gasped.

A huge creature, five times bigger than the others, dragged itself toward them, and its bright ruby eyes cast a thin glow over the ledge.

"Oh my *God*!" another woman yelled.

The slick black armaments covering the giant creature's torso glinted in the weak light. Retractable scales striped its back. Twelve-inch claws extended from each of its four limbs.

Ellen had been terrified of the other creatures. She had no vocabulary for how she felt about this new abomination.

The giant thudded forward, eyeing each woman in turn, and perched itself in the center of the circle. Its ten-foot tail whooshed from side to side, smashing against the cavern wall and spilling stones across the ground.

The creature swung toward Ellen and roared, blasting out a stench like rotting garbage. Saliva spattered across her face. She shut her eyes tight, praying somebody would wake her from this nightmare.

Hail Mary, full of grace, the Lord is with thee . . .

She sensed the creature inches from her face.

Blessed art thou amongst women, and blessed is the fruit of thy womb, Jesus . . .

A claw traced a line up Ellen's abdomen, exerting enough pressure to break the skin. She swallowed hard. It couldn't end like this.

Holy Mary, mother of God . . .

Warm blood trickled down her stomach.

Pray for us sinners, now and at the hour of our death . . .

The claw withdrew.

Ellen opened her eyes just a sliver.

The creature had moved on to the next woman.

Amen?

It ran a claw over the other woman's face and then down toward her stomach. The woman screamed and wriggled, but it did nothing to deter the creature.

Near darkness had scared Ellen shitless, but the creature's eyes illuminated the full terror of their situation. It moved on again, shuffling in front of the youngest-looking woman in the group, her body covered in a tattered yellow sundress. She stared up at it with wide-eyed fright and sharply inhaled, but didn't scream. The sharp edge of the creature's claw lifted her mucus-covered dress, revealing her pregnant belly, and it carved a circle into her flesh.

"Get away from me!" She attempted to twist her body. "Get the fuck away from my child!"

For a moment Ellen felt pride at the young woman's resistance, only to watch in horror as the creature's tail whipped around toward the girl's face. Ellen held her breath as she waited for the inevitable, but the vicious-looking tail abruptly stopped inches from stabbing through the woman's skull.

The girl in the yellow dress whimpered but said no more, bowing her head in submission, and Ellen's pride shifted to disappointment—more toward her own resignation than the girl's lack of resistance.

At least she *tried*, Ellen thought. *At least* her *spirit isn't completely dead.*

Swallowing back down a sob of anger, Ellen pulled her right hand upward as hard as she could, finally freeing it from the sticky bond. She grabbed a rock and heaved it at the creature, hitting it squarely on the head. "Get the hell away from us!" she shouted.

The creature spun and roared. It straightened in front of Ellen, towering almost twenty feet above her, and slammed two claws down into the ground on either side of her knees, splintering the ledge. But she was stronger than even she realized, and she was done letting the fear rule her.

"Fuck you! Do you hear me?"

The creature bent down and leaned close to her face. "Fuck you," it said, perfectly mimicking her voice. "Do you hear me?"

Ellen stared into its eyes with a look of defiance. If this was the end, she refused to go out dominated by this foul bastard.

The creature raised its tail and pulled it back for a strike.

She tensed, waiting for the inevitable, but didn't close her eyes.

Suddenly a brilliant white shaft of light burned onto the ledge and swept over each of the women. The beam focused on the massive creature, and deafening shrieks reverberated around the cavern.

She heard another noise—a muffled thud—and turned her head to see a lantern attached to a rope, bathing the area in a bright orange glow.

An artificial object.

Something from Ellen's world.

The giant creature screamed, and it raised a pair of claws over its eyes. It leaped into the air, flying through the darkness and disappearing into the void.

Two beams of light carved around the cavern, sending other creatures darting for the passages and other dark corners.

Fifty feet above, somebody in black clothing began climbing down, casting their flashlight in a protective arc around the women, while farther up, another light intermittently covered their savior's descent.

Relief washed over Ellen, and for the first time the creatures' shrieks sounded like a triumphant chorus in her ears. She turned to the crying girl to her left. "What's your name, sweetie?"

"N-Natalie."

"They're gonna get us out of here, Natalie."

Please, God, let them get us out of here.

The dark figure dropped to the ledge. Ellen squinted to see past the glare of the flashlight. She wasn't prepared to believe they were even close to safe, but whoever had descended was like an angel sent from heaven. Live or die, it felt like at least some of her prayers were being heard.

The figure came closer, and it became obvious it was a woman. She knelt by Ellen's side. "Are you Ellen Cafferty?"

"Yes . . . yes."

"My name's Sarah Bowcut. I'm here with Captain Larry Dumont from SWAT Team 415. We're here to help, but we have to move fast." She lifted her glove from Ellen's shoulder and scowled. "What the hell?"

"They covered us in it. We can't move."

"We'll see about that."

"Her first," Ellen said, jutting her chin toward the youngest in the group.

"Ma'am?"

"Free her first, then the others."

She appreciated how the officer didn't argue. As much as Ellen wanted to be released from the creatures' glue trap, she knew she wouldn't be able to live with herself unless the others were safe.

Bowcut approached Natalie and pulled a knife from her belt. "We're going to cut you free, all right?"

Natalie let out a shuddering breath and nodded. Bowcut worked the knife between her arms and body, chopping through the thick mucus, and then moving on to her legs. Once her limbs were free, Natalie unsteadily rose to her feet.

"Keep the creatures back by using this." Bowcut handed her the light. "Any get close focus exclusively on them."

"O-o-okay."

"I'm counting on you," Bowcut said firmly. "So are all these other women. This light is a powerful weapon against these things, so be alert."

"Okay," Natalie said, her voice much less shaky. She swung the light to the left and right, her eyes intent.

Bowcut winked back at Ellen and then moved on to the next woman. She repeated the procedure on the other five women, all under the protective glare of Dumont's light, and they crowded together in his beam.

"What now?" Ellen asked when she was finally freed.

"Mrs. Cafferty," Bowcut said, "now we get the fuck outta here."

CHAPTER TWENTY-SIX

Cafferty, North, and Flament moved Officer Spear's body to the side of the Pavilion and stood on the platform, awash in the glorious power of the IMAX projector. The creatures continued to screech from the tunnels, though none had returned to face the intense glare. With at least this solution firmly in place, Cafferty was able to consider his next steps. But first, he had two simple tasks to complete before launching his search for Ellen and the rest of the passengers: speaking with the command center staff to find out the latest situation and briefing the NYPD to take control of the train.

He eyed the tunnel determinedly as he mentally prepared to put his plan into action. However, David North, noticing the look on his face, read his longtime friend and boss' mind and caught him up short. "Tom, what are you thinking? I can't let you go into that tunnel. It's a suicide mission."

"You can't very well strap an IMAX projector on

your back, Mr. Mayor," Flament added, taking up North's cue.

"Which is why I'll take a few flashlights. Do you expect me to leave people behind?"

"We nearly died, Mr. Mayor," Flament said. "It's not just the light and oxygen, remember?"

"He's right, Tom. Not everything is within our power. Your duty is here, helping these people escape the hell we're in, not risking your life on a fool's errand. You need to let this go."

"You know I can't, David," the mayor replied, choking back his emotion. "She wouldn't have been on that train if it wasn't for me. None of us would have been here if it wasn't for me." Cafferty looked at his friend helplessly. All he could think about was Ellen, about how she had agreed to come to this, even though their marriage was on the verge of collapse, even though he had hurt her so deeply. It pained him to even *think* she was alive out there, scared and alone and prey to the creatures . . . it was enough to drive him mad.

North must have seen the desperation in his eyes, because he put his hand on Cafferty's shoulder. "Listen . . . I get it. Do you think I'm not worried about Sarah? She's down here, too. I'd give anything to know she's all right, to *see* her one more time. But I can't do something right now that's solely for her. These people are depending on us to survive. I expect you to help get us out of it. And like it or not, you're the mayor. Your place is here."

"My place is with her! I'm going to find my wife, and I'm going alone. I'm not going to risk anyone else's life. But I *am* going. David, you're in charge. And, Lucien, you've helped enough already. Please, return to the train."

Flament remained rooted to the spot, then tutted and dismissively waved his hand, ignoring the command.

"Return to the train," Cafferty repeated.

"I'm coming with you, Mr. Mayor," Flament said defiantly.

"Ah, fuck it," North said. "Count me in, too, Tom."

"David, I wasn't saying this as an option—I need you to take care of the people here."

"No offense, but I don't give a crap what you 'need.' My duty is your security—at least one of us should do their job. Anyway, there's nothing I can do here that Lieutenant Arnolds can't handle."

"Fine. Then how about I can't allow you to risk your life further. God, David, I've done enough to put you in danger already."

"What kind of friend would I be if I let you go alone, even if you are the asshole that got us into this mess?"

Cafferty reeled a bit at that, but it clearly wasn't the point North was trying to make, because he moved on, a hand on the mayor's shoulder.

"*À coeur vaillant rien d'impossible*," Flament said. "Nothing is impossible for a willing heart."

Cafferty frowned. "Eh?"

"We do this together with determination. More spotlights at more angles will increase the chances of success. Three is better than two."

"He's got a point," North said. "We go in a tight group, each covering a one-hundred-and-twenty-degree arc. It'll be much harder with two of us if the creatures come from all directions and almost certainly deadly for just one."

Cafferty peered back toward the train's scarred body. The survivors inside had already been through enough. They had achieved a sense of stability in the Pavilion, and he hoped they didn't view his next move as abandoning them. North's plan made sense, and though he didn't fully trust Flament, the Frenchman had offered his more than capable services, and he wasn't exactly in a position to refuse.

"All right. Gather flashlights and weapons. I'll speak with—"

"Mr. Mayor," Anna called from the command center entrance. "Come here. Quick."

Cafferty jogged to the battered blast door, hanging inward and peppered with dents. As he ran, his head throbbed and sharp pain stabbed in his temples. The elation of ridding his group of the creatures had made him momentarily forget about the threat of methane, but it was now rearing its ugly head once more. *If it's not one thing, it's another . . .*

He eased to a walk and entered the command center, and North and Flament followed him inside.

Six of Munoz's team, all wearing gas masks, stood at the far end of the room. All monitors were out apart from the one showing the Pavilion. A dried pool of blood surrounded a fire blanket covering something he had no desire to explore. Anna sat by the console, without a mask, and offered a faint smile. She had dark circles around her eyes, and a sheen of sweat varnished her face.

She depressed a button and leaned toward the mic. "This is the command center. Say again, over."

The speaker crackled. "*Sal Kirsch and Mike Esposito, engineers on diesel train 287-A. It's about damn time you answered.*"

"The relays are down. You've just come into range."

Cafferty raced over to the console. "Mr. Kirsch, this is Mayor Cafferty . . . are you in the Jersey tunnel?"

"It's Sal, and you got it. We're coming in to getcha out."

"My God," Flament said. "They'll blow us all to hell. Tell them to turn back."

"*I heard that,*" Sal replied. "*We're taking it nice and easy. We'll couple the engine to the car and pull you right out.*"

"Our last readings before the power went out showed that the methane was not at the LEL yet," Anna said to the group in the command center. "The tunnel explosion might have burned the level down further. If they get here soon enough, we *could* make it."

Cafferty inclined toward the mic. "Sal, I want you to listen to me very carefully."

"*Go ahead.*"

"Switch on every single one of your lights. Every single light. Do *not* stop that train until you reach the Pavilion. No matter who or what you see or hear on the tracks, do not stop that train. Any obstacles you come across, you barrel through. Do you copy?"

"Roger, Mr. Mayor. We'll smash through anything we see. Does this have something to do with that photo that got leaked?"

"Yeah," Cafferty said. "No matter what you see, for God's sake, just don't stop if you see any creatures."

"Creatures?"

"Sal, remember: stop for *nothing.*"

"Mr. Mayor, Jesus Christ himself couldn't stop this train. Over and out."

Cafferty would believe this plan had legs only once the engine arrived in the Pavilion. But it was the second victory after a long string of defeats. Sal and Mike potentially gave them another fighting chance.

"Anna," North said, "can the spare IMAX projector run on battery?"

"Anything can run on battery if the battery is big enough. So yeah, with the right wires and power, it's technically possible."

"Think you and your team can rig that thing to the front of the train?"

"We'll give it our best shot."

"I trust you can handle it—Diego knows how to pick a good team." Cafferty glanced around. "Where is he?"

"He never came back," Anna said. "We're hoping he took the sub, but . . ."

"You don't know if Reynolds left?"

"We lost connection with the docking station after the first explosion. I'm sorry, Mr. Mayor."

"I'll send some guys from the train to help your team. Strap everything that lights up to the body of that car. Hell, strap the oxygen tanks on the side if it stops any sparks from igniting. I'm relying on you to get these people to safety."

"Of course. But where are you going?"

"To find the missing passengers."

Anna forced a smile. "I hope you find her."

"Them. We'll need three of your spotlights."

"No problem . . . Mr. Mayor, if you're headed into that tunnel, there's a breach near where the attack happened. Marker 119. We lost one of our men when he went inside. I'd stay away from it if I were you."

"Sounds like a good place to start, actually," North said.

Cafferty nodded, then turned to leave. "Where's Lucien?"

"I don't know."

They ran back outside.

Flament had crossed the Pavilion and was quickly walking toward the Jersey tunnel, brandishing a spotlight.

"Lucien," Cafferty called out, "what the hell are you doing?"

"Testing to see if the light works."

Flament switched it off and fumbled for something in his satchel.

"We've already done that," North whispered to Cafferty.

"He's got my spider sense tingling, too, but forget about that. For now, we need his help. He's saved
our asses twice, remember? But, David?"

"Yeah?"

"Keep a close eye on him."

"Of course."

Assured that North was on it, Cafferty said,
"Anna?"

The young woman came over. "Yes?"

"Grab two spotlights for David." She immediately headed off to gather the lights. Cafferty turned
to North. "Once you have them, go find Flament.
I'll meet you at the Jersey tunnel entrance."

"Gotcha."

Cafferty jogged back toward the train. A few
people had disembarked and stared toward the tunnels with a mixture of fear and longing. He'd have
to nip that idea in the bud. At least DeLuca and
his team were continuing with their repairs, forti-
fying the subway car. Three of them crouched on
the roof and placed a strip of the vinyl floor onto a
section the creatures had ripped out. They tore off
strips of duct tape to secure it down. One of them
waved at Cafferty and he returned the gesture.

He boarded to a host of relieved faces, and a
round of applause rolled through the car. Even the
cop with bandaged lower legs winced a grin.

Cafferty raised his hands. "Settle down. Settle
down. We're not there yet. But I do have some
more news: a diesel engine's on its way to pull us
out through the Jersey tunnel and should be here
in minutes. But it's still dangerous out there, so I

need ten of you to report to Anna in the command center. We're going to strap the tanks to the sides of the train for the return journey. Those creatures won't know what hit them."

"But the train was originally attacked in the Jersey tunnel," one of the MTA workers said. "The entire front car was torn apart, and you want to go back the same way?"

"We haven't got a choice. But now we know how to fight these things. We fought them back before, and we'll do it again if we have to. Stick with the plan and we'll see this through. Nobody has more faith in you than me."

The crowd murmured its approval.

Cafferty waved Lieutenant Arnolds over to the platform. He glanced around to ensure nobody else was listening, and when he felt confident everyone else was on task, he said quietly, "I'm heading into the tunnels to look for the passengers and don't have time to answer the questions it'll provoke. If the engine comes and I'm not back, go. Don't even think about waiting. I'll make my own way out."

"Are you crazy? You'll die."

"If the creatures get me, and you're all safe, then I'm okay with that. But a small group needs to search for the passengers before we depart. I'm not sacrificing anyone's safety for my personal decision."

"Mr. Mayor, I don't mean this to sound critical, but you're running out on us. Do you know how this looks after what we heard on the train?"

"I'm not denying his accusations, but I can't walk

out of here with a clear conscience if we don't try to find the passengers."

"And your wife . . ."

"Yes. And my wife. It's the right thing to do, even if it costs me my life."

"You can't possibly believe they're still alive."

"There's only one way to find out. You're in charge now, Lieutenant. When that diesel train gets here, you promise me you'll head off immediately. And don't stop."

"I will. Jesus, Mr. Mayor, looks like I picked the wrong day to quit drinking."

"I plan on starting again when we get out. Stay safe."

A stream of people walked across the platform toward the command center, heading to carry out his plan. Cafferty felt confident he was leaving them in capable hands, and they'd execute his orders to the best of their ability. He couldn't shake the feeling, however, that their ultimate survival remained uncertain. He could only hope Lady Luck watched over the diesel engine, and the devil kept any sparks to himself.

North and Flament waited for him at the mouth of the Jersey tunnel, now wearing gas masks and aiming their spotlights into the darkness. Anna had gone above and beyond, apparently. He jumped onto the track and approached, searching the area beyond them for any signs of the creatures.

"You ready?" North handed him a spotlight and a mask. "I sent three of the command center team to the train. Thought we'd be needing these."

"Good idea." Cafferty pulled the mask over his face, and the sound of his breathing elevated inside the enclosed space. "What's our plan?"

"We stay in a close group and cover all angles. Shout if you see trouble coming. That's it."

"What if we meet the invisible force again?"

"Let's pray we don't."

Wasn't much of a plan, but then again, there wasn't really anything they could do about it *but* pray. So with a quick sign of the cross, Cafferty followed as North advanced, punching his spotlight into the darkness, watching as it sliced across the width of the tunnel. Flament moved to the left, shining his around the walls. Cafferty took the right-hand side of the track. He passed the ripped remains of an NYPD uniform and spatters of blood on the rail ties, but, thankfully, nothing else.

Raised voices came from the Pavilion, Arnolds' being the loudest of them all, but nobody looked back as the group pushed farther into the tunnel, away from the safety of the IMAX.

Distant shrieks echoed from the direction they were moving toward, and Cafferty's heart pounded against his chest. It would be so easy to go back and cower in the protective light of the IMAX. He was already finished in politics—even with Fields dead, there were enough reporters who would be compelled to spread his confession to the world. And the truth was he never considered himself the adventurous type. If he was being *truly* candid, he never thought he had the balls to do something like this. In an almost ironic twist, he couldn't help but think President Reynolds would have been way more suited for this kind of mission.

Yet here he was, step after step taking him farther from the lighted sanctuary of the Pavilion and closer to creatures that wanted to turn his body into ribbons of bloodied flesh. All because, as dangerous as all this was, Ellen was somewhere ahead, and he'd be damned if he'd sit around when there was a possibility of finding her. Especially if the Z Train was going to serve as a constant reminder of how much damage he had already caused to their lives. To other people's lives. He just hoped he wasn't too late.

They pressed on.

When they passed a curve in the track, the light behind them dimmed, until the wall completely eclipsed the Pavilion and the only light came from the ones in their hands. Cafferty swallowed hard but forced himself not to look back. The almost total darkness meant they were back in the creatures' territory, and he could sense both North and Flament tense as the same thought dawned on them.

As if on cue, a gleaming black creature dropped from the ceiling and screamed, revealing its three rows of bloodstained teeth. Its tail lashed out, not quite in range, but fast enough—and powerful enough—to make Cafferty flinch.

Flament, though, didn't hesitate and drove forward, locking it in his beam of light. The creature shrieked once more, but lurched back and bounded into the darkness. Somewhere in the inky tunnel, it waited for them.

And not just that one. Cafferty knew they faced thousands.

But he had known that from the moment he came up with this plan. He was thankful North and Flament had agreed to come with him. He wasn't sure he could do this on his own. Just the sight of that one had made him lose his cool. Still, he moved forward as the team pressed on. The darkness weighed heavy on him, and Cafferty clutched his spotlight with the fervor of a priest wielding a cross during an exorcism.

Step after step, they made their way down the tunnel until they hit the steady incline and started their ascent toward marker 119. One step after another, they came closer to the dream of Ellen, to potential death, and to certain evil.

CHAPTER TWENTY-SEVEN

Munoz had wrapped his finger around the laser's trigger as soon as he heard the creature's chilling howl from behind the Jersey tunnel's maintenance door. Every one of his natural instincts urged him to run, but they had nowhere safe to go. One way or another, he and the president had no other choice than to fight for their lives.

Reynolds held the conventional gun in a two-handed grip, aiming back up the passage, mumbling to himself about his administration.

"Put that goddamned gun away, Mr. President."

"We might not have any other option."

"We've got two options, but realistically neither involves a gun with bullets: face the creatures and a flood, or face the creatures in a methane-filled subway tunnel. I vote for the second option."

"I don't think it's much of a choice at all—that's our *only* option."

"I—"

Munoz didn't get a chance to finish his thought,

because a series of incredibly loud metal clanks drummed from somewhere overhead. Coupled with the shrieking, the sound led him to the conclusion that the creatures had followed through the engineering bay and were battering their way through the hatches, descending the levels and bringing a deadly amount of seawater with them.

Meaning they might not have any options at all.

Munoz raised his laser, aimed at the wall, and fired. A short red beam zipped from the barrel and blasted chips out of the concrete with tremendous power. At least the Foundation's weapon had passed the Samuels bullshit test.

"Christ, Diego," Reynolds said, instinctively ducking. "How about a warning next time?"

"Had to know if it worked before opening the door," Munoz said. "Let's move fast along the maintenance tunnel. I'll shoot anything that moves. You carry a strobe grenade."

"Let's do it."

The clanking overhead grew louder. Munoz imagined the creatures methodically smashing through the hatches and swirling down the passage at high speed on waves of ice-cold water.

He passed his strobes to the president, wondering if they had enough to reach safety, and turned for the maintenance tunnel door.

An extended boom groaned down at the end they had come from. Then another boom. And another.

A thin layer of water spilled around the corner and pooled at the far end of the tunnel, and it wasn't long before the flow increased to a steady stream.

Munoz's hand hovered over the keypad. "Ready?"

"As I'll ever be."

Munoz keyed in the code and extended his laser. His pulse pounded in his ears and his hands shook, but this was their only way out. He mentally readied himself for action. Reynolds moved to his side, holding a strobe between his fingers.

You got this, Diego. Remember, you're the crazy pendejo *who charged Sanchez's crew that Halloween . . .*

The door opened with a metallic screech, knee-high water rushed around them, and distant shrieks rang through the pitch-black maintenance tunnel.

"Why is it wet down *here*, Diego?" Reynolds asked.

"Cracks in the infrastructure. It'll only get worse because the pumps aren't working. If the explosion compromised the whole place, there's a risk of it imploding, including the Pavilion."

"So one more thing, I guess."

"Exactly." Munoz stepped through the open entrance, sweeping the laser's aim across the darkness. "Mr. President, now's a good time to activate the strobe."

Reynolds squeezed the sides of the silver sphere.

Blazing flashes lit up the immediate vicinity, silhouetting the stocky frames of four creatures within *much* too close a proximity. They roared, jumped out of the water, and raced away along the sides of the walls.

It worked. It fucking worked. An explosive sigh escaped Munoz, and he realized he had been holding his breath. *It fucking worked*, he thought again. *And that means we might actually get out of here.* Because from here, they had a relatively easy route along the maintenance tunnel to beneath the Jersey City station. Of course, that was if they had enough strobes to keep the creatures at bay. And if the ones behind them didn't catch up. And if . . .

And if . . .

And *if*.

Any elation he felt at seeing the Foundation weapons work quickly dissipated. There were just too many things that could go wrong before they made it to the surface, and it was *way* too early to be optimistic. One look at Reynolds, who was peering slack-jawed at the scene ahead, confirmed he wasn't the only one calculating their odds.

First things first, then. Munoz keyed in the code and the door rotated closed.

Reynolds held the strobe forward and leaned away from its dazzle. "Seems like Samuels told the truth for once in his life—"

A creature burst out of the water and howled, blasting out a fine damp mist.

Munoz staggered back.

Reynolds froze, feet away from the towering black figure.

The creature whipped its tail at the strobe and missed. But it did catch part of the cable housing, which sent shattered pieces of plastic flying across the tunnel.

Somehow ignoring the strobe, it spun to face Reynolds, growling, and crouched in preparation for a strike.

It was all talons and teeth. With the pitch-black

background of the deep tunnel, it was almost impossible to differentiate where the creature ended and the blackness began, as if the creature were darkness manifested in murderous, chitinous flesh. So close, it was pure terror for anyone unprepared for such a horrific sight.

Munoz's heart pounded, but not all that differently from when he had knelt in front of Malcolm Smith's crew in an abandoned warehouse in Gowanus, guns in his face, after a drug deal gone bad. He had survived that somehow—at the same moment vowing to get out of the game and turn his life around—and he was damned if all that was for nothing.

If this motherfucker was going to come after him, then all he could say was *I'm right here*, puta.

He composed himself, leveled the laser, and pulled the trigger.

A brilliant red beam seared out of the barrel, zipped through the creature's face, and blasted the opposite wall.

The creature gurgled and sank into the water.

Holy shit.

Munoz fired again, keeping his finger depressed on the trigger, and carved the beam across the creature's neck, slicing its head clean off.

Double holy shit.

The creature collapsed with a splash. Dark brown blood pooled around its body.

Munoz gazed at the weapon with a mixture of wonder and awe.

Reynolds opened his mouth as if to say something but managed to only produce stuttered gasps, before he croaked out, "Thank you. I owe you one."

"Trust me, I won't hesitate to ask you to return the favor, Mr. President."

They waded forward in the flashing light. Munoz swung the laser's aim to all parts, searching for any signs of movement, but for now, everything within the strobe's perimeter remained still. Reynolds followed closely by his side, turning every few feet to check for any creatures still lurking beneath the water. It was slow going, but the caution felt warranted.

Then another thunderous boom rocked the passage door and they picked up the pace, surging through the water as fast as humanly possible.

The strobe reduced to a flicker. Reynolds placed it on the wall's cable housing and activated another.

"We need to go easy on those," Munoz said.

"I don't think we've got a choice at the minute."

Creatures shrieked ahead, confirming their presence and intent, but the dazzling flashes of light kept them at bay, backing up the president's point.

A third earsplitting crack rocked the door, and Munoz spun to face it.

The first strobe Reynolds had left retained enough light to highlight a stream of water gushing through a fracture.

"Run," Munoz shouted. "We need to make it farther up the tunnel."

"I'm going as fast as I can. You've got at least twenty years on me."

"Those wall-mounted transformer boxes are live,

twenty thousand volts each. When the water rises high enough to hit them, I'll have no years on you."

That lit a fire under the president and he moved quicker. "Should have kept up the PT," he gasped.

Munoz splashed across, locked elbows with him, and heaved him forward.

Another boom resounded in the tunnel.

Munoz glanced over his shoulder.

The door had buckled and water now blasted through the sizable gap, creating a chest-high wave crashing directly toward them at a ferocious speed.

The realization hit him that they didn't have enough time, at least not as long as they stayed in the maintenance tunnel. He visually searched their immediate surroundings. The only quick way out was an emergency hatch leading straight up to the Jersey tunnel. That was dangerous, of course, but he guessed they had already made it past marker 119. And staying here was certain death, so he chose danger over deceased.

"This way," he yelled.

They plowed through the rapidly rising water, making for a steel ladder twenty yards away as the wave closed in, relentlessly roaring toward them. Reynolds lunged and grabbed a rung. He climbed the ladder, flung open the hatch, and scrambled up to the subway tracks.

Munoz was right behind him, but still that meant he gripped the ladder's rungs just as the wave hit him, and he clung for his life as the torrent tried to drag his body away. As if that weren't enough, a creature rushed past in the water, reached out a claw, and gouged his upper arm. He grunted as blood soaked his T-shirt, but that wasn't his biggest concern, nor was the creature in the water, already struggling to get back to him.

No, what had him truly worried was the wave—it was seconds away from hitting the transformer boxes and he was still very much in the tunnel, clinging to a steel ladder.

Another shrieking creature hurtled past, thrashing in the water, and its tail slammed against the wall next to Munoz's face. He jerked back to avoid it, causing his foot to slip, and once again he was hanging on to the ladder with all his strength.

"Swing your leg!" Reynolds shouted from above, holding his hand down for Munoz to grab. "You can do it!"

Gritting his teeth, he pulled himself back on to the ladder and practically threw his body up, using every ounce of strength left, fighting against the wave. Slowly, he climbed the rungs.

Too slowly.

Sparks spat from the transformer box. Then a loud snap filled the tunnel, and the shrieks of the creatures turned to agony as they were electrocuted. Munoz should have shared their fate, but at the last second, he had pushed himself upward and reached his hand out . . .

. . . which Reynolds grabbed. He may not have been in full marine shape, but the man still had a strong grip. *Probably from shaking all those hands.*

Dangling from the hatch, he willed the president to pull him up before the electrified water reached his legs. He could smell burning rubber, and looking down, he saw that the bottom of his boot was skimming the top of the water.

"Don't look down!" Reynolds screamed. "For God's sake, Diego, hold on!"

That's what he was doing, as inch by inch, the president hauled him up. He was close to the opening when, overhead, the distant sound of a train approached.

"Jesus . . ." Reynolds muttered.

Munoz said nothing, just held his breath, hoping it wasn't his last.

CHAPTER TWENTY-EIGHT

Dumont's overhead beam kept disappearing from the ledge, leaving the MTA lantern's orange glow and Bowcut's light as the hostages' only safeguard. She understood why. Creatures had stalked them from the tight passage leading to where their rope dangled, and he had to hold them back as well as provide cover.

Dark figures shot around every part of the vast football-stadium-sized space, looking for an opening while fleeing from the glare of Bowcut's light. The crackling in the cavern had risen in intensity, like somebody had tipped Pop Rocks into her ear. It was a disturbing sound, and it took some effort to concentrate on the situation at hand.

All the women had understandable fear in their eyes.

No, not all.

Not Ellen Cafferty. She held her chin up, unblinking, exuding every inch of her hardheaded reputation.

Now we just have to make sure she can keep *that head.*

It was easier said than done. Even as she thought that, a creature vaulted onto the far end of the ledge and quickly positioned itself to attack. But Bowcut acted faster, and she blitzed it with her powerful ray of light, sending it screaming into the blackness.

We have to get moving . . .

"Let's get out of here."

"Fine . . . but where the hell are we?" Ellen asked.

"A cavern underneath the subway." She quickly scanned the group once more. "Some of you look . . ."

"Pregnant?" Ellen asked. "Yeah. They've been clawing at our bellies for the last hour."

"You're pregnant, too?"

"It's a long story."

It seemed an odd and creepy coincidence, though Bowcut was past questioning anything that happened since her team entered the Jersey tunnel. She was solely focused on getting these women out of here alive. But pregnant women weren't exactly the most nimble, and that threw a bit of a monkey wrench in her plans for the rescue.

And then a large crash sounded from above, near the ledge where Dumont protected them with his light, and she knew another wrench was about to get thrown at them.

"Are you okay?" she yelled up to him.

"They're blocking the passage with boulders. We need a new way out. I'm coming down."

Fuck. "Make it fast. This place is *not* going to be our tomb."

Dumont gripped the rope and pushed himself out with his uninjured leg. He stopped every few feet and shone his light around the rock face, scanning for any creatures in the near vicinity before continuing his descent.

As he came down, Bowcut thought back to her first view of the huge cavern from its opposite side. Their original route was now blocked and they needed another way. Passages peppered the wall below the ledge, and it was more of a steep slope than a vertical drop, making it easier for anyone without climbing skills.

That's our way out.

Dumont's boots thudded next to her. He tugged the left rope; the quick-release knot unraveled, and it dropped by his feet. "What next?" he asked.

"I'll take a lantern down and find another way. Use my light to cover me, and yours to hold the creatures back. It's our only option," Sarah said.

"I'll go—" Dumont said.

"No, Captain. Not with your leg."

"You don't have to take the lead all the time. I'll make the climb." Dumont looked beyond her at the women, still partially caked in mucus. "It's better for you to stay with them. Try to keep everyone calm. You're better at that than I'll ever be."

Bowcut reluctantly nodded. He had a point. Dumont was an excellent leader in the field and fought to provide his team with the best equipment, but when it came to the softer side of their job, he was as subtle as a sledgehammer.

Dumont tied off the rope while Bowcut swept

her beam across the ledge, forcing back an increasing number of the creatures. The more the creatures attacked, the closer they got with each wave. She guessed it wouldn't take them long to figure out how to overpower their prey.

I'll keep that thought to myself, until . . .

"Who's taking this," Dumont said, holding up his light.

Ellen stepped forward and grabbed it. "Just shine on anything that moves close, right?"

"You got it in one."

Dumont attached the lantern to the side of his chest rig, leaned back on the rope, and disappeared over the side of the ledge.

Ellen stood on the lip and covered his descent.

Bowcut led the rest of the group away from the wall and stopped directly to Ellen's left. She waved them down to crouching positions, allowing her an unobstructed view of the cavern and any creature closing in for an attack.

"What're your names?" Bowcut asked while focusing on the passages and rocky overhangs. "Where are you from?"

"Melissa Santana, the Bronx."

"Erica Therese, from Staten Island."

"Gloria Omere, Upper West Side."

"Kara Dvorski . . . Bensonhurst."

"I'm Natalie Howard from Jersey City."

"What do you do for jobs?" Bowcut asked.

"Publicist."

"Legal secretary."

"Real estate broker."

"I'm an actor."

"I'm a cellist in the New York Philharmonic."

"And what's the last thing you remember from the train?" Bowcut asked.

"What train?" Natalie said.

Bowcut shot a quick glance over her shoulder. "The Z Train's inaugural run. Do you remember?"

"I wasn't on any train."

"Neither was I," another said.

"Same here."

"Me, too."

"Huh?" Bowcut forced three creatures back behind an outcrop and stepped closer to the women. "Kara, tell me your last memories before arriving here."

"We ventured into a surviving section of the old Sunswick Creek. My partner vanished and something grabbed my ankle."

"Sunswick Creek?"

"Check out an 1870s map and you'll see it. Stand in front of the former Sohmer Piano Factory building on Vernon and Broadway on a rainy day, and you'll hear it roaring beneath your feet. It's one of the oldest, deepest underground creeks in New York City, and long since forgotten."

"Gloria," Bowcut said, "what about you?"

"I was cave exploring with my boyfriend. He disappeared when my back was turned. I searched for him and something clamped around the back of my neck, and I woke up here. They've been force-feeding us on gross sludge."

"Where were you?"

"Howe Caverns."

"That's upstate, right?"

"You mean . . . we're not . . ."

"You're below the Hudson River between Manhattan and Jersey City. Erica, what about you?"

"Urban exploring in the Croton Aqueduct with three friends. It was freaky as hell, but this . . . Jesus . . ."

Three different stories from three very different parts of New York. It all spelled trouble. *Big* trouble. Bowcut had thought this strange and deadly occurrence was a one-off. She expected the authorities would fumigate the cavern, never speak of it again, and fact would pass into myth. From what the women said, though, it appeared that the creatures had a wide underground territory, and she wondered just how far this problem spread.

"My family must be panicked. I was due home Easter weekend—" Erica said.

"Wait. What?" Bowcut asked.

"Easter weekend. Tomorrow."

"It's July twenty-first. What date do the rest of you think it is?"

"May first."

"No, it's July seventh."

"March fifth."

"April tenth," Kara said in a quivering voice. "How's this even possible?"

"That'll soon be the question on the world's lips." Bowcut aimed her light at the sound of scampering footsteps. Several creatures perched on rocks scattered away and shrieked when the light hit them.

"One thing's for sure, though: blocking the breach won't end the problem."

"Then what are we going to do?" Natalie asked.

I don't know. Luckily, before she was forced to come up with some sort of answer, Ellen said, "He's found a passage!"

Bowcut backed to the edge. The rope disappeared into a hole thirty feet below, and the glow from Dumont's lantern emanated out.

"Okay, who's first?" Bowcut asked.

No one volunteered.

"We can't stay here."

Ellen Cafferty passed Bowcut the light. "I'll go. It's going to be all right, ladies—we can do this. Sarah will show us how, right?"

"Exactly." She handed her light to Kara and Ellen's to Natalie, and then showed Ellen what to do. "Okay, hand over hand, like this. Don't stop, and don't look down."

"Got it."

"Are you okay with only one sandal?"

"It's the least of my worries."

Bowcut took one light back and angled it onto Ellen as she unsteadily descended. Meanwhile, Natalie sliced the other beam backward and forward, brightening the immediate area around the group.

Once Ellen was down, Bowcut hauled up the rope, tied the end to her light, and lowered it gently down, where Dumont quickly untied it and provided the climbers with cover.

One by one, the women took turns edging down the steep incline, the strain of physical exertion showing on their sweat-drenched faces, warring with the stress and shock they were all experiencing in their own unique ways. Still, they did what they needed to do, each gripping the rope and scrambling down, successfully following Dumont and Ellen's path. Natalie went last, disappearing into the hole.

Now Bowcut stood on her own, surrounded by blackness and the deafening crackle. She cut her beam around the cavern one last time, memorizing the huge structure for future reference. It was truly massive, and with what the women had said about how they'd entered the caves, a sobering realization formed in her mind.

There had to be millions of these creatures.

One of them, closer to human in size, scrambled onto the ledge. Bowcut focused her light on its scaly chest and the creature darted to the left. She tracked it with the beam, never managing to get a solid fix as it ducked from side to side, closing in on her by the second.

She drew her knife.

The other creatures were unbelievably fast, but this one moved like greased lightning. She remembered seeing hundreds of these smaller ones surrounding the body of the construction worker when she first set eyes on the cavern, but its speed was a shock.

For some reason, though, the creature stopped twenty feet away and bared its teeth. She quickly got a fix on it, but her light failed to have the same impact as it did on the bigger ones she'd encountered. It checked the creature, but it didn't send it fleeing for the nearest dark corner.

It was such a startling discovery that she almost missed the moment when the creature swayed out of the glare again and drove forward, blasting out breaths through its flared nostrils.

It quickly dawned on Bowcut that the longer she spent driving this new challenge away, the more time others in the cavern were almost certainly rushing in from different directions.

The creature hunched, leaped forward, and wailed. It sprung ten feet in the air and dropped toward Bowcut, extending its claws toward her face.

She moved to the left, even as she thrust to the right. It was a desperate maneuver, and she was nowhere near fast enough to avoid the attack entirely. A claw ripped a gouge in the shoulder of her body armor, and a sharp jerking almost pulled her arm out if its socket—but somehow Bowcut had managed to sink her knife into the creature's rib cage. The thing was going so fast that she didn't have time to let go of her blade, which almost wrenched out of her hand. She held on, though, and actually felt a second of triumph, until the creature slammed against the ground, spun on its back, and shoved both heels into her stomach.

"Ugh!"

She staggered back, winded from the blow, and skidded to a stop inches from plunging off the ledge.

Bowcut glared across the rocky terrain at the creature. Blood oozed from the side of its mouth. It grunted to one knee, clutching the side of its chest, and rasped.

Shaking the cobwebs from her head, Bowcut suddenly remembered to flash her light in a circle to deter any other attacks. And there, at the far end of the ledge, thirty more of the smaller creatures climbed up and charged toward her, covering the ground in seconds.

Tackling one had nearly killed her.

What will thirty of them do to me?

She wasn't about to find out and sprinted for the rope—slamming her knife back in its sheath on the way—and grabbed the line, swinging over the ledge. Her boots skidded down the rocky incline, scrambling to find any kind of foothold as she slid down.

The rope burned through her tactical gloves.

A sharp outcrop slashed her thigh.

Finally, she swung into the hole.

The rope slithered away from her boots a moment after she let go, cut from above, and it dropped into the abyss below.

Shrieks rang out. Close . . .

The women lined the cramped passage in single file, brightened by the lantern's orange glow. Dumont crouched ahead of them, stabbing his light into the darkness.

"Sarah—" Ellen started.

"Fucking move!" Bowcut shouted.

Thankfully the group didn't hesitate, and the eight of them headed off at a crouching run, ducking and weaving through the tight space. She covered the rear, expecting creatures to pour into the passage at any moment and not knowing if there was really anything she could do about it. Because the fact was the safety of the light had just taken a significant downgrade. If these smaller creatures followed—and she saw no reason why they would back off—Bowcut had little doubt escaping meant facing a hand-to-hand fight to the death.

And the creatures had a *lot* more hands.

CHAPTER TWENTY-NINE

The diesel engine's wheels clanked slowly along the track. Sal peered through the cabin's front window for any signs of what he had seen in the grainy photograph. At this speed, they still had a few minutes before arriving at the Pavilion. Any faster risked creating sparks. Lots of them.

So far, nothing had appeared out of the ordinary apart from the lack of working lights. Still, the deeper they descended, the faster his heart raced.

"I still don't believe it," Mike said.

"You heard Cafferty. *Creatures.* Plural."

"You've read too many comics, buddy. And he's wasted on too much methane."

"Well, something's down here. And if we see something, we flatten them."

"I can live with that . . . if we don't, you know, *die.*"

Sal shrugged at Mike's worrying. He had no regrets about thundering through the police line, as it meant a shot at saving his friends and anyone else in the Pavilion, including the mayor and the president. Despite the fear building inside of him, he thought the only place worse than being here was back in the maintenance shed.

The diesel engine steadily continued toward their destination, when a movement caught his eye: down the track, a hatch flipped open on the left side of the tunnel.

Mike bolted from his seat.

Sal jumped, too, but quickly gathered his wits as he prepared for his first sight of the creatures.

Any minute now, he told himself. *Stay as calm as possible and don't lose your shit. People are relying on us. Stop for nothing.* That's what Cafferty had said. He thought he'd feel the crushing weight of their survival resting on his shoulders, but if he felt anything, he felt buoyed by the thought of saving all those people. He wasn't about to back down from anyone or anything.

The engine closed to within thirty feet of the open hatch.

A figure rose up and extended a palm in a halting gesture, partially obscuring its face.

"Holy shit, Sal," Mike said. "Should we stop?"

"It could be a trap. Remember what Cafferty told us? Stop for no one."

"We can't just barrel past—"

"We *can*. We stop for nothing. That's one man. There's loads more in the Pavilion."

As the train rolled by the figure, Mike leaned closer to the window. "Fuck, Sal—that looked like the president."

"It wasn't the fucking president."

"I'm telling you, it was John Reynolds."

"Are you certain it was him?" Sal asked.

"I . . . I can't be sure."

"Then we keep going."

The engine powered around a shallow bend and hit the straight descent toward the Pavilion. A smashed rail tie jutted from the ground at marker 119 and the track curved upward. It looked intact, though . . .

"Hit the brakes," Mike shouted. "Hard."

"And ignite the tunnel? Stop saying that."

"We'll derail, you dumbass."

Sal kept the throttle at a steady level. As the engine neared, the headlights brightened on a gaping hole in the middle of the track, but the metal rails on either side appeared mostly undamaged, apart from being bent upward.

"Stop," Mike said. "It's suicide."

"We're committed, my friend. Buckle up."

"We don't have fucking buckles."

"You know what I mean. This diesel engine weighs over four hundred thousand pounds. I'm telling you, we'll flatten that track."

"And what if the ground below won't hold us? It has to be damaged to raise the track, right?"

"It'll hold, buddy. It'll hold."

Farther past the damaged section, charred corpses were spread around the tunnel.

Mike crouched in the corner of the cabin and spread his arms against the walls, bracing himself for impact.

Sal tensed. He had no worries about the state of the track, but Mike's comment about the strength of the ground had put a fresh doubt in his mind.

The engine closed to within seconds.

He held his breath and squeezed his eyes shut. This was the moment of truth. If they couldn't get past or, worse still, crashed, it was all over. *They'd* be all over.

The diesel engine juddered . . . and smoothly continued forward, bending the track back down into place under the enormous weight of the loco-motive.

"What did I say?" Sal muttered, trying to force a smile. "Piece of cake."

Mike stared out the window and his jaw dropped. "Creatures."

A burned body lay against the wall, big and black. A scorched arm had frozen in the air with claws like talons. A tail. Skin had receded away from rows of sharp teeth. The engine passed another five twisted corpses that looked the same.

Cafferty had spoken the truth.

The picture in the TV van wasn't a lie.

One creature, missing both legs, dragged itself along the side of the track. It flicked its tail at the engine when they passed, leaving tiny shatter marks across the window.

"Holy shit," Mike said.

Sal swallowed hard and his grip tightened around the throttle lever, but that was a last resort. He knew he couldn't risk it. Not yet.

Shit was getting real.

Both stood in silence as the markers passed by the window. Sal said a silent prayer, asking for a clear run from here to the Pavilion and a safe return to the maintenance shed. He fished out his phone to text his family, a last message in case he didn't make it, but the signal had dropped out.

Something jumped from the middle of the track.

And another figure.

And another.

The engine's headlights hit a group of creatures bounding directly for them.

Hundreds of the damned things.

Behind the moving mass, three dazzling lights swept through the tunnel like World War II search-lights.

The creatures rushed past on either side, giving Sal a gut-churning closer look at their powerful bodies. Muscles and veins bulged on their arms, legs, and chests. They bashed themselves against the sides of the engine. A tail lashed the front of the cabin and took out a headlight.

"My God," Mike said.

Sal wiped sweat from his brow. They were committed, like whoever was shining the lights, sending the creatures hurtling in their direction.

The last few creatures in the tide raced past.

Another tail strike took out the remaining headlight.

The engine cruised past three people holding spotlights, focusing on the retreating creatures. One waved who looked like Cafferty, but he couldn't tell for sure.

Seconds later, the circular entrance of the Pavilion appeared in the distance.

"They've got some balls walking through the tunnel like that," Mike said.

"Not sure why they didn't wait for us."

"Maybe they're clearing a path?"

The Pavilion entrance grew bigger every second, along with the battered rear car where the survivors were holed up. People jumped out and cheered at the approaching engine. Two hugged, and another planted their hand on their forehead. Sal gently applied the brake, and they rolled to a gradual halt a few feet from the train.

"Check our alignment and the train's couple," Mike said. "Let's get this done as fast as possible."

"You see the state of this place?"

"That's why I said *as fast as possible*."

Dead bodies, with jackets spread over their upper halves, lined the far wall close to the Starbucks' splintered window. The command center blast door had been smashed inward and body parts covered the ground immediately to its front. People in MTA uniforms moved around inside.

"Just how strong are these things?"

"Dunno." Sal gazed up at the shattered overhead fittings. "But we don't need Columbo here to work out they don't like light."

Judging by the state of the barricaded train, the survivors had put up a serious fight before clearing the creatures from the Pavilion. A few cops and MTA workers stood outside the car, fixing spotlights and oxygen tanks to the sides. Sal flung open the door and stepped out into the glare of the IMAX projector.

"Thank God you're here," Lieutenant Arnolds said. He approached Sal and shook his hand. "Is anybody else coming?"

"This is it. You wanna get outta here, LT?"

"Does the Tin Man have a sheet metal cock?"

"Does a what? Oh, I get it. We'll hitch the train and head straight out."

Sal moved between the diesel engine and the train, checking that the couples were aligned, and he raised his thumb to Mike. He headed over to the command center, where several people clustered around wires and electronic equipment. He recognized Anna, who had come along to Friday drinks a few times with Munoz and had stonewalled his drunken advances, like pretty much every woman. None of the other faces was familiar.

"You're a sight for sore eyes," she said.

"Literally, by the looks of it. You guys must have been through hell down here. Where's Munoz?"

"He left with the president in the sub."

"What sub?"

All eyes focused on Sal.

Anna's smile vanished. "It hasn't been picked up?"

"Not that I know. But we saw a figure in the tunnel. Mike thought he looked like the president."

"What the hell? Was he near the breach?"

"You mean the hole in the ground? No. He came out of a hatch closer to Jersey City."

"Without Diego?"

"We only saw one guy. How'd he get from a sub to there?"

Anna moved over to a schematic of the system on the wall, placed her finger on the docking station and traced a route to marker 110 in the Jersey tunnel. "If that was Reynolds, they didn't get the sub. They probably went through the engineering bay to the maintenance tunnel. I don't see any other feasible route to the hatch. He couldn't have gotten there on his own, though."

"Munoz saving the president's ass." Sal shook his head and couldn't help grinning.

"Or his Secret Service agent who insisted on leaving us behind. Samuels. That guy made me show him around twenty times during the last week. He knows the layout, too."

"Let's hope they're all safe." Sal looked behind her at a pile of wires, batteries, and a large black projector. "What are you doing?"

"We're powering this baby up and attaching it to the front of your engine. Any creature in our way gets blasted with light." She turned to her team. "Attach the remaining oxygen tanks on there, too. As close to the wheels as you can. We'll keep them open with the smallest possible stream. It's a long shot, but with these tanks pumping out O_2, we're hoping any sparks we create don't ignite the methane."

"Every little bit helps," Sal said, though it sounded crazy.

A covered mass on the floor caught his eye. Rigid

pale white fingers poked from beneath a fire blanket, and the shape underneath looked like a torso with missing legs. Bile rose in his throat and Sal recoiled. For everyone's sake, Anna's plan had to work.

CHAPTER THIRTY

T he sight of the diesel engine speeding toward the Pavilion had boosted Cafferty's hopes that some would make it out of here alive. For the first time since the explosion in the Manhattan tunnel, the survivors had a physical prospect of getting out of the subway system, instead of failed promises. He angled his spotlight toward the creatures, bathing the back of the retreating mass in its glare, and another wave of screams erupted through the tunnel.

North led up the middle of the track, walking at a quick pace. Always selfless and never flinching, focused on the task at hand, he never took a backward step. Cafferty knew without him today, things would've turned out differently and almost certainly for the worse.

Flament advanced with smooth, deliberate strides, looking every inch a trained killer and a far cry from the unassuming journalist who had earlier asked Reynolds a question about funding. If they made it out alive, Cafferty had to ensure they didn't let him just wander off. He knew something about the creatures, and Tom wanted answers.

The two men moved with assurance and possessed skills more suitable for this environment, but Cafferty's sense of determination drove him on. So far, they had the situation under control, and marker 119 lay just minutes ahead.

There, Cafferty prayed he'd discover the fate of Ellen and the other passengers. And if he didn't . . . well, he had to know *something* before he even considered leaving. Part of him dreaded what he might find in the coming minutes. He could swallow losing his career and his reputation—those things were baubles in the grand scheme of life—but he couldn't face living without the woman who had burned so strongly into his soul.

North paused and directed his beam over several smoldering corpses toward the distant breach. The mass of creatures funneled down the hole until none visibly remained. "That's where we'll probably find any passengers," he said. "They can't be anywhere else."

"How do you know?" Flament asked.

"Look at the blood all over the walls. We didn't see them come our way, and they sure as shit didn't take any hostages to Jersey City."

"Quiet," Cafferty said.

The faint sound of flowing water rose through the ground.

"That's the maintenance tunnel filling," North said. "Jesus, if there's a breach . . . we haven't got much time."

"How much?" Flament asked.

"No idea, but hanging around discussing it won't help. Come on."

North broke into a fast jog, and they followed hot on his heels.

Running in a gas mask sapped Cafferty's strength and he struggled to keep up. Not that he was really much of a runner to begin with. *One more thing I need to do if we get out of this alive.* He squeezed out every ounce of energy to avoid falling behind. He was the main reason both men were here, and he couldn't allow himself to become the group's weak link on his mission.

North weaved his way between the corpses and arrived at the breach. Flament joined him and they crouched back-to-back, covering both directions.

Cafferty passed the last pair of bodies, locked in a death embrace, and he did a double take. One was human with a helmet and pistol by his side. His entrails had spilled out and were blackened from the earlier explosion. A dead creature's teeth were clamped around the back of his head and its claws were buried in his back.

The sight turned his stomach. The thought of finding Ellen in similar circumstances added to his stress. He fought down the urge to vomit and reached the breach. Leaning against the wall and attempting to catch his breath, he worked to push any negative thoughts to the back of his mind.

"Tom, you okay?" North asked.

"Fine. I—I just need a second."

"You got it."

North inspected a length of rope that ran from pipes on the opposite wall and disappeared into the breach. He looped the spotlight around his belt, positioning the glare downward. "I'll go first. We'll go straight in, a quick search, and straight out. Cover my descent."

Cafferty moved to the edge of the gaping hole and shone his light into the abyss, while Flament scanned the tunnel for any stray creatures lurking in the shadows.

North eased himself down, kicking off the wall and dropping a few feet at a time. His figure grew smaller as he lowered. The rope slackened, and his light disappeared as he moved farther down and in. "It's a cavern," he shouted frantically. "Creatures at the far end."

The dread in North's voice was clear, and Cafferty shot Flament a nervous glance. Millions of these things could be waiting below, far beyond anything the group could collectively handle, and it scared him shitless.

"You next, Mr. Mayor," Flament said, seemingly more relaxed about their situation.

In fact, oddly relaxed. Like he was playing an arcade game rather than descending to his potential death. But they had to proceed if they wanted an answer.

Cafferty had never been into outdoor activities, apart from the odd round of golf at Forest Park or a cocktail at the Knickerbocker Hotel's rooftop bar. So rappelling wasn't really a skill he had acquired. Still, he'd seen what North had done, so he copied his security chief and attached his spotlight to his belt, grabbed the rope, and edged back. The brittle rock face crunched under his shoes as he told himself, *Don't look down.*

Flament's beam swept overhead. North shouted encouragement from below, instructing him to lean back and relax, which was easier said than done. Cafferty's foot slipped and he tightly clutched the rope. His legs felt like jelly and beads of sweat dripped down his face, pooling at the bottom of his gas mask—a new level of discomfort he didn't think possible. He ignored that and found new footholds, descending into the cavern as fast as he could manage, until he landed on a pile of rubble next to the remains of a smashed MTA lantern and dropped to his knees.

North stood motionless, focusing his spotlight below a group of low-hanging stalactites. Cafferty freed his light from his belt, climbed to his feet, and shone it in the same direction.

"See that?" North said.

"What?"

"Pinned to the stalactites."

"Christ, who is it?"

"I'm betting it's the cop Anna told us about."

Cafferty strained to hear any sounds above the distant creatures and running water: a scream, a cry, a call for help—anything that pointed toward someone being alive and trapped deeper inside the subterranean network.

Flament's shoes thudded against the ground, his

spotlight brightening the cavern even further, and he shuffled between them. "What now, *mes amis*?"

"We head under—"

Smaller creatures exploded out of dark passages on the other side of the stalactites, at least twenty, tearing forward at unbelievable speeds. They dodged between the lights and their shrieks engulfed the cavern.

The three men's beams crisscrossed the area, breaking the momentum of the charge, but this time the creatures acted differently.

They didn't retreat.

Some snaked between the stalactites, others darted behind rocks. As soon as a light moved away, they moved forward again.

"We can't hold them like this," North shouted.

"No shit," Cafferty said. A creature leaped within spitting distance of him and hunched behind a boulder. He focused his spotlight on it, knowing one more leap and it would make mincemeat out of his guts.

But the creature didn't jump out. Instead, its tail whipped over the boulder and slashed his right forearm, cutting his muscle deep.

Cafferty screwed his face, and blood quickly soaked his shirt. The pain seared through his arm, but he held his aim.

The tail whipped over again and hammered the edge of his shoe, splitting the leather.

North swept his beam from left to the right, concentrating on several creatures who had ducked behind a pile of rubble. Flament, however, had lowered his light and unbuckled his satchel.

"What the fuck are you doing?" Cafferty yelled. "We're gonna die!"

"They're evolving," Flament said. "I haven't seen them like this before."

"You've never what? Never mind—put up your goddamned spotlight!"

The creature's tail lashed the ground by Cafferty's feet, splitting the rock.

"Get your goddamn light on those creatures!" North bellowed.

But Flament, almost nonchalantly, ignored them, reached into his satchel, produced a small silver sphere, and threw it into the center of the cavern.

Brilliant blinding flashes of light lit up the walls and ceiling.

The creatures screamed in pain and leaped toward the stalactites. They raced for the passages without looking back, trying to escape from the strobing light.

Within seconds, only the sound of the chattering sphere remained.

Cafferty and North stared at Flament. He drew an odd black gun out of his satchel. A green light winked on the top of it, and the transparent grip glowed pink around his fingers.

"You need to start talking," Cafferty said. "Like *now*."

"I saved our lives. The creatures don't like flashing light."

"That's it? What about the sphere you conveniently had in your satchel, and that gun? I've never seen anything like it."

"I'm helping you. You're helping me. That's all you need to know."

North moved to the Frenchman's side. "All you need to know is I'll kick your ass if you keep lying."

Flament's face twisted into a scowl, breaking his near constant look of composure. "Don't be an imbecile, Monsieur North. I've killed bigger and meaner men than you in a heartbeat. Try anything foolish like that and I guarantee you won't see daylight again. This is how things are going to proceed: I'll help you get deeper inside the cavern to find your friends and help you get back out. That's all that matters. We haven't got much time."

"What?" Cafferty asked.

"I'm a benevolent man, unlike the other member of my team. Everyone deserves a chance to survive, including your wife." Flament fished a digital timer out of his satchel, hit a button on the side, and a countdown started from twenty minutes. "The clock is now ticking, as you say. Nothing can stop the detonator automatically triggering the block of C-4 in my bag. I suggest we move."

"*C-4?* Are you a madman?" Cafferty said.

"We'll never make it out alive," North said. "You've been playing us."

"It's true I used you as human shields, but that's a mutually beneficial arrangement. I intend to leave the tunnel today. If you want to live, you'll stop asking questions you know I'm not going to answer and follow me."

Flament threw another silver sphere under the stalactites. It rolled to a stop in the next cavern, and light erupted from its surface.

"Follow you where?" Cafferty asked.

"To the nest. I'm destroying it. If any of the passengers are alive, they'll be there."

"A nest?" North said. "Who are you?"

"The man who will rid New York of these creatures." Flament pulled a disc-shaped device out of his pocket, flipped it open, and thumbed the screen. "The other charges are primed. We don't have long. Let's go."

"Wait," Cafferty said. "What other charges?"

"Mr. Mayor, it takes more than one block of C-4 to destroy the entire Z Train subway system. Your choice is clear. Run now or search for your wife. Either way, your legacy will be destroyed. Ask yourself what's more important: getting answers or staying alive. Because no matter what, these creatures cannot survive. It's us or them, and frankly, I choose us."

Nothing made sense, and North appeared in an equal state of confusion. Cafferty didn't know whether to strangle Flament or thank him. He was leaning toward violence, though. Because Flament had known all along. The precise theories, the strobing spheres, the blocks of C-4, and the mention of a nest made it obvious. And by knowing and being here, it meant he had prior knowledge of the attack and hadn't warned anyone.

"Who sent you here?" Cafferty snapped.

"We don't have t—"

"People are dying down here, and you want to keep playing games? Who the hell do you work for?"

"My employer is irrelevant."

"I'd say it's *very* fucking relevant," North said. "We want to get out of this alive."

"*This?* You still don't get it. *This* is nothing. *This* is just one more moment in a series of moments. Don't think you're a special case. It's a global problem and I'm merely a defender of our species. I wish to remain that way, so stop asking questions and do as I say."

Cafferty shook his head, trying to parse it all. "Why should we trust you?"

"*Il vaut mieux être marteau qu'enclume*, Mr. Mayor. It's better to be a hammer than a nail. Don't let the creatures or the C-4 drive you into a wooden box." With that, Flament keyed something else into his device, flipped the lid shut, and ducked below the stalactites.

"I don't think we have choice," North said to Cafferty.

There's always a choice, but he knew what North was saying. Sighing, he said, "You're right. Creatures and passengers are our concern, and he's got the weapons to beat them back."

Cafferty ripped the arm off his shirt, wrapped it around the wound on his forearm, and followed Flament underneath the stalactites toward the dark passages. As if he had expected them to come with him, Flament was waiting not too deep in the cave. He simply nodded and led them to where multiple passages split off from the one they were in. Without hesitating, the Frenchman entered the left one, pulled out another sphere, and activated it, brightening the way ahead. He extended his gun in his right hand and moved forward at a fast pace, aiming at any dark corner or large boulder, but always efficiently progressing into the blackness.

Shrieks echoed in the distance, growing louder as they plunged deeper into the underground network, and yet Flament led them ever closer to those brutal sounds through a series of small caverns. As they slid through the dark, they passed a handheld radio, a broken MTA lantern, pieces of ripped clothing, and, not unexpectedly, impressive spatters of blood over the walls.

North spun and aimed his spotlight back at regular intervals, but he didn't seem to ever see anything.

They moved on in silence.

Eventually, though, Flament said, "Something else has them distracted."

"What?" Cafferty asked.

"They're territorial and defend their nests with their lives. But they aren't attacking us in this cave. Another threat is in the cavern."

"I don't even know what that's supposed to mean. What could possibly be threatening these things?"

"Does it matter? Whatever it is that's drawing their attention, it's helped clear our path."

Cafferty thought it mattered a great deal. There were already too many deadly secrets in these tunnels, and this new one made him even more nervous. It didn't help that the air was growing thicker, more difficult to breathe even with the gas mask, and his headache had returned again. Sure, every step took him closer to discovering Ellen's fate, but he was also following a man whom he now not only heavily distrusted, but one he suspected might turn on North and him at any moment.

And that mattered.

CHAPTER THIRTY-ONE

Munoz lifted himself through the hatch into the subway tunnel and breathed a huge sigh of relief. Freezing water dripped from his pants, pattering against the ground. He scanned the area for any signs of life in the immediate vicinity.

Reynolds was taking no chances. He grabbed another strobe from his pocket, squeezed the sides, and tossed it onto the track.

Bright flashes flooded the tunnel, highlighting three distant creatures. They howled and bolted out of view, back toward the breach.

"I can't believe the train didn't stop," Reynolds said.

"We've got a good chance of making it from here. People in the Pavilion haven't—I say we go back down with the laser."

"We're not going back. It's too dangerous."

"We could at least try."

"You heard Samuels and saw the blast door report in the docking station. The chances of anyone in the

Pavilion being alive are slim at best. Someone needs to make it out to tell the story. That's you and me."

Unlike Reynolds, Munoz liked the fact that the diesel engine had roared past without stopping. It meant his team had a plausible means of escape . . . if they were still alive. Of course, he had some serious doubts on that score. But hope was a powerful thing, and right now, he wasn't prepared to give up on them. "I thought you didn't want to look like a coward," he said. "We know people on the train are alive."

"Do we? They've just ridden into hell—"

Munoz's pocket vibrated and let out an electronic ping.

"What was that?" Reynolds asked.

"Samuels' phone." He'd forgotten about it. He was actually pretty amazed the thing still worked. Then again, this was the same guy who had a laser pistol in his jacket, so . . . Munoz pulled out the disc-shaped device and flipped it open.

"One unread message" displayed in bright green text. The screen unlocked with the push of his thumb, the device's lack of security showing Samuels' level of cockiness. He tapped his finger on the envelope, which unfolded to reveal the text. "Holy shit."

"What?"

"It says, 'Planting C-4 in nest. Other charges primed. All tunnels to blow in 19 mins. Your status? LF.'"

"They rigged every tunnel?" Reynolds asked rhetorically. "With the methane that means . . ."

"The whole place blows. No, the whole place probably fuses together in a mess of molten rock. Either way, anyone inside these tunnels is dead."

"Which means we've barely got time to get out ourselves, Diego. I know it's hard, but we need to head for Jersey City. The train might already be on its way out."

Reynolds' simple truth hit Munoz hard. It seemed they would be the two sole survivors of this mess and had only one obvious way to go from here, not that the president needed the extra motivation. He'd already decided to cut and run.

Munoz scanned the message again. "What does he mean about a nest?"

"I'm guessing it's where these fuckers come from. But what interests me more is that someone else is down here working against us—someone allied with Samuels."

Great—two *of those assholes*. He snapped the phone shut. "Then let's hustle. And pray the train comes back with everyone from the Pavilion on board."

Munoz offered his hand and hauled Reynolds to his feet. They headed up the deserted tunnel toward the station, taking a wide berth around the scattered corpses of smoldering creatures.

As they walked, Munoz tried to go through everything he'd been learning ever since they'd tied up Samuels. The more he mulled the conspiracy, the more it chilled him. He thought back to surprise election results around the world, to the heads of state who had lost their lives in violent ways, to the seemingly stable, democratic countries erupting into chaos. And he wondered if they all connected to this shadow organization. The existence of these creatures was shocking enough. But that just seemed to be the tip of the iceberg.

"What are you thinking?" Reynolds asked.

"Just how deep this thing goes."

"That's the first thing I'm going to look into when we get out of here. Because this madness ends today. Starting with Blake fucking Mansfield."

The anger in the president's words echoed off the tunnel, almost masking the sound of multiple footsteps hammering against the ground ahead of them. But Munoz heard them: too loud, too heavy, and too fast to be human. "Strobe," he shouted.

Reynolds dug a fresh one from his pocket, crushed the sides, and held it forward.

Flashes brightened the smooth, circular concrete walls.

Shrieks split the air.

Munoz sprinted forward a few steps and raised the laser.

Three small creatures bounded around the corner, screaming, heading directly for him—*small* being a relative word, as they were still all bigger than any human. Their tails whipped in the air, and they raised their claws. They were more tolerant of the strobe lights than their bigger counterparts.

He dropped to one knee, fixed the closest one in his sights, and fired.

A red beam shot out of the barrel and scorched a hole in the creature's chest, and he moved his aim down, cutting through its stomach. Blood sprayed from the creature's torso and spattered the wall. It staggered forward with a gargling wail and crashed onto the track.

Munoz quickly switched his focus to the next, blasting a chunk out of its head with a red-hot laser beam. The creature lurched backward, and it slammed against the concrete.

The last creature hadn't stopped, though, and had closed to within yards of Munoz. With a snarl, the black horror lunged for the kill.

"Shoot it!" Reynolds yelled.

Not that Munoz needed the advice. The problem was these things were just so *fast* and it took so much to even disable one, let alone kill it. He fired again anyway, barely aiming, hoping to at least slow the last creature down. If he could at least give the president a chance to escape . . .

He'd underestimated the concentrated power of the laser, though. When the beam connected with the creature at close range, it ripped the thing's arm right off, twisting its body sideways. Encouraged, he cut the beam across its shoulders, slicing across its thick neck.

The creature's headless body skidded to the ground and stopped inches from his feet, giving him his first close look at its razor-sharp claws.

Those claws were almost buried in me. Dios mío . . .

With a shuddering breath, Munoz snapped himself out of his daze and swept the laser over the three twitching corpses, searching for any other creatures. As his heart started to slow down, he almost smiled. Slicing and dicing these sons of bitches to bloody pieces gave him a sense of satisfaction, no matter how small, knowing he had some payback for Donaldson and his team.

And the dark part of him he had abandoned as a teenager enjoyed the fuck out of it.

The stench of burning flesh hung in the air, but the tunnel had returned to near silence.

Reynolds gave Munoz an openmouthed stare. For a former marine, the action apparently rocked him. But maybe that was being unfair to the president. Even a leatherneck wouldn't be inured from fighting monsters.

Finally, Reynolds said, "Nice shooting."

"I guess I still got it," Munoz said with a wry smile.

"Maybe when we get out of here, you'll tell me how you learned to handle a gun like that."

"You already know." Munoz grabbed him by his jacket's shoulder pad and dragged him forward. "And I'd like to get outta here in one piece."

"Diego," Reynolds said between heavy breaths, "you're a goddamn hero."

I left my whole team behind.

And then Munoz remembered, adding to his guilt: *The diesel engine.* He had no way of warning whoever was on board about the impending C-4 detonations.

I'm not a hero, but someone has to tell the story of the people who are.

CHAPTER THIRTY-TWO

B owcut and Captain Dumont had handed their gas masks to the women, telling them to share every few minutes, allowing each some respite from the methane-clogged air. She took the lead in their attempt to escape and moved forward with conviction. Her eyes stung as she scrambled through the narrow passage, but she didn't slow, drilling her beam of light ahead and forcing back the creatures who packed the route. Luckily none of the small ones was ahead of them.

She didn't hold out a lot of hope for how long that luck would remain, though.

Still, she urged everyone on, even as waves of deafening screams came from both directions. It helped that the cramped confines gave the creatures no space to evade the glare of her light other than back down the tunnel. She hoped it meant they wouldn't be able to flank them.

Not that they were defenseless. Ellen Cafferty followed immediately behind, carrying the MTA lantern, and she seemed as capable in person as she always had on TV. And, of course, Dumont covered their rear. He had been her mentor and rock for most of her career, and she couldn't think of anyone she'd rather have on her six, holding back the tide of the smaller and faster monstrosities who had given chase from the vast cavern. Maybe David North . . .

She shook her head. *Can't think about him right now. Fight back the feelings. Need to focus.*

And she really did need to concentrate: the confusing twists and turns, along with breathing in the thick air, had fogged Bowcut's mind and destroyed her sense of direction. They were traveling upward. That's all she knew. Where to, she didn't know. Up was better than down, although after hearing the stories of the women being snatched from different locations, she feared they would end up lost in an endless labyrinth.

Worst still, she guessed the group had a few minutes of consciousness left at most before the creatures ripped apart their incapacitated bodies. Rotating the gas masks wasn't enough to stop the poisoning of their lungs.

"Slow down for a minute," Ellen said. "Let everyone catch up."

Bowcut skidded to a halt. Looking back over her shoulder, she realized just how spread out they'd become.

Dammit, I'm losing my edge.

She thought about all she'd seen that day, and it wasn't a surprise why. Christiansen and Dalton torn apart. The cop impaled on the stalactites. Discovering the creatures' massive lair and fighting one at close quarters.

It was enough to drive most people out of their mind.

And that didn't even factor in the rancid air down here. So far, she had downplayed the methane threat to the pregnant women, only acknowledging how hard it was to breathe.

We're inside the chamber of a gun, and we're one spark from making this all for naught.

We've got to move . . .

"Catch up!" she yelled. "We have to keep going."

"We're not all as fit as you," Ellen said.

She looked down the cavern and saw the girl Natalie stumbling along, one hand holding her large belly. "Sorry. I forgot—"

"No need to apologize." Ellen rested a hand on her shoulder. "Without you, we'd be dead."

If we stay here too long, we will be dead.

But she held her tongue on that point and waited for the others to catch up. Eventually she said, "How far along are you, if you don't mind me asking?"

"Two months," Ellen replied.

"I hadn't heard you were pregnant."

"No one has."

Bowcut frowned at the way Ellen said that. "Not even the mayor?"

"It's . . . complicated."

"Complicated sums up my life. No need to explain."

For the briefest of moments, Ellen's face softened, like she had met a kindred spirit. A moment later, it was gone, replaced by her trademark hard stare.

Three of the women caught up and crouched in a row behind Ellen. They slumped over, breathing hard. Their heads shot up when a new round of shrieks echoed in the tunnel.

"Pay attention," Bowcut shouted to the group over the shrieks. "We need to forget caution and move faster. I'm sure you're all feeling the effects of the methane, and it'll get a hell of a lot worse if we don't get to the surface. We're moving up, which means we're going in the right direction. But we have to dig deep and give everything we've got to it—and I mean *everything.*"

A few of the group nodded.

She turned and drove forward again, glancing back every few seconds to ensure everyone kept up with her pace. They still straggled, but she could see they were determined to at least *try.* And that's really all she could ask of them. These women had gone through hell—forcibly kept alive for weeks and immobilized in mucus, while their unborn children grew in their wombs unaware of the horror they would be born into. Yet they kept pushing, and that gave her strength even as her head pounded and every time she swallowed to moisten her parched throat.

Just.

Keep.

Moving.

The passage widened ahead.

Creatures shot through an opening from the opposite side.

Bowcut slowed her pace as she neared, crept forward, and swept her light through the dusty air.

The tennis court–sized cavern had other dark entrances to the left and right, each filled with dozens of the smaller, faster creatures. As soon as she focused on an individual passage, they exploded from the other two, extending their claws and thrashing their tails, and she quickly moved her light between all three to push them back. But there was only so much light, and she was only so fast.

With every sweep of the beam, they came a little bit closer. It was only a matter of time before the creatures were within striking distance.

The group bunched up and pressed against her back.

"Talk to me," Dumont called out.

"A big problem. Give me second."

Bowcut attempted to figure out a strategy to guide the group forward without being susceptible to attacks from the side. It was possible with the larger creatures, but the smaller ones were a different story. She needed to clear the opposite tunnel for the group to move, but Dumont had to cover the rear, holding back the creatures who pursued them, and the lantern wasn't powerful enough . . .

Think, Sarah, dammit!

Precious seconds passed while she racked her brain for a way out. But there was no obvious option in her mind, not without everything descending into bloody carnage. The only other direction led straight back to the main nest, and that meant certain death.

"My God," Ellen said. "Help her!"

A quick glance over her shoulder showed Bowcut that one of the women had collapsed. Another pulled off a gas mask and placed it over her face.

Two of the other women rested their hands against the wall for support.

"There's hundreds of creatures coming up the passage," Dumont yelled. "They're crushing the front ones toward my light."

Another woman sunk to her knees and slumped against the wall. The group looked in no condition to continue forward, let alone carry out a fast maneuver to see them through the cavern. Even if they were in peak physical shape, Bowcut wasn't sure it would matter. There were just too many of the creatures, and there was no escape.

We're dead.

A light-headed sensation overcame her.

It can't end like this. Not without some vengeance . . .

"Do something!" Ellen shouted.

But Bowcut just flopped against the entrance, straining to keep her light focused.

She couldn't keep herself focused, though. Disorienting images and emotions flashed through her mind.

The chance of her future happiness with David North was ebbing to nothing. He was the only man who ever really understood her . . .

Her brokenhearted mother had already lost a husband and a son. Bowcut hated every moment of her suffering: kissing a picture of the men in uniform every morning and placing it back on her fireplace, going to church every day and praying for them, sobbing behind her bedroom door at night . . .

The creatures killing Dalton and Christiansen . . .

And now this.

Extra grief piled onto the already immeasurable amount. Her left leg buckled and she dropped to one knee.

"No . . ."

"Sarah!"

"No!"

Bowcut roared with anger and drew her knife, refusing to go down without a fight. If the creatures were taking her down, some would taste cold steel.

Her vision blurred.

Screaming creatures flowed out of the opposite passage.

"Fuck you all!" Bowcut cried out in desperation.

She thrust her knife forward with all her remaining strength . . .

. . . and a metal sphere bounced into the cavern out of nowhere.

Brilliant flashes of strobing light erupted from it, clearing the area immediately, sending shrieking creatures hurtling away from the passage entrances.

Bowcut squinted and raised a hand to protect her eyes from the glare.

Three figures, wearing gas masks, raced toward them. One pulled a small black dome from a leather satchel and placed it on the ground, and green lights flashed around its base. Four metal tubes extended, blasting out powerful streams of some gas.

No, not some gas. *Oxygen.*

Bowcut drew in a deep breath.

The same man tossed another sphere beyond Dumont, flooding the passage with rapid flashing light. "Bring them around the oxygenator," he said in a French accent. "It only works for a limited period."

Strong hands grabbed Bowcut's body armor and dragged her into the cavern. Whatever they had used to emit the strobing light left them confident enough to ignore the entrances. The dome was a godsend.

The other two men stepped beyond her to retrieve the rest of the group.

"Tom?" Ellen cried out. "Is it really you?"

Tears welled in Mayor Cafferty's eyes. "You didn't think I'd leave you down here, did you?"

The mayor and his wife tightly embraced.

The other women and Dumont crowded around the dome and breathed in refreshing air.

Bowcut blinked and focused. She recognized the mayor and . . . no. It couldn't be.

"Hey."

"You're here. You're here?"

"I'm here," David North said.

She let out a deep sigh of relief, grabbed his arm, and hauled herself to her feet.

"Are you okay?" North asked.

"Took you long enough," Bowcut said, planting a kiss squarely on his lips and embracing him.

"You can yell at me when we get out of here."

"Sounds good. Who's the other guy?" she asked, looking at the Frenchman as he rifled through his leather satchel.

"It's a long story." North lowered his voice to a whisper. "We need to keep a close eye on him."

She looked once more. The man looked like a natural-born fighter, and the effective devices he had deployed seemed far from coincidental. Whoever he was, he came purposely armed for this scenario, which struck her as odd, considering the other two had come from the Pavilion.

Those questions could wait, and the man had helped in their rescue. For the moment, she continued to breathe and regain her strength, refocusing on leading the hostages to safety.

But then Ellen looked toward the stranger and said, "Lucien? What are you doing here?"

"What?" Cafferty said, confused. "You know each other?"

"Better than you realize," Lucien said, smirking at the mayor.

"What—"

"I've given you a chance to survive," Lucien interrupted. "I've done so against my orders, but I thought it was necessary. Now, though, I'm afraid this is where our journey together ends."

"I didn't believe your benevolent crap for a second," North said.

"I never said anything about being benevolent. I just said we had a mutually beneficial situation concerning our survival, and so we helped each other.

But I have a mission, and none of you are a part of it anymore."

Bowcut had no idea what was going on, but if David didn't trust this guy, she didn't, either. She slipped her knife behind her back.

The Frenchman pulled out a block of C-4 with an attached detonator and timer and positioned it in the center of the cavern.

North lunged toward him.

Flament spun and aimed a chunky pistol at his chest, stopping his advance.

"If you make another move at me, I'll rip out your stomach and replace it with this C-4."

"You're a piece of shit," Cafferty said.

Lucien shrugged with a weird grin on his face, and Sarah was pretty sure there was more evil in this cave than just the creatures.

CHAPTER THIRTY-THREE

S narls, howls, and shrieks reverberated around the Pavilion, raising the hairs on the back of Sal's neck. He stood by his cabin, waiting for the survivors to finish the train's modifications and to give him the go-ahead to drag everyone back to safety.

A team of six finished strapping oxygen tanks to the sides of the diesel engine, as close to the wheels as possible, and moved over to help mount the IMAX.

The time to leave couldn't come soon enough. Scientists had calculated that a single cigarette reduced a person's life by eleven minutes. He had no idea how they came to that conclusion, but he thought every minute spent in the Pavilion knocked at least twenty off his.

Mike connected a power cable to the train's socket. Lights flickered on inside the rear car, high-lighting thin gouges in its battered body.

At any moment, Sal expected the creatures to

storm the Pavilion and rip everyone to shreds. His paranoia told him the light wouldn't keep the creatures back forever, and he felt the presence of hundreds of eyes watching his every move, waiting for the right moment to race in and turn him into a pile of entrails.

Eight of the MTA workers mounted the IMAX projector to the front of the engine and positioned it ahead of the bank of batteries. Anna hooked it up while they angled the twin lenses toward the pitch-black tunnel.

A cop at the front of the engine raised his thumb. "That'll do it."

The workers lashed rope around the projector, securing it in place. Anna pressed a button on the side and a shaft of brilliant white light illuminated the tunnel.

"You guys really know your shit," Sal said.

"I guess," Anna said. "But any one of the creatures could pull it right off this train. It's all we've got, though."

"Then it's what we got. Are we ready to go?"

"Ready as we'll ever be. I'll grab the rest of the guys from the command center."

"LT," Sal shouted across to the car's open door. "Get everyone on board."

Lieutenant Arnolds nodded and started ushering people back in the Z Train car.

Sal walked by Anna's side, taking a final opportunity to survey the scene. Two days ago, he had wandered through the deserted Pavilion with a bottle of beer, marveling at New York's latest big-ticket item. Today, death and violence hung in the air, and he shuddered at the sounds emanating from the other tunnel and the sight of body parts strewn in front of the command center.

"What made you decide to come?" Anna asked, quietly snapping him out of his dark thoughts.

"I just couldn't stand by and do nothing. I saw a picture of those things. It must have been scary as hell."

"When the creatures attacked?"

"Yeah."

"I was behind the blast door when the first one appeared. To be honest, I thought we were safe and was worried about the people outside. Then they started smashing their way in . . ."

"Man, you guys sure have a story to tell. I'll watch you on the ten o'clock news."

"You'll probably see yourself, too, Sal. If we make it out, that is." She looked at him. "We're gonna make it out, right?"

"You're *damn* right."

Dull metallic thuds came from inside the command center. A woman and man, dressed in the same blue MTA uniforms as Anna, burst out.

A pool of water followed, spreading across the Pavilion's polished stone floor.

"They're hammering through from the emergency passage," the woman shouted.

Anna stopped midstride and peered at the shallow tide breaking around her shoes. "Holy shit. If it's flooded and the hatch breaks, we're all dead."

"What?"

"You know the Hudson River?"

"Yeah . . ."

"We're about to be part of it."

"Jesus Christ."

Sal spun to face the train. Imagination wasn't required to know the consequences. He sprinted for the diesel engine's cabin as the last few people boarded the car. He climbed up the ladder and flung open the cabin door.

"Go, go, go," he yelled.

Mike released the brake and thrust the throttle backward.

The engine jerked forward a few inches and ground to a halt.

"What the hell?" Mike said.

The engine roared and fumes filled the cabin, but they remained static.

"Goddamn it," he said. "Did you check the front car? The emergency brakes must be locked. You've gotta decouple us from it now!"

Sal grabbed a wrench. "Don't go without me!"

He leaped from the cab onto the platform and raced past the first car.

An increasing flow of water gushed out of the command center and spilled across the platform. Sal reached between the cars. The pin block locking the knuckle of the coupler was still in place. He slipped through a gap in the doors—doing his best to ignore the blood-spattered walls—rushed into the conductor's cab, and hit the foot pedal.

The coupler groaned, but the pin held.

Shit.

His only option was to do it by hand.

Sal exited the car and hopped onto the track. He banged the pin with the wrench a few times with all his might, but it didn't budge.

"All right, c'mon." He wrapped the wrench around the pin, tightened it, and pried with all his might.

It still didn't budge. Water was spilling off the platform onto the track itself.

"C'mon, you son of a bitch."

The pin loosened.

"Yes . . ."

Two more heaves popped it free from the knuckle.

"There!"

"Get your ass moving," Mike called out. "I've started releasing the oxygen."

Sal scrambled back onto the overflowing platform, trying not to get knocked over by the growing wall of water, and sprinted for the cabin.

A crash came from inside the command center, much louder than the one before.

Glancing over, Sal's eyes widened at the sight of thousands of gallons of water exploding out of its entrance and racing across the polished stone ground.

"Come on!" Mike yelled.

Sal ran for all he was worth, even as Mike got the train moving down the track. No one had ever accused him of being the fastest guy in the world, but he was pretty sure he could have at least medaled in the Olympics in both the sprint and long jump, because as the water came rushing toward him, he made a desperate leap toward the open door of the diesel. He landed hard against the steel frame and felt himself slipping, when a pair of soft but firm hands grabbed his wrists.

"I got you," Anna said, and, struggling, helped pull him in just as the water completely covered the Pavilion.

As the diesel train picked up speed down the tunnel, Sal looked back at the tons of water roaring into the Pavilion. They had gotten the train with the passengers moving, but he couldn't help wondering if he had saved them from one death only for the torrent to rush up the tunnel, consume the train, and spit it out of the Jersey City entrance like a cork, except filled with the mangled corpses of humans . . . and creatures.

CHAPTER THIRTY-FOUR

Reynolds activated another strobe grenade, lighting up the tunnel with rapid flashes. He had only a couple left, and they still had a decent stretch of the tunnel to cover.

Sweat trickled down Munoz's face as he advanced.

There might not be enough strobe grenades left to cover our escape. And the laser could die on me at any moment.

What he wanted right now was to hear the rumble of an approaching diesel engine. But so far, he heard nothing, and that scared the crap out of him. He checked his watch. They had sixteen minutes left to escape if the communicator message had told the truth, and he saw no reason to doubt it—the person on the other end would have no reason to believe anyone but Samuels would see the text. His chest heaved and his thighs burned as they jogged up the incline. He was running on almost pure adrenaline at this point.

"Not far now, Mr. President."

Reynolds just nodded, smartly saving his breath for the run.

The two of them kept going until a sight caused Munoz to hiss, "Stop!"

Two dead creatures lay on the ground to their front, both in pools of glistening blood. One had had its guts torn out.

"They weren't killed in any explosion," Munoz said.

"Hit by the diesel engine?"

"Maybe." But he doubted it. "Something about this feels wrong."

"Other than the dead monsters on the ground?"

Munoz ignored that and stepped onto the tracks—carefully placing his feet to avoid making a sound—and passed the lifeless bodies of the creatures. A quick glance told him that somebody or something had gone to town on them. Both had received multiple blows to the head that chipped away shards of their scaly armor and dented in their skulls. A pile of intestines, stinking like fresh horse manure, lay to the left of the closest corpse.

Reynolds shook his head. "Don't tell me we've got something bigger and badder down here."

Munoz continued forward, scanning the ground ahead, worried that was *exactly* what they could be facing. But then he came to a square grate lying on the track to his front . . . and a tiny silver sphere resting in a puddle. It glinted in the thin light.

A strobe grenade.

Munoz glanced over his shoulder.

A bloodied human figure leapt out of the wound

in the dead creature's stomach, raised a steel pipe over his shoulder, and crashed it into the side of Reynolds' head.

A dull crack echoed in the tunnel and Reynolds slumped to the ground, knocked unconscious. The gun spilled out of his jacket and rested by his side.

Munoz staggered back, but he still had the presence of mind to raise the laser and fire.

A red beam shot from the barrel, missing his intended target and zipping through the tunnel.

Damn.

The figure stood over Reynolds, covered in gore, a freak show with murderous intent. Whoever it was showed speed that belied someone skilled at killing. The pipe rose for the killer blow.

"Freeze, motherfucker!" Munoz shouted. "One more move and I'll slice off your head."

The figure looked up, and Munoz almost dropped the gun.

It can't be.

Can it?

The figure wore the same trousers and shirt as Samuels, except they were now shredded to ribbons and caked in blood. The back of his head had been gouged, exposing part of his skull, but the body shape made it an unmistakable match.

"Samuels!" Munoz said. "You've got two seconds to drop your weapon and move away from the president."

The pipe dropped from Samuels hands and he stepped clear of Reynolds' body, keeping his back toward Munoz.

"Hands in the air," Munoz said. "No sudden movements."

Samuels slowly turned to face him. Munoz gasped. He had claw marks across his chest and was missing two fingers on his left hand, and a tear across his left cheek exposed his teeth and gums, right down to his throat. A pool of blood formed under his feet, pouring out of his body from somewhere. The Secret Service agent looked like he was half dead.

Munoz wasn't sure how he was accomplishing the other half.

"We meet again," Samuels said coldly, his voice sounding altered from the gashes in his throat. Deeper, raspier.

"How the fuck did you survive?"

"I was . . . highly motivated," Samuels replied, smirking with the half of his face that wasn't ripped open. "Now, why don't you turn around and keep running, while I complete my mission?"

Samuels began to turn back toward the president's motionless body.

Munoz fired another warning shot with the laser, this time missing on purpose. "I didn't say you could move, asshole."

"You're awfully tough using *my* gun," Samuels replied.

"And you're delusional if you think I'm gonna let you kill the president."

"Delusional? One way or another, the president is a dead man. He gets finished here, or he gets finished if he makes it out. The Foundation *always* completes its mission. Your decision only affects *your* life. You've still got time to make it out before a blast wave destroys everything—the nest, the Pavilion, the tunnels, *everything*."

Munoz studied the traitor and didn't see a speck of remorse—or a lie—in his bloodshot eyes.

"Tell me something, Samuels. How is it that you can justify killing so many innocent people today? How is it that you don't give a damn about what you've done?"

Samuels glared at him, wincing every few seconds and sucking in deep breaths. Finally, though, he spoke. "How do I justify what? You owe your very existence to the Foundation. You live aboveground in the sun, but you're really in the fucking dark. You don't know the sacrifices *we* make every day to keep you and everyone you know alive. So let me fill you in: there can only be one dominant species on this planet. The creatures intend to take on that mantle and humanity is standing in their way. They don't feel remorse. They cannot be reasoned with. They're stronger than us, evolve faster than us, and . . ."

"And?"

"And they're smarter than us."

"Smarter than you, maybe," Munoz said. "But let's say I buy your bullshit that the Foundation is nobly trying to save humanity."

"That is precisely our mission."

"Well then, why would you be going out of your way to kill the president? Why not just destroy the nest and move on? It seems to me that Van Ness cares more about revenge than stopping these monsters."

Samuels grunted a laugh. "Van Ness doesn't care if Reynolds lives or dies. The key has always been the creatures. Once we saw the signs of potentially the largest nest on record, maybe topping a million creatures, our only concern was ensuring its destruction. Which is exactly what I've done. My C-4 will take care of the tunnels and my colleague is dealing with the nest. That's the only thing that actually matters." He shrugged. "Reynolds' execution? It was merely an added bonus, sanctioned by two of his own administration."

"You make it sound so nonchalant, like killing people is just another day at the office. That assassinating anyone who doesn't play your game is something you can just shrug off."

"I *can* shrug it off. Wanna know why? Because those assassinations *save* lives. You call this a game, but that's because you still don't get it." Samuels grunted. "Even after all this, you still believe in the world you've lived in your whole life. That world only exists because of the Foundation, and we're getting very close to a moment when even we may not be able to fight it."

"What do you mean?"

"These nests are growing rapidly, and they are evolving to tolerate higher levels of oxygen. Mark my words. The day will come when we'll face a battle on the surface. Men like Reynolds stand in our way, and the Foundation simply cannot tolerate that. Humanity can't tolerate that. He put your life—and the lives of every single person on this planet—in danger out of *ego*."

Munoz shook his head in disbelief. Clearly, Samuels had drank the Kool-Aid.

But then again, so had he.

How often have I been on my podcast, talking about shit just like this?

"How many of these nests are there? How many have you destroyed?"

"My personal handiwork? The Chicago 'gas explosion' of 2011, the Amsterdam tenement fire that wiped out three city blocks in 2014, the London sewer implosion in 2016. I could go on and on, but I'd rather finish my job . . ."

"Those were all cover stories for the Foundation destroying other nests?" Munoz asked, ignoring Samuels' comment.

"You're finally learning."

"I . . . but . . ." Munoz was trying to process all this. The creatures were real—he'd seen them, fought them, and killed them. There was no disputing that. But how had they never been encountered before? How was this simply hidden? Where—

"Where did they come from?"

"Hardly the time and place for a history lesson, *ese*."

Munoz held the gun up straighter at Samuels' head.

"If you insist. These monsters lived here long before the first bipeds wandered the plains of Africa. A few ancient civilizations dug deep enough to breach a nest. The Mayans vanished from Chichen

Itza in 900 A.D. and the Toltecs in 1300 A.D. They've been hiding in plain sight on some centuries-old rock carvings and paintings. Visit Wadi Mathendous in Libya, Kondoa Irangi in Tanzania, Kakadu National Park in Australia, El Abra in Colombia, Tassili n'Ajjer in Algeria, and Vernal in Utah if you want to see proof." Samuels cleared his throat and spat a thick globule of blood.

"If they've been around so long, then why the urgency to destroy their nests *now*?"

"Human advancement. Urban expansion and population growth have necessitated massive underground excavation. Tunnels for water management, mass transportation. Never before in human history have we dug deeper into the earth. Understand this: we've encroached on them, not vice versa. We've unearthed nests and expedited their evolution. I've witnessed them becoming more skilled at avoiding our traps, appearing higher and higher in the earth's crust. Apparently, sixty years ago they could barely move a chair with their telekinetic power. Five years ago, I watched a cluster of them drag a human down into the abyss."

"Telekinetic power?" Munoz asked. "You've got to be shitting me."

"Believe what you want. Just know this—these creatures are evolving faster than we are. They can no longer be contained. If we don't stop them, there won't be any humanity left to defend. Now, put down my gun, let me finish my job, and let's get out of this tunnel before it blows."

Reynolds groaned and rolled onto his side.

Munoz's finger twitched on the trigger and his eyes squinted. The clock was ticking, and he'd gained enough information about the Foundation to satisfy his immediate curiosity. His mind was reeling, but at the moment the main thing was what to do with Samuels before completing his escape.

This prick is responsible for killing my team . . .

"Don't be a fool," Samuels said. "I can see in your eyes what you're thinking. Let me pick up the pipe."

"So you can kill me? Get the fuck outta here."

Reynolds murmured and raised his hand to his head.

"You are not part of my mission. You have my word I'll let you go. But I *am* going to finish this no matter what. Don't do something you'll regret," Samuels said, and edged toward Reynolds.

"Step away from the president."

Samuels edged closer.

"Get the fuck away from the president!"

Samuels dove for the pipe.

Munoz fired the laser.

A brilliant red line speared from the muzzle and punched through Samuels' lower left side. Munoz shifted his aim up, diagonally cutting through the Secret Service agent's abdomen and chest, sending blood and guts splattering across the track until the beam sliced out from his right shoulder.

Samuels' upper half slid backward, his lower half fell forward, and both parts of his dead body landed in a heap.

Munoz let out a deep breath, staring at the corpse.

A groggy Reynolds came to and bolted to a sitting position. Munoz moved over to him and helped him get back on his feet. Blood trickled from a swollen cut over his left eye, and he blinked and flexed his jaw.

"What the fuck—he's back from the dead?"

"Not anymore," Munoz replied.

"Jesus. Thanks, Diego. That's about the fifth time you've save my life."

Munoz wasn't quite sure how he felt about that anymore.

Samuels' secret communicator buzzed in Munoz's pocket. He pulled it out and peered at the screen. A message read, "Confirm extermination." It was from "AVN."

"You might want to see this," he said, passing Reynolds the device. "Look at the initials."

"It's him. It's Albert Van Ness." Reynolds tapped a reply and flashed the display toward Munoz. "Let's see what he thinks of this."

You failed. Now I'm coming after you.

CHAPTER THIRTY-FIVE

Seawater jetted through a crack in the cavern's ceiling, soaking the ground. Lucien Flament edged backward, gun extended, and swept it across the group. The Frenchman's expression had transformed from perpetually neutral to a sneer, and Cafferty realized the apparent guardian angel turned mysterious creature hunter had quickly transformed into their enemy.

The strobe grenades Flament had thrown were losing power, and the shrieks from the passages grew louder by the second. With time running out, something had to give.

"What the hell are you doing?" North shouted. "You said you were saving our lives."

"I said many things. It served a purpose. Now please shut up—I can't stand to hear whining, especially in an American accent."

"Why are you doing this?"

Flament sighed and rolled his eyes, muttering something in French. "Does it matter?"

"You're about to kill us all. It fucking matters!"

"If you must know, there's something invigorating about seeing people on the brink of death. All emotions and senses are heightened. They do and say things you don't see in normal walks of life. I suppose I'm a collector of these snapshots. They intrigue me."

"You're a sick bastard," Ellen Cafferty said.

"I see your opinion of me has changed," Flament replied with an insincere smile. "I'm wounded."

"How do you know him?" Cafferty asked Ellen. "Who is he?"

"Not now, Tom. We've got bigger things to worry about."

"You never told him, did you?" Flament said. "He should thank my virility for giving him an opportunity to see you again."

"What's he talking about?" Cafferty snapped.

"Don't listen to him," Ellen said. "He's mad."

"Completely mad. But look around, Mr. Mayor. Does anything strike you as odd about the women your wife finds herself in the company of?"

Cafferty scanned the other survivors not in SWAT uniforms. All women. All frightened. Some . . . pregnant. But . . . Ellen and he hadn't been intimate for months. Ever since she learned of his marital indiscretion, that part of their life ended. Her angry stare at Flament told him everything he needed to know, though. He glared at the Frenchman, clenched his fist, and advanced.

"Very cute, Monsieur Mayor, but that's far enough," Flament said, pointing his strange gun directly at Cafferty's face. "We French are the best lovers because we don't treat seduction with negative connotations. It's just a game, something to be played out until the lure is irresistible. I seduced Ellen because, well, she's lovely. And because I knew I'd be seeing you here, and it amused me to know I had that over you. Then, today, I seduced you into helping me while you thought I was helping you." Flament glanced at his watch. "Truly, though, I must say my good-byes now."

Ellen gripped Cafferty's arm. "Tom, you have to believe me, I am so, so sorry. You and I were basically separated and he caught me at my most vulnerable. It only happened once. I promise. I've regretted it ever since."

"I . . ."

There were no words, though. Because he *did* believe her. And he knew he had no right to be angry—his own neglect and affair had clearly pushed her into Flament's arms. But that would be what a rational person felt. And everything about today was far from rational. The confession, both the words and the look on her face, tore at his guts worse than any of the creatures could have. Mostly, though, he felt sick at himself for feeling mad at her. He thought he would crumble right there.

"You should be thanking me," Flament said. The Frenchman smirked in a way that would drive a pacifist to violence. "You see, the only reason your wife is alive right now is because she's carrying my child. We don't know why the creatures are studying these women, but the Foundation for Human Advancement intends to find out."

"That's not happening if you blow us all up, is it?"

"There are plenty more creatures . . . and plenty more pregnant women. Don't worry—we'll suss it out." Flament took a step back. "*Au revoir*, my friends. My transport is waiting."

"You can't leave us down here, you son of a bitch!"

"I'm quite sure you're wrong, Cafferty. I *can* leave you down here, and I will. Because no one—*no one*—is making it out of these tunnels alive.

"Especially not you or your wife."

BOWCUT COULDN'T BELIEVE HER EARS. AN ORGANIZATION dedicated to fighting the creatures. One of its undercover agents engineering an affair for blackmail purposes and casually talking about the group's fate as if discussing the pros and cons of future picks for the MLB draft. All of this was irrelevant, though, if they couldn't find a way out, and fast.

She gripped the handle of her knife behind her back and shuffled forward a few inches, closing the distance between her and Flament. He needed stopping, immediately. Cafferty and the Frenchman continued their conversation, with the mayor becoming increasingly loud and red-faced.

The strobe light had reduced to faint flickers, reflecting off the water pooling around her boots. Creatures would be on top of them at any moment, and in her recovered state, she knew the peril of facing their massed ranks without the use of Flament's specialized weapons.

There was no way on God's green earth the Frenchman was swanning out of the cavern after he revealed himself. This had to end now.

Bowcut focused solely on his movements as he repeatedly swept his gun across the group, figuring out the best time to pounce.

"I'm quite sure you're wrong, Cafferty. I can leave you down here, and I will. Because no one—no one—is making it out of these tunnels alive.

"Especially not you or your wife."

Flament aimed at the far end of the group.

Bowcut lunged forward and closed to within three feet.

The Frenchman swung his gun toward her in a rapid, smooth movement.

He was fast, but he was also cocky. She'd seen him move earlier, and it was clear he was highly trained. And normally he'd probably have caught her between the eyes. But she was prepared, and she expected him to round on her with his gun. So she reached inside his arm before he had the chance to shoot and parried the weapon with her left fist.

The laser gun discharged, creating a red-hot flash as the beam of light pierced through the cavern.

A man roared in pain. Maybe Dumont . . . or Cafferty . . . or North.

Flament looked bemused, as if he couldn't quite understand why she wasn't already dead. Bowcut rammed the tip of her knife underneath his chin.

The blade drove through his jugular, up inside his open mouth, and plunged into his palate.

This should shut the sick fuck up.

The Frenchman's eyes bulged.

His gun thudded against the ground.

Blood spilled over his bottom lip and gushed down his chin.

Flament gargled and reached forward, and his hand weakly slid down Bowcut's chest rig. She brushed it away and looped his satchel off his shoulder, ripped out the knife, and took a step back.

He stared at her through half-closed eyes. His left leg buckled, and he reached out once more as if to ask her something. Bowcut answered his unasked question with a kick toward his chest. The sole of her boot smashed into his sternum, sending him skidding backward to the edge of a passage.

A dozen razor-sharp claws reached out, dug into his skull, and dragged Flament into the blackness. Dark figures thrashed, snarling and growling, ripping apart the Frenchman's body. Savaged body parts sprayed into the cavern, showering her boots and cargo pants with blood, followed by a broken pair of circular glasses.

Several of the women took sharp intakes of breath.

Bowcut didn't even flinch.

It was over, but the roar behind her . . .

North had crouched over Dumont's prone body.

She rushed over to see her captain clutching the upper left part of his chest. Blood seeped between his fingers, and his crimson lips made his face look an even paler shade of white under the glare of the weakening strobes.

"The prick fired a laser," North said while ripping out one of Dumont's field dressings. "Went straight through him."

"We're not leaving you behind, Captain," Bowcut said. "Hang in there."

North pressed the bandage over the wound. "He's bleeding out. Gimme some space."

Dumont clutched Bowcut's rig and tugged her closer. "Sarah, I need you to tell—"

"Don't give up on us," she said, more in hope, considering the area of the wound. "We didn't come this far to lose you."

"Get the hell out of here. All of you. Tell Marci I love her."

"No . . ."

Dumont's eyes fluttered shut and his head rolled to the side.

"Captain!" Bowcut lifted him by the shoulders.

"Promise me," he whispered. "You'll get these women outta here alive."

Dumont let out a deep sigh and relaxed in her arms.

"Captain!"

North checked for a pulse on Dumont's wrist and neck.

His gaunt face told her the result.

He lifted the soggy dressing and peered at the wound. Finally, he made eye contact with Bowcut. "You did the right thing taking out Flament."

"The right thing? It killed Dumont."

"That French fuck would've killed every one of us, and you stopped him. Dumont understood that, just like he understood we're all dead if we don't get moving."

He was right, and pure looks of terror on the women pressed against the wall told her, too. There was no time for regret. They still had a perilous journey through the methane-filled caverns to contend with, and their survival wasn't even close to being guaranteed.

North grabbed the satchel, set down Flament's communicator, a camera, and a pile of eight strobe grenades. He squeezed the sides of four grenades, tossing them in turn down each of the passages.

Flashing light erupted from all sides, back at full strength.

The creatures' shrieks faded into the distance as they fled.

"Can you disarm it?" Cafferty asked, peering down at the timer hooked up to the C-4. "Like immediately?"

"I'm not sure it matters," North said.

"What do you mean?"

"Flament told us they planted multiple charges in the tunnels, remember? Any one will ignite the methane."

"He might be lying," Bowcut said.

"We don't have the time to risk that," North replied. "Leave it here. We've got fourteen minutes and our only hope is catching that train. If it hasn't already passed the breach, that is."

"What train?"

"A diesel engine barreled into the Pavilion to drag out the train."

The train gave them another reason to get their asses moving. Bowcut picked up Flament's gun. It weighed more than she expected and a green light glowed on top of it, but more crucially, it didn't ignite the whole place when it previously fired. "We need to move."

"No argument here." Cafferty clasped Ellen's hand. "You ready to get out of here?"

"Tom, I'm—"

"Don't. You don't need to apologize. All this was my doing, and I'm just grateful you're alive. I lost you once. I don't want to lose you ever again."

"I love you so much."

"I love you, too—"

"No offense," Bowcut said. "But save it for later." She planted one final kiss on David North's lips. "Well, later beginning now."

"Let's move out," North shouted.

Bowcut took one last lingering look at Dumont before leading the group in an upward direction. Leaving the captain's body here went unsaid, but that was just another unwanted action forced upon them today. A necessary evil. She aimed her laser along the flashing passage and moved forward at a fast pace, driving back any stray creatures who lurked behind boulders and outcrops. She and North were as much a team down in the tunnels as they were partners on the topside. He wielded his spotlight deftly, always filling the space her laser wasn't covering. They were in sync, and the group progressed quickly. They raced through the tunnel, even as her own mind raced about the death of Captain Dumont . . . and the man who caused it.

She sliced apart a creature to her left, and they kept going.

Sarah Bowcut had grown up with a father and a brother who firmly believed there was right and wrong. Good and evil. Justice and oppression. Flament's Foundation seemed to think there were other rules to this world.

She refused to let that live in their world.

If I survive, these fuckers are going to pay.

CHAPTER THIRTY-SIX

Sweat poured down Sal's face, soaking the collar of his gray T-shirt as the diesel engine clanked into the tunnel. On the reversing camera screen, the IMAX projector pumped out fifteen thousand watts of light, clearing their route to freedom. Through the cabin's window, spotlights glared from the sides of the car, brightening the walls and ceiling, and the tanks hissed out oxygen.

Everything was set for their journey of no return.

It had to work.

Anything else didn't bear contemplating.

Water flooded onto the track, though they had the power to outrun it if necessary, providing the Pavilion didn't cave in. His hands trembled from the vibration of sixty thousand pounds of thrust driving the engine toward Jersey City. He kept the speed steady, reducing the risk of igniting the methane, and calculated that if he had to slow for the other group, they'd be back inside the maintenance shed in nine minutes.

"This is fucked up," Mike said. "Imagine what those creatures will do to our cabin if they can smash in a blast door."

"It's not like we have a choice, buddy."

"Holy shit, Sal. Look."

On the reversing camera screen, black figures clung to the top of the tunnel and hunched by the sides of the track, all with their backs turned. Sal's heartrate spiked. He knew increasing the throttle might blow them all to hell. The people in the car had clearly fought creatures off before . . . Maybe they could again.

"They might be sensing this is their last chance," Mike said.

"Who knows what they think? I ain't stopping to find out."

The train neared the creatures.

The full power of the projector washed over their bodies.

Piercing shrieks rose over the sound of the engine.

Within seconds, the train powered into the black mass. Sal and Mike watched on the camera as the creatures leaped to different parts of the tunnel, unable to find any cover from the brilliant light. The frenetic mess outside reminded him of a colony of bats in a cave somehow transforming into a swarm of wasps.

God, get us out of here . . .

But it was the devil who answered his prayer, as three creatures dropped onto the car and slammed their claws against the roof, again and again, ripping out slices of metal. Even from here, he heard the muffled shouts and screams from the train car. He was surprised his own voice wasn't joining them.

Mike backed away from the window.

Sal told himself to stay focused. His goal was to get these people out of here; panicking wouldn't help. Accelerating was their final and potentially deadly option, but they weren't there yet . . .

The engine juddered, followed by a deafening crack.

"What the hell?" Mike yelled.

Sal peered out the side window, trying to locate the cause. Several creatures threw themselves at the side of the engine. He lost his balance after the second blow and slammed into the dashboard.

"How can they be this strong?" Mike said. "It wasn't like this on the way down."

"I told you, I ain't stopping to ask."

The engine bashed through the main body of creatures, taking repeated blows, though none powerful enough to stop their advance. A heartbeat later, they cleared the writhing black mass and hit a clear section of the track.

But at least three creatures had latched on to the undercarriage. Their claws gripped the bottom edge and their tails whipped out.

Sal had to do something before they derailed. It was time to take a risk. "Hold on tight," he said. "Let's hope the oxygen tanks are doing the job."

"Wait!"

Waiting wasn't an option. Sal yanked the brakes.

The electronic traction-control system automatically activated the sand sprayers in front of each wheel, providing much greater traction. The sudden loss of momentum sent two of the creatures flying forward, tumbling out of control up the track. One fell from the car's roof. Sal released the brakes and pushed the throttle forward.

"Fuck you," he yelled.

The diesel engine plowed into the creatures, crushing them under the weight of the wheels. Blood and body parts splattered against the tunnel walls.

A razor-sharp tail lashed one of the cabin's left windows, shattering it to pieces. Fragments of glass exploded into Sal's face. He staggered back, grabbed the controls to stop himself from falling, and caught a reflection of himself in the front window. Tiny nicks peppered his face, but he was still alive, coherent, and determined.

"Keep your head down, Mike."

"I can't keep my lunch down."

Mike turned to the corner and heaved. Foul-smelling vomit splashed onto the floor.

A remaining creature ripped off one of the car's steel plates, revealing the passengers inside, weapons raised. It bashed the plate against a spotlight, shattering the glass and killing its beam. It dragged a cop through a hole in the roof. Its teeth clamped around his face and its claws raked along his body, slicing his shirt to ribbons and tearing open his torso.

Sal swallowed hard. It was his first sight of a creature attacking a human, and the lightning barbarity momentarily paralyzed him. He had expected to come across chilling scenes in the subway system after seeing the photo and the state of the Pavilion, but watching an attack in the flesh . . .

People in the car swung improvised weapons at the gaping hole, sending the creature scuttling to another exposed part of the roof. It dragged another cop's body through, thrashing him around like a rag doll.

Mike crouched by his pool of vomit, clutching his arms around his knees.

"Hang in there," Sal said. "We'll get through this."

Mike murmured a response.

Sal grabbed his radio. "Any station, do you hear me, over?"

Nobody replied.

"Any station, do you hear, over?"

Nothing.

The car's glare had stopped the creatures from venturing inside. That would change if they continued to gouge off sections of the roof and destroyed the overhead lights. Sal didn't know how much longer they could hold out, but it couldn't be long. And after the defenses had fallen, the creatures would be free to tear everyone apart.

He knew they had to speed up. They were going too slow to survive the onslaught.

The decision Sal faced was the toughest in his life. The oxygen tanks wouldn't last forever, and he didn't know the extent of the gas leak. Accelerating, causing repeated sparks, might kill everyone.

But it might also save them.

Might.

It was an impossible choice.

CHAPTER THIRTY-SEVEN

Munoz jogged up the track, moments from hitting broad daylight with time to spare before the C-4 detonated, and he rounded a sweeping bend that led to the mouth of the Jersey tunnel. He had no regrets about killing Samuels. The Secret Service agent had intended to leave Reynolds and him floating in the flooded docking station with bullet holes in the back of their heads.

Bangs echoed from deeper inside the tunnel, too faint to tell if they were from the diesel engine or the creatures causing more mayhem before being blown to oblivion. Whatever the source, it sounded far away—deep enough inside the subway system that if it were the train it stood little chance of making it to safety.

Munoz peered over his shoulder to check for any following creatures. Reynolds wheezed a few steps behind, but they had used their last strobe and only had the laser for protection, if it still had any juice left . . .

"Slow down," Reynolds said. "We need to chat before heading out."

Munoz eased to a fast walk. "About what?" he asked, though he was pretty sure he knew what the president was about to say.

"About how you need to keep quiet about Van Ness and the creatures. Pretend you never saw a thing. It's for my protection, and yours."

"It doesn't feel like it's for *my* protection. Besides, haven't there been enough lies? Isn't this a perfect time to expose him and the nightmare living below our streets?"

"And cause a worldwide panic? And let the people who perpetrated this find a way to escape? No, my first order of business is to root out the traitors involved in this conspiracy. I can't do that until I gather a team I implicitly trust and make plans to arrest every one of them in a single swoop—the secretary of defense, whoever else. I want to bring these sons of bitches down, trust me. But if we go public, they'll disappear."

"How are you gonna manage that?"

"I'll find out anyone involved with the contracts or who attended meetings with the Foundation. Blake Mansfield's personal phone and email records will probably say a lot. I need your cooperation, Diego. Promise me you won't say a word until I have these traitors arrested."

Munoz wasn't quite sure he could do this. He had been through a hell of a lot with the president, and that meant something, but it didn't necessarily mean he *trusted* him. There was a certain level of reasoning to Reynolds' words, but there was also a lot of political nonsense that Munoz couldn't stomach. He hadn't killed a man to keep this quiet. He wasn't about to let all those people in the Pavilion die for nothing, either.

But he also wasn't stupid.

Get out of here alive first, then worry about what happens next.

He nodded his promise, which seemed enough for Reynolds, then asked, "Do you think Van Ness will come after you again?"

"I'm counting on it. My second order of business is to destroy the Foundation and destroy Van Ness. I'll put forward a UN resolution to freeze his assets based on his election rigging and murders. Most countries and leaders are afraid *not* to pay Van Ness. They fear for their own lives. But my very survival proves that Van Ness can be stopped. The Foundation's axis of fear will crumble. And if any country doesn't follow our lead, we'll cut off all their economic ties to the United States. I'll starve the Foundation to death. Its monopoly will crumble. You can trust me on that. I'll strip Van Ness of his wealth and his arrogance. When only a shell of the man remains, I'll draft a secret executive order authorizing his imprisonment for the attempted assassination of the president of the United States. He'll spend the rest of his life locked in a hole somewhere in the bowels of Gitmo."

Munoz wasn't so sure about that. Hell, he wasn't sure he even liked how blatantly Reynolds was exposing himself. *Why tell me all this?*

"We don't know if anyone escaped through the other tunnels," Reynolds said. "I won't forget what you've done today. When it's all over, you'll be suitably rewarded. Have a think about what you want."

"A quiet life and big compensation packages for the families of the victims. It's as simple as that."

"That's a certainty, you have my word."

Munoz lied about wanting a quiet life, now that he'd had the time to finally contemplate his survival. Today's events had broken something inside of him, and his old aggression had resurfaced, but this time he aimed to channel it in the right way. He found the idea of simply shutting down the Foundation and imprisoning its leader unsatisfactory. It failed to punish everyone who had taken part in the Z Train plot. Killing these creatures didn't excuse cold-blooded murder.

Samuels had mentioned other members two times: once about an exfiltration team and a final unknown man from the Pavilion who activated the timers for the explosion.

Other people had blood on their hands. It was that simple.

Munoz refused to let anyone get away with doing this to his life. To the lives of his team. To the lives of the passengers and any victims in the Pavilion. Reynolds may be looking at the big picture, but Munoz saw things differently. The Foundation had made it personal. It had killed his friends. Destroyed the job he worked so hard to gain. Planned his death.

Those responsible had to answer for their actions.

I'm old-school Diego again, but with a genuine enemy.

They fucked up when they woke up these creatures by waking up one more monster.

Only a hundred yards remained and the first faint sliver of daylight appeared.

"Mr. President, one last question," Munoz said. "You plan on destroying the Foundation."

"That's correct."

"When Van Ness is finally gone, who's left to destroy these creatures?"

Reynolds stared at him without answering.

The sliver of light went dark, as if something had blocked it.

"What the hell?" Reynolds said.

Munoz crept forward and extended his laser.

An enormous creature moved in the shadows, bigger than any he'd previously seen. It turned its head away from the natural daylight, cowering.

Reynolds backed behind Munoz.

The creature let out a long hiss and moved closer, visibly struggling in the cleaner air. Its tail slowly flicked from side to side, and it raised its claws.

Munoz's finger sprung away from the trigger. He attempted to force it back, but it wouldn't move. The gun was frozen in place. "What the fuck?"

"Shoot!" Reynolds yelled.

The creature stomped forward, taking short, unwieldy strides.

Reynolds' left hand involuntarily rose to his own throat and his fingers crushed around his windpipe. "I'm not doing this! It's got some kind of hold on me," he gasped. "Fucking shoot!"

"I can't move my hand."

"What?"

The creature's tail whipped through the air, smashed into Munoz's ankles, and his ass crashed to the ground. It lumbered toward Reynolds, dug its claws into his shoulders, and raised him against the wall.

Reynolds screamed and kicked his legs. His face turned beet red as he fought against the creature's stocky forearms.

Munoz forced his shaking left hand toward the laser, but the invisible force stopped him from reaching the trigger. The creature's tail battered the ground next to his face, and its tip sliced his cheek.

"Fucking do something," Reynolds yelled.

"Fucking do something," the creature echoed, mimicking his exact tone, mocking its prey. It roared in Reynolds' face, pelting it with strings of sticky saliva.

The creature's tail rose for another strike, whipping above Munoz's head and thrusting down. He forced himself sideways, using every ounce of strength in his body, and rolled away. The tail slammed into the track, denting the rail.

"Diego!" Reynolds screamed.

Whatever was happening to him, he felt released from its control, and Munoz's finger tightened around the trigger. He swung the laser toward the creature and fired a beam across its stomach, holding down the trigger.

The creature's innards spewed out and dangled

between its legs, and its claws released from the president's body.

Reynolds dropped to his knees and scrambled away.

Munoz fired again, slicing the beam across the creature's head, and carved off the top of its skull. Its legs collapsed, and it slumped to the left. He fired again, blasting a hole through the center of the creature's face, and brain matter burst in every direction.

As the massive creature crumpled to the ground in pieces, the laser gun finally kicked out, spent of all its charge. Munoz let the now useless gun slowly fall to the ground, praying this creature was their last.

Reynolds edged behind him while maintaining a close eye on the smoldering corpse. "What the hell? How could it possibly survive up here? The oxygen level has got to be close to normal here, we're so close to the exit."

"Evolution, Mr. President. They're evolving. Let's get the fuck outta here."

This time, the president had no qualms about resuming their jog, grimacing and rubbing his neck as he staggered alongside Munoz.

The latest confrontation sent a chill down Munoz's spine. The creatures were adapting themselves to humanity's oxygen-rich environment. But he had also gone through an adaptation of sorts, and he was no longer prepared to lie down. The problem was he wasn't sure who was really on the right side.

Fuck what Reynolds wants. I refuse to be silenced. I am owed my revenge.

Maybe Samuels was right about the war to come.

Bright sunshine streamed through the mouth of the tunnel and sparkled off the glass pyramid of the Z Train Exhibition Center.

Confetti drifted across the deserted station platform.

A few hundred cops and soldiers were packed in behind a security line, staring down the track. Every barrel was pointed in his direction. A military helicopter thwacked overhead. Hundreds of the press in the parking lot and their cameras swung away from reporters to face him.

A wave of paranoia hit Munoz and he skidded to a halt.

"Is there a problem?" Reynolds asked.

"I bet the Foundation has backup plans for their backup plans. What if they have a sniper in one of the office blocks, waiting to finish us off the moment we walk out?"

"Well then, I'll walk out first," Reynolds said. "It's about time I saved *your* life for a change."

The men cautiously walked out of the subway tunnel, President Reynolds taking point.

A counterstrike team broke the line and charged toward them, weapons raised.

"Mr. President," one soldier shouted as he approached. "Who are you with?"

"Diego Munoz, from the command center."

The team surrounded Reynolds in a tight circle.

"Where's Agent Samuels?" another asked. "We

heard about him before we lost contact with the sub. What the hell happened down there?"

"There's no time. I need everyone to back away. An explosion is imminent and I don't want anyone here caught by the blast."

"Explosion, sir?"

"I'll explain when you get me out of here. Move everyone back."

"I'll call Marine One."

"No," Reynolds said. "That explosion is happening in minutes. Did operations command send any more rescue teams to the Pavilion?"

"Secretary Mansfield ordered us to stay back until we figured out a way of clearing the gas from the tunnel."

Reynolds gave a knowing nod. "I'm sure he did."

The agents stayed in a tight formation as they escorted him toward the line. Munoz followed closely behind, staring in awe at the hundreds of uniforms and vehicles. The day's events still hadn't sunk in, and he'd had no time to think about the outside world during his escape, only how to reach it with the president in one piece. But now that they were free, he kept on high alert, suspecting Samuels had spoken the truth about the Foundation eliminating all its enemies.

Sirens blared from the other side of the river, and a thin cloud of smoke drifted over Manhattan. Munoz walked past the diesel train maintenance shed and noticed the missing train. He knew a couple of diesel engine operators, one an old drinking buddy.

Then it hit him.

Sal Kirsch was one of the few mad enough to mount a rescue attempt against orders. His long-time buddy had a heart of gold and a strong head to match.

It had to be Sal's engine.

The crazy motherfucker.

Munoz peered back toward the tunnel and wanted the diesel engine to power out more than anything else in the world. Survivor's guilt was one thing. Living with the guilt of leaving his team, and them all dying in the subway system, along with Sal, would physically and mentally crush him.

CHAPTER THIRTY-EIGHT

Cafferty and North flanked Bowcut, stabbing beams of light through the misty water vapor. Ellen covered the rear with Flament's spotlight, behind the single file of freed hostages, one of whom carried Dumont's rifle. The group had under ten minutes to make it out of the subway system.

Bowcut wasn't sure they would make it in time, but instead of constantly checking her watch, she drove the group toward their only option for survival.

Her boots crunched over the rocky ground as she advanced, laser in one hand, her light in the other. The passage widened to twenty feet, snaking upward into the distance. Large boulders spread to her front. Cave entrances lined the walls, at least thirty of them, each providing a place for the smaller, lightning-fast creatures to shelter from the effects of their lights and reach anyone with a single leap. The stress of knowing that every step could be her last kept her heart in her throat, and it took all her strength to keep moving.

It helped having David with her. He was ever reliable, always by her side. She wouldn't have it any other way in their current situation. Cafferty was unproven, but it seemed the size of his balls matched his hubris.

North activated one of the last four strobe grenades.

Then shrieks rang out.

Creatures sprang from behind several boulders and shot into the cover of the pitch-black caves. Bowcut slowed her pace and surveyed the multiple attack points. They were basically in a killing field.

The *only* choice was to proceed.

She jutted her chin up the passage. "I see roughly thirty opportunities for the creatures to take a single lunge and rip us into the darkness."

"The strobe keeps them at bay," North said.

"For the most part. But we don't have many. And don't forget: there are thousands of them. There are nine of us."

"There's not much we can do either way," Cafferty said. "I'd rather *try* to get out than just give up and die."

Bowcut felt the same way. What else could they do? She continued forward.

Snarls, hisses, and growls filled the passage. She curled her finger around the trigger and crept between the boulders, searching for any signs of movement. Sweat trickled down her spine and the pain of her headache increased with every step taken away from the soothing air of the oxygenator. Maybe because of that, Bowcut increased her speed to a crouching run. The group's rapid footsteps followed, and they made it past half the caves.

A creature burst out of the blackness to her right.

It crashed into North, sending him skidding across the ground, and sunk its teeth into his leg. He roared and hammered his spotlight against its back. He might as well have been pounding on a rock. The creature thrashed its head, throwing his body from side to side like a dog with a toy.

Two of the women screamed.

The creature's tail lashed Cafferty's arm, instantly drawing blood. It raked its claws down the side of North's chest, tearing his shirt and exposing his rib cage.

No.

Bowcut dropped to one knee and aimed at its bulbous head, but at the same time, another creature raced out of a cave, leaped in the air, and dropped toward her with its claws primed. She fired.

A red-hot laser beam cut through its chest, and the creature's body slammed into Bowcut, knocking her backward, pinning her to the ground.

She stared into its soulless eyes.

It slowly opened its mouth, and blood dripped from the creature's teeth onto her face.

Claws tightened around her body chest rig.

Bowcut didn't even flinch. Calmly, she planted the barrel against the side of its head and fired again.

In a heartbeat, the beam drilled through the creature and zipped into a cave.

Deafening screams echoed out of the entrance.

The creature's eyes closed and its head slumped onto her shoulder like a spent, gruesome lover. She heaved herself free of the corpse, trained the laser on the one attacking North, and pulled the trigger. A red beam speared from the end of the barrel, punched through the creature's neck, and blasted chips from the passage wall.

The creature slumped into a puddle. Blood pulsed from the sizzling gouge below its jaw, each spurt smaller as life drained from its body. She was elated for a moment, but then reality crashed back down. She knew these were only two of thousands, and their attack might have encouraged others to ignore their instincts and charge into the strobing light.

And the clock was still ticking.

North wriggled away on his backside, his face contorted with agony. It dragged on her heartstrings, but she forced her emotions to the side and kept a vigilant watch on the caves surrounding them.

The group clustered around North, focusing their lights on the caves in their immediate vicinity. Everyone's face that didn't wear a gas mask displayed the desperation of their situation. To add insult to injury, jets of water hissed from more cracks in the ceiling, soaking the group, and a steady stream flowed around Bowcut's boots.

Cafferty winced and clutched his arm. "Nice shooting."

"They're getting braver," Bowcut said. "David, please tell me you're okay to move?"

"It's just a scratch," he said, and he unsteadily rose to his feet. "Don't worry about me."

It didn't look like "just a scratch," though. The shredded left leg of his trousers exposed deep teeth marks in his calf. He held his bloodstained hand over his ribs, covering where she had seen the creature expose his bones. But there was no time—he could either move or not, but the group couldn't stay here. It was cold—especially when knowing it was David she was contemplating leaving—but she had no choice. Her emotions meant nothing right now, because she had civilians she needed to protect. Bowcut swallowed hard and strained not to show any outward signs of emotion.

Even if it might leave her feeling dead inside.

Cafferty handed his spotlight to Ellen, ripped the remaining sleeve off his shirt, and one of the women helped him bandage the slice on the side of his biceps.

"Everyone stay tight," Bowcut said. "We can't stop for anything."

Some of the women looked at her in disbelief, as if no one could possibly be so calculating after the violent attack. Her mask remained in place, though. "The C-4 doesn't care that we're hurt," she said sharply, and risked a glance at David. For a second her resolve almost collapsed at the sight of his injuries, but he locked eyes with her and nodded his approval, so she quickly spun on her heel and proceeded up the passage, sweeping her aim across the caves' dark mouths.

The others followed without question.

The shrieks increased in intensity.

Tails whipped out from both sides and battered the ground, spraying Bowcut with water. She kept as close to the middle as possible, out of their reach, vaulting boulders and glancing back every few seconds to ensure everyone had managed to keep up with her pace. They couldn't afford to become strung out, not with their limited sources of light.

Then the creatures fell silent. Every single one within earshot. It felt eerie and weird, like they were up to something malicious beyond her already rapidly expanding comprehension of this new threat.

"Oh fuck," Cafferty said.

"What?" Bowcut asked.

She stumbled to the left, toward the mouth of a cave, as if somebody or something tore at her chest rig. But nothing physical had, and an unseen force continued to tug at her body.

"Go faster," North shouted. "Before we're all dragged away."

Bowcut had never heard David so audibly scared shitless—even if what he said made no sense to her—and she didn't hesitate in following his command.

She passed between the final six cave entrances, and with every step, the force became stronger, ripping her toward the silent darkness.

Cafferty bellowed behind her, encouraging everyone else to run for their lives.

The walls narrowed and Bowcut scrambled into a narrow passage. As fast as the force had gripped her, it vanished. She crouched and waved everyone forward.

North came first and traced his beam back on the survivors.

"What the hell, David?" she asked.

"It's like they band together, creating a magnetic power."

Three of the women made it into the passage.

Only Cafferty, Natalie, and Ellen remained between the caves, struggling the last few yards to free themselves from the creatures' invisible grip. It was like watching a car crash in slow motion. Their lights were useless against the power. Bowcut rose to help them but North dragged her back, wincing as he did.

"They'll make it," he said. "We'll make it."

Natalie, who was slower than the rest, stumbled toward the cave, fighting against the invisible force with all her might.

The creatures in the darkness appeared to focus their efforts on her, the weak link.

Ellen reached out, grasped Natalie's arm, and attempted to drag her the final few steps. But the smaller woman stopped dead in her tracks, as the force pulled her in the opposite direction.

"Natalie, no! Fight!" Ellen maintained her grip, trying to haul her to safety, seemingly oblivious to her cuts on her exposed foot. "Fight it!"

Natalie screamed, caught in a tug-of-war between life and death. "My baby! No! They're pulling me apart!"

Bowcut couldn't believe her eyes. Natalie's belly stretched and squirmed, as if the creatures were trying to rip open her womb.

Tears streamed down Natalie's face and her body shook. "Let me go . . ." she whispered to Ellen.

"No, Natalie, no!" Ellen cried back.

"Let me go—"

Blood squirted from Natalie's nostrils and dripped from her left eye. She broke free of Ellen's grip and uncontrollably lurched into the darkness, arms and legs flailing.

Silence followed a single scream.

Ellen staggered toward the passage and collapsed inside.

"She's gone, let's go!" Bowcut shouted. She charged up the rocky incline, laser at the ready, wondering if the creatures had any other terrifying tricks up their sleeves. She put nothing beyond them after witnessing their last sick display of power.

But grief for Natalie would have to wait.

Otherwise we'll all join her.

North grunted as he limped immediately behind, showing his renowned mettle by fighting the pain of his injuries and not slowing the group. Everyone in law enforcement circles knew of his glowing reputation, but to her, it was more than just a reputation—it was simply who he was. It was the reason she loved him and the reason it tore at her insides at how easily he sacrificed himself for others.

He was the one who was too good for this world, and he was too good for her. But for some reason he wanted her—loved her back—and if there was an option to get all these people out alive or simply die in his arms, she wasn't sure what she'd choose.

North tossed another strobe grenade ahead, leaving them with only two remaining.

Bowcut entered the familiar cavern where only stalactites separated them from the breach. She dropped to her hands and knees, crawled underneath the sharp points, and used her light to illuminate the path ahead.

The rope still dangled out of the shaft.

She breathed a huge sigh of relief, but then she realized they had a problem: the other women wouldn't have her climbing experience. Some were injured. All were pregnant. This was going to take some doing. But they were getting closer . . .

The dead cop hanging from two stalactites blunted any optimism, though. Because while she still had a chance to survive, his family and friends—like Dumont's and Natalie's—would never see him again. The impending explosion would see to that.

Just like my father. The thought almost froze her.

"Keep . . . moving," North wheezed.

The words urged Bowcut on. She scrambled to her feet, swept her light around the space, and walked over to the rope. She gave it a firm tug and it twanged rigid.

North, Ellen, and the other four women joined her next to the pile of rubble. Tom Cafferty stayed by the stalactites and blazed his spotlight back toward the passage, providing extra insurance on top of the weakening distant strobe.

"We've got no idea what's up there," Bowcut said. "But we need to move fast. The train might pass at any moment. I'll go first and clear any creatures."

She handed the laser to North. "Are you okay to cover me?"

"None of these sons of bitches will touch you," he replied, instilling confidence in her.

"Gimme the last couple of those light grenades."

North produced two silver spheres from his pocket. "I know you can do this."

"Everyone follow me straight up, use your legs as leverage to ascend up the shaft walls. We haven't got time to take turns."

Bowcut pocketed the grenades, slipped her light beneath a tight elastic fastening on her chest rig, and quickly ascended the mound of rubble. She wasted no time grabbing the first overhang and moved up the shaft with fast, smooth movements.

North climbed immediately after, grabbing rocks with his huge hands and hauling himself up. Dark figures followed, and their lights flashed around the cavern edges. Soon, everyone was ascending with Cafferty covering their rear, his spotlight glaring into the abyss.

Bowcut closed to within ten feet of the top when she heard a sound. Whirling, she saw a creature's snarling face looking down from the tunnel.

Another one joined it.

"Move to your left," North shouted.

Bowcut reached for an outcrop and swung to the

side. The rock below her boot snapped away and plunged into the cavern. She clung with her hands and attempted to find another foothold as the laser's beam shot past her shoulder and warmed her cheek.

One of the creatures screamed, until its head vanished in a puff of brown mist.

North fired again, punching the laser straight through the other's face. It slumped forward and fell into the shaft.

"Watch out!" Bowcut yelled.

The creature battered against the outcrops, its body twisting and crashing against both sides of the wall. It plummeted past Bowcut and she glanced down, hoping it wouldn't smash anyone back into the cavern.

The group hugged the wall and ducked under shallow ledges.

Moments later, the creature's limp body thudded on top of the pile of rubble and rolled off to the side. Bowcut sucked in a deep breath and continued her climb, keeping a close eye on the edges of the breach.

She paused a few feet from the top of the shaft, retrieved one of the grenades, pressed the sides until she felt a light click, and threw it into the tunnel.

Bright flashes erupted overhead.

Bowcut followed the strobe and pulled herself to the top, quickly panning her light around the deserted track as she climbed to her feet.

A faint, unrecognizable sound echoed up the tunnel.

She strained to identify the source.

As it grew louder, she picked out two distinct noises.

The roar of a diesel engine.

And shrieks.

This time, definitely thousands . . .

"Climb!" she shouted. *"Climb!"*

Their route to freedom was on the way, but it was bringing a sea of creatures. Bowcut feared with one strobe grenade and a single laser, a huge tide of monstrosities would overrun everyone as they tried to board. But they were out of options.

This was it.

CHAPTER THIRTY-NINE

The approaching roar of the diesel engine came as music to Cafferty's ears. He groaned to a standing position above the breach. Making it out of the creatures' underground network took them only halfway to safety and their ultimate survival was still out of their hands. The whole place was due to blow in just under four minutes.

North crouched next to Bowcut at the side of the track, aiming the laser down the tunnel. Ellen and the other women crowded behind, bathed by the orange glow of the MTA lantern, and she shone her spotlight in the same direction.

Shrieking and scrambling erupted from below, now that their lights weren't flooding the cavern. North repeatedly fired the laser beam across the creatures trying to scale the walls, slicing them to pieces.

The slashes on Cafferty's arms stung and blood soaked his bandages, but the adrenaline surging through his body kept him going strong.

And that just needs to last a little while longer . . .

Light illuminated the distant tunnel wall.

The diesel engine soared around the bend, dragging one of the Z Train's cars. A strong ray of light glared from its front—Anna and her team must have figured out the projector—and it closed to within a few hundred feet. But with the salvation of the train came a throng of creatures that raced by its sides, leaping and bounding over every part of the tunnel.

Spotlights dazzled on the sides of the car. Several creatures hunched on the roof and repeatedly slammed their claws into the metal. More hung off the sides, tearing away the steel plates. One leaned in an exposed window and ripped a man out. It threw him against the wall at a gut-churning speed. Huge black figures rounded on his broken body as they stole the life from him.

Cafferty joined Bowcut and North at the center of the track, squinting to protect his eyes, and he thrust out his palm toward the oncoming engine. "Throw your fucking grenades," he shouted.

"Grenade," Bowcut said, emphasizing the singular nature. "Not yet."

"But—"

"Trust us," North said.

And he did.

The train's air horn blasted. It closed to a hundred feet at a steady speed, allowing more creatures to surround the car.

"Ready . . ." Bowcut said.

"Now!" North yelled.

Bowcut launched her silver sphere. It arced through the air and bounced to the side of the track.

Brilliant flashes flooded the immediate area.

More piercing wails filled the air, creating an earsplitting sound.

The main body of creatures surged back. But the ones on the car continued their assault, letting out howls as the engine slowed toward the breach.

North thrust the laser up and fired, and a red beam swept over the top of the roof, cutting down four creatures. He switched his aim to the side of the car and shot another one in the back of its head.

Ellen focused her spotlight on a creature clinging to the undercarriage. It snarled and scuttled out, straight into a red beam that sliced through its stomach.

Sal rose from behind the cabin window. Cuts peppered his sweaty face; drops of blood speckled his T-shirt. "Get your people on board!" he shouted to the mayor, as the train kept moving. "I'm taking this baby outta here."

"Can you do it in three minutes?" Cafferty yelled over the noise.

"At full speed, maybe. But if we create sparks—"

"Fuck sparks. If we don't, we're dead. The tunnels are rigged to explode."

Sal nodded, seemingly accepting the high stakes. "Fucking hell. I'll let this sucker rip when you're all on board."

Cafferty looked at the Z Train car. DeLuca held a set of doors open. Cops and MTA employees manned the others, reaching out to the trackside survivors.

"Start running!" DeLuca yelled. "We'll pull you in."

The eight sprinted alongside the train.

The passenger car drew level with them, and arms reached out to pull in the pregnant women first, Ellen's spotlight aimed over their shoulders to keep any creatures at bay. One after the other, the ladies heaved inside.

"Get in!" Cafferty told Ellen, and, throwing her spotlight into the train, she grabbed the hand of a cop who hauled her in.

"You next, Mr. Mayor!" Bowcut said.

Along with him, only her and North remained outside the car.

With all his strength, Cafferty lunged forward, and a strong pair of hands clasped his wrists. The flesh on his arms burned like molten iron was being pumped through his veins as they jerked, and he let out a ragged scream.

"It's okay—I got you, sir," Lieutenant Arnolds said, and hauled him into car.

Cafferty spun around on his stomach to face outside.

North fired his laser beyond the strobes, rotating it across the width of the tunnel, cutting the first few ranks of creatures in half. How he kept moving with his injuries was nothing short of miraculous. "David!" Cafferty yelled.

North looked over and seemed to realize all the

civilians had made it safely inside. He rushed for the car and lunged for the open doors, and Tom grabbed him . . . only for his grip to give.

His strength had finally left him.

"No!"

But another arm thrust past him and grabbed North's jacket. Arnolds—with a few passengers hanging on to him as an anchor—heaved, and North collapsed inside.

Cafferty and North lay on the floor for a second, spent, but North somehow popped up and pushed his way along the aisle to the rear of the car.

The cars pulled away from Bowcut.

"Get in!" Cafferty shouted at her retreating fig-ure. Hauling himself up, he made his way back to North, stumbling down the aisle. Through the fi-nal set of doors . . . Bowcut fell farther behind.

The despair almost hit him. He had ordered her SWAT team here, and Dumont was already dead. Now it appeared he had brought her down into the tunnels to find death, too.

The diesel engine let out a thunderous roar, the train jerked forward, and they quickly built up speed, smoothly clanking up the track.

They were leaving her behind . . .

Except Cafferty had somehow forgot about Da-vid North.

At the rear of the car, David had already opened the door that connected trains, and for a mo-ment Tom had the irrational thought that people weren't supposed to ride between cars—that it was dangerous.

For what felt like an eternity, his security chief stood there against a backdrop of pitch black and wailing shrieks.

And then he pulled Bowcut inside, and they landed on the floor in each other's arms. Cafferty had never felt so relieved in his life.

Except they weren't out just yet . . .

He glanced around at the people in the blood-stained car, and any relief that was left quickly vanished.

How did it come to this . . . ?

So many missing.

Dead.

The body and roof of the project he had spent the better part of a decade on—the better part of his *marriage* on—had been torn to ribbons. Only two steel plates remained in place, and wind rushed through torn-out sections at the front and sides.

Roughly thirty souls remained alive, between the seats, resolutely holding their lanterns and improvised weapons. Lieutenant Arnolds barked orders, his determined face stained with the blood of those who didn't make it. A mix of cops, MTA workers, and guests crouched around him, fewer than half the amount who had originally barricaded themselves in for the desperate fight.

The car's suspension bumped and a shallow crimson pool spilled across the floor.

Cafferty checked his watch.

Under two minutes.

The diesel engine's roar increased in pitch.

"They're coming back!" North shouted.

Cafferty raced along the aisle only to lose his footing when his shoe slipped. He crashed against the floor and skidded through a thin layer of blood.

A cop reached down and grabbed his arm, sending a fresh wave of agony through the laceration, but he gritted down the nausea. Shuddering, he rose to his feet and wiped his hands on the front of his shirt. He carefully walked the last few steps and crouched by North, Ellen, and Bowcut around a torn-out section at the rear of the car. The creatures had peeled away enough of the body to easily drag a couple of people through, though it had created a space wide enough for the survivors to use their weapons.

Ellen edged out of the way, giving him a clear view.

Thousands of creatures surged forward, followed by a foaming wave of water that swallowed up the bottom half of the tunnel. In the darkness, it was hard to tell where the creatures ended and the water began, but he wasn't sure it mattered—either one would kill them all. The smaller creatures were easier to delineate, though, as they were at the front, charging at lightning speed, eating up the ground between themselves and the train in seconds.

The alarm on Cafferty's watch beeped, signaling one minute until detonation.

All this. We made it through all this, and we're still going to die.

But North didn't seem willing to accept that. He fired, punching the laser's beam through the closest creatures. Others bounded over the corpses and reached out their claws.

Ellen and Bowcut cut their spotlights to the left and right, attempting to slow the advance. It had no effect. The water appeared to have made up the creatures' minds, and whatever impact the light had on them was preferable to drowning.

"We can't outrun them—they're too fast," Cafferty said. He glanced over his shoulder at the survivors. "Get ready!"

North fired repeatedly, chopping down hundreds of creatures. Blood spurted from their limbs and bodies, and the rush of seawater quickly consumed the carcasses.

It barely seemed to make a dent in the ranks of the shrieking mass.

The train gained a bit more speed, and it looked like they were pulling clear of the main body.

But the small ones . . .

Three of them raced along the walls and leaped at the car.

Claws stabbed through the roof.

A tail whipped through a window and carved into the top of Lieutenant Arnolds' head, splitting it down to his nose.

Screams erupted inside the car.

The tail slithered around Arnolds' neck and lashed from side to side, battering his limp body against the internal walls.

Everyone ducked lower between the seats.

North spun and fired. Sparks fizzed from the ceiling. He cut a line through it, and the beam severed a creature's legs. It didn't seem to matter, though—the tail ripped Arnolds' body out the window.

"Sparks!" Bowcut shouted at Cafferty. "The methane won't ignite! Let's take these fuckers down."

She shouldered her Commando, aimed outside, and took rapid single shots. The bullets slammed into creatures' bodies, checking their stride. Head-shots took them down.

A few of the cops unholstered their weapons and fired out the sides through the open doors and broken windows.

The train pulled farther away from the chasing pack and approached the final bend leading to the Jersey City station.

Thirty seconds.

Cafferty turned to search for the first signs of daylight. He finally allowed himself to believe that they might make it.

A claw reached inside the gap, clamped around North's arm, and wrenched him out of the car. Cafferty dove down, reached for his legs . . . and grasped nothing but air.

"No!" Bowcut screamed as North's body tumbled along the track, entwined with a creature. "David!"

She stopped firing and went to leap from the train. Cafferty grabbed her chest rig, stopping her suicidal rescue attempt.

"Let me go, goddamn it!"

"No! These people need you! What would David want you to do?"

Bowcut growled and thrashed, but Tom was damned if he was going to let go. He had almost lost North once with a weak grip. He wasn't going to betray his best friend by releasing Sarah's rig and letting her kill herself.

Ellen focused her light on the head of security, and they watched out the back of the train as North fired while he rolled, shredding the creature to pieces.

North rose to his knees, gave Bowcut and Cafferty a single firm nod, and twisted to face the screeching mass. He fired, keeping his finger depressed against the laser trigger, and the red beam lanced through a tide of writhing black bodies he had no chance of stopping.

"Jesus Christ," Bowcut whispered.

Cafferty couldn't even speak. He also couldn't take his eyes off the scene: his selfless head of security, fighting with his last breaths to hold back the creatures, giving everyone else a chance at freedom.

North disappeared into a black blanket of snarling chaos. The laser continued to pierce bodies, and Cafferty could see the red cutting back and forth on all parts of the tunnel.

Then it went out, and he let out a deep sigh, his grip still on Bowcut's rig. Silently, Ellen wrapped her arms around both of them.

A hush filled Cafferty's head, only to be replaced by Bowcut's quiet sobs.

And then an explosion rumbled from deep inside the subway system.

Then another.

And a final one, closer to them.

The ground shook, jolting the train.

Breaking free, Bowcut yelled, "Everyone get down!"

A wall of smoke and water rocketed up the tunnel. Chunks of concrete dropped from the ceiling, crashing against the roof of the car.

Ellen grabbed Cafferty's hand. "Come on, Tom. I'm not losing you today."

Cafferty spun and ducked next to Ellen under a seat. The train powered around the bend toward the station.

He tensed, waiting for the shock wave to hit. From across the aisle, Bowcut had tucked herself under the opposite seat, staring at him with a mix of fury and sorrow.

Somehow that felt even worse.

Cafferty closed his eyes and thought about keeping them closed forever. But then bright light flooded the train. Daylight. He pulled himself out from underneath the seat.

Hundreds of uniforms and vehicles packed a distant police line, weapons aimed at the speeding train. He had no idea if they were a safe distance from the blast, but he also knew there was nothing he could do about it now as the train thundered past the platform and headed for the maintenance shed.

Glancing through the rear of the car, Cafferty watched in awe as water, smoke, and debris exploded out of the tunnel's mouth as the Hudson River retook the Z Train.

An earsplitting boom ripped through the air as

the tunnel simultaneously exploded and imploded, knocking Cafferty back down. Ellen reached for him and they wrapped their arms around each other, squeezing tight.

The force of the blast lifted the train, and for a second, Cafferty felt weightless. The diesel engine lurched to the right, dragging the car with it. He braced for impact as well as he could.

The train smashed into the ground and crashed through two concrete bollards, and the wheels screeched over the deserted pedestrian zone, heading directly at the center of the police line ... and the Z Train Exhibition Center's shimmering pyramid.

Soldiers and cops scattered.

The diesel engine pounded two police cars to the side, slowing its momentum, though not enough ...

They rammed through the Exhibition Center's front entrance, sending glass flying in all directions, flattening the reception desk, and driving through two more walls. The engine and car eventually groaned to a halt inside the main hall, surround by broken display cases.

For a moment, finally, there was a welcome silence.

All energy drained from Cafferty's body and he slumped on the floor.

Sirens began to blare in the distance.

Hundreds of uniforms rushed over from all sides with weapons raised.

Cafferty could barely find the strength to care about any of it.

Eventually, though, he surveyed the train's path of destruction and wondered how he had come through so many dangerous situations in three hours and lived to tell the tale. It seemed a lifetime ago since he stood on the Pavilion's stage.

"We're alive," Ellen said. "I can't believe it. Tom, we actually made it."

"I'm never letting you go again. I'm so sorry for everything."

"I'm sorry, too. I love you."

They embraced tightly.

Some survivors shook their heads in disbelief. Others exited and headed between the obliterated exhibits for the shattered entrance.

Cafferty led Ellen out through the rear set of doors. A model of the Z Train extension lay by his feet, broken into hundreds of pieces, much like the legacy he had intended to leave for the city. It seemed so small, considering the legacy of people like Arnolds. Like Dumont. Like David North.

Fresh air had never tasted so good, but he felt numbness, not relief. Everything was too much to comprehend.

Only thirty had made it out of the Pavilion.

It was staggering to think not only of how many people had died, but that this many had *survived*. Again, though, he thought back to the dead—one in particular. Because while Cafferty knew he shouldered some of the burden for the tragedy, Lucien Flament's organization nagged in the back of his mind. The Foundation for Human Advancement.

The creatures did the killing, but the Foundation's silence had *let* them. Further, it could have prevented it but instead was willing to kill *everyone* down there . . . just because.

All to preserve this secret.

Cafferty was a driven man. He had fought and struggled and begged and compromised to make the Z Train happen, and it had almost cost him everything. The one thing it hadn't changed, though, was his ability to accomplish his goals. And now he had a new one.

No matter what it takes, I will not *let my friends die in vain. One way or the other, the Foundation* will *pay for this.*

Bowcut approached, and for a moment the two just stared at each other.

"Sarah, I'm so—"

"Don't, Mr. Mayor. Not right now. Maybe not ever. But right now, I have to keep doing my job and debrief my bosses. I—I have to keep doing what I know how to do, because otherwise . . ."

"Otherwise it seems like this was for nothing," he said quietly.

Bowcut simply nodded.

"It's won't be for nothing, Sarah. I promise you."

"I hope so. And when you're ready, you know where to find me."

"Same for you."

Bowcut turned to Ellen. "Mrs. Cafferty."

"I owe you my life."

"We all owe David."

And with that, Sarah Bowcut slipped around the front of the train and disappeared.

Cafferty stood there for a moment, his heart aching for her. She would need time to heal—as they all would. But he had meant what he told her. This wasn't over. And by the look in her eyes, he was pretty sure she was more than willing to take this to the very end.

Leaning on Ellen, he made his way toward the diesel engine. As he approached, the cabin door flung open. Sal climbed down the steel ladder and helped his shaken colleague descend. He spun toward Cafferty and his eyes lit up.

"You're one crazy asshole," Cafferty said. "We're here thanks to you."

"Come 'ere." Sal grasped him in a tight bear hug, only letting go when he gasped from the pain. "Sorry, Mr. Mayor. But it wasn't just me and Mike. You're the crazy asshole going into the tunnel with spotlights . . . Holy shit—Diego!"

Munoz picked his way through the wrecked center, followed by soldiers and cops. He broke into a run, grabbed Anna from behind, and lifted her in the air. The surviving members of his command center team surrounded him, relief and joy plastered across their faces.

A smile cracked Cafferty's.

"Diego," Sal called out, "get your crusty ass over here."

Munoz broke away from his group, grinned, and approached Sal, Cafferty, and Ellen. "How'd I guess it was you who took the engine down?"

"I couldn't let you take all the glory. Where's the president?"

"They whisked him away five minutes ago."

"I never thought I'd be pleased to see you."

"Likewise." Munoz eyed Cafferty and his smile dropped. "We need to talk, Mr. Mayor." He motioned his head to the shattered display cases. "In private."

They left Sal and Ellen busily chatting about the escape.

"What is it?" Cafferty asked.

"Reynolds' head of security was a double agent for a shadowy organization—"

"The Foundation?"

"You know it?"

"It's a long story."

Munoz leaned closer. "Not as long as mine. I'm sworn to secrecy by the president 'cause I heard things you wouldn't believe. But I'll be damned if these assholes get away with this."

"They won't, Diego," Cafferty said, watching the cops and soldiers closing in. "We'll make sure of it, won't we?"

Diego and Cafferty stared resolutely at each other, and finally Munoz nodded.

Cafferty walked back to his wife. Seeing her there, talking with Sal, looking so beautiful and composed and *alive* . . . it was enough for him to want to take her as far away from here as possible and never look back. But he knew he couldn't do that. Not after what he'd seen. Not after what Bowcut and Munoz had gone through to get them all out of there. He might not be fighters like them, at least physically, and his political career was definitely over. But he had a new ambition, a new steely resolve: to avenge the memory of those who died today, to unravel the conspiracy, and to take down the Foundation for Human Advancement.

Ellen saw Tom coming and smiled, both warm and nervous. He shook his head quickly and took her in his arms, letting her know that the only thing that mattered was their future. Reluctantly pulling away from each other, they locked hands and headed through the front of the Exhibition Center into the brilliant sunshine.

CHAPTER FORTY

Albert Van Ness spun his electric wheelchair away from the BBC World News broadcast at the far side of his penthouse office. The footage of the president being ushered from the scene confirmed the failure of the New York mission, not that he needed telling. He glared down at the message from Reynolds on his smartphone and his hands balled into fists.

The Foundation for Human Advancement had a zero-tolerance policy for failure. Ultimately, it was all part of a giant mechanism created by his father and continued by him, fueled by cash from national governments. If components like Samuels and Flament died, they had their bank accounts stripped and his recruiters identified new targets. If a fuel source soured, like Reynolds and his country's funding, he had to be removed for someone with better compliance.

What angered Van Ness most about this public screwup was the previous work the Foundation had carried out to get the ungrateful Reynolds elected. Dark sites in multiple locations bombarded social media using thousands of bogus accounts. Online opinion polls were stuffed in his favor. Hackers broke into electoral systems and manipulated data, and they left believable trails of evidence for his opponent's fake affair with a prostitute. They had needed to shift public opinion only half a percentage point. By his team's estimation, they managed to double their target, and this wasn't even the Foundation's primary mission.

And now the fool had sent a threat to the man who made him.

Van Ness needed a moment to calm himself before dealing with his executives.

His father once claimed the key to success was stripping all emotions out of the decision-making process and to always use the cold, hard facts. An *SS-oberführer* would say that. The old guard had no idea when it came to juggling politics and business, didn't have a clue about the concept of an iron fist in a velvet glove.

Van Ness rotated his chair toward the bulletproof glass window. He peered at his weak reflection, wearing a perfectly pressed gray pin-striped Kiton suit made of vicuña wool. His shoes rested on the foot platforms at odd angles, and his knees buckled inward. Most never guessed the true power behind his frail figure.

Twenty stories below, hundreds of tourists walked along the Parc du Champ de Mars toward the Eiffel Tower. So many people, oblivious and naive. They would live, work, breed, and die without ever knowing they owed their survival, their very existence and place at the top of the food chain, to him, the all-knowing, all-seeing benefactor and puppeteer of the world. Protecting humanity from itself and these creatures wasn't a mission *from* God; it was God's mission.

Van Ness spun his chair back toward his polished walnut desk and tapped the pad on his left armrest. The office's two glass walls transformed to gunmetal gray. He knew various government agencies watched him like a hawk from distant buildings, hoping to catch a glimpse of his inner world.

He pressed a button on his desk. "Send them in, Henrietta."

"Right away, Mr. Van Ness."

The door smoothly swung open with an electric grind.

Werner Schulz, his tall, ambitious number three, entered first. His grandfather had served with Van Ness' father, and nobody was more committed to the Foundation's principles.

Allen Edwards, his shorter, dark-haired right-hand man, followed. He drove the projects with a strong fundamentalist belief that even Van Ness found mildly creepy, though lately he had become careless.

The sweat on Edwards' top lip told Van Ness he knew it, too.

The men stood motionless, waiting for Van Ness to speak. He stared at them, drumming his fingers on the desk. Neither moved or dared to break eye contact. He decided to get the trivial business over with first.

"Werner, what's the latest on the UK election?"

"Our favored party has a two-point lead going into the live debates."

"How are you mitigating a poor performance?"

"We've got four news stories of varying severity ready to run in the national papers. I'll let you know which we deploy. The nuclear option is to engineer a terrorist attack in Canary Wharf, but we won't need to go that far. Not this time."

"Everything used to be so simple. Governments paid and we carried out our work." Van Ness breathed out a heavy sigh. "We live in a cynical world today, gentlemen. A cynical world indeed."

Edwards pulled a handkerchief from inside his jacket pocket and dabbed his face. The Londoner had worked at the Foundation for the best part of twenty years as Van Ness' number two, but Van Ness knew age had caught up with him. Edwards' mistakes were becoming more regular, his excuses more outlandish.

"I'm sorry, Mr. Van Ness," Edwards said. "I take full responsibility for New York."

Van Ness tossed him the smartphone. "At least the creatures are under control. But this?"

Edwards read the message and his face turned a paler shade of white.

"Sir," Schulz said, "may I offer a suggestion?"

"You may."

"I've prepared a contingency plan and it's ready

for implementation, with your approval. It'll achieve our original objectives within twenty-four months."

Schulz placed a report on Van Ness' desk.

"Excellent work," Van Ness said, thumbing through the pages. He switched his focus back to his number two. "Do you have a contingency plan, Allen?"

"I'm working on our alternatives."

"So you don't?"

"Not yet, but I will."

"I see."

Van Ness scrutinized Edwards' face. He was facing nothing more than a tired old boxer, taking his last desperate swing before his punch-drunk body smashed against the canvas. It saddened him, but everyone had a shelf life.

"Sir," Edwards pleaded, "give me another chance. As you said yourself, things are harder nowadays."

"Don't misquote me. I can't tolerate failure, old friend."

A bead of sweat rolled down Edwards' cheek.

Van Ness glanced at an iris-activated sensor on the wall, which instantly lit up red. He immediately switched his focus above Edwards' eyes.

At the last moment, he shifted his glare to Schulz, his number three.

A red laser beam shot from the front of Van Ness' desk and drilled a perfect hole through his forehead.

Schulz rocked on his heels, staring vacantly ahead.

Van Ness eased back in his wheelchair, steepled his fingers, and watched with morbid curiosity. He had once heard a severed head retained consciousness for several seconds, and he searched his number three's eyes for signs of recognition. "Are you still there?" he asked.

Schulz collapsed. Blood pooled around his body. The sensor deactivated.

"Without loyalty, what do we have left?" Van Ness said introspectively.

"I told you we couldn't trust him," Edwards said. "He wanted to lead the Foundation and wouldn't let anything stand in his path. I'll get working on a real contingency plan right away."

"I know you will, old friend. Don't fail me again."

"I won't, sir." Edwards turned to leave.

"Oh, and Allen."

"Yes, sir?"

"Send someone up to clean this mess."

The door shut behind Edwards. Van Ness navigated his wheelchair from behind his desk, steered a wide circle around the dead body, and stopped in front of his mahogany bookcase. He keyed in a code on his armrest.

A section of the bookcase eased out with a pneumatic hiss and rolled to the side, revealing a brightly lit corridor. It led to the back entrance of his top secret test facility, where the most exhilarating find in the Foundation's illustrious history lay in wait. Excitement rose inside him as he accelerated forward toward the test rooms.

A creature lay dissected in the first. Originally

found by villagers in Slovenia and reported as a strange body in a cave, the Foundation's speech recognition software, monitoring global emergency calls, identified a caller saying, *"Bitje,"* the southern Slavic word for *creature*. Van Ness immediately sent a helicopter to the remote area, his team posing as a government agency. They collected the shriveled corpse and left before the real authorities arrived.

A woman dressed in scrubs and a surgical mask removed one of the creature's dark brown organs and dropped it onto a metal weighing scale.

In the next room, Van Ness' DNA sequencers worked on every available sample to see if they could detect any global patterns from recovered traces of blood. Most creatures died at the hands of the Foundation, usually in deep underground explosions, so Van Ness' scientists cherished anything they could lay their hands on.

During the last couple of years, the occurrence of nests had doubled in frequency and the creatures were reported at higher depths. He had suspected they had been evolving for some time, but he had received only anecdotal evidence about their physical changes in form. That was until a group of cavers was reported missing at a site deep in the Alps. What his team returned with blew his mind.

Van Ness nudged his chair forward to the next room. Blue mist shrouded the space inside. He drew his father's military swagger stick and tapped its brass sphere on the window.

A palm thrust out of the mist and thudded against the glass.

The creature's hand and arm had a smaller, humanlike appearance. The razor-sharp black fingernails reminded him of his hundreds of historical battles, until the early nineties when a creature's tail had broken his back in the depths of a Florida sinkhole.

Van Ness reached up and rested his palm on the opposite side of the glass. The creatures were evolving, and it was only a matter of time before they rose to the surface from beyond the abyss.

For a moment, he saw visions of creatures ripping the Austrian cavers to shreds, and he heard the creature's words.

Those who help us will survive our onslaught.

I will, Van Ness thought.

"I will," he said aloud.

His father once had a vision of global domination. Van Ness harbored the same ambition, though the Foundation had to take a new direction to achieve a dead man's dream. If they stopped hunting the creatures and found a way to *harness* their power instead, no government on the planet, no president, *no one*, could resist Albert Van Ness' demands.

CHAPTER FORTY-ONE

NINE MONTHS LATER

Cafferty made his way toward the blue room in city hall, flanked by Ellen and the new mayor, James Rattner. The assembled press had gathered for his speech, ready to broadcast it live across the nation. If they expected him to talk about creatures and be ridiculed on the airwaves and their front pages for a second time, they were sorely mistaken.

In the weeks after that fateful day, the subways had been sealed off as thousands of national guardsmen scoured through every inch of every tunnel, every station, every shaft in the five boroughs. They found only fragments of bones. A federal archaeologist, almost certainly controlled by Van Ness, identified them as unique finds from the Triassic period, but not the creatures survivors had described. The fireball and implosion had done their job.

Cafferty's official career had ended, but he was far from finished. He strode into the blue room, resolved not to give the slightest hint about his life's new mission.

The press eyed him with cynicism as he pulled his notes from inside his jacket pocket and spread them on the podium. Rattner stood by his shoulder; Ellen stayed at the back of the room, cradling their baby.

"Mr. Mayor," Cafferty said, "my fellow New Yorkers, my fellow Americans. I stand before you today as former mayor of this great city to make you a promise.

"I'll work tirelessly for the rest of my life to make amends to every victim's family, every traumatized survivor, and everyone else who the tragic event impacted. To achieve this goal, Ellen and I have created the David North Memorial Foundation."

That much was true, but two could play at creating foundations with concealed functions. Today felt a million miles away from his speech in the Pavilion. His arrival had sucked the life out of the room, though he didn't care. Nobody except a chosen few knew it marked the moment he started out on his quest to publicly uncover the creatures' existence and to expose the Foundation for Human Advancement.

"No matter what you believe, what version of the truth you choose to accept, the fact remains—many of our friends, our loved ones, our brothers and sisters, husbands and wives, died that day. I thank God Ellen and our newborn son are here today, and although I cannot change the past, I can affect our future."

A strange phenomenon had occurred since the disaster. Initially, fear and panic spread throughout the globe. But investigation after investigation in countries around the world uncovered no physical evidence, no proof, nothing to corroborate the survivors' stories. Three months of congressional hearings and a UN Security Council investigation returned the same results—nothing.

Van Ness' stranglehold reached far and wide.

"In the end," Cafferty continued, "history will determine whether the good I create is greater than the damage I've caused. I promise you this—I will never stop working to right the true injustices in the world. Thank you, and God bless."

"Why did the president pardon you?" a reported shouted.

Cafferty glared at Christopher Fields' replacement at WNBC, wondering if he faced a Van Ness plant. He had resigned as mayor and come clean about the corners he cut to meet the project's deadlines. The district attorney had indicted him on involuntary manslaughter because he was never aware of any danger in the completed tunnels. The judge sentenced him to fifteen years in prison.

The president had immediately pardoned him, much to the public's disgust, but for reasons Cafferty understood. Reynolds had used his injuries and near-death experience to propel him into office for another four years, without the need for Van Ness' fake news. The vice president unexpectedly resigned for health reasons, the secretary of defense retired, and half the president's cabinet got fired after the election. The David North Foundation gained a new silent partner in the top position of government for its global fight.

Cafferty blanked everyone out as he left the room. Cameras flashed at his sides and journalists fired more questions. His days of appeasing the press and regular public appearances were over. His mantra going forward was to trust nobody apart from his inner circle.

Ellen joined him in the corridor and they left the building at a fast walk. Cafferty led them down the steps and into a waiting black car with tinted windows.

"You did well, honey," she said.

"This is only the start. Do you think Mayor Rattner's in on it?"

"He asked me a few questions about our plans for the North Foundation. I guess we'll see."

The car's engine purred as it pulled away and sped along Park Row.

Everything from this point forward required precision planning and secrecy. Psychologists, unsurprisingly from a French institute, explained away the creatures as some form of mass hallucination brought on by the methane leak. The bloodstained car was blamed on a suicide bomber, and evidence to disprove the claim lay under millions of tons of water and rubble. It worked. Publicly stating the creatures existed attracted ridicule.

The survivors found themselves defending their stories against a skeptical and often abusive media. The events of that day had become the source of hundreds of conspiracy theories, a rapidly produced bestselling book, a graphic novel, and a reality show called *Sub Terranean*, where contestants spent days together underground carrying out embarrassing tasks and the loser of the episode got punished. People couldn't get enough.

It infuriated Cafferty how Van Ness continued to cleverly manipulate the situation into a source of mass entertainment, hiding the real truth in plain sight.

The car stopped at the side of Nassau Street. Cafferty changed into a casual jacket and tugged a Yankees cap over his head. He leaned over and kissed Ellen and baby David, shoved the door open, and headed along the sidewalk.

It never ceased to amaze him how easy it was to become invisible in Manhattan. He put it down to the flow of tourists and the rush of the streets. Not a single face flickered with recognition as he headed for his meeting.

Cafferty turned a corner and entered the Beekman Pub. Two figures sat at a table in the dark far corner. One turned as he approached.

"How'd it go?" Diego Munoz asked.

"As expected. They'll be watching our every move."

Sarah Bowcut pushed a pint of Guinness across the table. "And we'll be watching the Foundation's. I've booked my ticket to Paris."

Cafferty sat and took two refreshing gulps of his pint. The look of determination in their eyes matched his inner drive. This was just the beginning, but each of them had vowed to see it through to the very end. Whatever the consequences.

For the next few minutes, the team quietly discussed the rest of their European travel plans, until the owner of the pub fished a remote control from behind the bar. He increased the volume of a wall-mounted television in the corner of the room.

A bold CNN headline read: "BREAKING NEWS: PRESIDENT REYNOLDS MISSING."

The pub fell silent.

All eyes turned to the on-screen anchor. She reported that Reynolds went out for a jog and had never returned to Camp David's main lodge. Five of his security detail had been discovered during a search of Catoctin Mountain Park's wooded hills. Each with multiple gunshot wounds.

"It's Van Ness," Munoz muttered. "That asshole has a real hard-on for Reynolds."

Cafferty put his finger to his lips. He considered nowhere safe from the old German's grasp, and this latest move only added to the Foundation of Human Advancement's already mountainous list of crimes. Reynolds refused to play ball and this time they had successfully taken him. It was the only logical explanation in his mind, and it came as no surprise.

Events like these would only continue unless somebody stopped the disease that was blighting the world. Somebody needed to stop Van Ness. And that somebody was Tom Cafferty.

Albert Van Ness would regret the day he unearthed the terror below New York and crossed swords with a man who didn't know how to lose.

ACKNOWLEDGMENTS

I wrote *Awakened* on a dare thirteen years ago. Thanks to Chris Spear for daring me. A huge thanks to my friend Darren Wearmouth for being such an excellent writer and collaborator, not to mention an all-around nice guy. Read all his books—you'll love them. Thanks to David Pomerico from Harper Voyager and Lisa Sharkey from HarperCollins for their belief in the novel and their constant guidance. They have been an absolute pleasure to work with. Thanks to my best friends Joey, Sal, and Brian for giving me the courage to succeed after I thought I had failed. Thanks to Susan Travers for improving my life and my family's life on a daily basis. Thanks to Jack Rovner and Dexter Scott from Vector Management; Nick Nuciforo and Marc Gerald from UTA; Danny Passman from Gang, Tyre, Ramer & Brown; and Phil Sarna and Mitch Pearlstein from PSBM. The best team in the business.

Mom and Dad—thanks for raising me to believe I could achieve all of my dreams. I love you both.

And finally, thanks to all the *Impractical Jokers* fans out there who make all these amazing opportunities possible. You truly are the best fans in the world, and I hope you enjoy the *Awakened* trilogy!

—JAMES S. MURRAY

That James wrote this book a decade ago and the concept has stood the test of time is a big tick against who he is as a creator and writer. It's been an honor working with him on *Awakened*, and we've had a lot of fun along the way. I'd also like to thank three other people. First, Paul Lucas from Janklow & Nesbit. Paul is my agent and works tirelessly on my behalf. His advice is beyond value. Second, David Pomerico from Harper Voyager. If you ever look behind the curtain of any great book, you'll generally find a fantastic editor sitting there. David is one of those, and millions of people have unknowingly read novels containing his fingerprints. Third, Dawn, who puts up with my long hours in the office and my many moments of distraction, and unconditionally supports my endeavors. I love her for it. Lastly, and most importantly, a huge thanks to you for reading *Awakened*.

—DARREN WEARMOUTH

The terror started on a local train.

Now it's spreading global.

The horrors unleashed underneath the Hudson are threatening to wipe out humanity. A mysterious organization can stop them, but it comes at a hefty price. The world has a choice: pay the extortion money, or face extinction.

Because these are powerful, insatiable creatures. And they're putting us all on

THE BRINK

An Awakened Novel

The latest book from internationally bestselling authors James S. Murray and Darren Wearmouth

Out from Harper Voyager

Summer 2019

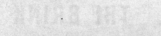